"Donna Thorland writes first-class historical fiction rich with textured detail. Above all, *The Dutch Girl* is a great read steeped in authentic history."

—Kate Alcott, author of *The Dressmaker, The Daring Ladies of Lowell*, and *A Touch of Stardust*

"Vivid [and] evocative, Thorland's newest novel about the Revolution reminds us that more than one kind of liberty was at stake. Rich in historical detail, overflowing with political intrigue and lost love, *The Dutch Girl* is a captivating and thought-provoking read."

—Sara Donati, international bestselling author of the Wilderness series

Praise for the Novels of Donna Thorland

Mistress Firebrand

"I loved this book from the first page and raced through it. The plot is seamless, the characters (all of them) compelling, and the romance just lovely. The two main characters are a perfect balance of equals. I consider this author a major find."

—Mary Balogh, *New York Times* bestselling author of *Only a Promise* and *Longing*

"Thorland's most amusing, clever, adventurous, and thought-provoking novel yet. Not only are there wonderfully vivid descriptions, fascinating historical events, and dynamic characters alongside a powerful love story, but Thorland depicts the revolution from several sides, giving readers a 360-degree view of the era."

—*RT Book Reviews*

"I loved *Mistress Firebrand* every bit as much as [Thorland's] first two books. . . . Her unique mix of history, romance, and adventure all add up to create stunning, sensual stories you cannot put down."

—Jennifer McQuiston, *New York Times* and *USA Today* bestselling author of *Her Highland Fling*

continued . . .

T0200808

The Rebel Pirate

"Authentic detail, amazing characters, and a dazzlingly broad sweep of action make this a richly romantic adventure that's hard to put down. Truly brilliant. Prepare to be blown away."

—Susanna Kearsley, *New York Times* bestselling author of
A Desperate Fortune

"A fast-paced, soundly researched historical intrigue with vivid characters and sharp writing, *The Rebel Pirate* is a compelling read."

—Madeline Hunter, *New York Times* bestselling author of
His Wicked Reputation

"Seethes with conflict, intrigue, and romance . . . richly vibrant and utterly believable."

—Amy Belding Brown, author of *Flight of the Sparrow*

"What fun! Totally captivating." —Alex Myers, author of *Revolutionary*

"Swashbuckling high-seas adventure crossed with desire-driven romance, all dished up with perfect historical detail."

—Bee Ridgway, author of *The River of No Return*

The Turncoat

"Very entertaining."
—Margaret George, *New York Times* bestselling author of *Elizabeth I*

"Cool & sexy."
—Meg Cabot, *New York Times* bestselling author of *Royal Wedding*

"A stay-up-all-night, swashbuckling, breath-holding adventure of a novel . . . an extraordinary book about an extraordinary heroine."
—Lauren Willig, *New York Times* bestselling author of the Pink Carnation series

"Thorland takes you on an incredible adventure through a wonderfully realized depiction of Colonial America."
—Corey May, writer of video game Assassin's Creed 3

"Fans of Philippa Gregory and Loretta Chase will find *The Turncoat* a thrilling read."
—*Booklist*

"A strong debut."
—Historical Novel Society

"Kept me up far too late . . . an absolutely gripping read."
—Meredith Duran, bestselling author of *Lady Be Good*

"Great storytelling—the very best of what historical fiction can be."
—Simone St. James, author of *The Other Side of Midnight*

"One high-stakes adventure. . . . Thorland's believable dialogue steals each scene."
—*New Jersey Monthly*

OTHER NOVELS BY DONNA THORLAND

Renegades of the American Revolution Series

The Turncoat
The Rebel Pirate
Mistress Firebrand

The Dutch Girl

RENEGADES OF THE AMERICAN REVOLUTION

DONNA THORLAND

NEW AMERICAN LIBRARY

NEW AMERICAN LIBRARY
Published by New American Library,
an imprint of Penguin Random House LLC
375 Hudson Street, New York, New York 10014

This book is an original publication of New American Library.

First Printing, March 2016

For more information about Penguin Random House, visit penguin.com.

LIBRARY OF CONGRESS CATALOGING-IN-PUBLICATION DATA:

Names: Thorland, Donna, author.
Title: The Dutch girl: renegades of the American Revolution/Donna Thorland.
Description: New York City: New American Library, [2016] | Series: Renegades of the American Revolution; 4
Identifiers: LCCN 2015042073 (print) | LCCN 2015045295 (ebook) | ISBN 9780451471024 (softcover) | ISBN 9780698166875 (ebook)
Subjects: LCSH: Manhattan (New York, N.Y.)—History—18th century—Fiction. | United States—History—Revolution, 1775–1783—Fiction. | BISAC: FICTION/Historical. | FICTION/Romance/Historical. | FICTION/Biographical. | GSAFD: Romantic suspense fiction. | Historical fiction. | Love stories.
Classification: LCC PS3620.H766 D88 2016 (print) | LCC PS3620.H766 (ebook) | DDC 813/.6—dc23
LC record available at http://lccn.loc.gov/2015042073

Printed in the United States of America
10 9 8 7 6 5 4 3 2 1

Penguin
Random
House

Scrappy Thorland
1997–2014
Promoted to Glory

The Dutch Girl

One

The sampler above the fireplace was a beautiful lie. Everything about the silkwork picture was a fantasy, from the house and trees at the bottom to the inscription stitched at the top: *With utmost care I've wrought this piece according to my skill. Anna Winters, daughter of Charles and Hannah Winters, in the 14th year of her age 1764.*

The six girls stitching earnestly beneath it did not know. To them it was the standard of excellence to which they aspired. Their parents did not know either. For them it was a symbol of the status they hoped to acquire for their daughters. A good dame school could teach a girl to sew, to spell, to darn, and to mend, but finishing academies such as Anna's offered more: a polite education for females, acquisition of the ornamental domestic and social skills that materially improved a provincial girl's marriage prospects.

The picture was a lie, but Anna delivered on its promises. She taught the daughters of New York's wealthy merchants embroidery, mathematics, geography, decorative painting, and drawing in charcoal and pastel. For extra tuition her charges could attend the Tuesday-morning dance class where Mr. Sodi taught the minuet, the louvre, and the allemande. For another fee they could study voice, composition, and the harpsichord with Mr. Biferi.

It was a complete education for ladies, and the finest available in New York, sufficient to make an American girl show to good effect in even a London drawing room, but Anna's visitor was not impressed.

"Geography is an unusual discipline for a finishing school," said her neatly attired guest, observing the scene in the parlor. Anna could not tell whether she approved. Then she added, "But you offer an otherwise narrow curriculum, and a deceptive one"—her eyes moved from the silk picture on the wall to the girls stitching below it—"when life's hardest lessons are sure to be learned outside these walls."

Anna had heard similar sentiments from parents before, particularly those in the more volatile trades, whose fortunes were at the mercy of the changing market, although something about this woman's manner suggested that money was no obstacle.

"Education," replied Anna smoothly, "is an investment in a woman's future. It is a dowry that cannot be squandered by a spendthrift husband. It is an evergreen inheritance that can be passed to her children no matter the condition of her husband's estate."

"And if the times call for a woman who can do more than dance and sew?"

That was *not* one of the usual questions.

It forced Anna to turn and examine her visitor. They had been talking for a quarter of an hour. Anna had led her on a tour of the house, shown her the parlors and garden and a selection of her most advanced students' works in progress, but somehow in that time Anna had failed to look at her guest closely.

The woman had given her name as Ashcroft. Anna had addressed her as "Miss," and the woman had not corrected her. Miss Ashcroft was young, probably the same age as Anna, in her middle to late twenties; too young to have daughters old enough for finishing school, but not too young to be entrusted with the education of a sister or a niece.

From a short distance, Miss Ashcroft was pleasant-looking, but she wouldn't turn heads on the street. Her linen gown was that shade of beige that blends into every background. Her straw hat was practical and plain. But the face beneath it . . . Anna was forced to take a closer look.

Miss Ashcroft was more than pleasant-looking. She had flawless skin, Cupid's bow lips, and wide, dark brown eyes. The hair tucked into her plain straw hat was a rich chestnut. The body beneath the dun-colored linen was classically proportioned.

Miss Ashcroft was in fact beautiful, but it was not

the sort of beauty that advertised. She wore no paint or powder, no rouge to color her cheeks. She did nothing to court attention and everything to divert it from her.

The simple costume struck Anna all at once as a disguise. Her heart skipped a beat. She had ever known only one woman capable of such artful subterfuge, and the Widow was dead. That dangerous lady had taken her secrets—and Anna's—to the grave with her, and this enigmatic stranger could not possibly know the truth.

"We offer Latin and French to girls who will need it," said Anna, putting the Widow and the treacherous past from her mind.

Miss Ashcroft turned her penetrating gaze on Anna, and their eyes met. "And what about Dutch?"

Anna's heart raced. This woman knew. It did not matter how *much* she knew. When you lived beneath layers of secrets piled like blankets against the cold, losing a single covering meant you'd freeze to death. She pulled them close around her now and brazened it out as her late mentor, the woman who had shaped the path her life had taken, would have done.

"There is no demand for it," Anna said. "The Dutch rarely marry outsiders, and they speak their language only amongst themselves."

"But you speak it fluently," said Miss Ashcroft.

Anna could feel all the color drain from her face. The girls went on stitching as though nothing had happened while Anna's carefully constructed world fell down around her ears.

With it went all hope of safety. Anna Winters, English

gentlewoman of disappointed hopes and modest means, mistress of Miss Winters' Academy, did not speak Dutch, but Annatje Hoppe, fugitive from the law, the girl she had once been, did.

"We can arrange special tuition in a variety of subjects," said Anna. She said it for the benefit of the girls, who were definitely listening, no matter how dulcet and absorbed in their embroidery they might pretend to be. The Widow had always said that women made the best spies because, being so seldom invited to speak, they were forced to cultivate the habit of listening.

The girls' parents, of course, would withdraw them if and when they found out about her. But not yet. Not yet. She had weathered so much to get here. She was not ready to give it up. Each hour, each *minute* she could bargain for counted. "If you'd care to discuss a program of study, we can take tea in my office."

Miss Ashcroft inclined her head and followed Anna out of the parlor. Every detail of the house she had worked so hard to buy seemed suddenly precious to her: the painted floorcloth in the hall, the sturdy banister on the stairs, the fine chintz curtains on the windows. Her childhood had been one of austerity, her adolescence despair and poverty, so when prosperity had come to her, she'd furnished her home with all the domestic comforts she had never known.

Her students were used to finer things, of course. Their families were among the richest in Manhattan. But no one expected a schoolmistress to keep a luxurious house, and there were comforts enough for the girls who boarded.

There had been more students before the war began in '75, when travel was easier and families from as far away as Albany sent their daughters to Anna for finishing. But then the trouble had started at Lexington in April, and by October the Liberty Boys and the Livingston family between them had driven the royal governor and the British garrison off Manhattan Island.

For months it had been unclear who really controlled New York: the governor, from his floating office aboard a ship in the harbor; the Rebel Committee of Safety; or the mob. Anna's personal sympathies lay with the Rebels, but their war was endangering her livelihood. Anyone with money, anyone whose business was portable, took it elsewhere, and half of Anna's girls had departed with their families.

Then Washington's army arrived in New York in the summer of '76 and enrollment swelled. The Virginian general brought with him a coterie of officers, wives, and, *naturally*, daughters—whose needlework and dancing skills could be improved upon, especially with so many eligible young men of the right political persuasion on hand and so many balls being given in their honor.

It was not to last. By November General Howe had driven Washington and his army out of New York and into the Jerseys, and the school had emptied once more. Fire had broken out as the Rebels fled, and for months the city had reeked of smoke and all the sills in the house had been black with soot. Anna had despaired of the school's recovering.

Her salvation had come from the enemy. Anna would never love the King or the government that ruled in his name, but General Howe had made her prosperous. He had fortified Manhattan and created a safe haven for loyalists—at least the ones wealthy enough to leave their homes and businesses behind—from all over the colonies. War may have been raging off Manhattan Island, with armies pursuing one another through the Jerseys, but in New York life went on. Now Anna was turning students away and putting girls from the finest families in America on a waiting list.

That morning she had been prosperous, successful, *safe*.

If this woman exposed her, she would be none of those things. If this woman exposed her, the bailiffs would come, and the same corrupt courts that had killed her father would try her. It didn't matter who controlled New York—the British or the Rebels—some things never changed. The law would always be on the side of the rich.

The light filtering through the window at the top of the stairs suddenly seemed wan and gray, as though the day had darkened with Anna's future. Miss Ashcroft followed Anna into the little office behind the second-floor parlor, where she had her writing table and her secretary and four comfortable chairs. She'd learned that comfortable chairs made meetings with parents, which were sometimes strained, a little easier, but today the soft green damask worsted on her armchair felt suffocating and she fought a sudden urge to run as she had run so many years before. That impulse had only led her into different—and deeper—danger. She had learned since—no, she had been *taught*—to know when to stand and fight.

She shut the door, closeting herself and the enigmatic Miss Ashcroft in privacy. Anna wished that the woman would have the courtesy at least to seem threatening. Instead, she untied her hat and arranged her skirts until she was sitting comfortably and then said, "Did you mention tea?"

It was such a commonplace question. The sort of thing the Widow would have asked. That lady had always leveraged the domestic and the familiar, the feminine and delicate, to her advantage. Tea with the Widow had been like lifting the dome on a silver platter to find a coiled adder.

Miss Ashcroft was so very like the Widow that Anna did not know how she had missed it. It wasn't just the costume. It was something about her manner.

"You're not here for tea, or to look at the school," said Anna.

"Whiskey, then, perhaps?" said Miss Ashcroft setting her hat on the baize-covered table. "I'm told New Yorkers like to conduct all their business over strong drink, and I expect you kept a bottle, for her."

"I did keep one, in the kitchen," admitted Anna. "But I poured it out when I learned she was dead." She'd poured it, to be specific, in a wide circle over the ground in the garden, a libation of sorts. It had been a sentimental gesture, an offering in honor of a woman who disdained sentiment. Anna had never learned the trick of it, how to detach herself from people and things. Sometimes at night she still closed her eyes and ached to be back in her family's cottage with the smoky jambless chimney and warm sleeping loft.

"Then I suppose there's nothing for it—tea, it is," said her mysterious visitor. She took the liberty of rising and pulling the bell. When she was seated again, she said, "Now, Anna—or do you prefer Annatje?"

"Anna will do. I presume your name is not Ashcroft."

"No, it's not. But Ashcroft is a familiar name. That was one of the things I learned from the Widow. Never use a name you will not answer to instinctively, immediately, even—or especially—when you hear it called in a crowded room. Anna is close enough to Annatje, but Winters is an interesting choice, since your family name is Hoppe."

If she knew that much, she knew everything that mattered. The only question that remained was whether she would prove friend or foe. "Winters was my mother's name."

"A sensible option, then."

The door opened. Mrs. Peterson entered with a tray. Miss Ashcroft smiled and asked how many girls were usually enrolled at one time. Here at least was a scene Anna could play to perfection. She made all the right noises about the school, as though she were conversing with the parent of a prospective student. When Mrs. Peterson was gone and the door was closed again Miss Ashcroft said, "Is there no one in New York in your confidence?"

"No."

"That must be very lonely." Miss Ashcroft sounded as though she was intimately acquainted with loneliness.

Anna had never been lonely. She'd kept her secrets gladly. Talking about them would not change the past. It would only destroy the adoptive family she had formed at the school and shatter all the joy she had found there. Some things were better kept close to the heart. "How do you know who I am?"

"Angela Ferrers willed me her estate. Property, money, and . . . contacts. At least the ones she did not divulge before her death. Her intention was unwritten, but plain enough. I have taken up, in a small way, the work the Widow once did, gathering information. As you observed, though, the Dutch keep themselves to themselves. That is why I am here."

Anna did not have to ask for whom Miss Ashcroft gathered information. The Widow had been in French pay when Anna met her, though Anna had not learned that until later. Angela had worked for many flags and diverse factions in her varied career, but always against British interests. If this lady was the Widow's protégée, she worked for the Americans, or one of their allies.

It didn't matter. All that was behind her.

"I have not spoken or read Dutch in ten years. You would do better to look for a translator elsewhere." She heard Dutch, of course, on the street, almost every day, but it was not the Dutch she had grown up with. The accent was different, closer to the way it was spoken in the Netherlands. The Jerseys had their own dialect too. Anna rarely heard the soft cadences of the Hudson Highlands in Manhattan, and when she did she walked quickly away.

That life—that world—was behind her. She did not want to be reminded of all she had lost.

"I do not need a translator. I need a teacher. One who knows Dutch but appears to be wholly English. Someone who can be my eyes and ears on Harenwyck."

Harenwyck. Anna could not hear the name without feeling her chest constrict, even after all this time.

She'd passed by the Dutch Church on Pearl Street one day just after a wedding. The bride and groom had been glowing with youth and optimism, and a well-wisher had asked them where they planned to set up house. The couple announced that they were bound for Harenwyck to take up a lease. They did not have the money to buy land themselves, so they would rent acreage on the manor until they could afford to buy.

Only they would *never* be able to afford to buy. Anna could have told them that. But she hadn't. She'd hurried away down the street, face flushed, unable to conceal her reaction. *Harenwyck.* An estate so large she had never set foot off it in the first seventeen years of her life. Fields so golden, cattle so sleek, soil so black it should have been impossible for a family to go hungry there, but hers had.

"No." She said it automatically, but the answer would have been the same after long deliberation. "I can never go back there."

"You were barely seventeen when you left. A child. The chances that anyone would recognize the woman you have become are slight. And *Miss Winters* is so well established as a genteel New Yorker—a decidedly English type—that no one will see a fugitive Dutch girl when they look at her. I cannot claim that you will be in no danger, but I can assure you that the game is worth the candle. Harenwyck occupies a vital position on the Hudson. If we lose control of the valley, the way to New England will be open to Howe's army. Make no mistake— if we lose the river, we will lose this war."

"My family lost everything—my father lost his life— playing at revolutions with the Widow." She could not speak of what she alone had lost. It was in the past, and she wanted it—*needed* it—to stay there. "I will not make the same mistake with her successor. But I will give you this for free: Cornelis Van Haren will never support the Rebels. He'll play both sides for every advantage he can get, but when pressed he will defend his ancient privileges." His great fiefdom, his seat in the assembly, his influence over the courts.

"Cornelis Van Haren is dead. His son is patroon of Harenwyck, and an entirely different kettle of fish."

"Gerrit," said Anna, remembering the quiet, dark-haired young man only a year older than herself. He had been kind. A very different character from his father. Even as a child. One of her earliest memories of the big house at the manor was of Gerrit.

Her father had taken her to pay their tithe to the landlord. She'd been nine years old, dressed in her best linen gown, shiny new *klompen* on her feet, painted bright yellow with pink flowers and red laces.

Ten-year-old Gerrit had spied her *klompen* and furrowed his brow. "It's not raining out. Why are you wearing pattens over your shoes?"

At first she did not understand his question. *Klompen* were shoes. Everyone wore them, except for coachmen and soldiers, who wore boots. And hers were special for today. Painted and pretty. Her father had pronounced them little drops of sunlight. Not like the bare wooden ones she wore in the fields.

Then Anna spied the patroon's lady and her friends. They were sitting on the high, deep porch of the house, shaded by the gently sloped roof, drinking tea at a table with legs carved like the claws of a great bird. The ladies looked like fairies. Their dresses rustled like tall grass, yards and yards of bright silk shining like water, and their shoes . . . their shoes were not *klompen*. They were not made out of wood. They were not carved with stars or hearts, or painted sunny yellow or sky blue. They were delicate silk slippers, colored like jewels, embroidered and trimmed with ribbon.

Before she could fully grasp the gulf that separated a poor tenant's daughter from a lord—far wider than the stretch of lawn between herself and the tea table—he did. She saw it on his face. His cosseted childhood came to an end in front of her. He saw for the first time the walls that separated the patroon's family and peers from their tenants—walls both physical and social. The sandstone of the old manor house and the lacquered panels of a liveried carriage, buttressed by inward- and outward-facing retainers: the servants in the hall and the *schouts*, bailiffs, and other agents that insulated Gerrit's class from hers.

With all the gravity a ten-year-old could muster he took it upon himself to salvage the situation. He bowed low, as though she were a lady and an equal, and introduced himself as Gerrit Van Haren.

It was seven years before he spoke to her again. She saw him nearly every week, though, standing up at the front of the church during services in the broad Van Haren box pew with its tiled stove and silk cushions, his broad shoulders cased in brown velvet, his chestnut hair falling loose down his back. Every time she thought about talking to him, she looked down at her feet. She was still wearing *klompen*, and he was still wearing shoes.

It was her growling stomach that brought them together again when she was sixteen and he was seventeen. He had heard it, all the way at the front of the church, three rows forward from the Hoppe pew.

After the service, Gerrit offered her *koekjes* from his pocket. Up close it was impossible to ignore the changes in him, the broadening of his shoulders, the deepening of his voice, the shadow about his chin.

They ate the cookies together in the burying ground behind the church. Or more accurately she devoured them while he entertained her with wild stories—entirely fabricated—about the men and women buried in the graveyard. Flights of Gothic fancy complete with ghosts and witches and haunted abbeys and brooding old mansions.

He'd been too kind to remark on her hunger, or ask the source of it. Or maybe he had been too embarrassed, because he knew where the tenants' beef and butter and corn went: to the manor house, to pay the rents that increased each year. They were called a tithe out of tradition, but they had long since ceased to be just a tenth of tenant crops. But you paid because you'd cleared the land and built the cottage yourself—had invested everything in someone else's land—and to lose your lease was to lose all.

The following week Gerrit brought enough cookies for Anna and himself; buttery treats, tasting of cardamom and orange water. They infused the pockets of his velvet coat with their perfume, and the scent blended sweetly with the bay rum he wore.

When it turned cold they met in the old barn where the wheat was threshed and the flax was carded in summer. Their meetings continued for a year, until Anna's mother found out about them, and beat her. She told Anna that there was only one thing that the patroon's son could want from a tenant's daughter.

The lecture had made her skin crawl. She had felt the way Gerrit must have done that day on the lawn, when he had become suddenly aware of the gulf that separated him from most of the people on the estate. Only this wasn't just the gulf that separated the rich from the poor, the powerful from the weak. This was the chasm that separated men and women, and according to her mother, it could not be bridged by friendship or affection.

After that Anna's mother kept her home from church for a month. And sometime during that month, Gerrit left for school in Leiden, and she never saw him again.

"He will recognize me. I knew Gerrit when we were

children." More than knew him. Even now she could remember the bay rum and cardamom scent of him, the lazy hours spent together in the woods or up in the hayloft.

Miss Ashcroft shook her head. "Gerrit is not patroon. He ran away to join the Rebels in 'seventy-five and Cornelis disinherited him. It is Andries, the younger brother, who is lord of the manor now."

Andries. She remembered him too. A tall blond boy. "There were three children," said Anna. "Gerrit, Andries, and a younger sister."

"Yes," said Miss Ashcroft. "Elizabeth. Information about what goes on among the more remote patroon families is hard to come by. As you know, New York's gossips and broadsheets waste little time on the Hudson aristocracy in general—despite their wealth—*because* they are of little interest to young women, and the parents of young women, of marriageable age: they've long sought spouses, and been content to socialize, almost exclusively among their own. For the most part, families like the Van Harens keep themselves to themselves, and their tenants are reluctant to share 'intelligence' for fear of reprisal. But by all accounts Elizabeth eloped to get away from her father. It is presumably her children—twin girls—that Andries is raising. Cornelis Van Haren was not well liked, either by his tenants or his family. Andries, it seems, is doing his best to make amends."

As a boy Andries had possessed a quick wit and a cold demeanor. He and Anna had never spoken, but she had overheard him cutting one of the *schouts*, the private bailiffs who answered to no law but the patroon's, down to size. He had been aloof like his father. He would not know her from Eve.

"Andries Van Haren," continued the woman who called herself Ashcroft, "controls two hundred thousand strategic acres on the Hudson, including Harenhoeck."

Anna could picture it now, that narrow point on the Hudson. On a clear day you could make out what a man was wearing on the other side. It had been considered a great feat to swim it when she was a child.

"The current there," said Miss Ashcroft, "is such that a chain can be stretched across the river without breaking. Van Haren is ready to declare for the Americans, to give us Harenhoeck, but he wants something. Washington needs to discover what."

"I know a little of revolutions." Anna had been there in '65 when the tenants had risen. She could still close her eyes and see the mob. She could remember the light in their eyes, her father's ringing voice and rousing words. And what had happened when the sheriffs had come for him. "Why do you think it will turn out differently this time?" Anna demanded.

"Because this is more than an uprising of tenants. Because men—and women—of every station are risking their lives and fortunes. Because the times are right to do now what your father tried to do then. There will be no lords and tenants in this new America. Only freemen and freeholders. The same vision your father swayed a multitude with."

His vision had ended in failure and Anna too had paid the price for the risks he had taken. She believed in the

American cause because it was rooted in the same ideals of equality that her father had espoused, but she had already fought one revolution, and lost. It was for others to fight this one.

"Why me?" Anna asked. "Surely you can find someone else who speaks Dutch to listen at doors. There must be hundreds of families on the patroonship who are chafing under the Van Haren yoke and would gladly spy on that family."

"True enough. And we have allies already at Harenwyck, but none so well placed as you could be. Andries Van Haren has sent his man of business to New York to sell his wheat, his linen, his flax, and his beef, and to hire a teacher for his nieces. This is our opportunity to place an agent directly in his household, one he will speak freely in front of because he will not know that she is Dutch."

"And once I am there? I am not the Widow. I have no skill at espionage."

"She would have disagreed. According to her notes, you ride, you shoot, and through her you acquired some skill with lockpicks and a certain . . . agility in difficult situations."

"A lifetime ago," said Anna. When she had been young and scared and determined never to fall under another's power again.

"And you understand men."

Anna did not reply at once. She could see how a woman who was like the Widow—but not the Widow herself—might arrive at such a conclusion. It would suggest itself in the broad outline of Anna's life, the events that had taken her from Harenwyck to New York, from Annatje to Anna.

"I thought you wanted *eyes* and *ears*."

"What I want, what Washington needs, is Harenwyck. If the Widow were alive, she could deliver it to him. Did you know she was at Trenton? Or, more accurately, she was at Mount Holly with the Hessian commander when *he* should have been at Trenton, and by her wiles Washington snatched victory from the jaws of defeat."

"She was a singular woman," said Anna. The Widow had rescued her and given her a new identity and a new life. She could have been no older than forty when she was killed, and might have been a good deal younger— she had the sort of spare beauty that seemed ageless—but Anna had always sensed that the Widow had experience in excess of her years. "How did she die?"

"She was murdered," said Miss Ashcroft, looking Anna straight in the eye, "by the same British intelligence officer who has fixed his eyes on the narrows at Harenhoeck. A man named John André. He had her tortured, and then he stood by while someone else slit her throat."

Anna stilled the impulse to touch her own neck. She had known that the Widow had died violently. The lawyer had implied as much with his silence. But she had not been prepared for the visceral horror of it. Whatever else the Widow had been or done, the woman had saved her, helped her build a new life on the ashes of the old. The ashes of her and her father's lives on Harenwyck.

"I realize that I am asking you to give up the relative safety you enjoy now," said Miss Ashcroft, "but the Widow thought highly of you. And I do not believe that a thinking woman with integrity can remain neutral in this fight—especially not one who has experienced injustice firsthand."

"Why should I trust you," asked Anna, who, however deep her reservations, could not deny the force of the woman's argument, "when I don't even know your real name?"

"Because I will do what the Widow did not, even in death. I will give you *my* real name. It is Kate Grey. My father is one of Washington's commanders. They call him the Grey Fox. My husband is an English lord who has been attainted a traitor. He is wanted by the Crown for treason and by the army for desertion. I spied for the Americans in Philadelphia, and while I was there, I killed a British officer. There is a price on my head, and I still thought it worth coming to New York, entering the lion's den, to beg your help. You hold my life in your hands. I have some of the Widow's skill, but none of her ruthlessness. If you ran to the fort now, I would not escape Manhattan alive."

"If I go back to Harenwyck, if someone recognizes me, *I'll* hang." She was trying to talk herself out of it. She was safe here. She had Mrs. Peterson and Miss Demarest and the girls, and even if she could not marry and start a family herself, she had a role in shaping such futures for the young women she taught. There was value in that. And security.

"It would be safer to stay here," agreed the woman who said her name was Kate Grey.

Anna believed her. She'd been a terrible judge of people when she'd arrived in New York, but a decade teaching adolescent girls had schooled her in the art of mendacity as her years with the Widow never had.

"But not by much. And this," her visitor continued, "is your opportunity to make your father's death and all that you have suffered mean something."

Miss Ashcroft—Kate Grey—was nearly as good as the Widow. She was fired by the same zeal. She made no false promises or assurances of safety, simply laid out what was at stake. But Anna was not naive enough to think she was free to choose. She had seen the carrot, but the Widow had taught her to keep one eye out for the stick.

"Safer, you say, but not by much. So what happens if I elect to stay here, at the school, and you have to find some other spy to send to Harenwyck?"

"You own an empty house on Pearl Street," said Kate Grey. "The deed is in your name, and there is a body in the basement."

"If you know that, then you know that I didn't put it there."

"Yes. But you will have a difficult time convincing a jury of it."

"So the high ideals of your revolution embrace blackmail, then."

"Your position as a finishing school teacher has insulated you from the suffering in the countryside, Miss Winters. There are families who have had everything taken from them. They were not given a choice in the matter. The Widow rarely acted out of sentiment. She rescued you for a reason and educated you for a purpose.

I doubt that it was to teach watercolors and dancing lessons."

Miss Ashcroft stood up and tied on her plain hat. "The patroon's man of business will likely call on you tomorrow, or the day after. He is here to sell Van Haren's produce, and to buy seed and pots and pans and kettles and harness to sell to the tenants of Harenwyck at prices that will keep them forever in debt and tied to the land."

She knew it. Her butter and her flax had made that journey. She'd bought buttons and needles and copper pans in the manor house store at dear prices, and every year, no matter how much more her family had produced, they found themselves a little poorer.

"If you accept his offer," continued Kate Grey, "and travel to Harenwyck, you can write to me care of your housekeeper here. Mrs. Peterson will forward your letters."

Of course. The Widow had found Mrs. Peterson for Anna. Mrs. Peterson alone knew what Anna had been before she became a teacher, though not where she had come from, or what she had fled.

"And what do you expect me to *do* at Harenwyck itself?"

"Whatever it takes to bring Andries Van Haren to our side."

A picture of Gerrit's chilly younger brother, glittering, blond, handsome, and decidedly aloof, swam into her mind. "Just because I understand the patroonship doesn't mean I have any insight into the mind of the patroon. I am only a tenant farmer's daughter."

"You are surely more than that, but your adversaries are as well. Beware of John André. He is charming, accomplished, clever, and quite deadly."

"Am I expected to seduce him too?" asked Anna, sourly.

"Expectations are dangerous where someone like Captain André is concerned, except perhaps that feminine wiles will leave him unmoved. He is ruthless and all too willing to sacrifice his pawns. If you encounter him, be on your guard. Use your instincts. The Widow thought you were a sound judge of character."

"I cannot imagine why."

"Perhaps because you never trusted her."

Anna stood in the door and watched her visitor disappear into the traffic on the street. She did it very well, this Kate Grey, walking with her head tilted so the brim of her hat obscured her face, elbows held close to her body so she took up hardly any room at all. The dun-colored gown blended into the dusty cobbled street, and then she rounded a corner and was gone.

Kate Grey was right about the Widow. If she had been alive, she would have expected Anna to go to Harenwyck. But Kate Grey was wrong about Anna's life in New York. It was not lonely. It was full of companionship and sometimes even gossip and drama, usually the harmless kind that young women relished and which Anna enjoyed vicariously through them.

Only today's gossip was not harmless. Anna knew as much from the few words she caught as she approached the parlor, terms that did not belong in the vocabulary of gently reared young maidens. When the boards in the hall creaked beneath her feet, the voices inside fell silent.

She entered the room to discover the scene she had expected. All six of her students were stitching with extraordinary concentration.

Anna marched straight up to Becky Putnam and put out her hand. "I'll take the letter, Rebecca."

Becky looked up from her embroidery loom, all wide-eyed innocence. "What letter, miss?"

"Why, the one you were just reading aloud. From a gentleman, I gather."

"But I don't know what you mean, Miss Winters. We were only trading recipes for blackberry preserves."

Anna weighed her choices. She knew exactly where the letter was now, because every schoolgirl ever born thought she had invented that particular hiding place. Knowing where girls hid things could be useful. If she showed her hand, none of those present would ever use such a hiding place again. They would have to become cleverer about their indiscretions—which might be inconvenient for Anna. But then, if Anna allowed Becky to get away with her deception, the girl might become an incorrigible liar.

Anna decided that the benefits of this particular lesson outweighed the costs. She placed her hand on the top of Becky's embroidery loom. It was a pretty thing, a slender frame of polished tiger maple on brass casters, easy to move about the room as the sun changed position, the perfect height for a seated needlewoman to stitch away the afternoon. It was hinged at the top and could be tilted this way and that, or flipped entirely in case any stitches needed to be picked out. It was finer than the other frames in the room, finer than what the other girls had, and maybe because of that, because wealth and position made her bold, Becky gripped the bottom hard and held it fast.

Anna raised both her eyebrows. Becky withered beneath her stare, and released the frame. Anna flipped it over. She was unsurprised to find an elaborately folded letter tacked to the back of the canvas. The sender had taken a great deal of time with his love token, inking and folding it so that the verses made sense no matter which way one read it. Anna opened the puzzle purse to find that the illustrations inside were no less . . . ardent.

"Where did you get this?" Anna asked.

"I had it from Mrs. Peterson," admitted Becky. "She did not know the contents," the girl added hastily.

Anna handed the letter back to Becky. "Take it to the garden. Read it, by yourself," instructed Anna, "and then burn it."

"I can't burn it," said Becky. "He must have spent days writing it."

And illustrating it, no doubt. "Your parents are unlikely to find it as amusing as your friends do. Nor will they be as understanding as I am."

"I would keep it hidden," insisted Becky.

"And someone would find it, just as I have."

Becky paled at the unwelcome prospect. "I shall take it out to the garden now," she decided.

Becky departed. Anna sent the remaining girls up to the studio at the top of the house, where the light was very fine for sketching in the afternoon, and descended to the cellar kitchen.

Mrs. Peterson was mixing dough. She was an excellent baker, and she looked the part, plump and homely in her saffron linen jacket and skirt. Her little cakes were as fine as anything Mr. Fraunces offered at his tavern or sold from his bakeshop in Vauxhall Gardens. They were light and airy confections, made with the finely milled wheat flour that Anna's prosperity afforded. And yet, just at that moment, Anna hungered for the homely little *koekjes* from Harenwyck, Dutch treats, leavened with potash and spiced with cardamom and orange water and stretched with cornmeal.

"You've been passing letters for the girls again," said Anna, helping herself to one of the ginger cakes cooling on the rack.

"There's no harm in it with Becky," said Mrs. Peterson, pouring her batter into a buttered dish. "She's too sensible to do anything foolish. It's the other one, Mary, you'll need to watch."

Anna decided against mentioning the illustrations in the letter, because Mrs. Peterson was right. Becky was sensible. She would burn the love token, no matter how cleverly inked and folded it was.

Mary Phillips, though, was not sensible. The girl had been in one scrape after another ever since she had arrived at the school. Anna had tried talking with her, warned her of the dangers she courted, but ultimately realized that the girl would have to make her own mistakes, just like Anna had. Still, the fewer opportunities for those mistakes, the better, for all concerned. "Could Miss Demarest watch her, do you think, and manage the school, if I went away for a while?"

Mrs. Peterson halted on her way to the oven and set her dish down. "And where would you be thinking of going?"

"North, on a private tutoring engagement."

"She did a fair bit of traveling, in her day," said Mrs. Peterson. She did not have to say who "she" was. They were speaking of the Widow.

She did, Anna thought. *And one day she didn't come back.*

Two

Anna had never traveled so far in such style. More than a decade before she had made the journey from Harenwyck to New York on foot, mile after mile in her sturdy *klompen*. It had taken her days—she had lost track of how many on the road—to reach the ferry, and hunger and cold had been her constant companions.

Today was different. She was warm and well fed in Andries Van Haren's well-sprung coach, and the slippers on her feet were soft pink silk. They were not the most practical footwear for a trip into farm country. They were, in fact, the finest shoes she owned, and she kept them stuffed with paper in the bottom drawer of her good chest, reserving them for the recitals parents attended, the ones where her students showed off their progress on the harpsichord and the dance floor. She had chosen to wear them to Harenwyck precisely because they were inappropriate, because they would mark her as the city creature she pretended to be.

And because they were not *klompen.*

The carriage was an elegant four-seater with black lacquer pillars and gilded panels, the doors emblazoned with the Van Haren coat of arms: a black wolf grasping a dead lamb in its jaws on a yellow shield, doubtless "earned" from some medieval feat of butchery.

Her personal possessions and those items of school equipment too delicate to ride atop the coach were heaped on the seat beside her: a basket of embroidery floss to occupy her on the journey, the atlas she used to teach geography, the book of engravings that her students sketched copies from, the standing loom for large projects, and a box of fine paints imported from London.

On the bench opposite, facing backward because he had insisted that she have the finer perch, sat Theunis Ten Broeck, Andries Van Haren's estate manager and "man of business."

He had called on Anna, as predicted, the day after Kate Grey. Ten Broeck was a genial, lively man in his fifties who, unlike Kate Grey, had expressed delight over everything in the house. In a mellow baritone—whose guttural *R*'s and staccato rhythms recalled the language of her childhood—he had praised every detail in Anna's needlework landscape: the fine trees, the little ducks, the fishing lady and her beau, the stately house and well-kept grounds. He had declared the tight little parlor they used for dancing practice a "grand space for a whirl." The skylit attic where she taught painting was a "dazzling aerie," the kitchen a "testament to sound home management."

The estate manager, it turned out, had three daughters, and was keenly interested in the latest ideas in female education. He wanted his girls to be able to compete for husbands with the fashionable young women in New York. "To marry better than their unfortunate mother did," he said with a twinkle in his eye. But his silk suit and clocked stockings and the silver buckles on his shoes told Anna that Ten Broeck had done well for himself at Harenwyck. His daughters would have good portions to take into their marriages, and a little city polish went a long way for a girl with money. Anna had never envied her students that. Not the money. It was the love their parents lavished on them that she coveted, the thought and care and *caution* invested in their futures.

Ten Broeck had also sung the praises of the patroon's new house on the estate, the fine English mansion that had replaced the old Dutch cottage which had itself seemed so grand to Anna. But Ten Broeck was uncharacteristically silent on the subject of the patroon and his nieces. It didn't matter. She had already decided to accompany him back to Harenwyck. It was that, or wait for the bailiffs to appear at her door, and she had decided a long time ago that she would always meet fate head-on.

All the same, her heart had ached when she stood on the stoop of the house, looking back at Mrs. Peterson and Miss Demarest and the girls—even the troublesome Mary Phillips—assembled to bid her farewell. The school was in good hands with Miss Demarest. Anna had no fears on that account. It was what might happen if Anna was found out as Annatje Hoppe that terrified her. The school would be destroyed, along with the reputations of her friends and colleagues. The only way to safeguard the academy's future—and her own—was to journey into her past, to Harenwyck.

The carriage trundled through the early-morning streets of New York, past the soldiers, who were everywhere now, always searching the docks for extra work. Their red coats made the merchants feel safe, but the mechanics and laborers resented the competition, and Anna had given Mrs. Peterson strict orders not to hire any of them for odd jobs while she was gone. If the British lost control of the city, the mob would have its day, and Anna did not want her school or her girls to be objects of retribution.

At the ferry they were obliged to get out and wait while the coach was unhitched and horses, vehicle, and passengers were rowed across the swift-running Hudson. It was only the second time Anna had crossed the churning body of water that separated the mainland from Manhattan, her old life from her new.

Ten Broeck helped her to disembark on the other side. For several minutes she continued to feel the toss and pitch of the boat on dry land, and she was still swaying slightly when a troop of horse from the British Legion, smart in their short green jackets and leather and bearskin helmets, trotted up to meet them.

"Our escort," explained Ten Broeck, his deep voice almost apologetic.

"Does the patroon's carriage always merit a detachment of cavalry?" Anna asked Ten Broeck as the troop's young commander slid from his horse with practiced grace. He was not as tall perhaps as he had appeared in the saddle, but he was exceedingly graceful and well made, and he had the darkest brown eyes she had ever seen.

"No, but his strongbox does."

The patroon's strongbox was maple banded with iron and required two men to lift from the cart. And it merited not only thirty horses, but a lieutenant colonel as well: one whose name Anna had often heard whispered in her parlor. He removed his helmet and bowed just a trifle too deeply before her.

"Banastre Tarleton, at your service."

Ten Broeck presented her as Miss Winters of Miss Winters' Academy, and Tarleton's brows knit.

"Surely not," said Tarleton. "I have it on the best authority that Miss Winters is a snaggletoothed dragon, not a lovely young lady."

Now she understood why her girls whispered about this ambitious man—barely in his twenties—in such breathy tones. He wasn't just handsome, with his compact, horseman's frame, fine features and thick auburn hair glinting red in the sunlight. He was charming.

"That 'authority' would be Mary Phillips, I'll wager," said Anna.

His crooked smile made him more charming still. "*Do* schoolmistresses wager?"

"Yes, but only rhetorically. And, occasionally, on horse races," she added. Miss Demarest had a passion for racing.

She even won a little money at it, from time to time. "I hope Miss Phillips is acquitting herself well in the social whirl."

"She is indeed. Along with her charming sister. They are very accomplished young ladies and a credit to your school."

"Either you are a flatterer, or you have never seen her needlework," said Anna.

The colonel laughed. "I have never seen her needlework. Nor asked to. But she *dances* very prettily."

Mary did dance prettily. And her father owned two wharves and an estate in the Jerseys, which made her dancing prettier still to ambitious young men in search of a fortune.

The colonel loaded the strongbox into the carriage himself. It took up most of the room on the floor of the coach. Between Anna's school equipment and the fortune in gold at her feet the carriage became very cramped indeed. Tarleton apologized for the inconvenience and took the time to rearrange her baggage. He secured Anna's paint box, atlas, and embroidery loom to the strongbox with a lattice of leather strapping so that she had a little more room on the bench.

And then they were off, rumbling through an autumn tunnel of dense forest roofed with a canopy of red oak and sugar maple and black birch. She didn't remember the road being so beautiful, mysterious even, when she had traveled it before. Thinking back, she had not really *seen* the road or appreciated the scenery at all. She'd made that entire journey from Harenwyck looking over her shoulder, listening for signs of pursuit. Now she was returning, because there was no other way forward.

Viewed through glass windows flanked by velvet curtains, the landscape looked almost painted, like the backdrops at the theater—save for the presence of the horsemen. Tarleton's cavalry rode ahead, alongside, and behind the coach. Their green coats and bearskin helmets blended into the forest. Anna could see why this unit was so famed for horsemanship. They maintained their distance from the carriage and intervals one from another with precision and seemed to glide along the rutted road, while the carriage pitched and dove over every stone and furrow. Even with the jolting, though, it was idyllic, and difficult to imagine that bandits lurked around the bend.

"Are the roads really so dangerous?" she asked Ten Broeck, as Tarleton cantered past them for the second time that hour to confer with his scouts. She'd heard, of course, about bands of cattle thieves and gangs of armed loyalists on the roads.

"The 'Cowboys' and 'Skinners' are mostly interested in forage. You won't see a beast out to pasture within a mile of the road from here to Harenwyck. But they turn their hand to robbery readily enough when the opportunity presents itself."

And opportunity sat at her feet in an ironbound box.

"I had heard," she said carefully, "that the patroon favors the Rebels; and yet, Howe has given him a troop of horses to protect his gold."

"The patroon has thus far resisted local pressure to take the Rebel oath, and the British know he cannot make a public statement of loyalty to the King without risking the retribution of his neighbors. General Clinton asks for private assurances that the patroon is on the side of government. And the Rebels and their Committee of Safety ask for similar assurances. It is a damnably delicate business, miss."

He smiled at his own choice of words. "And 'business,' in part at least, it is. The patroon must sell his beef and butter *somewhere*. At present, the Continentals are not paying for their provisions in hard currency. The British are. The Rebels tolerate this trade because it funds the patroon's militia, buys powder and shot, and pays the men to defend the estate, and they hold out hope that the patroonship will go over to their side. Clinton knows that buying supplies from Harenwyck in hard cash is funding a militia that could be turned against him, but he has twenty thousand mouths to feed and must get his provisions where he can. For now, as long as the patroon sells his beef and butter and flour in New York, General Clinton will see that his gold gets to Harenwyck."

Ten Broeck said it with confidence, but Anna had her doubts. Her neighbors in New York had tried to maintain that same tricky balance at the beginning of the war. Avoiding oaths if they could, taking them and then breaking them as the city changed hands. Whatever it took to survive. But sometimes it wasn't enough, as she had seen close hand.

The Americans had arrested her dancing master, Mr. Sodi, and thrown him in the sugarhouse on suspicion of spying for the British. The British had let him out, but then decided that he might have agreed to spy for the Americans while he was in their custody, and arrested him again. It had played merry hell with the school's dancing lessons until Anna could get him released. It had taken three days of visiting well-connected parents, trying to find the right string to secure Mr. Sodi's freedom. For several months afterward he would flinch every time there was a knock upon the door, sure that someone was coming to imprison him again.

It sounded to Anna as though the situation at Harenwyck was, if anything, *more* precarious than in New York.

Their coach stopped at an inn a little after noon to rest the horses, and Anna was glad for the opportunity to stretch her legs. Even with Tarleton's careful packing, she found it difficult to be comfortable for long in the confined space. Ten Broeck ordered a hot meal for himself and the King's soldiers, but Anna wasn't really hungry. She asked the innkeeper if it was safe to walk on the path behind the house, and he assured her that it was. Anna followed the trail past the outbuildings and down to a pleasant little brook. The woods there were so like the ones where she had grown up that she could close her eyes and almost imagine herself a child again.

It was an illusion. She was traveling into danger, not the security of childhood. She had played in woods like these, and sat by a brook like this, and even kissed a boy under trees like this.

Even after everything she had experienced after leaving Harenwyck, it was still difficult for her to believe that

Gerrit had been the villain her mother made him out to be. Their kisses had been thrilling, and mutual. She'd felt her heart race, her pulse quicken, her head become light as air, but there had been nothing taken, or surrendered, in those exchanges. It had been a shared coming together, like two kittens butting heads with their eyes closed. Perhaps it was only possible in adolescence, before their paths diverged so sharply into the roles expected of them, that men and women could meet as equals. She had never had the opportunity to learn for herself.

Being back in the woods of her childhood revived that memory, restored the details that had faded over time: the texture of birch bark, the babble of running water, the perfume of the forest. But Gerrit Van Haren was no more welcome here than she, be he heir to Harenwyck or no. And reminiscence was a tricky beast; with it came the other parts of her past she wished she could forget. Anna resolved to eschew nostalgia and be on her guard. But the hazard she met on the path back to the inn was not the kind she had prepared herself for.

The colonel was walking down to meet her. For a moment she thought that she had tarried too long, that the meal was finished and he was impatient to be on the road again, but her timepiece and his appearance told her otherwise. Only a quarter of an hour had passed. He had removed his crested helmet, washed his face, and combed his thick auburn hair.

And sought her out now, alone on the path, when he might have spoken to her in the company of Mr. Ten Broeck anytime that morning, or during their arrival at the inn. He was handsome, well-spoken, well connected, and well respected, but that did not make him safe. Safe men weren't, as a rule, whispered about in finishing school parlors.

"I thought you might enjoy some company on your amble, Miss Winters," he said. In the light filtered through the canopy of leaves above their heads, his brown eyes seemed almost black.

She was conscious all at once of how well he blended into the forest in his dark green jacket and brown breeches. Like a predator. Going deeper into the woods with him seemed like a very bad idea. "I was just returning to the inn, actually."

"Then permit me to escort you." She felt a ripple of unease when he offered her his arm. It was the wrong gesture to make to a lady one barely knew. In public, in view of Mr. Ten Broeck, it might have been courteous. Alone on the path, out of earshot of the inn, it bordered on effrontery, and placed her in an impossible position. If she refused, she risked giving offense. It would be as provoking as a slap to the face. It would suggest that she questioned his motives, which she did. Which was why he shouldn't have offered his arm at all.

The Widow had made her own way through the world and must have encountered dangerous situations— dangerous men—like this all the time. *When in doubt, play the scene through as though it is of your own making.* Anna took her advice, and Tarleton's arm, and prayed she knew what she was doing.

"How long will you stay at Harenwyck, Miss Winters?" He placed his hand over hers, which she did not like at all. With each step he pulled her a little closer until they were hip to hip. It was entirely too familiar for the shallow depth of their acquaintance. The Widow had taught her how to extricate herself from physical danger, but Anna was unpracticed in the far trickier art of evading this kind of subtle encroachment.

"It is difficult to say how long I will be," she said truthfully. "Much depends on what sort of curriculum the patroon has in mind for his nieces, and of course how quickly the misses Van Haren progress."

"Then allow me to tender a piece of practical advice: charge the patroon by the day, and dearly, and we'll have you back in New York before the month is out."

It was an invitation to flirt. She ignored it. "Is Harenwyck so grim, then?"

He gave her a sidelong glance. She doubted that many young women declined an opportunity to flirt with him. "Harenwyck is a pleasant enough countryseat," he said. "The new house is very English and very modern. The patroon is another matter. You will find these rural Dutch even more boorish than their city counterparts, and their entertainments and diversions rustic at best. They think a cider pressing the highest sort of social occasion and account their greasy oil cakes a great delicacy."

He did not know she was Dutch, of course. He did not know that she had eaten hot *olykoecken*, her lips and gown frosted with sugar, her fingers sticky, standing next to the bubbling pot, while the cider that leavened the dough was pressed on the great granite stone. It was like drinking in pure autumn, the perfume of apples and wood smoke and frying oil.

"The Dutch are notoriously mean," continued Tarleton, oblivious to the offense he gave, "but that parsimony may work to your advantage—if you are eager for a swift return to New York, where I might call on you."

She did not in fact like that idea at all.

"I am certain that the patroon will expect at least a complete sampler from each girl," she said, "if not other accomplished works from his nieces before I depart Harenwyck, and that will likely keep me in the Hudson Highlands at least into the new year."

"Teaching the patroon's nieces embroidery will be like throwing pearls before swine. They are sure to marry some country cousin with a desirable mill or sandpit or some such thing, who will not care a whit whether his wife can embroider an angling lady scene on a fire screen or not."

"You know a remarkable amount about the current taste in schoolgirl embroidery, Colonel Tarleton," she said. She did not altogether disguise the suspicion in her voice.

To her surprise he laughed. "I assure you that is not because I have been *fishing* among your young charges."

"No?"

"No. Though surely no man could blame me if I had."

Their fathers might, thought Anna.

"Some of your young misses," continued Tarleton, "are decidedly saucy pieces, and wise in the ways of the world beyond their years. Impossible to avoid, I'm bound, with so many lambs all in one fold." There were some men, Anna had long ago realized, who could not conceive of a gathering of unrelated women in any other context than the one with which they were most familiar: a brothel. It said more about those men, she believed, than about the essential nature of female education.

"It is my sister," continued Tarleton, "who writes to me about the fashion in stitchery. She is tutored at home, of course"—*of course*—"but she debates a choice of motif for her silk picture with the seriousness Parliament reserves for taxes."

"And how do you answer her?"

"That any man who cares more about the quality of her stitchery than the quality of her conversation isn't worth her time or effort."

She had been starting to dislike him, intensely, but it was impossible to despise a man who took his sister's part, no matter how unenlightened he might be on the subject of females outside his own family.

"What?" he prompted. "Aren't you going to lecture me on the importance of feminine accomplishments?"

"I expect that your sister already has, so I will spare you the lesson."

"I'm certain there are other things you could teach me."

Banastre Tarleton, the brother, and Banastre Tarleton, the man, she decided, were tolerable, even engaging. Banastre Tarleton, the seducer, was a decidedly unsavory character.

When she did not take the bait he said, "I expect to be sent south in the new year, but if you are able to return before then, you could write to me, and I could come up with some pretext to visit Harenwyck and escort you home. It would not be so very difficult to arrange. There's always unrest in the highlands and the territory is so vast that cavalry is the only answer. We could make it a very pleasant journey, you and I, and I could cover any expenses you might incur."

It was a proposition, and nicely done considering his aims, with no open vulgarity, and only an oblique reference to money changing hands. It had been a long time since she had received such an offer, and never one so delicately phrased.

That was because her new profession rarely placed her in proximity to men like this. Anna spent most of her days surrounded by women. The gentlemen she did meet were fathers in the company of their wives and daughters. Such men were always on their best behavior. The tradesmen and artisans she dealt with valued her custom and would never risk losing her business.

Tarleton, though, was neither a parent nor a tradesman. He saw her as a *demimondaine*, a woman on the fringe of polite society. Because she sold her services as a teacher, he assumed that she sold herself as well. That made it all too likely that he would take her refusal personally. She wished they were closer to the inn.

"It is a very flattering offer, Colonel," she said carefully, "but my livelihood in the city relies upon my reputation as a snaggletoothed dragon."

"And you conceive that I might play a swording Saint George to your toothy dragon."

"I think that is rather the point."

He smiled now, a wide, knowing grin, and she realized she had made an error. He mistook her frankness for another form of coquetry, or indeed for mere haggling. "The Hudson Highlands are *not* New York, Miss Winters. I know an establishment nearby that is both comfortable and discreet."

She had to make her answer plain. "I am sorry, but I am not in a position to accept," she said.

He stopped on the path and because her arm was entwined with his she was forced to stop as well. "I enjoy games," he said. "I truly do. But *not* coyness. Not in a grown woman. It is unseemly and unflattering."

"I am sorry if I gave you a false impression, Colonel, but I'm not the sort of woman who conducts casual liaisons."

"But *I* know that you are. Your young ladies are very well-informed on a variety of subjects not usually taught in finishing schools."

Her stomach lurched. Anna knew she had taken a risk explaining the dangers of intercourse, of disease, and pregnancy—and how to avoid them—to Mary Phillips. It was the lecture the Widow had given her, more or less. Anna had deliberated for weeks about whether to have such a talk with Mary, but after four months with the girl under her roof—one narrowly averted disaster after another—she had decided that it would be unforgivable to let the girl go on without a full understanding of the dangers she courted. And because Anna was a realist and could remember the temptations of youth, she had given her the resources to avoid them.

She had carefully considered the danger to the school if Mary Phillips tattled, but never the danger to herself in the form of men like this one.

"There is time enough for a short lesson," he suggested, pulling off her cap and brushing her lower lip with his thumb.

For a second she froze, incapacitated by memory. Sound dwindled, her vision dimmed, and the world narrowed to the space between them. There was not enough of it, not nearly enough. She stepped back, felt rough bark impress its pattern on her shoulders through the cotton of her gown. She stepped to the right and met Tarleton's arm, like a boom gate barring her path. She darted left and he moved to block her with his body, bringing them into closer contact than she could tolerate.

He laughed. It was a game to him, a hunt, and her feelings mattered as much as those of a fox. "I must get back to the inn," she said.

"In a little while," he said.

She tried to push him away. He captured her right hand in his. She struggled, but he was stronger and it took an act of will to stop herself from fighting him, to soften and melt as the Widow had taught her.

This was the difficult part. Every fiber of her being screamed to push him away, but safety lay in pulling him close. Men are, as a rule, bigger, and generally they are stronger, at least physically. That does not mean you must play the victim. It means you must learn to use their size against them, as a wrestler might.

Anna slid one hand to Tarleton's collar and took hold

of his lapel. She grasped his sleeve with the other, stepped in close . . . then turned, dropped, and threw him over her shoulder.

Then she took off running.

She wished then that she had not worn the dainty kid slippers, but there was nothing she could do about that now. She could hear Tarleton crashing through the underbrush after her. She knew better than to look back.

When she reached the rear of the inn she smoothed her skirts and hurried on to the bustling taproom, where she found Mr. Ten Broeck making an end of his meal, and promptly sat down beside him.

"Your walk has put color in your cheeks," said Ten Broeck cheerfully.

"Yes," agreed Anna. It had probably put another shade of red in Tarleton's complexion. She brought her breathing back under control, grateful now for the Widow's lessons—which had often seemed tedious and painful at the time—and that practicing at dancing with her charges had gifted her a reasonable stock of wind and speed.

Ten Broeck frowned now. "But you have lost your pretty cap."

"Have I? It must have gotten snagged on a tree branch."

It was a terrible lie, and Ten Broeck's pursed lips told her that he did not believe it, but he did not press her, and she knew better than to tell the true tale herself. Such incidents so seldom had repercussions for the men who instigated them, but always cast a shadow over the women who related them.

Tarleton came in a few minutes later and called for a

glass of ale. From across the room he flashed her an unpleasant smile that warned her he wasn't done with her just yet. She slid her chair closer to Mr. Ten Broeck, and he tried to ply her with pudding, but the thought of food did not appeal.

After that she did not stray far from the estate manager's side.

Their journey resumed, and the afternoon passed if not comfortably, then supportably, the leagues rolling by in Ten Broeck's pleasant, *safe* company, until the sun dipped below the horizon, and they slowed to a halt on a flat stretch of road that felt smoother than the previous miles.

"Are we here?" she asked. Her back had begun to ache from sitting so long and she was hungry and eager to be done with traveling—and to bid farewell to their escort.

"No," said Ten Broeck, a note of concern entering his voice. "This is the border of Harenwyck."

Ten Broeck opened the carriage door and Anna craned her neck to see beyond the horses. A red sandstone arch straddled the road. It was weathered, but the inscription was still legible:

Harenwyck 1630

She could not remember seeing the arch on her way off the estate, but then she had come miles through the woods, off road, to avoid the men searching for her.

Tarleton sat his horse at the head of the column. He signaled his men and they wheeled as one to fall in behind him. A picture of equestrian grace, he trotted up to the carriage window.

"We shall leave you here, Mr. Ten Broeck," announced Tarleton.

Even in the failing light Anna could see that Mr. Ten Broeck's face was a mask of concern. "We are twenty miles from the new manor house."

"We are twenty *feet* from Harenwyck," said Tarleton. "The patroon's gold has been delivered to the patroon's very gates. What happens on Van Haren land is, I think, still very much the patroon's responsibility. 'Lord of the manor,' and all that, yes?"

Tarleton did not wait for Ten Broeck's reply. The colonel spared Anna a look that promised he would not soon forget her, or their brief engagement in the woods. Then he spurred his horse down the road. Thirty mounted men followed in near-perfect order, creating earthly thunder and leaving a cloud of choking dust behind.

"How very like our English masters," said Ten Broeck drily, watching them go, "to give with one hand and take away with the other. A warning from General Clinton, no doubt. A reminder that he can withdraw his protection at his will and pleasure."

Anna listened to the sound of the legion's hooves dying away in the distance. Mr. Ten Broeck's distress was genuine, but all she felt was relief. Tarleton was gone. It was likely that if their journey together had continued, he would have cornered her again, and she doubted he would be so easily eluded twice. She had surprised him—in seizing the initiative and in exhibiting some modicum of skill—but the colonel was an active man, strong and agile, and now forewarned and forearmed.

"Surely we are safe now that we are on Van Haren land," she said, recalling the neat cottages and tirelessly tended fields, orchards, and gardens of her childhood.

"Just so," said Mr. Ten Broeck, but something in his tone did not convince.

Mr. Ten Broeck tapped the roof of the coach, his walking stick making a dull thump on the canvas headliner, and the carriage lurched and began rumbling forward again into the landscape of her childhood.

It was changed beyond recognition. The first cottage they passed had been burned, the fields with it. The second a few miles later was boarded up.

"What has happened here?" she asked.

"There has been some unrest," admitted Ten Broeck. "Some incidents with the Skinners and Cowboys. Unhappy consequences of this war."

"But the patroon has a militia."

"He has a militia, but the estate spans two hundred thousand acres and they cannot be everywhere at once."

"It looks as though they have been nowhere at all," she said, after a moment's pause. She knew how close to the bone tenant farmers lived. The families whose homes they were passing would never recover.

"The Skinners and loyalist cattlemen are often better armed and better mounted," said Ten Broeck.

"Why do they raid Harenwyck when the patroon sells his butter and beef to their side?"

"Because Clinton needs provisions too badly to scruple over where they come from and the Skinners and Cowboys can undersell the patroon. They don't have to bear any of the cost of raising the cattle they steal. It's pure profit for them. But you needn't fear. They dare not come near the manor house. And some of the destruction you see here is tenants against tenants. Old grievances given new life by politics. I assure you there is no threat to the patroon or the manor."

And that she knew for a flat-out lie, because starving tenants were dangerous tenants, especially to the man who collected their rents, but she was too unsettled and exhausted to argue.

She'd had no appetite earlier in the day, but now her stomach was growling and her back ached. She wanted her own bed and dinner in her own parlor with Mrs. Peterson and Miss Demarest, but she wouldn't be home for weeks, possibly months, and her homesickness became suddenly acute.

Anna shut her eyes, and discovered the peculiar, disjointed sleep of the traveler, where the motion of the journey incubates and invades dreams.

She woke, her body falling into space, as the carriage lurched forward and then sprang back. Hands gripped her shoulders and steadied her. For a moment she did not know where she was. She had dreamed she was asleep sitting up in her chair at home. But the seat beneath her was too hard and the windows beside her were too close and too small. She struggled to remember where she was and then, for a second, *who* she was. A name. A name. Her name. She reached for it, as if searching for the doorway in a dark room at night. *Annatje*. Annatje Hoppe of Harenwyck. She was at Harenwyck. Only that wasn't right.

"Miss Winters?"

She looked up into Mr. Ten Broeck's face; the weak light from the coach's lanterns was reflected in his kind brown eyes. She was Anna Winters now, because there were years between Annatje and Anna. But she *was* back at Harenwyck, where they had wanted to hang her.

But if they were at Harenwyck there should be lights and footmen and the sounds of a busy household. Outside the carriage windows were only trees and the deep, quiet dark of full night.

Something was wrong. She knew it the same way she had known it in the cottage that night so long ago, before she heard the rustle of movement on the path, before the heavy knock upon the door. That same queasy frisson of fear ran from the top of her head to the tips of her toes.

"Why have we stopped?" Her voice sounded calm. She was anything but.

"I'm not sure," said Mr. Broeck. He wore that reassuring smile of his, but as soon as he'd let her go, his hands had wrapped themselves around his walking stick, and he held it now like a club.

She wished she had a weapon. Thanks to the Widow, she could probably make better employment of Ten Broeck's stick than he could, though she couldn't think how to convince him to relinquish it. There was a pistol in her chest on top of the coach, but that wasn't going to do her much good at present. There were knives in her paint box, tucked among the brushes, where a casual observer might mistake them for artist's tools, but her case was strapped to the strongbox on the floor. All she had in her embroidery basket—which had tumbled off the seat and was now lost in the mess on the floor—was a set of lockpicks hidden amongst the skeins.

Then she heard voices: the coach driver's, which she recognized, and another. It teased at her memory, the tenor familiar, but the tone new. It came to her in a heartbeat, triggered by the growling of her stomach, the hunger that had been her constant companion in childhood and today had dogged her since the inn. The voice belonged to a man who should not be here. The boy who had remarked on her *klompen* when she was nine, and brought her cookies at sixteen, and kissed her—whom *she'd* kissed—in the woods. The one man, alone, who would be *sure* to recognize her, and to get her hanged: Gerrit Van Haren.

Three

Gerrit lay in the brush on the side of the road, flat on his stomach, watching the cat cross back and forth. The dark-furred beast had already made the trip twice, bold as brass, strutting like he had every right to be there. Certainly he had as much right as Gerrit and the dozen renegade Harenwyck men hiding in the trees.

The feline bore more than a passing resemblance to the barn cat that had patrolled the stores at the manor house when Gerrit was a boy. He could remember being ten or perhaps eleven years old, and sneaking the tom inside to sleep with him on cold winter nights. They'd kept each other snug, Gerrit and the tom, and he could still recall the comforting warmth of having that heavy, purring body slung across his feet at night.

Then Gerrit's father had found out. He had beaten Gerrit and banished the cat, ordered the estate manager to take the tom to the gates of Harenwyck and leave him there. That had been more than a decade ago, and this spry creature could hardly be the same feline, but Gerrit liked the idea that this was one of his descendants. Gerrit felt an instant kinship with the creature. That the cat was prowling an empty road twenty miles from the manor house meant that like Gerrit, he was not a welcome visitor at Harenwyck.

Tonight they were both hunters in the dark. The difference was that Gerrit was after far more dangerous prey.

The night was inky black, the moon barely a sliver of tarnished silver in the sky. The coachman would not see the felled trees in the road until it was too late to stop and turn around, and by that time, Gerrit's men would be behind the carriage, dragging another barrier into place, stopping the road like a bottle and cutting off all retreat.

Gerrit had chosen this spot with care. The Continental Army had been god-awful at drill and discipline, particularly the loutish New Englanders he'd been handed to command. The retreat from New York had been a shambles and a sickening waste of lives. Though his highland Dutch compatriots this evening might not show to best effect on the drill field either, they were unmatched at *this* form of warfare. They had been practicing it for the past hundred years, against the Indians and the French and occasionally one another. No one exceeded them at ambush and highway robbery.

That was a good thing, because they could not afford to fail. Not if he meant to wrest Harenwyck from his brother, Andries. It was all that mattered to him: justice for the tenants. He wanted the power of the landlords broken. Congress ought to want the same, but even though Gerrit had joined their army and fought for them, the Rebels had sided with his younger brother over the estate. Andries now had the New York courts, at least the ones controlled by the Americans, on his side. Gerrit could never hope to fight him there. But if he was successful tonight, if he could capture the carriage and its cargo of gold—a far bigger prize than anything he had attempted heretofore—the British would be forced to take him seriously.

And he would become a traitor to the American cause. He didn't like it, but there was no other way open to him. He was no saint. If he *had* to choose between the independence of his country and the best interests of the tenants who had sweated to keep his family in luxury this past century and a half, he would choose the oppressed of Harenwyck. Every time.

"Damned cat," muttered Pieter, lying beside him. Gerrit had known Pieter Ackerman since they were both ten. That was the year everything had changed. The year the little girl in the yellow clogs had come with her father to pay their family's rent and Gerrit had learned the truth about his charmed life at Harenwyck: it was built on injustice and lies.

Gerrit had shoes on his feet and wood in his fire and food on his table when—*because*—others did not. Because some dead Dutchman in Amsterdam had decreed it so a century ago, all the land in the valley belonged to the patroons, and all the work was done by the tenants. Farmers paid the price of their land in rent ten times over in a single generation but would never own it.

His father had kept all that from him. Until that day, Gerrit had never even talked to one of the tenant children. Then and there, Gerrit had resolved to change that, but it hadn't been as simple as bowing to the girl in the sunny *klompen*. His efforts to talk to the children threshing wheat in the barn or shelling peas in the kitchen were failures. The tenant children knew better than to pause from their work to speak with the patroon's son. Except for Pieter.

"The cat's just hungry," said Gerrit.

"So am I," said Pieter. "Think your brother bought us any of those fancy almonds again?"

"Probably," said Gerrit. "Maybe a more generous supply, since we left none for him the last time." A month ago they had robbed Andries' wagon from New York and come away with six bolts of good cloth, a box of sugared almonds, a jar of Spanish olives, four hams, a Parmesan cheese, and a case of Madeira. Gerrit's brother enjoyed his luxuries.

"I liked the almonds," said Pieter. "The wine was too sweet, though."

"You drank it all down anyway," Jan observed, from somewhere in the thicket beside them. "And *I* liked the wine."

Gerrit was resolved to sample some of Andries' delicacies himself this time, before Pieter devoured them. The stuff was impossible to sell for hard cash at Harenwyck, so Gerrit and his men might as well benefit. Farm wives had little use for Jordan almonds or Madeira wine.

He scanned the road once more. The damned cat was crossing again. The white streaks in his coat betrayed all his feline stealth. This time the little brute had something stuffed in his mouth, a plump gray mouse or baby rat, and that must explain the repeated trips. The tom, at least, had found his prey. Gerrit envied him. He wanted the Harenwyck coach in *his* grasp. He wanted the strongbox and the fortune in gold that Andries would need to keep his militia paid and his favorite tenants bribed. Gerrit was going to deprive his brother of everything useful, everything he needed to hold on to Harenwyck.

Gerrit wished he could keep Ten Broeck. The man was an able estate manager, and depriving Andries of his services would cripple the patroonship, but Ten Broeck was well-liked by the tenants—a fair man, all agreed—and Gerrit could not hold Ten Broeck without risking the ire of the populace.

The doxy was another matter. His sources on the road reported that she was a higher-priced strumpet than Andries usually sent for. *Her* he could keep from his brother, and his brother would know why. Gerrit would send her back to New York on foot. It would make Andries look like a fool, and *that* would weaken his position with the Rebels and British alike.

Gerrit checked his pistol, and then finally he heard the sound he had been waiting for all night: the jingle of harness and tack. The cat heard it too. The tom froze in the middle of the road and turned, ears pricked, in the direction of the sound. His dinner took the opportunity to struggle free. The wriggling burden dropped to the ground and let out a plaintive mew.

It was not a mouse. And the tom was *not* a tom. Just as the glow of lanterns diffused the gloom, the mother cat took off running, leaving her kitten behind.

Gerrit cursed and stood up.

"Not yet!" hissed Jan, who had been doing this long before Gerrit turned outlaw, and knew his business. "They aren't close enough."

The kitten mewed again. Gerrit sighed and strode to the middle of the road, scooped up the trembling animal, and dropped the warm bundle of fur, claws, and teeth in his coat pocket.

By then, of course, it was too late. The driver had seen him, and the barricade as well. The coachman reined his team in thirty paces shy of the intended ambush spot and Gerrit's carefully laid plans evaporated. The driver began the dangerous business of trying to execute a turn on a dark road with skittish horses.

His men were waiting for a signal. If Gerrit did not attack now, the carriage—and the patroon's strongbox—would get away, and Harenwyck would slip even further from his grasp.

Gerrit's father had told him never to aim a weapon he didn't intend to use. It had been, perhaps, the only piece of good advice old Cornelis had ever dispensed. It had served Gerrit well in the army but was proving useless here, where there were no uniforms and it was too often impossible to distinguish enemies from friends.

Like the coach's driver. Gerrit recognized his face, or the blurred shape of it moving in the dark, anyway. He could not remember the man's name. The driver had been a groom or stable boy when Gerrit was a child—something to do with horses at any rate. Gerrit did not believe he had ever spoken with the man, which was unfortunate. He had no memory of kindness or cruelty to hang his next move on. The driver might be a good man or bad, like any of those Gerrit had fought—and killed—in the war.

Without doubt this was a Harenwyck man, a tenant, one of the people Gerrit was risking his honor, his freedom, and his life, to liberate from the grinding serfdom of the patroonship—and there wasn't a hope in hell of doing that without hurting some of them.

Gerrit strolled to the center of the road with the nonchalance of a man who had nothing left to lose, because that, in fact, was what he was.

"*Stand and deliver*," he intoned. A ritual greeting, the highwayman's litany. His voice, trained to give orders in battle, carried on the air. It had the weight and ring of gospel authority in it, but the driver did not appear to be a God-fearing or highwayman-fearing man. He snapped the reins and urged his skittish horses forward.

Gerrit raised his pistol and aimed it at the driver's head.

The coachman found religion and reined up. The horses did not like it, and if they had been a whit friskier, Gerrit would have been trampled. As it was, they came to a stop so close that he could feel the heat of their breath in the night air.

"Climb down, sir!" Gerrit shouted.

The driver shook his head. He had a pistol beside him on the bench. Gerrit suspected it was loaded. "The patroon will evict me if I give up his coach."

Gerrit had almost forgotten. This was Harenwyck, and on the estate, the tenants tithed to the patroon.

"Then join us and become a free man with no lease, no rent, no tithe."

The coachman snorted. "It's all fine and good for you to play these games with your brother, my lord, but I have a family to feed. And a brother and a cousin who have their own leaseholds to protect. Apart from Van Harens, there are no 'free men' at Harenwyck." He cast a jaundiced eye over the bandits emerging from the woods to surround the carriage. "Not honest ones, anyway."

Pieter strolled up beside Gerrit and cocked his head. "Honest or not, you're no use to your family dead, Gerardus Bogart, and even if the patroon here won't shoot you dead, reach for that pistol, and I will."

Gerrit watched Bogart weigh his choices: *bad and worse*, no doubt. Edwaert and Dirck emerged from the brush and stepped into the lantern light. The sound of another eight men hurrying up the road carried through the night air.

Only a fool or a madman would take those odds.

Bogart was neither. He climbed down, leaving his pistol behind on the bench. Pieter sprang up to take the reins. Gerrit realized then he'd been holding his breath. But he could not relax—not yet. He circled to the door, approaching it at an angle, just in case Ten Broeck was armed. Something scratched his upper thigh.

He looked down. His pocket was putting up a fuss. The kitten inside was distinctly unhappy, and trying to claw its way out, but there was nothing Gerrit could do about that at the moment. If his information was wrong, if his associates had betrayed him, there could be a troop of dragoons following just behind the coach. Speed was of the essence. They needed the passengers dealt with and the carriage off the main road before they were detected.

The coach had been repainted recently. The gilding looked fresh. So did the damned coat of arms. *The wolf and lamb*. Andries wanted the world to know that he was patroon, second son or not.

Gerrit opened the carriage door.

Inside was the same canvas lining Gerrit remembered from childhood. His parents had always sat facing forward, the position of privilege, reserved for adults, with he and Andries on the bench opposite. It had meant that whenever he rode with his family the world seemed to be rushing away from him.

Gerrit had expected to find Ten Broeck in his father's place, but the estate manager had ceded pride of place to a woman.

One from whom Gerrit could not look away. She had a face of extraordinary character, even if she was not the usual sort of beauty Andries paid to keep him company. If she wore paint, it was so skillfully applied that Gerrit could not detect it. Her face was a neat oval tapering to a pointed chin. Her eyes were a pale gray that might have been blue—it was difficult to tell in the lantern light. Her hair was artfully dressed to fall over one shoulder in loose curls. It wasn't blond, quite, but it wasn't brown either. More the color of clover honey shot through with streaks of gold. She wore a jaunty little fichu and matching apron all in light translucent silk with white embroidery, the sort of things schoolgirls made to show off their needlework.

Only she was anything but a schoolgirl. She had a woman's body, delightfully outlined in a gown of soft Indian chintz, airy folds of white cotton printed with pink and orange flowers. It made him think of sunlit bedcurtains and summer afternoons. It made him hungry for sensual pleasures, the kind he had not known these three long years. The kind Andries was starving Harenwyck's tenants to pay for.

Gerrit lifted one of the coach lanterns and held it up to get a better look at her face. When she blinked in the bright light, like a woman waking to her lover's touch, he knew he wasn't going to send her back to New York. The roof of the coach was laden with boxes. They would be filled with all the other delicacies Andries ordered from Manhattan. Pieter's sugared almonds and Jan's Madeira wine. They could have it all. The only thing Gerrit wanted from the coach—besides the gold, of course—was her.

Anna blinked in the lantern light, blinded by the brightness after so many hours in the dark.

"Get out, Mr. Ten Broeck," said Gerrit Van Haren.

The cultured voice was the same one that had beguiled her with ghost stories and fairy tales in the woods behind the church, but as her eyes adjusted to the light she could see that his had changed. They were colder—harder—than she remembered. She searched his face for some trace of the boy he had been. His thick brown hair still had an unruly curl to it, but the softness of youth had been carved away—as if by a sculptor—to reveal high cheekbones, a wide mouth, and a firm jaw. A handsome villain, and if the pistol steady in his hand and the battered sword hanging at his hip were anything to judge by, a ruthless one.

"Get out," he repeated, this time with an impatient edge in his tone.

Anna lifted her foot over the box on the carriage floor.

"Not you."

She hesitated and looked at Mr. Ten Broeck.

"This is madness, Gerrit," said Ten Broeck. "Your brother will overlook a little petty thievery, a box of sweetmeats or a case of wine, but not this. Not robbery on the King's Highway."

"There is no robbery taking place, Mr. Broeck. And we are not on the King's Highway. This is Harenwyck land. *My* land. Your driver will reach home tomorrow, after a night at our expense in suitable accommodation, with the contents of his purse intact. And so will you. As for the contents of the coach . . . well, everything my brother claims to own is mine by right. Andries has stolen the estate from me by lies and judicial legerdemain, as I'll prove, eventually. For now, though, I'll be taking the Harenwyck gold into custody for safekeeping, along with all the other luxuries my brother imports from New York."

His eyes swept over Anna in a frank appraisal and she suddenly realized the truth: he *didn't* recognize her.

She should have felt relief. Instead, she felt something very much like jealousy. She had never been jealous of her students, never resented them for being born with more than she had worked to have. But those afternoons with Gerrit behind the church had been the closest she had come to romance in all her thirty-two years.

And he had forgotten her. And, like Tarleton, he assumed she was for sale.

"I think you mistake the nature of my business with your brother," she said.

He looked as though he was surprised that she could speak. "Do I?" he asked, one dark eyebrow subtly lifted. "Then pray tell me, what does bring you to Harenwyck, milady?"

His mock courtesy galled her. She wanted to wipe the superior expression off his face. She wanted to tell him that he'd once been better than his father and his brother. She wanted to tell him the truth: that his wretched family had cast a pall over her life that stretched as far as New York—but telling him that would only get her hanged, so she said, "Your brother has hired me as a tutor."

"For private instruction and from a very fine *academy*, I have no doubt."

She should have kept the pistol with her in the carriage, or at the very least made her knives more accessible. One of the slim blades might do quite nicely. Gerrit Van Haren had not only grown up, but had inflated into a bladder much in need of a sharp poke.

"I do *not* run a cavaulting school. It is a finishing academy for young ladies."

"I will take your word that it is a proper nunnery," replied Gerrit, easily. "And I do look forward to enjoying the tuition that Andries has paid for, but just at this moment, I'm rather preoccupied. Mr. Ten Broeck, you may step down, and join Edwaert and Dirck and your driver for a lovely evening walk to the old mill, or you can be dragged out of the carriage and frog-marched cross-country barefoot. The choice is yours."

Gerrit stepped aside. Mr. Broeck shot a worried look at Anna and then climbed down. Before she could follow, Gerrit vaulted into the compartment and blocked her escape. Without ceremony he snatched up her stockinged ankles and lifted them back onto the bench. Instinct, honed under the tutelage of the Widow, took over, and she twisted and dove for the opposite door.

In the enclosed space his superior size was a decided advantage. He reached around her and seized the door handle before she could touch it, then held it fast. "You're very lithe for a schoolteacher," he said pleasantly. "But I confess I am wounded. Was Mr. Ten Broeck such better company?"

He didn't wait for an answer before settling comfortably on the bench opposite. Then, quite coldly, he added, "Don't try it again, or I'll tie you to the roof with the other baggage."

She knew that he meant it. She might have mistaken his *immediate* intentions, but no matter what kind of boy

Gerrit Van Haren had been, he was clearly a different man now, and a dangerous one.

She tucked her feet up under her on the bench. The carriage seemed far smaller than when it had been occupied by just her and Broeck, especially with Gerrit leaning over the boxes on the floor. He produced a knife from his pocket and cut the leather strapping that held her possessions together atop the patroon's strongbox.

The carriage swayed on its springs. A long gaunt face framed by poker-straight white blond hair appeared in the open carriage door. The man standing on the running board looked sharply up at Gerrit. "Any almonds, then?" he asked in Dutch.

Gerrit lifted Anna's prized book of engravings by one corner and held it carelessly up to the lantern light. "Does this look like almonds to you, Pieter?" Gerrit replied.

"That," said Anna, "is Domenico de' Rossi's *Raccolta di statue antiche e moderne.*"

The loose pages, the ones too often copied by the girls, where the binding had grown weak and failed after endless hours lying open in the sun of the school's third-floor studio, slipped out in a papery rush and fluttered down like leaves in a gale. Anna snatched the Laocoön and Apollo Belvedere plates from the air as they fell.

Gerrit stared at her and suddenly she could not recall if he had asked about the book in English or in Dutch. To cover her mistake she said, "Please be careful with that. It's old and delicate and very valuable."

Gerrit set the book down on the bench beside him. "In New York, maybe, but up here, if you can't eat it, plant it, ride it, or kill someone with it, it won't fetch much."

The man named Pieter sighed. "No olives either, I suppose," he said in Dutch.

"No olives either," confirmed Gerrit in the same language. He was still looking at her, she realized, studying her face. *"Spreek je Nederlands, juf?"* he asked.

Do you speak Dutch, miss? He had asked the question informally, as he would a child or a servant or a woman of low status, but addressed her—with a tinge of sarcasm—as one might a school mistress. It took an act of will not to reply in the same language, in the fine accents she'd practiced with him when he'd corrected her speech as a child. Of course, that was why he had spoken as he did: to see her reaction.

I know you, she wanted to say, *and you are not this man.*

But fifteen years was a long time, and she was not Annatje Hoppe anymore. She gave him the blank look she had perfected in New York and said, "It's very rude to speak another language in front of a person who doesn't understand it."

That, apparently, was schoolmarmish enough to satisfy her captor. "What use, I wonder," he asked, "does a pretty girl have for such a book?"

"I told you. I've been hired to tutor the Van Haren girls."

He nodded at the engraving of Laocoön in her lap. "Is that really a suitable area of study for young ladies?"

Anna stopped smoothing the page with her hands

and set it on the seat beside her. "Drawing is thought to be an essential element of a polite education."

"I meant the subject matter."

"For some obscure reason the ancients are always considered respectable, no matter their state of dress."

His eyebrows rose at that. "You're not my brother's usual type."

"Does your brother have a usual type in schoolteachers?"

"My brother has a usual type in *women*. The quiet, biddable sort. And he prefers it when they belong to someone else."

She had never heard him speak with bitterness before. Not even about his father. But they had been children when they had known each other and experience had obviously changed them both.

Gerrit tapped on the roof, just as Mr. Ten Broeck had, and the carriage lurched forward.

"Where are we going?" she asked, as the vehicle began to turn around.

"Your night won't be as rustic as Mr. Ten Broeck's. We're bound for an inn."

A look of alarm must have crossed her face.

"Don't worry. I'm not always bent on debauchery. In fact, I have a meeting there with some associates."

"In a stolen coach?" Which was now picking up speed at an alarming rate. Anna braced her arms on the walls. "With a fortune in stolen gold?"

"The coach is mine," said Gerrit, settling back comfortably onto his bench. Anna envied him. He was a head taller than her and his shoulders were too broad to be buffeted by the jostling of the coach, while she could barely keep her seat. "The courts only found in favor of Andries and his pack of lies because they are controlled by the Rebels, and the Rebels want Harenwyck whole."

"I thought that your father disinherited you."

Gerrit sighed. "He did. Perhaps. Once upon a time, he said as much, in his study, with my brother at his elbow. Or perhaps it was more of his bluff and bullying. Of one thing I am sure: he never made a will to formalize it. If he had, be certain Andries would have presented it in probate. He did not.

"Without a will, under Dutch rules of inheritance, Harenwyck passes to me. So my brother of necessity concocted a story, plausible enough, that Cornelis Van Haren *had* made a last will and testament naming him as sole heir. Then I came home, shortly after my father's death, refused to accept its terms—and burned it. In truth, I came home to find that Andries had already declared himself patroon and hired a militia to keep me out. I never even got near the house.

"To settle matters, Andries produced men who claimed to have witnessed this will, and recalled its basic terms. As far as the courts are concerned—the New York Court of Chancery in particular, where my brother applied all his considerable influence—Harenwyck is now the lawful inheritance of Andries, just as my father wished it. You see, at equity, a rogue like me cannot be permitted to unjustly profit from his misdeed. By destroying my dear father's will I sought to pull his estate back into intestacy, where the common law would make me heir. The will, and fair play, must be upheld! Never mind the damned thing never existed, and Andries and his 'witnesses' were perjurers. Such is the course of justice, as twisted by my brother and his Hudson peers."

"But the New York courts are controlled by the Rebels," she said. And Kate Grey's allies. And Kate Grey had said nothing of any of this. It was possible that she had not known. And equally possible that she had known and decided against sharing all the facts with Anna. "Surely it must count for something that you fought for them with the Continentals."

"It appears the teacher has done her homework on the Van Haren family."

Anna knew she had made another mistake. She must be more careful. She was supposed to be a stranger to Harenwyck. "It seemed only sensible to find out as much about the patroon as possible, before accepting his offer."

"How much is he paying you?"

"Enough," she said.

"I'll double it."

"You would like to brush up your English grammar and improve your needlework?"

"Just now, I would *like* to reach my chest of gold, but find it buried beneath a heap of female impedimenta."

He set her book down and resumed rummaging through the baggage. He plucked Anna's sewing box out of the jumbled mess on the floor and examined it in bafflement, unfastening the clasp and flipping it upside down.

The lid swung open with the motion of the coach and

Anna's silks spilled out like tumbled jewels. Glinting among them were streaks of shining silver. Her lockpicks clattered over the mahogany paint case and the maple strongbox to land ringing upon the floorboards and dislimn Anna's painstakingly crafted identity as Miss Winters, headmistress of Miss Winters' Academy.

Four

Anna held her breath as Gerrit raised an eyebrow and fished a steel pick out of the tangled heap. He held it up to the light and it glinted. She kept them polished because that made them easier to work with in the dark. With a sinking heart she knew that he knew what it was.

"Is burglary among the normal subjects for a finishing school?"

"Adolescent girls are much given to drama," said Anna. It was, after all, true. "They have a tendency to lock themselves in rooms when romance disappoints." Also true, if not the exact reason she had brought the lockpicks.

"And how often is that?"

"Most Tuesdays," said Anna. "That is when the post arrives."

"Now you sound like a schoolteacher," he said. "But I find it difficult to believe you are only that."

"Because I own a set of lockpicks?"

"Because you're too pretty not to make more profitable use of your looks."

"You have a very low opinion of the female character, sir."

"Not uninformed by experience," he replied, continuing his investigation of the contents of the coach. "My strongbox had better be at the bottom somewhere."

"It is beneath my loom and paint case."

He tossed the loom aside and lifted her case of paints onto the seat beside him. Anna could hear the brushes rattling with the motion of the coach from inside the box. When Gerrit leaned forward again, something mewed. "Blast it," he said. He shifted and dug in his coat pocket and produced a small ball of wriggling gray fur.

"By your logic I should now conclude that you are a ratcatcher," she said.

"It's not a rat; it's a very small cat." He plucked up her empty silk basket and deposited the creature inside.

"Why do you keep a kitten in your pocket?"

He snorted, seemed amused in spite of himself. "I don't, as a rule. In this case, it's expediency: the little beast was about to be run over by your carriage."

Anna took the basket out of his lap. That brought her into closer proximity with her captor and the surprising scent of bay rum. He'd worn it at seventeen when they had kissed behind the church and ever since she had associated the fragrance with the thrill of intimacy. It mingled now with the woodsy scent of the pine needles that still clung to his coat.

Up close she could see that he was not dressed like an *ordinary* gentleman of the road. His suit was fine chocolate wool, the cuffs worn and frayed but the cloth unmistakably soft and rich. His shirt and stockings were cream silk, his shoes brocade with silver buckles. Everything he wore had once been of the highest quality and remained scrupulously clean, if not tirelessly mended.

"What was such a tiny kitten doing in the middle of the road?" she asked.

"His mother was crossing, and he wriggled free of her jaws just as your carriage thundered into view."

"She abandoned him," said Anna, heartsick.

"She would have been run over otherwise. She was *not* a small cat. I thought her a tom at first. The carriage would have struck her for certain, but the kitten was little enough that the coach and team might have missed or passed right over him."

Anna peaked inside the basket. The kitten was mottled gray with giant yellow eyes—perhaps not long opened on the world—and a decidedly stocky build. And it was trembling like a leaf.

"It's too young to be on its own, poor thing," she said.

For the first time all night Gerrit had the good grace to look ashamed. "I will go back in the morning and find his mother. We could hardly do it tonight. The militia patrols the estate."

"How do you know it's a he?" Anna asked.

"He's too scrappy to be a girl. He squirmed out of his mother's grasp in the middle of the road."

Anna lifted the kitten out of the basket and turned it over. "Be that as it may, *he's* a *she*." The kitten scrabbled madly up onto her shoulder and began chewing her hair. "Scrappy, though, is certainly an apt name for her."

"She thinks you're her mother," said Gerrit, clearly amused.

Scrappy began kneading Anna's shoulder with determination, eyes screwed shut and paws flexing. "She wants milk."

"She shall have cream when we get to the inn. And a fish, if they have any."

He liked cats. She remembered that. Gerrit reached across the carriage to stroke the kitten's head. The back of his hand brushed Anna's cheek. His touch was warm and electric, just like it had been in the woods behind the church.

For years she had told herself that what they shared as children had been the thrill of infatuation, the fleeting passion of youth, a fairy kingdom impossible to revisit as an adult.

She had been wrong.

The truth was that she had met too young—and across an impossible divide of wealth and station—the one man above all others for her. And the circumstances, God knew, were just as impossible now.

She disentangled the purring kitten from her hair and passed the warm, furry body to Gerrit just as they hurtled over a bump in the road. He put out his hands to steady her and the contact was illicitly thrilling. If only he knew it was her. But he could not. Ever. She deposited the kitten in his lap and drew back. "What sort of inn gives refuge to highwaymen?"

The kitten rolled over in his lap. Gerrit rubbed its soft white belly, and she felt a flash of affection, saw in this strange man a glimpse of the boy who'd touched her heart. Loud purring filled the carriage.

"I prefer to think of myself as a land-going privateer."

"I thought you said that the Rebels had sided with your brother over your inheritance."

"They have. Which leaves me with no choice but to turn to the British."

"So the British Army is licensing brigands as well as pirates now."

"In a sense. The Skinners and Cowboys are authorized to forage. How foraging differs from robbery and cattle thieving is difficult to say. Still, the British do not issue letters of marque for foraging. I've never understood why robbery on the King's Highway can only get you hanged while robbery on the high seas, under the right circumstances, will get you knighted, but then that's probably because I'm not a naval man."

"And how, exactly, does stealing your brother's gold endear you to the British?"

"It's not his. And, unlikely as this may sound, I don't want the gold for myself."

"Am I supposed to believe that you're a latter-day Robin Hood, stealing from the rich to give to the poor?"

"I'll answer to Robin Hood, if that makes you my Maid Marian."

He flashed her a roguish smile and she glimpsed again

the boy who had charmed her in the woods behind the church. She remembered what it had been like to while away long afternoons in his company. With him, Annatje Hoppe, the farm girl with no fortune and no prospects, who wore homespun and *klompen*, had always felt clever and beautiful. This was Gerrit's gift: a natural ability to bring out the best in others. A half-remembered ballad came bubbling to her lips.

"Alas," she said, "I'm not a bonny fine maid of noble degree."

"I thought all schoolteachers were disappointed gentlewomen."

"Gentlewomen, not noblewomen."

"A degree without a difference."

"That is easy to say if you are already standing on the high ground."

"Or have no further to fall."

"Even dressed in rags, you will always be the son of a patroon. If you are disgraced, you do not fall. You are cast *out*, not *down*. It is only those of us in the middle who must cling to each slippery rung of the ladder for dear life."

"Unless you jump. Leap off the ladder into the unknown." His voice was almost wistful.

"In a man that would be called boldness. In a woman, it is called something else."

"That is a surprising point of view for a bold woman."

"What makes you think I'm bold?" she asked.

"For one thing, you are arguing with a highwayman, a notorious *struikrover*, and for another, you *are* a veritable Marian, ranging *the wood to find Robin Hood, the bravest of men in that age.*"

He knew the ballad too. Of course he did. She'd found it in one of the books he'd brought her. And they were back to flirting. She wished she did not like it so much. She wished that fragments of that ballad were not percolating to the surface of her memory, waking up part of her that had been asleep too long, like black coffee in the morning. "Marian," she said earnestly, "searched for Robin dressed as a boy."

"I grant that you would not make a very convincing boy, but I doubt Marian did either. Or most of Shakespeare's heroines, for that matter. And you won't hear me complaining. That's a very pretty gown."

It was the best thing she owned, her very proper schoolmistress gown, bought secondhand and altered to fit her by Mrs. Peterson, with Miss Demarest's help. And, just now, Anna had never felt so pretty in anything in her life. She struggled to ignore the feeling. "Nor am I *armed with quiver and bow, sword, buckler, and all.*"

"But I could still draw out my sword," he suggested, his meaning clear, "and to cutting we could go."

It was the same proposition Tarleton had made earlier that day, based in large part on the same assumptions, that as a woman in commerce among the goods and services she traded would be those of her body. With Tarleton the idea had repelled her. With this man, she had to admit, it thrilled her. It was truly the world turned upside down. Tarleton was a respected member of the gentry, a rising star in the army. Gerrit was a disgraced aristocrat turned highwayman. And she had never felt safer with anyone in her life, even though he held, all unwittingly, power of life and death over her.

There was nothing and no one to stop her climbing across the heap of boxes and into the arms of the only man she had ever wanted. Except that it wouldn't be real, because he didn't know it was her. And, outlaw of sorts though he was, he was still so honest and so good—he'd nearly gotten himself run down to save a kitten—he would be honor bound to turn her over to justice if he found out the truth: that she was Annatje Hoppe, the fugitive Dutch girl, the one who had killed a *schout* and fled Harenwyck for her life all those years ago.

The thought stole all the joy from their banter. "I seem to remember that Marian got the better of Robin in that version. *The blood ran apace from bold Robin's face*, didn't it?"

"Ah, but when she realized it was Robin," said Gerrit, still delighting in their wordplay, still hopeful it would lead somewhere, when she knew it was a door already closed, "*with kisses sweet she did him greet, like to a most loyal lover.*"

"That is because Robin and Marian were reunited sweethearts," said Anna. "We are not." Of all the lies she had told across the years, this was the first she regretted. "And I will not call you Robin unless you distribute your largesse, flinging coins like a Roman emperor or a Venetian doge, when we get to this inn."

He appeared to consider it. "I suppose Pieter could hold the reins while I toss coins from the running board, but it wouldn't do my brother's tenants any good. The only thing they want is the land they're working, and he won't sell it to them."

"And you would?" She couldn't keep the surprise out of her voice. It was too pronounced for the woman she pretended to be—a stranger to the patroonship—but he was too caught up in their exchange to notice.

"Yes. I would sell to them. America has no future without land. A republic can't be built out of plantations and patroonships. It needs freeholders with a stake in the government."

"That is a very revolutionary sentiment for a man on his way to the King's Arms."

"I believe in independence. It is the Continental Congress that does not believe in me. I fought for them for three years, but when my father died, Andries told them that I planned to break up the estate, to sell Harenwyck to the tenants. He claimed that my father had disinherited me—even though he could produce no proof and the will has conveniently disappeared. The courts sided with Andries because the courts are controlled by Rebels, and the gentlemen running this revolution don't trust all of Harenwyck's tenants to side with them: don't trust them with the rights to vote, or without a master to move them. Propertied men in New England are one thing; poor Dutchmen, apparently, are another."

She felt something tighten in her chest and realized it was grief. This was the idealistic boy she remembered, the one who stole books from his father's library and brought them to her all summer long. The one who championed underdogs—like her father. Like her. A decent man who knew right from wrong. And that was why she could not reveal herself to him, because she ought to have hanged fourteen years ago for killing that bailiff. She had lived a decade on borrowed time. These moments were borrowed too. She knew that. And still, she could not resist matching minds with him.

"So you are more like one of the Gracchi than Robin Hood. A land reformer with republican ideals. Does that make you Tiberius the elder, or Gaius the younger?"

"That's like asking if I'd rather be clubbed to death or compelled to suicide."

"And which would you rather?"

"Suicide," he replied without hesitation.

"You are equally dead," she replied, "but in that instance you've done your enemy's work for him."

"There's a nobility in taking that away from your enemies. He can't kill you if you're already dead."

"But *dum spiro spero*. Where there is breath, there is hope. How do you know that you mightn't have prevailed, in a fair fight?"

"Gaius knew it wasn't going to *be* a fair fight. He saw his older brother murdered in the forum by the senate. They would not even give him the honor of dying by the sword. They beat him to death with broken staves from the senate benches and cast his body into the Tiber."

"And yet," she said, "he had tried to continue his brother Tiberius' work. More than that. Gaius went further and tried to expand the vote, to enfranchise all Latin-speaking people. He knew the risks, all too well. And he still thought the game worth the candle."

"But was it?" asked Gerrit. "The franchise was extended to the whole Roman world two hundred years later without bloodshed or loss of life."

"Only because Caracalla wanted to expand the tax base," said Anna. "And you forget all the men and women who lived and died in the years between. How different might their days have been as full Roman citizens with citizens' rights?"

"That is exactly what Congress fears, I suspect. Thousands of new freeholders, entitled to vote by virtue of their landownership. Representation is a tricky thing. We wanted it for ourselves in Parliament, but we're not sure we'd trust our neighbors with it. Sturdy New Englanders maybe, but not Dutch tenant farmers, no better than peasants—men stupid enough to sign themselves into serfdom for a few acres of uncleared land."

She could feel her hackles rise, even though she knew he was being sarcastic. "It is not stupidity if you have no other real choices. There are far worse things than tenant farming. Worse things than serfdom." She had experienced some of them, alone, cold, hungry, and friendless in New York.

"I know that." All levity had left him. They had been speaking, she realized, for some time now, as equals, about things she cared about. About things that were important, the subjects that had drawn her to books and learning and kindled her desire to be a teacher in the first place. And none of it touched on needlework or dancing or decorative painting.

"If you have no faith in Congress and no love for the Continental Army, then what will you do with the gold?" she asked him.

"Keep it—and everything else he desires—out of my brother's hands."

Gerrit knew that he should not have kept the girl. He ought to have had her marched off with Mr. Ten Broeck to spend the night in the old Peterson barn and be released at dawn. There was bound to be trouble over it, and he found he didn't care. He could not remember the last time he had enjoyed a woman's company—anyone's company— so much.

No, that was wrong. He could remember. It had been the summer before he left for Leiden, when he had courted his *klompen* girl behind the church. He had forgotten about her for a time after their first precocious meeting as children, but then suddenly girls had been all he could think about, and one girl in particular who wore sunny yellow clogs seemed to be everywhere he looked.

He had prayed for an excuse to talk to her, and the Lord had answered him. Her stomach had growled louder than the homily and added a distinctly off-key note to the singing. He'd watched her devour the cookies, sitting cross-legged on a weathered tomb behind the church, and he'd found the sight inconveniently erotic. She had turned into a beauty, his *klompen* girl.

But that was not why he had loved her. There had been plenty of girls, some even prettier than Annatje, who had tried to attract his attention. Annatje was different. He had never met anyone, before or since, who was so curious about the world. Her mind ranged across a vast expanse of subjects. She craved books and stories and he had delightedly shared whatever could be found in the sorry Harenwyck library. He had thought, more than once, that she was a better candidate for Leiden than he.

But Annatje had not been there when he came back from college. His father had told him she was dead. He had not believed that, or the other things that were being said, but the *schouts* brought him her clogs as proof that she had taken her own life, and he had decided that if he must marry someone, it might as well be Sophia.

He had been struck by Sophia's beauty when they first met. Her father was land poor but cash rich, the opposite of every patroon, and Gerrit's father had been keen on the match. Gerrit himself had been determined to dislike her. He'd been fresh from his studies in Leiden, fired by the liberal ideas gaining currency in the Dutch Republic, and had come home with plans to reform the estate. But his father was having none of it. Gerrit's chief responsibility as the next patroon was to marry advantageously. They could discuss reform as soon as the succession was secure.

The beautiful Sophia had surprised him by seeming to like him. She was tiny, delicate, and moved in a rustling cloud of silk and gardenia. She ate daintily, shared all his preferences in food, agreed with all his opinions on politics, estate management, and domestic arrangements. It did not occur to him until too late that she evidenced no opinions of her own. He had never met any ladies who did. Except for the girl in the yellow *klompen*.

There had been women in Holland, of course, but mostly dairymaids and serving girls with no education. The occasional burgher's wife or pretty widow wasn't interested in him for conversation. And certainly hadn't read Cassius Dio on Caracalla.

Miss Winters was a decidedly unusual lady. Sophia, of course, had been regarded as very accomplished. She'd been educated at a school something like Miss Winters' Academy. She sang and danced and painted and stitched. But he did not think he had ever seen her open a book. Not even a recipe book. Apparently not all finishing schools were the same.

There was another tome on the pile of baggage separating him from his brother's gold. He picked it up—more carefully this time, lest he earn another scolding—and flipped it open.

"What does a finishing school teacher want with an atlas?" he asked.

She met his gaze with the directness that had teased at his memory and delighted him all night. "It's my belief that a woman ought to know her place in the world."

Maybe he would let her go on to Harenwyck after all. He liked the idea of Grietje and Jannetje poring over an atlas, learning Latin and history and something more useful than embroidery. His daughters were the only good thing to come out of his mess of a marriage and he wanted them to have lives beyond the borders of the patroonship.

And he liked Anna herself. She was easy to talk to, like the girl he used to kiss in the barn before he went off to college. He thought of his own childhood at Harenwyck and wished there had been someone as tart and wise as Miss Winters to challenge him. He could give that to Grietje and Jannetje if he let her go. But he wanted an excuse to make her stay, to keep her for himself.

"How good are you with those lockpicks?" he asked.

Her face turned guarded now. "Good enough. Why?"

He tapped the strongbox, a lead weight on the rumbling carriage floor, with his foot. "Because I'd like to get this open without recourse to a hatchet and pry bar, if at all possible."

"That would make me an accessory to your crime."

"It's not a crime if the gold really belongs to me."

"That's for the courts to decide," she said primly.

"I've had my day in court, Miss Winters. The New York bench is in the pocket of the landlords, and justice is reserved for the rich and powerful."

"All the more reason," she said sensibly, "for me to stay out of them."

"I'll make a bargain with you," he said.

She did not look like she welcomed the idea. He pressed on anyway. "If you will open the strongbox for me, I will send you on to Harenwyck."

"And if I won't?"

"Highwaymen don't sign articles, like pirates, but as gentlemen of the road they do make agreements. Money we split evenly, because everyone can agree upon its value. Gold never fails to please sweethearts or flatter complexions. Powder and shot are shared out evenly because every man benefits from his compatriot having a full cartridge case. Everything else is negotiable, but each man must have some prize from the night's work. Jan will want the Madeira, and Edwaert something pretty for his wife. Dirck is after a timepiece for his father and if we do not luck into one soon I fear he will hold up the reverend in broad daylight and liberate his. Pieter will trade everything for a case of those sugared almonds. And if you will not open the strongbox for me, the one thing I will keep is *you*."

Five

She had already made two mistakes. She could not risk making another. And the longer she remained in Gerrit's company the likelier she was to betray herself. She'd shown too much understanding when they were speaking Dutch, and she'd displayed far too much knowledge about Harenwyck for an outsider. She needed to get away from him as quickly as possible. Easier said than done while she was trapped in a moving carriage with him, but she must be ready to make her escape as soon as they reached the inn.

"Give me my lockpicks."

Gerrit pursed his lips and closed his eyes. "The speed of your reply wounds me, Miss Winters. Maybe I should keep you and resort to an ax with the box."

"You gave your word. And *ignis aurum probat, miseria fortes viros*," she prompted.

He sighed. "Fire tests gold, but adversity tests men."

He bent to move the paint box and the loom, and at last the strongbox lay revealed on the floor between them.

"My tools, please," she prompted.

He searched the seats, the skirts of his coat, and the floor until he had five of her lockpicks, but not the one most likely to be of use. "Keep looking."

"Yes, ma'am. If I had any doubts that you truly were a schoolteacher, you have dispelled them. Ah." He plucked one of her picks out of a corner of her embroidery loom where it had gotten stuck between the canvas and the frame. "Good God, what is this thing?" he asked.

He held up the stretched canvas, which he had discarded earlier that night, and in the lantern light filtering through the window the pattern was unmistakable.

"That is your family's coat of arms, as you well know. I thought it would encourage the girls, especially if their skills are rudimentary, to work on something familiar."

"Let them embroider something else." He opened the door of the moving carriage. Trees rushed by. The night air raced in, cool and bracing. Without warning, Gerrit threw the frame out into the night. Anna heard it strike something—a tree most likely—with a sharp crack, and then clatter to the ground, gone forever. She had been quite fond of that particular loom.

"Do you object to heraldry in general or just your family's in particular?" She did not bother to hide her irritation.

"Both, actually," he said, latching the door. "What do seven-year-old girls want with slaughtered lambs and ravening wolves?"

"Armorial subjects are very popular," said Anna. "Almost obligatory, if your family claims a coat of arms."

"Did you make one yourself?" he asked.

"Hardly. Mine was not that kind of family."

"That's right. Teachers come from gentle, but not noble birth." She couldn't tell whether he was mocking her or not. "What sort of embroidery did you make? A devotional sampler?"

"Do I look like I arrived with the Puritans on the Mayflower?"

"Decidedly not. If biblical platitudes are out of fashion, then what is the current vogue?"

"Fishing lady scenes remain very popular."

"But you're not fond of them," he surmised.

"They are copied from prints. Invention is always superior to mimicry. A truly accomplished needlewoman is also an accomplished draftswoman. She can draw her own scene, and paint it in with thread."

"And what was your invention?"

Her invention was just that: the story she had fabricated for herself, made up out of whole cloth with the Widow's guidance, memorialized in the silkwork picture that hung in the school's parlor and attracted students from as far away as Albany.

"I stitched a portrait of my family's home," she said. "Before we lost it, of course." She *had* lost her home, but it hadn't been the redbrick manse in her embroidered picture. "And the trees and the pond. There is even a fishing lady, but she is my own, not copied from an engraving."

Gerrit clasped his hands together and leaned forward.

She recalled the pose from their youth. It meant he was about to embark on a story. "I picture your father as a learned man. A lawyer or a divine. No, scratch that. A doctor. He taught you Latin and instilled in you a love of science. You read Pliny instead of Catullus, and sketched ducklings and carpenter ants with equal ardor. You lived in one of those severe New England houses with the steep roofs and tiny windows, the kind the Puritans built and everyone slaps a coat of yellow paint and a portico on and tries to pretend are classical. But they aren't. They've got a medieval soul that sash windows and dentil moldings can never banish. You loved the house anyway because although you were raised on reason, you have a romantic nature, and you whiled away hours holed up in that maze of tiny, irregular rooms, lost in the pages of a novel. How am I doing so far?"

He was a natural born raconteur, a lover of words, and she had listened to his flights of fancy for hours in the barn, sometimes adding her own embellishments. He'd made up a plausible background for the woman she presented herself as, for the woman she had become. "It was a very good story," she said truthfully. "I like it better than my own."

Her own was as much a work of fiction as his. The only difference was that it was not a spur-of-the-moment invention. She had been telling it for years. It had not seemed so sad and gray before she heard Gerrit's version.

"My father was a surveyor," she recited. "He was away from home a great deal and often traveled in inclement weather. He caught a chill while working in the backcountry and died. My mother succumbed to grief shortly thereafter. The estate passed to my brothers, who my parents expected to provide me with a good portion, but whose wives persuaded them against settling enough on me to make a good marriage. My options were become the unpaid governess to my nieces and nephews, and housekeeper to my sisters-in-law, or teach. So I taught."

"Did I at least get the house right?" he asked.

Anna thought about her real childhood home, the one-room tenant's cottage with the sleeping attic, built Dutch-style on an H-frame, the two end walls of rough red sandstone, the rest narrow clapboard. There had been no privacy for reading, but then there had been no books save one battered old Statenbijbel. She liked Gerrit's version of her life better.

"The house," she said, thinking of the fantasy in silk-work hanging in her parlor in New York, "was brick."

"You don't sound as though you liked it."

"I like the house you described better."

"Then you should have stitched it."

"But that one is only a fantasy."

"No more so than the Van Haren coat of arms. Do you know its origin?"

"No. Something to do with knights and swords and services to a king, I expect."

"Hardly. The first patroon was a jeweler. All you needed—provided you knew the right people—one hundred and fifty years ago to be granted a patroonship under the West India Company's Charter of Rights and Exemptions was to settle fifty persons over the age of fifteen in New Netherland. In other words, all you needed was money. Money to recruit them and pay their passage and supply the basic needs of life for a few years. After that, the land, and the people on it, in effect, belonged to you. A perpetual profit machine powered by human lives. The first patroon of Harenwyck never even set foot in America, but he wasted no time inventing a coat of arms for himself. The heraldry of the Van Harens is purest fantasy— and I can't help feel its allusions cut rather too close to the bone. If Grietje and Jannetje are going to embroider a fantasy, it might as well be something entirely their own. Not that of a grasping old gem cutter, or, come to that, of my good father and brother."

"They won't be embroidering anything at all," said Anna, "until someone makes me a new frame."

For a second he looked sheepish. Then he said, "Get my box of gold open and you may have a dozen frames."

He handed her the collected set of lockpicks. There was just enough room on the floor of the coach for her to crouch beside the strongbox—and discover that it was facing the wrong way. It was wedged in tightly between the walls of the coach, with no room to turn, and the side with the lock completely inaccessible.

She explained her problem.

"We'll wait until we reach the inn, then," said Gerrit.

She wanted to ask him which inn he meant. She wanted to get her bearings. She had thought she would remember more about Harenwyck, but the gates had been strange to her, and they'd traveled some ways from there by now. Anna knew she must take the first opportunity to escape, but that would be easier if she had any idea where she was.

. . .

Gerrit was enjoying himself. Things could have gone very, very wrong on the road, but they hadn't. He had possession of Andries' carriage. That was good. No one had gotten hurt. That was better. And the girl made him feel alive and excited, like the world was full of opportunity again. He could not remember the last time he had felt that way.

He probably shouldn't have thrown her loom out the door. It was amazing how the sight of that coat of arms set him off, how anything to do with Andries and his family could set him off. He *knew* there was a world beyond Harenwyck. His *raison d'être* was to dismantle the damned place, for God's sake. But as long as the patroonship stood unchanged, it would cast its shadow over his life.

Talking with the pretty teacher was like a glimpse of that wider world.

He'd been so smitten that he'd gone and spun her a story, the kind his father had hated, but that the pretty girl with the sunny *klompen* had always loved. Annatje had done more than listen to his tales, though. She had joined her invention to his. When she didn't like the ending of a story, she changed it. *The heroine*, she used to say, *ought to get to win once in a while, and live happily ever after.* Annatje had not lived happily ever after, but she had convinced him that endings could be changed, that just because something always had been didn't mean it always had to be.

He'd said something to that effect to his father, and the old man had shipped him off to Leiden.

Gerrit had tried to explain to his father that his mind

had always worked that way, that people and places and things suggested stories. He'd explained to his father that he knew it was just an amusement, something to entertain ladies—that at least was something the old goat, who had chased everything in petticoats on the estate for decades, would understand—but his father had seen the deeper truth: Gerrit would never look at a tenant and see just numbers in a ledger. He saw families, histories, whole lives and lines being subordinated to someone else's—all because Gerrit's great-great-great-grandfather had made a few sharp trades in cut diamonds, and known whose palm to grease in Amsterdam.

He probably shouldn't have threatened to keep Miss Winters, as if she were a case of wine or a crate of olives. He was not Cornelis. People's lives were not his to play with. But he had thought—just for a moment—that she might feel the same thrilling attraction that he did, and want only for an excuse to act on it.

Of course it was possible that she did feel it but knew better than to act on it. And she was right. No matter how far he fell, he would always be the heir to Harenwyck, a patroon's son. That was why this meeting was taking place at all. Howe's officers would not be courting the son of a tenant farmer, no matter how successful his raids. It was Gerrit's claim to the patroonship they were after, the ability to deliver two hundred thousand acres and two thousand able-bodied men to their side. He would always be able to trade on that, no matter what his situation.

Whereas Miss Winters had nothing to trade upon but her reputation.

Her caution was probably well-founded. He liked what he knew of her, and he most definitely wanted her—in a way that made him feel like a whole man again after Sophia's betrayal had burned away all his appetites—but a gently raised bluestocking had no place at the side of an outlaw, and no place in the Hudson Highlands for that matter.

Gerrit had spent endless hours arguing with his father after he returned from Leiden. He had believed Cornelis ought to sell tenants their land anytime they could come up with the money, because it was the right thing to do, but Cornelis had been a blasphemous rake of the old school and hadn't given a damn about right and wrong in the eyes of God or man. He liked money and he liked power, and he didn't see why he should give up any of either. "You won't talk such nonsense when it's all yours," his father had told him.

Gerrit had never wanted Harenwyck. He had never wanted to sit at that table in front of the old castle and collect rents, watching his coffers fill with money other men worked for. But he did want Miss Winters, and keeping her was just as wrong.

"I promise to set you free after we open the strong-box," he said. "I'll hire you an escort at the King's Arms. You can go on to Harenwyck, and my brother, if you insist, in the morning, but I'll pay you double whatever Andries has offered you to turn around and go home to New York."

She had settled back into the shadows of the seat after the strongbox proved inaccessible and her face was unreadable now. "I wish I could," she said. "But I have already agreed to your brother's terms and taken his money. Even if I had not, circumstances would not permit me to change my plans."

He knew determination when he heard it. He'd had a Latin master who knew how to use that tone. If Miss Winters insisted on traveling to Harenwyck, Grietje and Jannetje—or Hubble and Bubble as they were known around the estate—were in for a surprise.

He would have liked to draw her out again, to find out why she was compelled to go on with this journey, but it was clear she did not want to share her reasons with him, and he contented himself for the moment with looking at her. It would have been rude, bordering on insulting, in another context, to stare at a lady so, but he'd already engaged in robbery on the King's Highway—the law would see it that way, even if he did not—so drinking in the appearance of a lovely young woman was surely the least of his crimes that evening.

Anna recognized the stepped roof and the slate tiles gleaming in the moonlight as soon as the carriage rounded the bend. The Halve Maen. Although Gerrit had called it the King's Arms. Her father had liked to drink there. He used to say the air was freer because it was in sight of the river, which the patroon did not own, but Anna suspected he liked to drink there because it was a long walk from the cottage and her mother only seldom thought it worth the trip to roust him from his cups.

Whatever the name, Anna was glad, because she knew how to get home from there. Or more accurately she knew how to reach the cottage where she had grown up and from there how to reach the manor house—if only she could slip away from Gerrit long enough to make her escape.

She could not leave the kitten behind. It needed warmth and milk, both things that a band of rogues on the run in a stolen carriage could hardly be relied upon to provide. She double-checked that the basket contained no silk threads for the kitty to eat, then took her fichu and tucked it in next to the purring kitten so there would be something soft for the creature to curl up against. She'd be cold without it covering her shoulders, but the kitten needed it more.

Gerrit helped her from the carriage with perfect courtesy and Pieter and Jan, who had ridden on top, pardoned themselves before sidling past her to haul out the heavy strongbox. Come to think of it, she had been the victim of an uncommonly courteous robbery. Gerrit's men behaved less like rogues and more like soldiers, but as Ten Broeck had explained, the line that separated the two was illegibly blurred on the Hudson just now.

It had been a long time since Anna had set foot in a tavern like the Halve Maen at night. Rural alehouses weren't like their counterparts in New York. She never thought anything of stopping in at the Fraunces Tavern to take a break from her errands, and she had been entertained there more than once by parents come to town to visit their daughters. Manhattan's public houses were not exclusively male domains—at least not the better sort, anyway—and Anna would have felt perfectly comfortable walking through the door of any of them after dark.

The Half Moon—or whatever it was called now—was different. It had not been built for entertaining. It had been built for defense. Four solid stories with three-foot-thick walls pierced by arrow slits. The windows had been a later addition, and they looked it: small and oddly shaped. The ground floor housed the kitchens with their massive jambless hearths, and through the open batten doors Anna could see that at least three cooking fires were burning. A busy night, then. The sound of the bustling taproom above carried to her on the brisk night air.

She climbed the wooden steps beside Gerrit, with Pieter and Jan following, the weighty strongbox carried between them. The stairs creaked just as she remembered. At the top Anna discovered that the tavern sign still bore the image of Henry Hudson's ship entering New York Harbor, sails full and Dutch colors flying, though the *vlieboot*'s name had been painted over with the inn's new moniker.

The wide front hall was as she recalled it, running from the front to the back of the building with a narrow stair leading into the upper rooms and wide doors to either side opening onto the public spaces. The main taproom was full, and Anna's heart skipped a beat when she saw with whom: Tarleton's green dragoons.

Six

The uniforms of the British Legion were unmistakable. This was their erstwhile escort to Harenwyck. Their bearskin helmets were stacked on benches against the wall, and they were drinking and dicing and playing at cards. The aroma of hot meat braised in wine with onions filled the air. While Anna and Mr. Ten Broeck had traveled into danger, the green dragoons had been dining on fresh crusty bread and stewed rabbit at the King's Arms.

There were, as she had expected, no women present, save the landlord's wife and daughter, busy serving tables, and an old woman sitting beside the cage bar, reflexively holding out her cup for a refill anytime one of the family members came by. Anna remembered her. Like the other fixtures—creaky rush-seat chairs, plank tables, tarnished tavern lamps—Mevrouw Zabriskie had changed little. Perhaps her straw yellow hair was whiter, but the old woman who lived in the woods and told fortunes for beer at the Halve Maen looked much as she had more than a decade ago. She wore her pale mane long and loose down her back like a young girl, and dressed in brightly colored castoffs, tonight a striped pink silk jacket and lampas petticoat in clashing ochre with a pair of riotous bargello shoes. Anna's mother had called her a witch. As far as Anna knew the cunning woman paid no tithe for her cottage and produced no crops, but the old patroon had always tolerated her presence on his land, and it seemed that the new one followed precedent.

Mevrouw Zabriskie had told her fortune once when she was a girl. She knew now that tarot was pure nonsense, but it had been frightening at the time: all hanged men and falling towers. Even so, Anna would take a witch over a certain dragoon any day.

"What is the British Legion doing here?" she asked.

"Perhaps they've had favorable reports of the season's ale," said Gerrit.

With a sinking heart, she surveyed the room. It wasn't difficult, even in that sea of green coats, to spot the man Gerrit must have come to meet. His auburn hair was burnished red in the firelight. He was playing five-card loo with several of his dragoons and a man in a civilian suit of dark gray wool.

"You've come to meet Tarleton, haven't you?" she said.

"Do you know him?"

"He was our escort to Harenwyck. And it would be better if we did not meet again," she said.

Just then Tarleton looked up. He nodded at Gerrit.

Then his dark, coffee-colored eyes found Anna and she felt her empty stomach revolt.

"Too late now," said Gerrit, as Tarleton got up and started through the crowd toward them. "Is there something else I should know?"

Anna watched the way Tarleton's men—hard, confident men—made way for him. She spent her days surrounded by women, but power worked much the same in all groups. It would be a mistake to underestimate the colonel. "I rebuffed him on the road to Harenwyck. I suspect that he is not a man to take such slights graciously."

"I have a room spoken for upstairs if you would prefer to retire," Gerrit said.

It was her chance, and she ought to take it, ought to go upstairs and then slip down while Gerrit was speaking with Tarleton and disappear into the night. Gerrit was intent on Harenwyck. He would not be thinking of her. She knew she could sneak past him. But Tarleton . . .

Would be waiting for her. Anna weighed her chances of evading him a second time, found she did not like them one bit. "I would prefer to stay close to you," said Anna, "while Tarleton is about."

"When you say you rebuffed him, what sort of overture did you discourage?" asked Gerrit tightly.

"It doesn't matter."

"What makes you think that?"

"Experience."

"I am very sorry to hear it, Miss Winters. I promise you he will not insult you again."

It was pure Gerrit, the outraged sense of justice and

the instinct to do right—even for a woman he barely knew. If she did not already know him, she would have fallen a little in love with him then.

Tarleton was almost upon them when Gerrit offered her his arm. He could not have known that Tarleton had done the same, but perhaps he had guessed how the man might react. The colonel's smile was stretched tight when he reached them.

"Van Haren," said Tarleton. He did not acknowledge Anna. "I thought we had agreed that the passengers would be held overnight and released on the morrow."

"Mr. Ten Broeck and the driver are even now on their way to the old barn."

"And the girl?" asked Tarleton.

"The services of *Miss Winters*," replied Gerrit, "like my brother's wine and his olives and sweetmeats, have been bought for Harenwyck, and because Harenwyck is rightfully mine, that makes them mine to dispose of as I see fit."

"You cannot just hold the girl," said Tarleton.

"Technically he *cannot*," said the man with whom Tarleton had been playing cards. The stranger was dressed in a suit of dark gray wool, exceptionally well-tailored, and it set off his coal black hair and gold-flecked hazel eyes. His approach had been the very opposite of Tarleton's. He'd threaded his way through the crowd, creating not so much as a ripple and come upon them all but unnoticed—until he spoke.

"In theory," he continued, "the patroons have not had the power to establish and administer their own courts of justice for almost a hundred years. But theory is one thing, and practice is another where the manors are concerned. Your father followed the old Dutch ways, did he not? Cornelis Van Haren had his own *schouts*, sheriff and bailiffs, to enforce the traditional laws of the patroonship."

"You know a great deal about the business of Harenwyck, sir," said Gerrit, examining the stranger with wariness.

"It is my business to know the character of all the strategic positions of interest to our government."

"Then I presume you are the gentleman that I am here to meet."

The gentleman nodded. "Major John André, at your service."

For a second, Anna forgot to breathe. Kate Grey's words about the Widow came back to her: *She was murdered by the same British intelligence officer who has fixed his eyes on the narrows at Harenhoeck. A man named John André. He had her tortured, and then he stood by while someone else slit her throat.*

Anna was face-to-face with the Widow's killer.

"I'm not sure an Englishman can fully understand the character of a place like Harenwyck," Gerrit was saying, to the man who had murdered her mentor. "It is the Middle Ages come back to life. My father took it on himself to settle everything except capital matters in his own court, where he was judge and jury. When he did deal with capital offenses, he referred them to Albany, which always handed down the verdict he desired, because he and the other patroons owned the courts. But I am not my father.

There will never be another sheriff of Harenwyck. The job got the last man killed, and not without reason. There will be no more estate courts when I am patroon. The Middle Ages can rest in peace."

"Reform is inevitable," said André. "But the patroons are understandably reluctant to accept that reality. Many of them have sided with the Rebels on the promise that they may retain their ancient privileges under the new American government." He was good, thought Anna, as good as the Widow. He had the trick of sincerity and he knew exactly what to say to appeal to Gerrit's amour propre. "Shall we retire to discuss the situation in detail?" André indicated the door, and Gerrit fell into step beside him.

Anna did not want to be left behind with Tarleton, so she moved to follow, but the colonel smoothly intercepted her. "I shall take charge of Miss Winters, and escort her home to New York."

Her heart hammered in her chest. Tarleton had thirty men to enforce his will. And he was bent on more than seduction now. After their encounter in the woods he would want revenge.

Gerrit slipped his arm beneath hers and pulled her out of Tarleton's orbit. "No need, Colonel. I'm rather warming up to the idea of the girls having her for a teacher."

"Miss Winters," said Tarleton, "is a lady with influential friends in New York. She's an Englishwoman and not subject to your authority."

"Actually," said John André, "we're well within the bounds of Harenwyck now. If we acknowledge that Mr. Van Haren is indeed patroon, and the estate has contracted with the lady, she is subject to his authority by local custom, if not by law."

Tarleton laid a hand on the hilt of his pistol. "My British Legion is not subject to 'local custom.'"

It was a threat. There was no way around it. Gerrit had perhaps a dozen men that Anna had seen. He might have more, but there was no way to know. Tarleton had thirty dragoons, and he was clearly willing to use them to get what he wanted.

"Your *troop*," said Gerrit, sounding just the sort of medieval patroon he despised, "is eight miles inside of Harenwyck at the moment, through woods controlled by my men. So unless your horses can swim the Hudson, Colonel, you won't be leaving the estate with the girl."

Tarleton's men, as Anna had suspected, were as naturally violent as their commander. A green-jacketed sergeant— a brawny, lantern-jawed man—rose suddenly from a table nearby and, almost before Gerrit had finished speaking, clapped a hand on his shoulder, seizing hold of it in thick, tightening fingers like a vise.

"You need a lesson in manners, cheese-head," he said.

Anna heard the slur on occasion in New York. She had never heard it uttered at Harenwyck, and definitely not against a member of the patroon's family.

Gerrit made no reply, but calmly turned, catching the wrist of the hand grasping his shoulder. The sergeant pulled up a knee, thinking to batter his adversary's chest, but Gerrit shifted position smoothly, hooked his free arm underneath the knee even as it rose. Twisting and lifting—almost without effort, it seemed—he used the larger man's momentum and weight against him. The dragoon voiced a great roar of surprise as he found himself thrown bodily backward, almost somersaulting, to crash down against the hardwood floor.

Anna was also surprised, almost amazed, at just how expertly Gerrit had dealt with the burly soldier. As readily as she'd dealt with his colonel in the woods, she thought, but this man was much larger than Tarleton, and had been spoiling for a fight rather than taken unawares.

Further intelligence of the sort of man the boy she'd cherished in her memory had become, but there was no time to examine her feelings on the subject. The sergeant, the wind knocked out of him, gasped for air and glared at Gerrit, standing above him, with murderous intent. Gerrit gave a quick, ambiguous nod to Pieter, who had lingered near the door when they entered, while all around the taproom, soldiers now pushed away from tables, balling fists and looking to their weapons; at any instant, the tension looked to dissolve into chaos and bloodshed.

"Ban," said John André in a soft warning voice. He did not seem alarmed by the prospect of the violence about to explode around him, only impatient. "This is not the time."

It was not an order. A major could not give orders to a colonel. But clearly, André had some authority that trumped the hierarchy of command. Banastre Tarleton smiled, lips thin and tight, then lifted a hand to quell his men. The effect was impressive. Those who saw the gesture sat back down almost immediately, as though nothing untoward had occurred; those who had not were very quickly restrained and informed by their fellows.

"Thank you, Sergeant, but I will handle things my own way," Tarleton said to his vanquished champion. "And when I want you to teach anyone *anything*—or indeed, to kill someone—I shall make that very plain. See you remember that."

"Yes, sir." The big sergeant picked himself up off the floor and rejoined his comrades with no more than a few black looks back at Gerrit.

The colonel's tone had been calm, almost amused, but Anna was not the only one to observe that his hand was still on his pistol.

"Perhaps it would be better to consult the lady herself," suggested André equably. He showed no reluctance, Anna noticed, to come between these two "killing gentlemen."

The three men turned toward Anna. "I am traveling on to Harenwyck."

When Tarleton started to voice his protests, André interrupted. "Miss Winters is not a dragoon, Ban, and you can't exactly *command* her to return to New York with you."

Tarleton did not like her answer, but André obviously had some hold over him, because he removed his hand from his pistol with great care and said, "Have you actually *seen* the girls since you have been back, Van Haren?"

There was malice in the question. Anna could feel it, even if she didn't know its source.

Gerrit's voice was frosty in response. "I have not seen Grietje or Jannetje in four years."

"What a pity," said Tarleton. "They are quite a striking pair. Quite. And there is a marked family resemblance. They have the Van Haren coloring, with all that golden hair."

"I would have thought that the Van Haren girls were too young even for you, Ban," said André, his patience appearing to wear thin at last.

He turned to Gerrit. "I have a private room spoken for above, my lord, if you and the lady would like to join me. And I am certain that the colonel is eager to return to his game."

Anna glanced back at the table where Tarleton, André, and three dragoons had been playing cards. The bank was heaped in the center of the table, and it told its own tale: a pile of coins, some paper money of dubious value, a ring, a seed pearl pin, and a pair of very fine silk kneebands with silver buckles.

She did not, as a rule, pay attention to gossip, or much credit it when she did. But when her students talked a great deal too much about a man, she thought it wise to learn the facts. In Tarleton's case the facts were these: He had gambled away a fortune before twenty and nearly ended in debtors' prison. With his inheritance exhausted, he had prevailed upon his mother to buy him a commission. He had made a success of himself in the army, rising fast on pure merit and élan. It surprised Anna that he still played, even for small stakes, when he had skirted so close to disaster, but she suspected that the sort of risk taking that drove him to gamble was precisely what distinguished him on the battlefield.

Anna realized that she was thinking like the Widow now, and that was probably just as well, since this was the Widow's arena: politics and war. And now Anna was facing the man who had killed her.

John André was difficult to read. She studied him as he led the way up the stairs. He was dressed appropriately enough for the highlands. His suit was simple wool, but finer and better cut than any farmer could afford. If she had met him on the street she would be hard-pressed to say whether he was a city lawyer or a country gentleman, although—she must admit—an exceptionally well-formed one, to judge from his coat's breadth of shoulder and trimness of waist.

Anna had never been up to the second floor of the Halve Maen, but she found it achingly familiar, because it was the first truly Dutch home she had entered since leaving Harenwyck. The room André had been given must have been the best in the house, because there was a massive carved and painted *kas* against one wall, and the jambless fireplace was surrounded by blue and white tiles and hung with a fine wool curtain on brass rings.

A cold meal had been laid on the sideboard. Anna knew she ought to eat—she hadn't had anything since breakfast—but she was too wrung out to take any food. Not so the kitten, which must have smelled the rabbit below, and now the roast turkey, and was mewing mournfully. Anna slipped a slice of meat inside the basket before joining Gerrit and André at the table by the fire.

"I understand," André said to Gerrit as he passed him a glass of brandy, "that you studied at Leiden."

"Yes," said Gerrit. "Before the war."

"Then perhaps Miss Winters will forgive me if I take the opportunity to practice my Dutch with you."

André favored her with a smile that was meant to charm, but it chilled her to the bone, because this handsome, cultured man had tortured the Widow and presided over her murder. Anna forced herself to smile back. She had only one advantage at the moment. André did not know that she spoke Dutch.

Gerrit was glad that Miss Winters could not understand their conversation. He had convinced Dirck and Pieter and Edwaert and all the men who had followed him into the Continental Army—and back out of it—of the necessity of switching sides, but now that he was drinking brandy with the enemy he felt like a traitor.

"I was educated on the Continent myself," said André, speaking in the flawless accent of an Amsterdam burgher. "At Geneva. I would have liked to have gone to Leiden—the observatory there is extraordinary—but Leiden's Calvinism wasn't strict enough for my Huguenot father's tastes."

André was trying to put him at ease with what some would deem treason, searching for common ground. Gerrit *had* been to the observatory once. The student he shared lodgings with had invited him. He had accepted the invitation with eagerness, excited at the idea of seeing the stars up close. At Harenwyck Gerrit had whiled away hours lying in the fields looking up at the night sky. The constellations had fascinated him, an ever-changing pageant of lions, bears, monsters, women, and witches, an irresistible brew of lurid adolescent imaginings and respectable classical learning—but through the lens of the twelve-foot telescope, divorced from their neighbors, the stars had turned out to be nothing more than pinpoints of light.

On the subject of fathers steeped in Calvinism, however, Gerrit suspected that he and André saw eye to eye. "My father wanted me to study law," admitted Gerrit, "no doubt to help him contest the Wappinger and their land claims, and the tenants and their lease disputes. So I read history instead." He had never been able to see the point in the law, since his father had always been able to bend it readily enough to serve his will.

"Mine wanted me to pursue mathematics," said André, "and become a merchant, like him. I did indeed study mathematics—but as part of military science—along with drawing, which my father despised as a feminine pursuit."

Gerrit spared a glance at Miss Winters, who was slipping a fish into her basket and cooing in a very unschoolteacherish manner. He had to remember to do something about that kitten. If he could not keep his sworn oaths to nations, he must keep his small promises, must fulfill his lesser obligations, or he would be nothing at all.

"A continental education must be unusual in the British Army," observed Gerrit. It had certainly been almost unheard of amongst the colonists, particularly the New Englanders, who often took provincialism to new heights.

"A foreign education—along with foreign blood—is both curse and blessing," said André. "The English, in my experience, alternate between despising and envying foreigners. They discount our bravery and dismiss our military acumen, but hire our mercenaries by the thousands. They are suspicious of all but the plainest English cooking, and yet covet European chefs. I was born in England, but my family name ends in a vowel, so the children at my grammar school pretended to detect a whiff of garlic whenever I entered the room. I am acquainted with the prejudices that you face among your countrymen and in trying to deal with my colleagues. I want you to understand that I do not share them, and that they pose no obstacle to our negotiations, but there are other factors in play that will cause my superiors to be circumspect."

"You mean," said Gerrit, "my late service with the Continental Army."

"No," said André, with some amusement. "General Clinton finds it entirely credible that a man—particularly a Dutchman—might recant his revolutionary fervor when faced with the prospect of gaining, or losing, a great inheritance. There, at least, prejudice works in your favor. And your military experience in this case is an asset. The general is not one of those officers who underestimates American fighting men."

"Then what is the obstacle?"

"Your brother," said André. "He has not taken the Rebel oath. Oh, he meets with them in secret. We know that. And he has expressed the greatest sympathy for their aims. He even fancies himself something of a leveler, which must involve some very creative thought for a man who holds more than a thousand souls in leases that last three lifetimes, not to mention slaves. But, most important, he holds the patroonship in a quiescent, tractable state. Other manors are plagued by riots and riven by civil strife, while Harenwyck remains relatively calm."

"That is because he uses my father's tactics," said Gerrit. "He keeps his favorites on his side with patronage and bribes, and the troublemakers in their place with threats." Like the driver tonight.

"But keep them he does," said André. "And whichever faction your brother sides with will be able to march an army through Harenwyck straight to the Hudson, the highway to the north. Harenwyck whole, Harenwyck with unfettered access to the Narrows is what General Clinton wants. He will not back you until you show that you can deliver him that. Harenwyck splintered into a bloody patchwork of hostile territories is worse than useless to him."

"The tenants will back me," said Gerrit, hoping it was true, "once they no longer have Andries to fear."

"I do not doubt you, my lord, but my superiors will require proof."

"What sort of proof?"

"A show of capability and commitment. Raise two hundred Harenwyck men to fight for the King by the end of this month, and we will bring you six hundred to subdue and secure the estate: cavalry, infantry, and fieldpieces. But it must be done quickly. Events are in motion on the Hudson. Harenwyck is not the only strategic asset that the general has his eye on."

It would be enough. Gerrit's brother, Andries, had only eighty men under arms and no artillery. Eight hundred men together would be overwhelming numbers. Eight hundred would mean that Andries' militia would lay down their arms just like the coachman had, and no one would have to get hurt.

"I can do that," said Gerrit, praying it was true. He would have barely two weeks to raise the men, but he had an idea how to do it. "I will need powder and shot. They'd be fools to join me with empty muskets."

"You have gold," said André, rising from the table. "Transmuting that commodity into gunpowder and lead shot is no great alchemy, or at least should prove a little easier than turning water into wine."

But not by much. There were no working powder mills in the Hudson Highlands. Powder had to be imported to the estates, just like their iron and glass, and it was scarcer now than ever. The only way Gerrit was going to acquire enough for two hundred men was by stealing it from Rebel stockpiles, as André well knew. "And when I have these two hundred men, how will I contact you?"

"Correspondence left with the publican here will reach me," the Englishman replied, rising from his chair. "A piece of advice in the meanwhile. I have another appointment tonight and, unfortunately, I cannot take my impulsive friend downstairs with me."

"Is that wise?" asked Gerrit. "You can hardly be taken for a spy, even out of uniform, when you are traveling with Tarleton's dragoons, but on your own, hereabouts, with lines between armies ever shifting, you could find yourself in some difficulty." He could find himself hanged, in point of fact, and with very little fanfare, given the dispositions of Washington's officers.

"Spare no worry on my account," said André. "But do not, I pray you, leave Ban alone with your pretty teacher, or delectable as she is, she will go the way of your brother's olives and sweetmeats."

Anna watched the door close behind John André. While Gerrit and the British agent had been talking, she had been feeding the kitten—and listening.

After Scrappy had inhaled the initial slice of turkey, Anna had returned to the sideboard and decided that someone ought to eat at least a fraction of the luxurious—by highland standards, anyway—repast that had been laid out.

There were tiny river fish grilled whole. Her father had called them sunnies for their golden hue. As a small child, she had loved to go to cast a line with him on the rocky banks of the Hudson, though she had not understood until later that he only fished when their crops failed or their hens refused to lay. She could not bear to eat one herself, but the kitten thoroughly enjoyed the offering, crunching one up, bones and all.

She was going to have to get a new sewing basket.

There was squash baked with a crust of Parmesan cheese. Anna wondered where the Halve Maen was getting Italian cheese in the highlands; then she realized that she had ridden in with the answer: from a highwayman.

She did not think that kittens as a rule ate squash, but she knew they liked cheese, and the little beast accounted the Parmesan crust a great delicacy, licking her paws thoroughly clean afterward. And all the while Anna had listened to John André talk.

Anna remembered what Kate Grey had said of him. *He is ruthless and all too willing to sacrifice his pawns.*

John André was going to get Gerrit killed.

There wasn't a damned thing she could do about it without risking herself.

Anna knew what men like André—and women like the Widow—did. She knew what late-night meetings in private rooms led to. Anna had sat on the bench in front of the jambless hearth shelling peas while her father and the Widow talked that first time, her mother busy about the fire cooking a meal for the woman whose schemes were going to destroy her family. It was the same conversation, then as now: men and arms and numbers and odds. Undertakings and promises. Her father and the Widow had drunk cloudy homemade gin and after Angela Ferrers had gone, Anna's parents had argued the whole night through.

The second meeting had followed a similar pattern, and by the third her mother was gone, decamped with a Huguenot tin peddler from New Paltz. Anna never saw her again.

It was that third meeting that changed everything. It was spring by then, and her father had gone out and gotten a bottle of the corn whiskey that was sold illegally on the estate—only the manor store and the Halve Maen had the right to sell spirits on the patroon's land—because the Widow had mentioned she preferred it to gin. And the talk that night had not been about leases and suits and lawyers and the natural rights of tenants, but about rough music and bringing the patroon—lofty Cornelis Van Haren—to his knees.

By autumn her father was dead and Anna was . . . no longer Anna.

She could not let the same happen to Gerrit. He had been willing to put himself between Anna and Tarleton and Tarleton's thirty dragoons. And in some strange way—for all he had changed—he was still the youth she'd cared so much for, all those years ago.

She watched Gerrit now as he reached across the table for the bottle of brandy that André had left. It was nearly full. He poured himself a brimming glass and drank it off in one go.

He needed advice. He needed someone like the Widow. And the only person like the Widow within a hundred miles and on his side—which John André was decidedly not—was Anna.

"Gerrit," she said. It came naturally to her lips, his given name, though their acquaintance, as far as he knew, had been far too short to merit it.

"Forgive me," he said looking up. "You must be starving. And exhausted. Have something to eat, and I shall arrange a room for you here. In the morning we can send to the manor house; no doubt Andries will dispatch one of his other conveyances for you. At last count he had five, including a chariot and a chaise."

"Thank you," she said, "but I have something I need to tell you first."

His puzzlement was plain on his handsome face. He picked up the bottle once more and said, "What?"

"I lied earlier, about not speaking Dutch."

For a moment he was utterly still. All was silence in the chamber and the sounds of the taproom, a muffled music of talk and tankards, played in the space between them. Then he set the bottle down very carefully. "Why?" he asked.

"Habit. Because no one wants a Dutch woman for a finishing school mistress." That was true, even if it wasn't her truth.

"Does my brother know?"

"That I speak Dutch? No."

He was silent for too long, and when he spoke, his voice was cold. "Then the real question becomes, did you come to the highlands to spy on him, or on me?"

"If I had come to the highlands to spy on you, would I be telling you now that I speak Dutch?" It was amazing how easy it was to sidestep the truth.

"Why are you telling me now?" She could hear the impatience in his voice.

"Because the man with whom you have been dealing, this John André, is dangerous."

"I should hope so," said Gerrit, "since he is a British officer out of uniform in contested territory. If he weren't a dangerous man, he wouldn't stay alive for very long. The Americans could hang him for a spy. I gather, from his deportment, that the prospect does not worry him over-much. That is all to the good. If I'm to wrest Harenwyck from my brother, I will need the help of dangerous men."

"But not that one," said Anna. "He is more than dangerous. He is a murderer."

"How do you know that?"

"I'm not free to say." She could hardly tell him about the Widow, but she had to convince him. "But I know of what I speak. I have met people like him before. They are manipulators, puppet masters. They plot and pull the strings of people like us as though we are marionettes. They play at revolutions and insurrections, but they are very seldom there when the killing starts. That man does not give a damn about you or Harenwyck or the tenants. All he wants is British control of Harenhoeck on the Narrows, so the Rebels cannot lay their chain across the river. John André will have done his research on you and your family, and he will say whatever he thinks will win you to his side. He woos you with talk of rigid Calvinist fathers and promises of reform. He is trying to seduce you to his cause."

"I rather thought he was trying to seduce me in general," said Gerrit. "And that kind of attraction can cut both ways."

"He prefers men," agreed Anna. "But spymasters with his sort of cunning do not make fools of themselves over pretty faces. Even ones as pretty as yours. John André might allow you to think you are playing him, but it will be his hands upon the strings."

"Thank you for that detailed appraisal of my gullibility and stupidity."

"I have dealt with people like him before and you have not. That hardly makes you stupid."

"Just naive, then," he said. "After all, I was taken in by you. Anna Winters, English gentlewoman. Who are you really?"

"Miss Winters and her school are very real." Both seemed like a fever dream. She was back at Harenwyck. It felt so strange. Perhaps she would wake up in a moment and discover she had never left. But she was here with Gerrit, so it must be real, and she could not let him share her father's fate.

"What about the brick house and the ducks and the fishing lady?"

Inside her a voice cried out to reveal herself. *I am Annatje Hoppe, don't you remember? You kissed me behind the church and terrible things happened to me later but I survived and I have come home.* But that would get her hanged and do Gerrit no good at all.

"I stitched them." The embroidery was still there above the mantel in her parlor in New York.

There was a scratch at the door, interrupting her thoughts, and Gerrit said, "Come," without taking his eyes off her.

The door opened. Pieter entered, smiling and smelling of fresh air and the outdoors. "The coach is taken care of, and the gold with it," he said in Dutch, eyeing the sideboard. "Aren't you going to eat some of that?"

"I think we're quite done here," said Gerrit.

"Are the sunnies any good?" asked Pieter, again in Dutch.

"I don't know," replied Gerrit, in the same language. "Ask Miss Winters."

"Did you try the fish?" he asked in English.

"No," said Gerrit. "Ask her in Dutch."

Pieter's brow knit. "I don't understand, *baas*."

"Of course not," said Gerrit. "That is because you and I, Pieter, are gullible rustics."

"Please stop," said Anna.

He didn't. "We're such chawbacons that we can't see beyond a pretty face and a pretty—"

"Don't!" she cried out. "You are better than this."

"Ah, but you understand Dutch, so you know that I am *not* in fact better than this. You know what André and I were talking about: betraying my oath to the Americans."

"Can I have the turkey?" asked Pieter.

"Good God, of course. Help yourself."

For a moment, Anna watched Pieter heap his plate with turkey and coleslaw and rice fritters and a generous scoop of the baked squash with cheese. Her appetite woke at last, but she could hardly eat now. Gerrit was still regarding her with something like disgust in his eyes.

"Just what am I supposed to do with you?" he asked her.

"I will go on to the manor house tonight," she said, "and relieve you of the dilemma." She could not bear to have him look at her like that. She would happily tramp three miles in the dark to be away from him now.

"No, you won't. You heard everything that André said. I can't let you go tattling to my dear brother."

"I have no plans to tell your brother anything," she said truthfully. But if she did not reach Harenwyck, Kate Grey would set the bailiffs on her.

"Please, Miss Winters, we both know I can't believe a word that comes out of your mouth. As the proverb has it, deceive me once, the fault is thine; when twice, 'tis only mine."

"The only thing I have deceived you about is myself. Everything I said about André is true."

Gerrit shrugged. "True or false, we need his help."

"So are we with the British now?" asked Pieter between bites of rice fritter.

"No," said Gerrit. "Or at least, not yet. They don't think I can take Harenwyck with thirty men."

"Could be that's because you can't," said Pieter.

There was another scratch at the door, and this time when it opened the one called Dirck stood on the threshold. He didn't spare a glance for the heaped food on the sideboard. "The patroon is going to repossess Edwaert's sheep tonight for nonpayment of rent."

"How do you know that?" asked Gerrit sharply.

"Mevrouw Duyser overheard two of your brother's *schouts* talking. They'll be getting a tithe each from the herd for the job. They would not do it for less, because they know Edwaert rides with us. And they mean to see it done before dawn, because they heard we were out a-roving tonight. They think they are free to take his property."

"Right," said Gerrit. "Saddle the horses."

"What are we going to do, *baas*?" asked Pieter.

"We're going to help Edwaert to steal his own sheep, before my brother does."

"What about the girl?" asked Pieter.

"There is not enough Parmesan cheese in the world to convince Mynheer Duyser to hold a girl prisoner for us," said Gerrit flatly. "She comes with us."

Seven

Gerrit did not know who he was angrier with, Miss Winters or himself. He'd been taken in by her, even after he'd seen the lockpicks, because she was pretty and smelled like oranges, and he'd wanted to drown in the folds of that airy cotton gown and sink into her softness. She'd lied to him, spied on him, and as good as called him a simpleton to his face—and she knew that he was a traitor to the country of his birth.

The very worst of it was that he still wanted her.

"I'm not exactly dressed for riding. Or sheep rustling," she said. She was standing by the ransacked buffet and she still had the damned basket with the damned kitten in it, and it was impossible to hate a woman who was kind to small animals.

"Would you prefer to go back to New York with Colonel Tarleton?" he asked.

She paled, and he felt disgusted with himself. "No," she said.

"Then find some other shoes in your baggage. It's in the room next door. Pieter will take you. And remember, the only way out of here is past the green dragoons. If you end up in Tarleton's clutches, I won't put my men at risk to get you back."

The look of disappointment on her face cut him to the quick. He knew he was lying, but it was just as well that she didn't. Twelve against thirty were poor odds, and he could not be certain how many of the Halve Maen's regulars would side with him in such a fight.

When they came back a few minutes later, Miss Winters had traded her silk slippers for leather shoes with sturdy pinchbeck buckles, and Pieter was somehow still eating. He returned to the buffet and began wrapping the remaining rice fritters in one of Mynheer Duyser's fine linen napkins. Gerrit doubted that André had paid quite enough to cover lost linens. Pieter reached for the last of the grilled fishes, but Miss Winters intercepted him and snatched the fish away. "Scrappy needs it more than you do," she said.

"You have already fed that cat twice its weight in fish," said Gerrit.

"It's a kitten, and it's growing," she said.

"It's all right," said Pieter. "Rice fritters travel better."

Gerrit very much doubted that.

Downstairs Tarleton was nowhere in sight, but there were dragoons sleeping on the benches in the taproom and on bedrolls in the hall and Mynheer Duyser and his wife treaded softly among them to clear glasses and plates.

He ought to be thinking about Edwaert's sheep, but all he could think of as they crossed the yard to the stable was Miss Winters. She kept pace with the men easily, her skirts flowing in the slight breeze, cotton gown ghost pale in the moonlight. He did not know what to do with her.

And she was far too quiet. When they reached the barn she waited in silence while the horses were saddled. She was too smart to try to run away while Tarleton was about, but he suspected she was plotting something.

"We haven't any sidesaddles," said Pieter, as he threw Gerrit his gear.

"Miss Winters will ride with me," said Gerrit.

"I'm quite capable of riding myself, astride," she said. They were the first words out of her mouth in the last half hour, and they were cool and clipped.

"That's what I'm afraid of," said Gerrit. "You ride with me."

She surprised him when she made no further protest. They led the horses out into the yard. Gerrit gave Miss Winters a leg up onto Konjin's back, and then slung himself into the saddle behind her. He did his best to ignore the supple curves of her body and the citrus sweetness of her scent. Pieter passed up the sewing basket with the kitten in it, and Gerrit heard it clink. A very unkittenlike sound.

Miss Winters stiffened. "I'll take Scrappy," she said, shifting in the saddle to try to get hold of the basket. And that made it impossible to ignore the fact that he had a woman in his arms for the first time in three years.

But it did not rob him entirely of his wits. He held firm to the basket and began to walk Konjin out of the innyard and down the rocky track that would take them to Edwaert's farm the back way. Edwaert and Dirck and Pieter and the others followed.

When they cleared the overhanging trees and came out into a wide field where the moon lit their way, he flipped open the lid on the basket. "Whatever have we here, Miss Winters?"

Anna ignored Gerrit's question. There was enough moonlight for him to see exactly what the basket contained: one kitten and an assortment of implements pilfered from the Halve Maen to aid her escape.

Gerrit looped the reins over his wrist and dipped his hand into her basket.

"I hope she scratches you," said Anna.

"She's licking me."

"A thoroughly undiscriminating beast, then. One can only hope that with age will come wisdom."

"She seems quite advanced for her tender years—or weeks. Already she has mastered the use of fire." He plucked up the candle she had stolen from its sconce while Pieter's back was turned and flung it into the field, along with the little flint she had found in her baggage. "And table manners withal—she apparently intends to cut her own food." He pocketed the little knife the Widow had taught her to use. Anna would rather have seen it between his ribs just at that moment.

"Ah. Our clever kitten is even a budding burglar." He held up a handful of her picks and tossed them into the corn.

"But a poor accomplice," replied Anna. "You take altogether too much delight in discarding my property."

"What were you going to do with it?" he asked, placing Scrappy's basket back in her hands.

"Find my way to the manor house, of course."

"At night? Across three miles of unfamiliar country?"

"I possess an excellent sense of direction."

"That may be, but a sense of direction wouldn't have saved you from the witch."

"If you mean the woman telling fortunes at the Ha— at the King's Arms, then you are sadly mistaken."

"How did you know the inn used to be called the Halve Maen?"

"Pieter must have said."

"No, he didn't."

"The sign above the door still has a painting of the ship on it. And not every old woman who sells cures or reads tea leaves is a witch," she added, hoping to change the subject.

"I did not mean Mevrouw Zabriskie. I meant the English witch. She of the velvet gown. Have you never heard of her?"

"Should I have done?"

"Perhaps she is not so famous in New York. Or wherever it is you're really from."

"Obviously not," said Miss Winters. "But then you wouldn't expect New Yorkers to be entertained by such rustic nonsense as scare tales about witches and hobgoblins when they have concerts and lectures and the theater to amuse them."

"But it is the English theater that birthed this particular witch, so your sophisticated New Yorkers ought to own her. I'm told she was an actress on the London stage during the reign of Charles the First. Very young, very pretty, and part of that first generation of females allowed to tread the boards in England. A star on the rise—until Cromwell and the fifty-nine commissioners cut off King Charles' head and closed all the theaters. You can imagine what might become of a pretty young girl thrown penniless onto the streets of London in those times."

She did not have to imagine it. "I don't think I want to hear the rest," said Anna.

"It gets better, I promise you. But like all good stories, it gets worse first. Hardly had she time to say a prayer for the soul of the late king before she herself was *preyed upon*—and by the same pious hypocrites who closed the theaters. Public vices like the playhouse were an affront to Puritan virtue, but apparently using young women for your private entertainment was of rather less moment in the eyes of the Lord. A certain baronet who was one of the commissioners—and also a provost marshal—had her arrested for vagrancy and abused her while in his custody, and allowed his 'worthy' friends to do the same."

"Please tell me that the story improves *soon*," said Anna.

"It does. I do promise. Barbara Fenton—for that was her name—decided that the god of the Puritans was neither merciful nor just, so she turned in her despair to his ancient adversary, and pledged herself, body and soul, to dark powers. She signed the Devil's book, like all good witches, and after enduring the loathsome attentions of the baronet and his friends for months, I can only imagine that consorting with the Devil was something of a relief."

It would have been.

"*Oude Nikken* gave her the power to free herself, right enough. But if it was a bad time to be an actress in England, it was an even worse one to be a woman suspected of witchcraft after a seemingly impossible escape from a locked room."

"I thought you said that the story was going to get better." Anna found that she was clutching Scrappy's basket so tightly that the wicker was printed on her fingers.

"It does now," said Gerrit. "I told you that Miss Barbara Fenton was an actress, and a fine one. The equal of Kitty Clive or the Divine Fanny in our own century. Had she been born just a few years later, she would have been Susanna Centlivre or Nell Gwynn.

"In any case, Barbara *had* played the Witch of Edmonton. She knew Elizabeth Sawyer's fate, and she was determined not to share it. She disguised herself as a Puritan and so thoroughly did she inhabit the role that she was invited to join one of those communities of emigrants setting out to build their Jerusalem in the New World. She traveled with them to Holland, where the first patroon was still energetically recruiting. Every fifty settlers he dispatched to Harenwyck earned him the right to more land. Barbara met and married a poor but large-hearted Dutchman, and they set out for New Netherland to take up one of the patroon's leases.

"They lived happily in a cottage not far from here for many years, but though she loved her farmer, she sometimes put on her velvet gown—a relic of her former life that she had not been able to part with—went out into the woods, and called up hare and deer and owls to be her rapt audience.

"Then one day a rumor reached Harenwyck that two of the regicides who had signed Charles the First's death warrant had been forced to flee the Netherlands one step ahead of the English sheriffs charged with capturing them, and were now in New Amsterdam. The monarchy had been restored and the theaters reopened by then, if too late for Barbara Fenton. Fame and fortune, you see, had passed her by. But now at least her opportunity for revenge was at hand.

"She walked all the way to Manhattan, and there she played the greatest role of her life: devoted Puritan good-wife succoring the English 'martyrs.' She sought and found these men, who were among those who had abused her, and such was the quality of her acting—perhaps, admittedly, aided by the passage of time—that despite past, all-too-close acquaintance, they neither of them recognized her. She told these gentlemen that the patroon was a godly man in sympathy with their plight, that he would gladly offer them shelter at Harenwyck, but that they must come with her quickly and in secret, lest their pursuers catch their trail.

"The gentlemen—heroes still in their own minds, albeit *justly* afraid of *unjust* death—quickly agreed and left with her at once. She took them to her cottage in the woods, where she had laid a repast in readiness, all of it most richly seasoned and most carefully poisoned. They ate and they drank and they thanked her for her generosity, even as the venom began to course though their veins.

"It was important to Miss Fenton that they know who she was and why they were going to die, so she chose a slow poison that paralyzes first. And when they were incapable of movement, she brought her dressing table and her chair and her looking glass down to the parlor and arranged them before her attentive audience. She applied her paint and dressed her hair and donned her paste jewels and her velvet gown, then turned to face them. And so, with the finality of a clashing gong, the Puritan goodwife was revealed to be the actress they had so misused, like a vengeful specter raised from their common past.

"When the poison had at last separated the gentlemen's gross physical bodies from their immortal souls, she cleaned the house very thoroughly, because she did not want her husband to accidentally ingest poison. And as the sun set, he arrived home from the fields to find a pair of strangers seemingly frozen at his table, and quite dead. His wife, who was dressed in finery he had never seen before, looked almost equally a stranger to his eyes.

"She loved him, so she explained what she had done

and why, what horrors had befallen her all those years ago. He loved her too, so he said he would not expose her and that he would help her to bury the bodies, but after that he must leave. He vowed he would never love another woman, but he was in truth a godly man, and could not share the bed of a murderess. And so like so many tenants did in those days, he fled his lease. He changed his name and searched for a better life somewhere else in the New World, and Mevrouw Fenton never saw him again.

"After he left, they say, she cried every night for ten days. Then went out into the woods and hanged herself in her fine velvet gown. Her ghost has haunted these parts ever since."

"I think," said Anna, "that I *wouldn't* mind meeting Barbara Fenton."

Try as he might, Gerrit could not stay angry at the maddening Englishwoman in his arms. If she really *was* English. He still did not know how or why she spoke Dutch or even if Anna Winters was really her name, but when he had seen the embroidered fichu folded up beneath the sleeping kitten all his ill humor had faded away. That scrap of translucent silk was the work of many hours, embroidered, he recalled from when it had covered her collarbones and décolletage, with lifelike strawberries and vines in pure white silk thread.

And she had given it to the cat to sleep on. She had, of course, been planning to knife Gerrit in the ribs and then escape with said cat with the aid of a single candle and a piece of flint, but he preferred to believe that she would have avoided piercing any vital organs. She had enjoyed his story about the witch. Certain parts had been rough going, and he'd worried that he had breached some kind of finishing school teacher rule with the details of Barbara Fenton's plight—but she had plainly liked the ending, and that was what mattered. It was possible she was part witch herself. He'd never seen anyone take food away from Pieter Ackerman and live to tell the tale.

"Would you have abandoned her?" asked Miss Winters, interrupting his thoughts.

"Abandoned whom?"

"Barbara Fenton. Would you have abandoned her as her husband did?"

Gerrit thought a moment. He had walked away from his marriage to Sophia over less, but had he ever really loved her?

"I don't know. I like to think that real love is two people, or a family, standing together against the world. Perhaps he should have stood by her. But if I had been Barbara Fenton's husband, I should have wanted her to come to me *before* she made that trip to New York."

"So you could have stopped her?"

"So I could *understand*—and then perhaps plot vengeance *with* her."

"How many men, do you think, would still love their wives if they found out she had been with so many others?"

"I suppose that depends on who their wives had slept with, and why and when. But a fair number, I should think, including more than a few 'godly' Puritans and worldly English monarchs."

"But not," said Anna sadly, "Barbara Fenton's Dutchman."

Anna saw the steep roof of the cottage at the top of the hill, distinct even by moon- and starlight. She knew its outline intimately, because her childhood home had been nearly identical. Most of the old cottages at Harenwyck had been constructed along similar lines.

The first patroon had required all of his settlers to build in brick, but brick was expensive, and thus each tenant was supplied only so many. If a tenant wished a larger home he had to *buy* more bricks—from the patroon naturally, who sold his bricks at a dear price. The result had been hundreds of tiny one-room cottages with sleeping lofts above, built on the traditional Dutch H-frame, with the steep curving roof and a jambless chimney at one end.

Glass had been another luxury the patroon did not provide. This house was more prosperous than the Hoppe farm. There was glass in all the windows, and the original cottage was now the kitchen of a larger house built of clapboard and sandstone. For a time at least, Edwaert, or his predecessors, had done well at Harenwyck.

And now they were reduced to stealing their own sheep before the patroon took them. Anna looked up at the night sky and the curved roof and knew that nothing had changed at Harenwyck in the time that she had been gone. Nothing ever did. It was changeless as the stars. Kate Grey had been wrong. The time wasn't right to do what her father had failed to a decade ago. It never would be. And because of Kate Grey, Anna was caught fast in Harenwyck's grip again.

But Gerrit did not have to be. He thought her a liar and a spy—and she was both of these things—but she was speaking a lived truth when she said, "You are going to get these men and their families evicted, or worse."

"Are we back to your very low opinion of my competence? Because I have discovered that it is not my favorite topic."

"This isn't about your competence. And it isn't about what's right or what's really yours. Places like this don't change. Neither do men like André. He won't support you when the time comes, not unless you're sure to win, anyway. And you *can't* win here. Sheep rustling and coach robbing won't secure you your inheritance. It will only goad your brother into retaliation. And not just against you. These men and their families will suffer as much, or more. And your conflict will degenerate into mob violence like it always does, until the patroon calls out his militia."

"His militia of eighty. By that time I will have *eight hundred* to stand against him."

"And as soon as he hears that you are recruiting, he will do the same."

"Then we must prevent him hearing until he's behind the times. There's logistics for you. And in that light, isn't it fortunate for me that I've deprived my brother of both his carriage and his spy?"

"I am not your brother's spy. I've never even met him. My reasons for going to Harenwyck are my own. But the second you set up your drum *someone* is sure to run and tell him. That's why the patroonships will never change. Human nature. There will never be a shortage of tenants willing and eager to sell out their fellows to earn the patroon's favor or buy a few extra privileges."

"Someday you will have to tell me from whence your remarkable perspective on the highlands derives. For now, try not to spook the herd."

The sheep were in a pen beside the barn. It was a sizable flock, close to a hundred head by Anna's estimate. She could smell the tang of the dairy house nearby, fresh curd drying on cool stone slabs. Her stomach growled, and she wished she had thought to make up a napkin of food like Pieter's.

Edwaert got down to open the gate, and Pieter—hair silver white in the moonlight—slipped into the enclosure and began urging the sheep toward the opening. There were a few surprised bleats and a great deal of sneezing, but finally the whole flock was out of the pen, with Pieter urging them toward the pasture and Gerrit using his horse to round up the lambs at the back.

It had been done with remarkable speed and quiet.

"You've left a lamb behind," said Anna, turning as far as she could in the saddle.

"Where?" He peered back toward the enclosure.

"In the pen."

"There's no time," said Gerrit, quite reasonably. If they did not get the sheep onto the road fast, they would disperse over the pasture, and every minute they wasted increased the likelihood that his brother's men would arrive.

"You can't just leave him without his mother."

Gerrit sighed and slid from the horse.

As she knew he would.

"Wait here," he said.

She waited a moment, stranded in a sea of sheep contentedly grazing.

As soon as he disappeared into the enclosure, she lowered herself to the ground and began searching his saddlebags.

She had just enough time to find and load his pistol.

When he emerged she aimed the piece with care and said, "No closer, please."

He stopped where he stood. "I presume from the way you are holding that thing that you know how to use it."

"Very well, in fact," she admitted.

"My father always told me never to aim a gun you don't intend on firing."

"It's good advice."

"My brother would be grateful if you pulled that trigger," said Gerrit, "but you might find Edwaert and Pieter less appreciative."

"I told you, I don't work for your brother. At least not as a spy."

"But you'll level a loaded pistol at me because I won't let you fly to him." Gerrit took a step forward.

She cocked the pistol and he stopped. "I have to reach

Harenwyck," she said. "For reasons you could not possibly understand."

"Now you're making Barbara Fenton's mistake. Give me the benefit of the doubt and tell me these reasons. I might just surprise you by understanding them after all."

"Yes, perhaps you might understand them—but, much like her Dutch farmer, you wouldn't be able to live with them."

Because she was a murderess, just like Barbara Fenton.

Her stomach chose that moment to growl again. Louder this time, like an animal yowling. A distinct and distinctively embarrassing sound, the same one Gerrit had turned toward in church that day all those years ago.

He cocked his head and took a step closer. He was studying her face in the moonlight with disbelief writ large over his own.

"It can't be."

Her stomach growled again. "Not another step," she warned.

Recognition, full and absolute, lit his eyes. It was the same wonder he used to show when they looked together at the stars. He shook his head. "You're not going to shoot me."

"I never intended to." She raised her arm and fired into the night sky.

Eight

The pasture erupted into noise and motion. Sheep bleated and bolted, men cursed, hooves hammered the ground. Gerrit started toward her, but frightened livestock surged between them. For a second their eyes met across a sea of confused sheep.

"Annatje!" Gerrit's voice was loud as a shot.

He knew. Anna threw the pistol down on the grass. She swept up Scrappy's basket and took off running.

The grass was wet and slippery. She clutched the basket tight to her chest and ran, dodging upset sheep. Strands of hair came free of their pins and tumbled in front of her face. For a second she was blinded and slammed into a body—thick with scratchy fleece—but the sheep was as frightened as she and ricocheted away in another direction.

She scrabbled on as the ground became rockier and more uneven. When she hit a steep downward slope she stumbled and sprawled, knees cracking against fieldstone so hard that it brought tears to her eyes—but she got back up and kept going. She could hear shouting behind her, thought she might be able to discern Gerrit's voice in the tumult crying her name and calling, *"Don't go"*—but it could just as easily have been a trick of the wind and her own wishful thinking.

She went on, because *he knew*. And if he caught her, even if he wanted to save her, she would surely hang. Because this was Harenwyck, the same Harenwyck she'd grown up in. It hadn't changed at all, and she would be held accountable for what she'd done, if not by the law, then by the mob. Because at Harenwyck, they played rough music at night.

If she reached the trees, he would not—*could* not—search for her, or Edwaert would lose his flock, and to lose your livestock was to lose everything. Gerrit would never let that happen to a friend. He cared about people and animals and even as a young boy, he had felt deeply that the strong ought to protect the weak. If he had to choose between apprehending a murderess whose crime was a thing of the past and the survival of an innocent family in the here and now, he would choose the latter, to save Edwaert.

At least she prayed that he would. She was counting on that to make good her escape.

As she slipped and slid through dung and rocks and mud, she was thankful that she had changed out of her kid slippers and into her more substantial walking shoes. As she reached the tree line and crashed into the dense forest, though, she wished she had worn her thick wool stockings and not the fine clocked silk. The sheer fabric was no protection against the forest. She could feel it shredding to ribbons as she plunged through the undergrowth, brambles and branches whipping and scratching at her ankles.

Her chest grew tight, her lungs burned, blood trickled down into her shoes, but she plunged on.

The woods grew thicker. The sound of outraged livestock dwindled and finally ceased. Anna stopped. Her chest ached. She leaned against a tree and sucked in ragged gulps of cool damp air. It sounded unnaturally loud and ugly in the stillness. Once she caught her breath she set Scrappy's basket down on the soft earth and fumbled with the clasp. She wished she had thought to hide the candle and flint in her pockets.

The moon was bright enough to reveal poor Scrappy's predicament. She was sitting up in her basket looking as disgruntled as a ball of fur could look. The fish Anna had tucked in with her at the Halve Maen had not traveled well. It had broken apart during her flight, and now lay mashed and crumbled in Anna's fichu. It had gotten all over Scrappy's coat during that jostling journey from the sheep pasture, and now flakes of fish clung to her fur in sorry clumps.

Anna doubted she looked much better herself, and unfortunately she could not lick herself clean as the tiny cat was attempting to do.

At least one of them would look presentable by the time they reached the patroon's house. Anna latched the basket and took a moment to get her bearings. She'd entered the woods on the north slope of Ackerman's rise. That meant she should be able to strike east through the forest and find the old mill path, and that would take her to the manor house.

As a child she had flown through these woods heedless of low-hanging branches and snarling brambles. She'd worn fewer petticoats then, of course, and no cumbersome hip roll. The trees plucked at her with green fingers, and when she stopped to disentangle herself from a sweet birch, she discovered that her hair, which had come entirely undone in her flight, was full of twigs and leaves. She slipped twice, sliding flat on her bottom down a gentle slope that was carpeted in pine needles, and wished she still owned a pair of sturdy *klompen* with hatch-marked soles.

She almost missed the path when she came upon it. It was narrower than she remembered, more a tunnel through the forest than a road. It stretched unbroken into darkness behind and before her, and suddenly she did not want to turn her back on such deep shadows.

But now, just as on the day she had fled Harenwyck, there was no going back. She picked up her skirts and plowed onward.

His father had told him she was *dead*. She was nothing of the sort. She was gloriously, maddeningly alive, all the promise of her girlhood come to fruit in a woman who was as competent—as formidable—as she was beautiful. She was alive and a moment ago, here with him again.

And he could not go after her.

"Gerrit!" Pieter reined up beside him and followed Gerrit's line of sight into the woods. "We don't have time."

"I know." They were likely to lose half Edwaert's sheep as it was.

He couldn't look away from the woods.

"You can't go after her."

"I wasn't thinking about it."

"You're a terrible liar, *baas*. I heard you in the pasture. You called her Annatje. That was Annatje Hoppe, your *klompen* girl."

He was a fool. He should not have said her name out loud. But he had been so surprised—so desperate to keep her—that he had shouted out her name for the whole bloody estate to hear. Annatje Hoppe. The girl the *schouts* had tried to hang.

"Are you going to tell anyone?" Pieter had been his friend since they were both eleven years old. He had followed Gerrit into the army and back out of it. The ties of friendship bound them, but Anna—no, *Annatje*—had been right: he would always be the son of the patroon. Cast out, but not cast down. Men like Pieter, women like Annatje, had fewer choices, and Gerrit had no right to make demands on them.

"No," said Pieter. "But I'm not the only one who'll have heard you."

Dread ran through Gerrit like fever. He climbed into his saddle and guided his mount to follow Pieter's along the edge of the road, where so many of the sheep were now stamping in a confused huddle. "Who else?" he asked, queasy with the thought that anyone had.

"Edwaert, for certain. Jan maybe. Good ears, that one."

And Pieter did not need to tell Gerrit: Vim Dijkstra, the man Annatje had killed, had been Jan's uncle. The brother of Jan's mother, and that good Dutch *mevrouw* grieved him deeply still.

Pieter began urging the sheep up onto the road. "What do you think he will do?" asked Gerrit.

"I don't know," admitted Pieter. "His mother, Rie, was out for blood back then. She only gave up because we all thought Annatje Hoppe was dead and gone. If Rie finds out the girl's alive, she'll raise a mob and hang her. That much *is* certain. It will be rough music all over the estate."

"It doesn't have to be," said Gerrit. "You didn't recognize her. I didn't recognize her at first." And he had never been so close to anyone in his life as he had been to her that year. Never shared and exposed so much of himself. Not to his brother, even before the business with his wife; never to Sophia, who had not been interested in the workings of his mind or his heart; not even to Pieter, the closest friend he had ever had.

Pieter looked sidelong at Gerrit. "For a man who didn't recognize his childhood sweetheart, you certainly spent a long time in that carriage with her."

"I didn't know it was her then." But he knew now that some part of him *had* recognized something in her. He had explained it to himself as mutual attraction, the magnetic pull of kindred spirits, the earthy tug of lust, but something in him had known.

"I believe you," said Pieter, "but most won't. You can't have her and keep *them*." He nodded at the shadows in the darkness ahead of them where Edwaert and Jan and the rest were doing a remarkably quiet job of rounding up a hundred far-scattered sheep in the dark—probably because they were no strangers to impromptu livestock removals . . .

"But she's one of them," said Gerrit. Although that wasn't quite right. She *had* been one of them. The fierce little revolutionary who followed her father everywhere, who rioted right along with the farmers and the Indians and had even marched on the manor and confronted the patroon—before his father called in the army. Only she wasn't that girl anymore. She had become someone else even more fascinating. A woman with a mastery of the feminine accomplishments his wife had been so devoted to—but who also knew how to load and fire a pistol and was clever enough to start a panicked stampede to aid her escape. "Her father was a tenant," Gerrit added, less convinced that would make a difference.

"*Her* father got *their* fathers beaten, jailed, even evicted. Bram Hoppe's revolt ended in disaster. There were dozens of arrests that night. And almost as many evictions. Take up with Bram's daughter and everyone will think your revolt will follow the same path. Doomed and foredoomed."

"I just want to talk to her," said Gerrit. "To find out why she's here." And how Annatje Hoppe had become the equally extraordinary Anna Winters.

"You were long past talking by the time we got to the Halve Maen," said Pieter. "Half the valley saw you challenge that mad bastard Tarleton for her. That's not a scene they're likely to forget anytime soon. If the tenants find out that she's Bram Hoppe's runaway daughter, some of them will take your part, but at least as many will wash their hands of you. There is no earthly way you can raise two hundred men on this estate with that girl at your side, *baas*."

"Then I'll just have to raise the men before anyone finds out about her."

"You mean *if* Jan didn't hear you and *if* he isn't already on his way to Rie with the news."

Gerrit looked down the road. In the darkness, spread out among the sheep, the men were just so many dark shapes: impossible to tell one from another, or if one of them was missing.

"If Jan knows, there will be no place at Harenwyck that's safe for the girl. Vim Dijkstra was your father's favorite *schout*. Everyone knew he spoke for the patroon, and he used that to good effect, to make himself big and powerful among the tenants. His widow *still* has influence. Rie's not the only one who will want Annatje Hoppe's blood. Ida Dijkstra uses the pension the patroon awarded her for her loss to make loans to the other tenants. She uses Jan as an enforcer. If you don't pay, he pays a visit to you with some friends. If Mevrouw Dijkstra learns that Annatje is here, they will come for her."

"Then they'll have to come through me."

"They will. Right through you. And you'll never be patroon."

"Vim Dijkstra may have been feared," said Gerrit, "but he wasn't loved. Annatje's father was." Gerrit had heard him speak, felt the power of his oratory.

"Bram Hoppe is dead, and his daughter is wanted for murder."

"She's no murderer." Gerrit knew that in his heart, whether she'd killed a man or not. And Vim Dijkstra had been no saint. The *schouts* had gotten away with much brutality under the old patroon because a man would rather be beaten than evicted.

"You weren't there that night, *baas*. You don't *know* anything. It was chaos on the manor. Your father called the army in to put down the tenants after Bram Hoppe was arrested. There was violence of all kinds that night. And everyone on the estate knew how devoted that girl was to her father. It's not hard to imagine her shooting down the sheriff who arrested him."

It *was* hard—almost impossible—for Gerrit to imagine it because he knew her, but Pieter was right. On the manor Annatje had been branded a murderess, an unnatural woman, an unfortunate, but perhaps an inevitable product of her leveler father's revolutionary principles.

Anna Winters was such a completely different animal. Somehow his wild and freethinking *klompen* girl had transformed herself into the image of a prim spinster. And become an adept liar. As a girl she had been a creature of pure emotion, her feelings always on the surface, easy to read in her expressive gray eyes. No longer. He had been thoroughly taken in by her in the carriage, had even believed her sad story of the brick house and the unsympathetic brothers.

And somewhere along the way from his "Annatje" to this "Anna" she had acquired an education. Though that was less surprising. Even as a girl she had loved books. She had hungered for them, and he had brought them to her, spirited out of the small library at Harenwyck, along with the cookies he stole from the kitchens. The cooks, he realized later, had known that he was taking them—and with whom he shared them. They turned a blind eye because Bram Hoppe had been a hero to them.

But everyone who had followed Bram Hoppe, who had rioted and marched on the manor to demand their rights, had seen exactly where that led: to imprisonment, ruin, and death. Bram Hoppe's supporters might pity Annatje, but they would not risk themselves for her.

But someone had to. "What would you do?" asked Gerrit.

Pieter looked him square in the eyes and said, "If Annatje Hoppe was my girl, *baas*, I'd get her the hell away from Harenwyck. And make damned sure she never came back."

Anna had begun the day warm and dry in the patroon's carriage. Now she was cold and damp, with miles to go to the patroon's manor. As she penetrated deeper into the woods a feeling crept over her: she was being followed. There were no sounds of pursuit. There were no footfalls or broken branches, just a deep and unsettling sense of a presence *behind her*.

It was nonsense, of course, but the feeling became so acute that she finally gave in to it and turned around.

Of course there was no one there. She kept going.

And yet the feeling persisted. The back of her neck tingled. Her shoulder blades twitched. She found she was often holding her breath, listening for a broken twig or skipped pebble. She looked over her shoulder again, but the shadows were so deep beneath the trees that all she saw were pools of deeper darkness, and if she stared into them too long, they seemed to move, black surging upon deeper black.

That was no good at all, so she forced herself forward, but now all she could hear was the raggedness of her breathing. Until the twig snapped. It sounded like a mighty crack of thunder in the forest, and she whirled around to see a pale figure standing in the moonlight.

The witch in the velvet dress.

Anna screamed. No sound came out, just a dry croak. She turned and ran, heart pounding, dread coursing through her, terrified to look again. The path went on and on with no end in sight. Surely she had to reach the road soon. But by now she had lost all sense of how far she had come. And *something* was behind her.

It had been a woman in a pale gown.

Or at least light-colored petticoats and a jacket.

With white hair. Or at least blond.

Had the witch in the story been blond? She could not recall. And the woman on the path had been wearing some rich fabric that shone in the moonlight. It could have been velvet. Or not. Anna had only a vague impression of the woman's pallid face. Maiden, mother, crone—or milkmaid, for that matter—she could not have said.

Reason reasserted itself. She did not know *what* she had seen. Anna stopped running. When she turned to look behind her, there was no one. She had imagined it, or the moon had played tricks on her or some *jonge vrouw* had been slipping home from a late-night assignation. If that was the case, the girl in question had probably been just as terrified of Anna as Anna had been of her.

No living woman could be so pale . . .

Anna cursed herself for a fool. If she had started at every shadow like that when she had been seventeen and fleeing the bailiffs, she would not be alive today. And she would never have tolerated such flights of fancy from her students. She lived in an age of reason. When Anstiss Ward had told all the girls at the academy that a ghost was scratching at her walls at night, Anna had switched bedrooms with her to get to the bottom of the matter. It had turned out to be one of Mary Phillips' more ardent suitors scrabbling up the drainpipe.

There were no such things as ghosts.

She must find the manor house. Once she was safely under the patroon's roof, it would not matter what some outlaw claimed. She was Anna Winters of New York, mistress of a respected academy, property owner. And Gerrit's credit in the courts was, by his own admission, rather poor.

She had expected the trees to thin as they so often did

at the edge of cultivated land, but she emerged onto the manor road with no warning and found herself standing in the middle of a broad, empty lane. For a moment she thought that she had stumbled upon the wrong road. This stretch did not look familiar. There had always been beeches flanking the road to the patroon's house: tall, stately, clipped to shade, but not obstruct, the lane.

Anna saw no sign of them, but then it occurred to her that she had never seen them at night. She had always come this way with her father to pay their tithe or bring their complaints before the patroon, but that had invariably been by day. Perhaps the beeches would look different at night.

She went a little way farther in the direction she believed the house lay, and then she saw them at last, their waxy leaves shining in the moonlight. They were not shaped as she had thought. In her memory they were tall and narrow, an honor guard for the patroon's parade of carriage, horses, and carts. Now, they were wild and overgrown, heavy branches hanging out over the road and almost touching the ground in places. She did not know how a coach could have driven up this road without damaging the limbs, or itself.

Whether they looked as they had when she was a child or not, they indicated that she was very close to the manor—and safety. Anna slowed and finally looked back down the path. The dark tunnel she had emerged from was utterly empty.

Perhaps she had imagined the woman in the velvet gown.

But she did not think she had.

And she did not really believe that any sane young woman would have come that way by herself at night. Anna did *not* like to leave that darkling tunnel at her back, but she must look away and plod on to the house. She had told Gerrit that she would like meeting the witch in the velvet gown, because she had felt a kinship with the woman. They had both found themselves on the street at a tender age. Barbara Fenton's story was like something from the theater—only unlike a heroine from the stage, she hadn't waited for the hero to avenge her; she'd done it herself. Anna tried to convince herself that if she met the witch of the Harenwyck woods, that lady would harbor no resentment against her. Then again, if Anna herself had suffered so, she might very well be angry at the world.

Anna forced herself onward down the drive. Gerrit had never told her the story of the witch when they were young. Perhaps he had only just made it up. That was a comforting thought but an altogether unlikely one. The story was too neatly shaped to be a spur-of-the-moment invention, and more likely was an old, familiar one that young Gerrit had simply deemed too disturbing, too lurid, to share with a sixteen-year-old girl.

Anna came upon the lawn without realizing it. She had expected a neatly shaved carpet of green velvet. Instead she discovered knee-high grass gone to seed. Perhaps the new patroon did not much care for lawns. Or beeches.

It struck her then. Far too late. She had become fixed on the idea of escaping to the manor house after Gerrit had waylaid the carriage, but they had never been going to the old manor house. Both Tarleton and Mr. Ten Broeck had spoken of a newer, more modern mansion, completed by the current patroon.

Surely the new manor house had been built on the site of the old. Or at least hard by.

A quarter mile farther on, and she saw the distinctive sloped roof, bigger than any she had seen until she went to New York. Tip tilted in the Dutch style so the steep slope ran down over the attic and then curved gently up to shade the wide wraparound porch. *Familiar.*

And thanks be to God there was a light burning. *Someone* was home in the old manor. There would be warm rooms, maybe even the heat of banked coals to soothe her aching legs and feet. A bed. It did not matter if it was a servant's room, a straw tick with no curtains. She would sleep on anything she could lay her head upon, although the unwelcome thought crept upon her that the patroon might see her as a servant, on the same level as his cook and his gardener. Scratch that. He had obviously discharged the gardener. But the cook at Harenwyck had always slept on a pallet on the floor in the kitchen, and that she must refuse to do.

The grass was just as high in front of the house, creeping all the way to the beaten earth where the cooks used to set their trestles for drying fruit in the summer. Now that she was close, signs of habitation—besides the light— were nowhere in evidence. And the house seemed to loom over her, just as much as it had when she was a child.

Like the Halve Maen, the manor house was built on top of a ground floor devoted to cooking and housework. The thick walls were local fieldstone. The porch was half the depth of the house itself, reached by a broad double stair atop the entrance to the kitchens.

She had run so far to be there, but suddenly the house seemed just as dangerous as the woods. She did not want to climb those stairs, did not want to disturb the deep shadows of the porch. Which was nonsense. There was a light on. That meant that someone was home, even if the patroon did not live there anymore. Someone who was beholden to the lord of the manor for a roof over his or her head, and would send to the main house—wherever that might be now—and tell the patroon of her arrival.

And she could hardly spend the night standing in a field of overgrown grass.

She climbed the first riser. The wooden treads creaked. A wind picked up, rustling the piles of leaves that blanketed the packed earth in front of the house. Another step, another creak, this one louder. At least no one could fault her for sneaking up on them in the middle of the night. She was making enough noise to wake the dead, which was an entirely unwelcome thought.

Anna reached the top and stepped onto the porch. Up here all was stillness, a pocket of utter quiet beneath the painted blue roof. The light was coming from a window at the far right. The other three along the front façade were shuttered.

A branch broke somewhere out in the woods and suddenly Anna felt exposed, standing there at the edge of the porch. She rushed to the door and rapped three times with the cast-iron knocker.

The light in the window went out.

Her heart skipped a beat. She did not believe in ghosts or witches. She might have grown up among country people steeped in superstition, with a Calvinist dread of the Devil and a firm belief in his material existence, but she was an educated woman, and she lived in an age of reason. There was a rational explanation for everything. Unfortunately she could not think of rational explanations that she liked for the light blinking out so suddenly.

She tried the door knocker once more. She could, of course, walk to the window that had been lit and peer in, but that idea did not appeal. The ends of the porch were shrouded in darkness. And whoever was inside had snuffed their light for a reason.

The silence stretched. At last she put her hand upon the latch. The door swung away from her and stale air rushed out.

She had never been inside the patroon's house. As the daughter of a poor tenant farmer, who was decidedly *not* one of the patroon's favorites, she had never been invited. She was not invited now. She crossed the threshold anyway.

No one lived here. Anna could tell that at once. The broad center hall that ran from the front to the back of the house had not been swept for some time. Leaves had blown in and dirt crunched beneath her feet. Cobwebs infested the dark corners and doorways. There was a dining room to her left, the tables and chairs relics of the previous century, great bulbous legs black with age and caned seats chewed through by mice. The paintings and sconces that had once brightened the chamber were gone, leaving only suggestive shadows on the wall.

It was the parlor to the right where Anna had seen the light burning. She turned and entered that room, finding it paler and brighter, the paneling painted a shade of seafoam green that made the most of the feeble moonlight that reached it.

She had readily understood why the patroon might leave the carved table and chairs in the dining room behind. They were worn and out of fashion. The parlor was another matter. Some of the furnishings had been removed. There was a shadow on the wall where a settee had once rested, its camelback like the memory of an ocean wave on the sea green paneling. Nail holes above the windows showed where draperies, most likely in matching silk, had also been taken down.

But clustered beside the window were three items that no sensible person would leave behind.

The first was a wing chair upholstered entirely in needlework with a tiny vignette on the back of—naturally—a fishing lady scene. It was good if not accomplished work, stiff, with the figures as ramrod straight as their fishing poles. Pushed against the wall was the stand and frame upon which it had most likely been made, lengths of dusty linen still lying ready for the needle. A basket much like Anna's own sat on the floor beside it.

The second was a fire screen bearing another silk picture, this one of a shepherdess. An earlier work by the same hand, Anna judged, if the lamb's wild-eyed expression was anything to go by. Faces were always difficult, animals' especially so. One aimed for Carracci, but so often ended up with Brueghel. The effect was not improved by the amateur mounting. Someone had failed to stretch the canvas properly over a stiff backing before framing it and fixing it to the pole. Skilled craftspeople, no doubt, were difficult to come by in the highlands.

The third item was a large table, decorated with by far the most advanced piece of needlework: a flip-top gaming surface adorned with flowers and cards and mother-of-pearl counters, stitched in an almost successful mix of wool and silk on a green baize ground. It had been properly mounted to the surface by a professional cabinetmaker and would not look out of place in a New York parlor.

What she could see of it anyway, because most of the surface was covered in *doed koecks*. Anna remembered them from her childhood. "Dead cakes" were like English short-breads spiced with caraway, cut into four-inch squares, and given away at funerals. They lasted for months, sometimes years, and she could vividly recall the taste of them: sweet, buttery, and lightly spiced. She was tempted to eat one now. Anna had never seen any left over after a funeral, but here were stacked dozens, some wrapped in black paper, some not, pressed with the letters *C* and *H* linked by a small *V*. The man who had destroyed her life: Cornelis Van Haren, the old patroon.

The cakes suddenly lost all their appeal.

Outside the stairs creaked. Someone—or *something*—was coming.

Nine

Anna wished she had kept Gerrit's pistol. Or that she still had her knife. Or that the Van Harens had left something useful behind like a weighty iron candlestick or fireplace poker, or even an empty water jug. All she had currently on her person was an exhausted kitten in a greasy basket. She spied a candle sitting in the window and grabbed it, only to discover that it had no holder, just a chipped plate.

And the top was still *warm*. Someone *had* been here.

Now they were back. And she had trapped herself in a room with no exit. She heard feet crunching over the dirt in the front hall and she turned to the parlor door and called out, "Who is there?"

No answer. Just more steps in the dark.

"This is the patroon's house," she said, trying keep

the quaver out of her voice. "You have no right to be here."

Another step and a figure filled the doorway: tall, lean, and male. For a second Anna thought that it was Gerrit, come to track her down, and like a fool her heart surged at the thought, but then the figure crossed the threshold, and she saw that this was someone else entirely: a man dressed for riding in high boots and a short coat, his hair guinea gold in the moonlight. His face, though, remained obscured by shadow.

"You don't look much like the patroon yourself," he said. The accent was cultivated, and someone had worked hard to take the Dutch out of it. But she could still hear the vestiges of his first language in the flatness of his vowels, because that was what had long tripped her up too.

"How would you know?"

"Because every morning I stare at his face in the mirror."

"You are the patroon?" Anna tried to conjure a portrait of Andries in her mind, but all she could recall of him was his height, his coldness, and his golden hair. And his gold-tressed sister. They had been so like each other, so like all the gilded Van Harens, and so different from Gerrit.

"I am," he said, as though speaking to a simple child. "Who, may I ask, are you?"

She could hear the ill-concealed impatience in his voice, so similar to his father's. Cornelis had always disliked dealing with tenants. She'd once overheard him complaining of the garrulity of the lower classes. *They talk and talk when they have nothing to say, and it is impossible to get them to come to the point.*

"My name," she said, coming to the point, "is Anna Winters. I'm the teacher you hired for your nieces."

He advanced a few steps farther into the room and scrutinized her. She could only imagine what she looked like. She'd lost her cap, and her hair was wild and full of leaves. Her fichu was currently inside a basket containing fish, turkey, and a kitten, and it was very likely that the fish was beginning to smell. Her stockings were in shreds, and she doubted her gown was much better.

"How did you come to be here, Miss Winters? And in such a state?"

Your brother. But it felt disloyal to say it, because the truth was that Gerrit was not responsible for her current state of dishevelment. If she hadn't tried to warn him about André, she would most likely be sitting snug by the fire at the Halve Maen feeding Scrappy tidbits and waiting for the patroon's chariot to pick her up. Gerrit had promised to release her, and he was a man of his word. He had only reneged when she had put him—to his mind anyway—in an impossible situation. She did not know how she could have done things differently—or at least lived well with herself thereafter—but that didn't change the fact that she had only herself to blame.

"There was trouble on the road," she said at last. "We were held up by a highwayman. I believe Mr. Ten Broeck and your driver are to be released at dawn." The patroon's expression was unreadable in the half-lit room. "I escaped," she added. And then, because it would be strange if she did not say it: "The bandits were led by your brother."

He took another step forward. His face was still shrouded in shadow, but a band of light had fallen across his pale blue eyes and she saw them turn very, very cold.

"You were supposed to have an escort," he said.

"We did. They left us at the gates to Harenwyck." *And they sold you out.*

She was supposed to be at Harenwyck on behalf of the Americans. Kate Grey had wanted her to bring Andries decisively into the Rebel fold. There was probably no better way to accomplish this end than to tell him his older brother was plotting against him with the British.

She said nothing.

"Come," he said. "We must get you to the manor and organize a party to search for Mr. Ten Broeck. Do you feel well enough to ride? I could send for the chaise, but I dislike the idea of leaving you here alone."

She did not much fancy the idea of sharing a mount with the patroon of Harenwyck—he was as cold and aloof as she remembered and possibly as much a snob as his father—but neither did she want to spend another minute in that house alone. "I will ride."

She moved to smooth her skirts and realized that the warm candle was still in her hand. She set it down beside the *doed koecks*. That's when it occurred to her that these were his father's funerary keepsakes.

Good manners demanded some acknowledgment of that. In this case good manners demanded a bold-faced lie. "I am very sorry for your loss," she said.

He seemed to notice the cakes for the first time. "A quaint custom," he said. "But the cook should not have baked them. I have never seen so many left over after a funeral. My predecessor was not much loved on the estate, and it seems that not even his hungriest tenants were willing to eat free bread in his memory."

Neither was Anna. She was ravenous now. Dawn could not be far off and she had not eaten anything since breakfast—but she was certain she would not have been able to choke down even one of the patroon's cakes.

She followed Andries Van Haren out of the desolate house and down the porch. He did not bother to lock the door behind him. Anna wondered if that was because there was nothing of value to him in the house—or because he knew that no Harenwyck tenant would dare vandalize the patroon's property.

At the bottom of the steps he had a fine brown mare tied to the post. She had been so engrossed in exploring the house she had not heard the approach of hooves. Andries gave Anna a leg up and as soon as she settled into the saddle exhaustion struck her. The chaise sounded like heaven, but she would not have remained in that house by herself for all the carriages in the world.

Andries slung himself into the saddle behind her, leaving as much distance between their bodies as was possible on a shared mount. She tried to recall if she had ever seen his father as much as shake hands with a tenant. She did not think so. Evidently Andries had inherited the old patroon's distaste for the people who worked his lands and put food on his table.

They set off up the road that used to lead from the house to the old castle and the church, and Anna could see that it was even more overgrown than the way she had come. The wheel tracks were full of wildflowers. No cart or carriage had come this way for years. That made the patroon's presence in such an abandoned place in the middle of the night very odd indeed. The strangeness of it bothered her. He had not been out looking for her. He had not even been aware his carriage had been stolen. And he had approached the house so quietly that she had not heard him until he was inside. He must have had some other purpose in the woods.

"What were you doing here so late, my lord?"

"My father styled himself lord of the manor, but it is not a tradition I wish to maintain. 'Mr. Van Haren' will do."

"What were you doing here, Mr. Van Haren?"

"I was coming home late and saw your light."

"I did not have a light." But someone had. Someone who had been sitting at that table with the *doed koecks*.

"Then it must have been a trick of the moon."

"It wasn't."

"Trespassers, then."

He did not seem particularly concerned or even interested in the fact that someone else had been in his house.

"Your brother told me there was a witch in the woods." She felt like a fool as soon as the words were out of her mouth.

"There is a cunning woman who lives in the woods, but she is no harm to anyone."

"Not her. The English witch in the velvet gown. The one who murdered the regicides."

"Good God. *Gerrit*. Our nurse told us all that one when we were children, and my sister would not sleep for a week. I haven't thought of it in years. Do not, I pray you, share *that* story with my nieces."

Her hackles rose. "I would never frighten my students like that."

The patroon sighed. "You have not met Grietje and Jannetje. They do not frighten easily. More likely, if you told them there was a witch in the woods, they would set out to bag her, and soon we would have old ladies caught in snares from here to Rensselaer's place. I do hope that Mr. Ten Broeck was candid with you about the girls. They are hardly delicate young misses. Nothing like their mother, either of them. They do not even have her coloring. My nieces are true Van Harens: their father's daughters."

It took her a moment to grasp his meaning. *Their father's daughters.* Kate Grey had told her that they were the children of Elizabeth Van Haren, Andries' runaway sister, but if their mother was not a Van Haren . . .

"They are Gerrit's daughters?"

"You are on a first-name basis with my brother. What an exciting evening you must have had. You wouldn't happen to recall where he was when you saw him last?"

"I'm not certain," she lied. "I don't really know the area."

"Then you were remarkably lucky to find your way to the old manor."

"Yes. Very lucky," she said.

For years she had wondered if those afternoons behind the church had meant the same thing to Gerrit that they had meant to her. She had known how unlikely that was. She had convinced herself that it did not matter, that it was only natural that what they had shared should mean more to her. He was the heir to a fortune—destined to lead a richer life than hers. But some part of her, inherited from her dreamer of a father, had held on to a secret hope that she had not been one among many—that she had been special. Earlier, in the carriage, when he had flirted with her, she had hoped the same thing: that it was more than the expression of a physical attraction, that some part of him recognized her. She was such a fool.

Gerrit was married.

Gerrit was bone tired by the time he reached the old block-house. They were straggling in, his little band of sheep rustlers, some leading their horses and carrying recalcitrant lambs over their shoulders. Dawn was not far off and everything was wet with dew, including the hundred sheep they had just herded up the hill. Even better, he could smell rain in the air. It smelled nicer than damp sheep.

The blockhouse would be warm and dry. He wished he could stay. Gerrit had found the abandoned defense work when he was a boy and used to wander the woods for hours on his own. His father hadn't known it was up there, nor, when Gerrit had told him about the place, had the old man cared. The Indians had long since stopped attacking

Harenwyck with war cries and tomahawks. They preferred now to battle the patroons in court, suing to get their land back, even crossing the ocean to petition King George.

Long ago all this land had belonged to others, and once its theft was fresh. And once upon a time the blockhouse on the hill had been all that stood between the tenants and the just retribution of the dispossessed. The tower had been built in the Dutch manner out of local stone with a tiled roof—all but impossible to burn—and entirely forgotten by the time Gerrit was a boy. The terrain surrounding it was too rocky and steep to plant, and the trees that some early tenants had cleared to create a defensible line around the tower were beginning to grow back, but there was enough room for Edwaert's sheep to graze for a little while.

Gerrit led his horse inside the blockhouse, where most of the men were already rubbing down their mounts. Pieter came to take his saddle.

"Please tell me we have my brother's wine upstairs," said Gerrit.

"The whole case," said Pieter. "Along with the almonds. There was a box on top of the carriage. And there's a cask of little green things. Like raisins, but salty." He made a wry face.

"Those would be capers," said Gerrit. He doubted they would prove very popular in the blockhouse. "All I want is a bottle of the wine and an empty basket. I'll be back before noon."

"You've been up for twenty-four hours, *baas*. A man

goes too long without sleep, he gets careless, and you can't afford to be that now. Your brother can see you hang for what we did tonight."

"Unfortunately this errand can't wait."

Pieter looked skeptical but kept his peace, disappearing up the hatch to the room above where the men were already settling in to dicker over their spoils. There would likely be nothing left *except* the capers by the time Gerrit got back, but he realized then that there was nothing he truly wanted from the carriage in any case—*except* Annatje Hoppe.

Gerrit had promised her that he would go back and find the kitten's mother. He had promised her other things too, lying in the hayloft, and out behind the church staring up at the stars. She had not believed him then, and perhaps youth excused such oaths, but he did not excuse himself. Not with all that had come after. He'd nearly forgotten about her in Leiden, just as she had told him he would, and when he came back there was another family living in the Hoppe cottage. Bram Hoppe was dead, and his runaway daughter was wanted for murder and believed to have killed herself.

Pieter, of course, was right about the men. Gerrit risked losing them—he risked losing Harenwyck itself— if his band of displaced, evicted men found out he'd recognized and concealed her. But he risked losing respect for himself if he failed her now as he had failed her when he was seventeen.

And *she* had risked herself tonight trying to protect him. He winced now at how cruel he had been to her at the Halve Maen after she tried to warn him about André. A prim schoolteacher calling him naive had been an insult to his manhood. Annatje Hoppe warning him about the fate of revolutionaries . . . he had been Agamemnon ignoring Cassandra.

He owed her an apology. He owed her more than that. And he wanted to know where she had been all this time, and why in God's name she had come back to Harenwyck . . . and if kissing her was as thrilling as it had been when he was seventeen. Because nothing had ever been so thrilling since.

Pieter was right about the danger—both to his ambition to reclaim Harenwyck and to Annatje herself—but Gerrit could not just walk away from her. He would talk to Jan. The man had not known Annatje. And even if he had been devoted to his uncle—or moved by his aunt's and mother's grief—he must have known that Vim Dijkstra had been a violent bully on behalf of the old patroon. Gerrit would make Jan see that whatever had really taken place that night—and they had only ever known half the story, because Annatje had disappeared—his own father, the late patroon, was the one at fault. That the girl was not a cold-blooded murderess.

He would *make* Jan understand.

By the time Pieter returned with a basket and a bottle, Gerrit was the only one left downstairs.

Pieter handed him the basket. "The girl's not going to fit inside."

"The basket isn't for the girl."

"Whatever you say, *baas*."

Pieter had gone upstairs wearing one pistol. He had come back down with three. "We're after a cat, Pieter, not a lion. And it will be morning before my brother knows his carriage is missing."

"It's not your brother I'm worried about, *baas*. I took a head count when I went upstairs."

Gerrit knew what he was going to say before he said it. There was only one man whose absence mattered after Gerrit's indiscretion at the farm.

"Everyone came back from Edwaert's. Everyone except Jan."

Ten

Dawn was coloring the sky by the time Anna and Andries Van Haren reached the new house. She had nodded off once in his arms, and the young patroon had shaken her ungently awake, evidently unwilling to have an unconscious woman drool on his shoulder.

The new house was far grander than Mr. Ten Broeck had let on. He had told her it was modern and well lit, with good windows. It was much more than that. It was the largest house Anna had ever seen, built of red sandstone, trimmed in sparkling granite, four stories tall and nine windows across with a pillared portico entrance atop a granite stair and two massive wings projecting out the back.

The patroon slid from his horse and helped Anna down. He took her basket first, quite sensibly, as though assisting women sodden with dew who had spent the night in the woods was an expected—if somewhat distasteful—chore, and then helped her to the ground with the same impersonal touch he had used all night. The short grass was almost as wet as her skirts.

He made no effort to conceal the fact that he was trying to have as little physical contact with her as possible. Gerrit had implied that his brother brought courtesans from New York. Anna wondered if he displayed the same disdain for common people with them. If so, she hoped they charged him double.

No one came to take his horse, which she found odd. *No one knows he was out*, Angela Ferrers would have surmised. Just at that moment, though, Anna did not care whether Andries Van Haren had been communing with nature in the woods or with King George at Buckingham House. She wanted a meal and washing water and a bed.

A plaintive mew reminded her that Scrappy also had wants.

"Your basket appears to have become upset with you," said the patroon.

"That would be my kitten. She needs a sandbox, rather urgently, I suspect." Anna was not actually certain that Scrappy knew how to use a sandbox, but that doubt was unlikely to make the kitten a welcome guest in the patroon's home.

He made no comment about the kitten.

The patroon tied his horse to the railings and knocked on the kitchen door below the granite stairs. It did not open at once, but finally a bleary-eyed kitchen boy in wool socks and a long shirt appeared, and then things moved almost too quickly for Anna to keep track.

The boy was told to rouse the housekeeper, the groom, and the steward, in that order. The housekeeper, who was also, apparently, the head cook, appeared in her bed-gown and received her instructions. Miss Winters was to have a hot meal, washing water, a change of clothes, and a bed made up. And a sandbox for her cat. This necessitated two maids being sent for, who goggled at Anna's state and asked, in Dutch, if the witch in the woods had gotten her.

The patroon's expression quieted them immediately, but their reaction still sent a chill down Anna's spine. She forced herself to stare quizzically at them as though she did not understand the language and let the cook, Mrs. Buys, shush them back to their work. Mrs. Buys had very good English, and spoke to Anna in the kind of running patter that soothed children and small animals and—just at that moment—exhausted schoolteachers.

"We'll have your breakfast up in a jiffy. My girls bank a good fire, and the coals are always hot and ready to go of a morning." She proved her point by digging a scoop of glowing embers out of the pile against the fireback and layering them first with fatwood kindling and then with a small split log. It was hot enough to cook in less than ten minutes, and the chimneys were so new and so modern that there was hardly any smoke. The kitchen began to fill with delicious smells as the rest of the fires were lit.

The meal set before Anna was fit for the upstairs table, and Anna's fears that she would be treated as a servant here evaporated. There was half a chicken swimming in butter with parsley, a bowl of green peas dotted with bacon and crunchy *koolsla* with poppy seeds. It was better food and more of it than she had ever sat down to in her years living on the patroonship, but it was not what she wanted.

A fine English lady would not ask for such a thing, but at that moment, after all she had been through, Anna did not care. "May I have some of the porridge, please?" It was bubbling in a big pot hanging on a crane over the fire, and the aroma of sweet corn and butter and brown sugar made her mouth water.

Mrs. Buys did not seem to know that genteel school-teachers should not eat porridge. "I prefer it myself, even though the patroon doesn't stint on meat for his servants' meals." She smiled and bustled and filled a porringer for Anna, and then one for herself. She shaved a tablespoon of extra sugar off the cone for each one, and Anna had to stop herself from digging in before Mrs. Buys was done stirring.

It was the best thing Anna had ever tasted.

Scrappy did not know what to make of her sandbox, and, watching her throw sand all over the immaculate kitchen floor, Anna's heart sank. Mrs. Buys just tutted and sent the maids for another scoop from the sandpit, watching Scrappy roll around in the material she was supposed to use to answer the call of nature.

"She doesn't like being able to dig down to the bottom of the box," explained Mrs. Buys. "Did you bring her all the way from New York?"

"No. Our carriage almost ran over her in the road

and we could not find her mother." It was very near the truth.

Mrs. Buys was right. A second generous scoop of sand did the trick, and Anna was able to put Scrappy in a fresh—thank goodness—basket and follow one of the maids, a flower-faced girl whom the cook called Tryntje, to her room.

It was not in the attic. It was on the second floor, at the back of the house, with easy access to both the back and main stairs.

"The young misses are in the front, through that door," explained Tryntje. She said it apologetically, but Anna was just happy not to be relegated to an attic. She had hoped simply for a room she could stand up in. She had been given a room finer than her bedchamber in New York. The ceiling was so high that the bed's finials did not even come close to touching it. The bed frame itself was mahogany with carved posts and a fretwork tester dressed in blue and white chintz. The entire chamber was carpeted in a pleasing pattern of gray, green, and blue blocks, and the fireplace was surrounded by a full wall of paneling painted cornflower. It was a thoroughly *English* room. The only concession to Dutch taste was the tiled fireplace—but these were popular enough in English homes as well.

"There's water in the jug," the maid was saying as she bustled about the room opening the bed-curtains and laying brushes and soap out on the dresser. "The clothes are mine and Mrs. Buys'. The patroon said to apologize—there are no ladies in the house to borrow something better from."

No ladies in the house. "What about the girls' mother?"

Tryntje stopped bustling for a moment. She arranged the brushes on the dresser, lining them up left to right, largest to smallest. Then she picked them up and did it again, reversing their order. Anna recognized this for what it was: a delaying maneuver.

"Does she not live at the manor?" prompted Anna.

Tryntje gave up on the brushes and began fussing with the clothes. "Mrs. Buys would not like me gossiping. Now, this is my best shift and that's Mrs. Buys' Sunday gown."

And that was the subject closed. Anna didn't blame Tryntje. Jobs were hard to come by on the patroonship. A maid's salary would be a lifeline for a tenant family if there came a bad harvest. Positions at the house had been sought after even in Anna's day, when the old patroon had been well-known to corner maids in empty rooms. Even so, they were good positions, and Anna would not be the cause of Tryntje losing hers.

Anna turned her attention to the clothes on the bed. The chemise was fine cotton, but so old that it was transparent as glass around the elbows and knees. The gown was good silk but had obviously been remade. The large damask pattern was thirty years out-of-date, and the shoulders had most likely been reshaped with remnants of old robings. It was the best they had, and they were giving it to her. And the maid was embarrassed because their best was old and worn. Anna did not know what to say. She was not Gerrit. She had not been born with the best of everything and only later discovered that others did not have as much. She *was* one of those others—one of these people. She had nicer things now, but inside she had not changed.

"They're as pretty as anything I had in my baggage," she said. "Thank you, Tryntje. I'll be sure to return them as soon as my gown is laundered."

The maid's weak smile told Anna that laundering, or even mending, was unlikely to save her gown. She didn't care. The room was warm and dry and the linens on the bed looked smooth and cool, and she was almost falling asleep on her feet. She thanked Tryntje again for the water, declined her offer to heat it in the kettle, and then for the first time in nearly twenty-four hours, Anna was alone.

She stripped off her clothes, washed in the tepid water provided, put on Tryntje's shift, and climbed onto the bed. Scrappy seemed content to curl up on the carpet. Anna thought briefly about bringing the kitten up on the bed to sleep with her, but the drop to the ground was too far for such a tiny animal, and Scrappy had spent enough time trapped in the basket. She could have the run of the room.

Anna had already learned a great many things that Kate Grey and her Rebel friends would wish to know. There was probably paper and ink in the desk by the window, but she had not decided just yet how much to tell them. Gerrit's involvement changed everything. She probably ought to write some of what she had gleaned in a letter to Mrs. Peterson, but her heart was slowing down and the feather pillow beneath her cheek was soft, and she was too tired even to draw the bed-curtains.

It was midafternoon by the time she woke. She had slept through the whole morning and a good part of the day with the sun streaming in on her face, bed-curtains still wide-open. Someone—Tryntje, probably—had come and gone, leaving behind a pot of tea, a bowl of sugar, a pitcher of cream, and a bowl of porridge wrapped in towels to keep it warm. Someone had also brought a small sandbox for Scrappy and a chicken leg that was already more than half gone.

The kitten herself had clawed her way onto the upholstered chair by the fire and was sleeping contentedly on a cushion. Anna did not feel too bad about the snags on the arms. Her kitten might have spoiled the patroon's chair, but the patroon's feud with his brother had cost Anna her best clothes, her favorite loom, her paint box, her atlas, and her prized book of engravings. Not to mention her lockpicks, her knives, and the very fine muff pistol the Widow had given her. Anna did not, however, begrudge Scrappy her ruined sewing basket. The cat had at least made use of it, as opposed to flinging it from a moving carriage.

Anna ate. Scrappy got up and worried her chicken leg and then went to sleep again atop it, looking forlorn. *Probably missing her mother and siblings.*

The Van Harens were home wreckers to a man.

Anna made the best of the gown she had been given, folding back the excess fabric and pinning it closed over her stays. The silk was a rich shade of orange, like fiery autumn leaves, and Anna felt fortunate that it could be made to fit as well as flatter.

Her clothing, in reality, was the least of her problems. She had lost all of her school equipment. The Van Haren girls could not embroider a sampler out of thin air. Farm-dyed wool was not a reasonable substitute for silk thread, and linen thread was of no use at all. She had a great deal of work to do.

Last night she had come up the back stairs and seen little of the house. This morning she went down the front stairs. They were massive and branched upon a landing where family portraits hung amidst a display of weaponry. The halberds and harquebuses, Anna supposed, served the same purpose as the coat of arms: to lend an air of legitimacy to an estate earned not on the battlefield but in counting houses. Anna doubted that the display convinced the Wappinger Indians, who had been trying to reclaim their land for the last century, first from the Dutch and now through the English courts. The colonists *had* resorted to arms to defend their land over the years—from the natives, from the French, and even from their neighbors in Massachusetts—but Anna could not help but wonder how many of the pikes and hackbutts and muskets ranged along the wall had actually been wielded by Van Harens.

The portraits at the top of the double staircase were the oldest, all of gentlemen with wide-brimmed hats and ladies with dinner-plate ruffs. As Anna descended, the fashions became lighter and more modern but the faces that looked out from the frames changed little. The Van Harens were a distinctive-looking family. The first patroon might have been a merchant, but he'd had a long, aristocratic face with laughing blue eyes and thick blond hair, and he had bequeathed these—along with two hundred thousand acres on the Hudson—to his heirs.

The last patroon had a place of honor at the foot of the stairs. He had chosen to be painted with his favorite hunting dog, a long, lean hound, as black and fearsome as the wolf on the family arms. Cornelis could have been no more than forty when the portrait was done, and there was a loose grace to his pose that had been lost to age by the time Anna knew him. He stood beside a tree, a long fowling rifle in one hand, the old manor house in the background. Like all the bygone Van Harens the old patroon had been tall and slender and blond.

All the Van Harens except Gerrit, whose coffee hair and eyes set him apart from the rest of his family. Anna supposed he took after his mother, although she could not remember what Cornelis' wife had looked like—only an impression of rustling petticoats and silk shoes—and hers was not among the family portraits in the hall. Gerrit's likeness must have been painted after he returned from Leiden, for he looked older than when Anna had known him, but not as mature as he looked now. The picture was very fine—its subject strikingly handsome, though some quality of physiognomy or pose gave the younger Gerrit a serious, brooding aspect, worlds removed from the easy grace, and almost palpable sense of *entitlement*, reflected in his father's portrait.

Anna reluctantly turned her gaze from Gerrit's likeness. There was a companion picture beside his, and the lady had to be his wife, because the two portraits faced each other and had the same classical backdrop: a fantasy setting of stone pillars and red curtains with the fields of Harenwyck and the sparkle of the Hudson visible beyond.

Gerrit's wife was everything Anna was not. Raven-haired, petite, and fine-boned—so delicate in fact that it seemed like the breeze ruffling the curtain behind her ought to blow her away. The sort of woman Fragonard always painted sitting in a swing.

Anna wondered that the family had not taken these portraits down. She could not imagine the old patroon leaving up his renegade son's portrait, but perhaps Andries was cut from finer cloth. He was raising his brother's daughters, after all, even while that same brother robbed his coaches and stirred discontent among his tenants.

And there was no portrait of Andries himself. A second son, not destined for the patroonship, would not merit the expense. One might think that a usurper would rush to acquire the symbols of legitimacy, but Andries Van Haren had not.

The floor of the front hall was real marble, and there were four grain-painted doors framed by elaborate carvings. Three were open, revealing carpeted parlors and a dining room lined with a fancy painted floorcloth.

The fourth door was closed, and Anna could hear raised voices coming from inside.

The patroon, speaking Dutch, fast and angry: "He has our butter and our beef, and if he is backing Gerrit, then he has our gold as well," said the patroon.

"General Clinton is using your brother to force you to choose a side." Ten Broeck's gravelly voice was lower and more reasonable. Anna was glad to know he had been released safely.

"Then he could have spared me the trouble of driving the Harenwyck herd to market and just had his Skinners and Cowboys rob me here."

"Obviously he preferred to save *himself* the trouble of having to milk your cows and churn your butter. And he still hopes you will choose the side of government."

"When the government is backing my brother's attempt to overthrow me?"

"They will disown and discard Gerrit the minute you let them station a British garrison here. All they want is Harenhoeck. They do not care who gives it to them."

"You know I cannot do that, Theunis."

"What I know," the older man said patiently, "is that though you may believe in the American cause, our supposed allies have given us no powder, no shot, and no muskets with which to defend the estate if Clinton runs out of patience. We have had nothing from them. And our stores are running dangerously low. If either army were to invade in force, they would take us easily. And if the tenants should rise, we are virtually defenseless."

"It isn't polite to listen at doors."

Anna whirled to find two girls watching her from the parlor across the hall. They were twins, and looked identical, dressed alike in robin's egg blue silk gowns. Anna had been told that the girls were eleven, but they were tall for their age, as so many Dutch children were. They would have looked at home in any New York parlor—if not for the mud caked to their hems and the grass stains on their silk slippers. Both girls wore their blond hair loose down their backs, long tresses woefully in need of a brushing.

"It isn't polite to spy on people either," said Anna, guessing that the girls had been watching her for some time. "But I won't tell if you won't."

The girls looked at each other. When they turned it was possible to see that they were not quite identical. One was slightly taller and had a small scar above her right eyebrow. She spoke for both of them when she said, "That seems fair."

The smaller girl took a step forward and scrutinized Anna. "Are you the teacher Uncle Andries brought up from New York?"

"I am."

Excitement lit the girl's face. "Did you bring any novels?"

"Grietje," warned the taller girl.

"Yes," said Anna, "but my baggage has not yet arrived." *Because your father stole it from me.*

They were Gerrit's daughters. Anna supposed that explained his strong feelings about her choice of embroidery subjects, but it did not help the fact that he had deprived her of all her school equipment.

"You mean you will let us have novels?" asked the taller one, who must be Jannetje.

"As long as you do your other reading and advance in all of your subjects, I see no reason that you should not read novels."

"Reverend Blauvelt says they give women ideas."

"Well, someone has to," said Anna.

The door opened behind her. She was glad she had taken a few steps closer to the dining room while talking to the girls, so it did not seem quite so much like she had been eavesdropping.

"Miss Winters," said her employer. Anna turned to face Andries Van Haren.

Last night she had been too exhausted, and it had been too dark, for her to study him. Now she saw what she had missed in the moonlight. He was handsome. Not like Gerrit, who would always be the standard by which she judged masculine beauty, but like the rest of the Van Harens, who were tall and blond with laughing blue eyes, only his did not appear to be laughing right now. If she was trying to capture their likenesses, she would have to render Gerrit in the rich pigments of oil paint and Andries in the delicate coloring of pastels.

She saw something else as well. It was only a suspicion for now, but a heartbreaking one, the sort better kept to oneself.

"Mr. Van Haren," she said. As a child she had been told to always curtsy to the patroon. She refused to do so now, though her knees itched to bend.

"I see you have met Hubble and Bubble."

Behind her the girls giggled.

"Yes. We were just getting acquainted." If a backdrop of mutual blackmail could be called "getting acquainted."

"Excellent. What sort of lessons do you have planned for today?"

He asked in the manner of a man who does not particularly care to listen to the answer, but who does want credit for asking the question. She gave him the answer that his hauteur deserved: "Our lessons today will have to be improvised. Your brother stole all of my school equipment."

"That's all right," said Jannetje. "We don't like lessons very much anyway."

The patroon had the good grace to look embarrassed. "Make a list for Mr. Ten Broeck. As soon as certain matters are taken care of, he will have everything that was stolen replaced."

"What matters?" The question bordered on rudeness, but she was not a servant or a child, and she needed to establish that she would not be treated like one.

Ten Broeck appeared in the door. When he saw Anna he came forward and took her hands. "Miss Winters, I am so relieved to see you safe. I must apologize. I fear I did not acquit myself particularly heroically last night."

"You have nothing to apologize for, Mr. Ten Broeck. The bandits outnumbered you ten to one. I'm afraid the patroon's gold was as good as lost from the moment our escort abandoned us, along with all my school equipment and personal possessions. I hope you will be able to send someone to New York today."

"Not today, Miss Winters," said the patroon, in a tone that was meant to dismiss her and her concerns.

"But I *will* send a man tomorrow," said Mr. Ten Broeck, who was obviously used to his employer's imperious manner and understood the need to temper his dicta. "There is no one to spare at present. Our kidnappers were busy

last night, and the patroon's coach was not their only tar-
get. They stole a flock of sheep from one of the tenants.
This afternoon the outlaws were overheard boasting of
their plan to drive their stolen sheep to Wyckoff's ferry."

"With a little luck," added the patroon, "we will catch
our bandits tonight and have the gold, my carriage, and
your possessions, of course, back by morning."

"You say 'our bandits,' but you mean *our father*," said
Grietje, who obviously did not like that idea at all.

Neither did Anna. If Gerrit was captured, the first
thing that he would tell his brother was that Harenwyck
was sheltering a murderess.

"Come, girls. Let us see what sorts of books the
patroon keeps in his library," said Anna.

"It's not a very good library," vouchsafed Jannetje, as
she led Anna up the stairs.

"There aren't any novels," explained Grietje.

There weren't any novels. There was, however, an
atlas. It was not Anna's trusty English *Universal History of
the World* by Bowen. It was a Dutch atlas, printed in
Amsterdam and written in French. It was the very book
that had opened a door for her all those years ago, had
shown a provincial little Dutch girl that there was a world
beyond the borders of Harenwyck. She had not been able
to read it then, of course. She had not known French.
Gerrit had smuggled it out of the house in his coat one
winter morning and hidden it in the barn for their afternoon meeting.

He'd been late that day—delayed by his father after
church—and she had found the book herself, buried in the

hay. She'd been disappointed at first. Usually he brought her plays or poems or novels or, very occasionally, books of engravings. Anna had not known what to do with maps. They were just so many lines on paper—until Gerrit showed her how to read them. He had lain down with her in the hay and explained the points on the compass, latitude and longitude, the prime meridian, and the use of the key—and they'd adventured together through that ocean of pages like Henry Hudson on the Halve Maen. She'd lost track of time that afternoon, so that the sun had set while she was still in the barn with Gerrit and she was forced to run all the way home to get there before supper.

That was the day Anna's mother first became suspicious about how she spent her Sunday afternoons. The meetings in the barn had ended too shortly after that—after Gerrit had shown her the world.

"That is one of the boring books," announced Grietje, breaking in upon Anna's thoughts.

"Not if you know how to read it. I'll show you."

Both girls gave her a dubious look.

"I promise that if you give it a chance, this will be your favorite book by morning."

"But it's in French," said Jannetje. "You can't teach us French in one night."

"You don't need French to enjoy this book."

Jannetje eyed her suspiciously. "There's a trick to it, isn't there?"

"There may in fact be a trick," admitted Anna. That was the magic of education. Learning one new thing could change how you saw the whole world.

Clearly intrigued, despite themselves, by this unexpected confirmation of their suspicions, Jannetje and Grietje flopped on the damask sofa. Comportment was going to have to be tomorrow's lesson.

"Don't sit, girls," said Anna. "We're going on an adventure. We're going to travel the world, without ever leaving this room."

Jannetje raised a skeptical eyebrow, but Grietje was standing up and peering round at the parlor. "How?"

"Look at the sofa. Tell me, what is it made of?"

Jannetje remained resolutely silent, perhaps not sure she liked the flavor of this "trick."

"Wood," said Grietje. "And silk."

"Where did it come from?"

"New York?" asked Grietje.

"*Everything* comes from New York," said Jannetje.

"Everything comes to Harenwyck *by way of* New York," said Anna, "but the mahogany for the sofa came first from the Bahama Islands."

Jannetje perked up. "You mean where they have pirates?"

"Yes," said Anna. "Where they have pirates. How far do you think that is?"

"I don't know," said Jannetje. "Farther than New York," she said, putting her eleven-year-old reasoning skills to work. "Two times as far," she decided. "At least twice as far as New York."

"About *ten* times as far," said Anna. "The Bahama Islands are more than a thousand miles from here. Would you like to see?"

Jannetje streaked across the room to look as Anna opened the atlas on the tea table. "Here is New York," she said, pointing at the dot and label.

"And here are the Bahamas." She dragged her finger across the page.

"Where is Harenwyck?" asked Grietje.

"Right here," said Anna, finding the place on the map.

"Why isn't it marked?" asked Jannetje.

"Because it isn't big enough."

Jannetje took that in, just as Anna had all those years ago. *Harenwyck is not the world.* Grietje was also fascinated, puzzling out the key and tracing the current outlines of the colonies on that antiquated French map.

"Now," said Anna, looking around the room, "what about the jars on the mantel?" There were five of them, two beakers and three vases with covers, prettily decorated with pink and red flowers and collared by painted gold grilles. The rich burghers in New York all had sets like it.

This time Grietje shrugged. "They've *always* been there."

"Grandfather bought them," said Jannetje. "In New York."

"I've no doubt he did," said Anna. "But they weren't made in New York. The designs were drawn by a Dutchman in New Amsterdam and sent by the Dutch East India company to China, where the porcelain was fired and painted. Then it went to New York, probably by way of the Netherlands."

"How far is China?" asked Grietje.

"Oh, I should say about ten times as far as the Bahamas. Maybe ten thousand miles?"

"Show us," said Jannetje, hooked at last.

Evening fell while they were still exploring. From China, they went to India by way of the contents of the tea caddy. They visited France via the wallpaper, England via the silk draperies and ingrain carpet.

When Mrs. Buys interrupted with a tray of cookies and a pot of chocolate they journeyed onward to the kingdoms of the Aztecs and Spain, and the twins would not let the cook go back to the kitchen until they had interrogated her about everything on the plate. They even made an expedition to Pulau Run when Mrs. Buys admitted that there was nutmeg in the *koekjes*, and they returned to the West Indies through the sugar dish.

By then it was time for bed. Jannetje marched upstairs with the atlas tucked under one elbow and Grietje following, clamoring for another look at the book. Mrs. Buys watched them go with obvious amusement.

"That was a very nice day's work," said Mrs. Buys, with approval.

"I doubt table manners and hair brushing will go as well," said Anna. There were few other subjects they would be able to tackle until Mr. Broeck replaced her school equipment. That was the problem with teaching girls in a finishing school. The things that excited them were not the things their parents and society cared most about. The things that excited them were the same things that excited boys: history and politics and art and science. The things that excited parents were the accomplishments that could be displayed publicly—the singing and dancing and needlework—not the products of their engaged minds.

"Best to fortify yourself, then," advised Mrs. Buys. "Take the *koekjes* up to bed with you."

They were exactly the sort of cookies she had been longing for in New York: rich with fresh butter and cardamom and scented with orange water—and just the tiniest bit sandy from the cornmeal. They had been Gerrit's favorites, the ones he brought to her after church, until the day her mother had beaten her and forbidden any further meetings.

"I couldn't eat them all." The plate was heaped. Grietje and Jannetje had done yeomen's work eating them with their hot chocolate, but Mrs. Buys served everything in farm portions.

"Go on and take them, just in case you're hungry later," said Mrs. Buys.

Anna took the cookies.

She picked her way up the front stairs in the dark, hem in one hand, plate in the other, under the painted eyes of the patroons and their ladies. It struck her then, as she was climbing their stairs into the heart of their domain, that this family had done its best to destroy her. *And I survived.*

At the top of the stairs Anna could hear the girls behind their door still poring over the atlas. That made her smile. She felt her way down the dim hall to her room. There was a light burning, visible beneath the door, and though she still longed for her own bed in New York, the small army of servants that made up the fires and boiled water and aired linens at Harenwyck certainly made life here exceedingly comfortable. It would be far too easy to become accustomed to it.

She opened the door and set the cookies on her bed-side table. She'd expected Tryntje to be waiting for her—good maids didn't leave fires burning and sconces lit in empty rooms—but the girl was not there, so Anna began unpinning the front of her gown. It would be a relief to be out of her stays.

She plucked the pins free, sticking them in a tidy row on the bed-curtains as the Widow had taught her. *At times you will not be forewarned, so remain forearmed. Always have something sharp near to hand.*

Her advice proved prophetic when a voice came out of the darkness between the windows.

"I don't suppose you'd like some help with that."

A form detached itself from the shadows, familiar and unfamiliar, longed for and dreaded: *Gerrit*.

Eleven

If she had been just an object to be taken, only a prize to be won, he would have watched until she was naked in her shift, but Annatje Hoppe had never been that to him. He could vividly remember how close they had come to consummating their love in the barn, all those years ago, lying in the hay, clothes loosened, full of breathless anticipation.

He had stopped because he was not his father; even if she had wanted him as badly as he had wanted her, all the risk, all the consequences were hers to bear. Like the maids who—once their bellies swelled enough to show— were never seen again at the manor house. He had not wanted that for her. Never that.

Annatje was special. He had known that even then. And, young fool that he had been, he had said as much to his father.

"What are you doing here?" She did not look pleased to see him. Not displeased, necessarily, but the unpinning had come to a decided halt. She stood frozen with one hand in the air like one of those statues of classical goddesses, all sublime grace and arrested motion.

"I could ask you the same question. This, after all, is my house, while you—*you*, Annatje Hoppe, are supposed to be dead." He took a step closer, and she did not move away. That seemed a good sign.

"My death was a necessary fiction. Yours is an all too likely reality. Gerrit, your brother has the militia out hunting for you as we speak. If you are caught, you could hang."

"You tried to warn me at the Halve Maen, and I dismissed you. I'm sorry for that. I thought you were insulting my intelligence. You weren't. There are few women who know the consequences of the hand I'm playing better than Bram Hoppe's daughter."

"Please tell me that you didn't come here just to apologize."

She was the most sensible woman in the world and somehow also the most foolish. "Annatje, this is me, and this is you. That is why I'm here."

He closed the space between them. She didn't move, and that seemed a *very* good sign, but now he was at a loss. Because he was afraid that if he touched her she would evaporate like the mist. He had already touched her last night, of course, but he had not known then she was Annatje. They had ridden for miles together. He *knew* that she was real—yet he was still somehow afraid to believe it.

She was not a phantom, not mist. She came lightly into

his arms as though she had never left them, had *always been there*, and in some ways she had. He had known other women and even married one, but none had ever seemed as real to him. He and Annatje fit together, then and now, like puzzle pieces. She tilted her head back, and he kissed her, soft and warm and startlingly erotic and wet.

She broke away just when he wanted to pull her closer, and he worried for a moment that he had transgressed, but when he looked into her eyes he found them just as wide and full of wonder as his own must be.

"Gerrit," she said, "you cannot be here." He thrilled to note a flicker of irresolution behind such sensible words. "Your brother—"

"My brother will be halfway to Albany by now, chasing shadows." And the bed was tantalizingly close.

"But the sheep—"

"Are grazing in contentment in the shadow of the old blockhouse. Rumor is a powerful tool. I learned that from your father." He reached for her.

And she danced away. "Then take his final lesson to heart, Gerrit. Give up this madness. Your brother holds Harenwyck. You never wanted it anyway. Even if you had it, you could not dissolve it the way you dream. My father may have been a man of vision, but he was willfully blind to some realities. There are other forces holding the estates together than just the naked will of the patroons."

"Annatje, this war is likely to bring a king, a parliament, a great nation to its knees. Surely a patroon or two can be toppled as well."

"Not if the people who are busy toppling kings and

humbling nations want to keep that patroon in power. I want independence, Gerrit. I do. I have no love for the British, but I have no illusions about the men in Congress either."

"And yet you are working for them, aren't you? If you were in British pay you would not have tried to warn me away from André. But you didn't tell my brother where we were last night, or the Halve Maen would have been crawling with militia this morning. You are playing a deep game, Annatje Hoppe."

"It's Anna now," she said.

"Since when?"

"Since it became impossible to be Annatje."

"You are still my Annatje to me."

She pursed her lips and said, "I cannot be *your* Annatje if you are married."

"Annatje, my wife is dead."

"I am sorry."

He did not know how to explain Sophia to Annatje, so instead he kept silent. It had been a terrible marriage, but that did not excuse his part in it. "Did you never marry?"

"I *am* the spinster schoolteacher I appear to be."

"You are more than that, even judging solely by the contents of your luggage."

"You mean the remnants of it that you did not toss from a moving carriage?"

"I mean the knives, the muff pistol, and the codebook."

"I don't suppose you brought any of my baggage with you? I'm not sure how many days' lessons I can improvise out of Harenwyck's library and the rules of feminine deportment."

"I didn't bring your baggage because you won't be needing it. I'm taking you back to New York tonight."

She shook her head. "I can't leave Harenwyck, Gerrit."

"Why not?"

"There is a woman in New York who knows my real name, who I really am. If I do not secure Harenwyck for the Americans, she will expose me, and there is absolutely nothing you or I can do to stop her."

Anna wanted him to stay. She wanted to invite him to climb into the high feather bed with her and shut the curtains and pretend that they were back in the barn. She wanted him to tell her stories. Not about witches or adventurers but about himself. Of where he had been, what he had done, when and why he had married. About all the years of his life she had missed.

She wanted him to stay, but she needed him to leave because every minute he spent here was perilous.

"Annatje," he said. "You must leave Harenwyck. Too many people heard me call out your name last night. Vim Dijkstra's family will not have forgotten you, and they will not trouble themselves an instant with the letter of the law if they discover you are here."

"And what will they do to you, Gerrit, when they find out you recognized me? Or worse, that you helped me get away?"

"I can handle myself. Two years with the Continentals—commanding surly, sometimes mutinous New

Englanders—taught me a good deal about how to avoid a knife in the back."

"I have heard that discipline is very poor among the Continentals," said Anna.

"Even drilled and disciplined, I doubt the New Englanders I was given charge of would like me any better. They are the same men who think Harenwyck belongs to Massachusetts. Ten years ago we were fighting against them. General Washington had hoped that we would all see the British as our common enemy, but they did not prove so inclined."

"Can you blame the man? Washington knows he was chosen to bring the southern states into the Rebel fold. No doubt he welcomed the son of a Dutch patroon to try to win over the valley and the highlands. It sounds an excellent strategy, but even excellent strategies fail."

"You possess an impressive amount of military acumen for a schoolteacher."

"Said by a man with little experience of adolescent girls." With so much left unsaid, unknown, she tried to keep reproach from her tone.

"I would change that if I could," he replied, "but the girls are better off here than with me. There are some very rough customers among my men. Vim Dijkstra's nephew is perhaps the least of them."

She had feared the bailiffs, because they had always been on the side of the patroons, and it was the law, after all, that had killed her father. She had not feared private justice, because "right," and the mob, had always been on the side of Bram Hoppe, but now she feared that she must.

"Do you really think Dijkstra's family will still be out for vengeance," she asked, "after all these years?"

"If they are even half certain it is you, they will drag you to the nearest tree and hang you."

"They will have to get past Andries' militia first."

"You mean like I did tonight?"

"You had help, I suspect." She held out the plate of *koekjes*. "Mrs. Buys baked these for you, didn't she?"

"I am not the only one with friends at the manor house," he observed, taking a cookie. "If I can get in here, so can the Dijkstras."

"It's a pity, then, you did not bring my pistol."

"That pistol of yours is a very unusual weapon. Finely made. Hard to come by. Where did you get it?"

"From the woman who threw the *schouts* off my trail and helped me to become Anna."

"She sounds like a formidable ally."

"She was that. She could also be a very dangerous enemy." Anna would never forget the day the Widow had returned to New York, the efficient, calculated way in which she had dealt with those who had failed her.

"Tell me about this woman, about what happened between you and Dijkstra—and how you escaped," asked Gerrit, climbing onto the bed with the plate of cookies.

"It is not exactly a bedtime story." And she had never told anyone all of it, not even the Widow.

"I didn't think it was. I want to know what happened to you, how you survived and made your way back here."

"Barbara Fenton's Dutchman probably said the same thing."

"Now I'm sorry I told you that one."

"I was too, last night. I ran nearly three miles through those woods—all the way to the old manor house—because I was half convinced I was being chased by Barbara Fenton's ghost."

"Did you see her?" asked Gerrit with a twinkle in his eye.

"Yes."

He sobered then. "What did she look like?"

"I'm not sure. I'm not really even certain I saw anything. A pale figure—that is all I am certain of. Now you must go, Gerrit. Your brother does not strike me as a stupid man. He will realize, at some point quite soon, that he is being led on a wild-goose chase, and then he will come back here with his *schouts* and his militiamen."

"I'm not leaving until you tell me what happened that night, and what became of you afterward."

"And I won't tell you—later—unless you go *now*."

He sighed and popped the last morsel of cookie into his mouth. When he was done with it he said, "If we'd had a few more officers with your resolve in the Continentals we might have kept New York. And unlike General Washington I recognize an impossible position when I'm in it. I'll go, on the condition that you promise to meet me next week, and tell me everything. And then we will figure out what to do, *together*."

He was not going to leave unless she promised, and if he did not leave soon he was very likely to get himself killed. So she promised.

Gerrit came around the bed into the firelight and he

kissed her again, and this time she could not resist pressing closer to him, mapping the changes that time had wrought in his body with hers. He had been tall at seventeen, and wiry, but now he was fleshed with lean, sculpted muscle. He had washed and changed his clothes, and he smelled of soap and fresh linen. His dark coat was weather-beaten homespun, soft from many launderings, and his breeches were the silky deerskin the Wappinger tanned. He tasted like sugar and cardamom, and his heart was beating fast in his chest, echoing Anna's.

Everything she had missed. Everything she had been cheated of. Everything she had told herself she could live without because no man could ever be trusted with the secrets she lived with.

She pushed him away with regret. Looking up into his face was like looking up into the sun. She had always felt more alive under his gaze.

She buttoned his coat against the night air. From afar he would be able to pass as a tenant. Up close an observant man—or woman—would know he was not. His bearing was all wrong, even near exhaustion; his fingernails were too clean, and while his hands were callused they were not convincingly weather-beaten. She saw other things as well. "When did you last sleep?"

"The night before last," he said.

She could see as much in the dark circles beneath his eyes, the fine lines at the corners. "What was so important that you could not rest your head for a few hours?"

"You."

Something inside her broke then, like a cord stretched

too tight, or a dam holding back too much water, and she was caught fast in the flood. The rising tide threatened to overwhelm her. "Leave now," she said, backing away from him, "before you can't leave at all." *And before I drown.*

"Meet me after the cider pressing next week," he said.

"Where?"

"You'll know where, my *klompen* girl. And for God's sake, Annatje, until then, be careful. Stay near the house. And away from the old manor."

"And its ghosts?" she asked teasingly.

"And its ghosts," he said, with a seriousness that prickled the hairs on her neck. "Yours are not the only secrets on Harenwyck."

"Kindly bring my pistol. And my knives," she said as he slipped out the window.

He paused there on the sill for a moment. "I am sorry about your things, but I have left you something downstairs in the kitchen that might go a little ways toward making up for them."

Then he was gone. For a moment she allowed herself to be carried high by the thrill of their meeting. Then she had to fight back the floodwaters again because it was just as impossible now as it had been then, only now she had the bitter experience to know it. Finally, she took refuge in the practical. She dusted the crumbs Gerrit had left on the coverlet and picked up the cookie plate. That was another skill the Widow had taught her. *When passions threaten to overwhelm, focus on the details. And go forward. Always forward.*

She had taken the Widow's advice when she learned

of that lady's death and focused on work. The school had been whipsawed by the changing fortunes of New York during those months, and it had been easy to put off thinking about the Widow's demise.

No longer. She was treading in the Widow's footsteps, as she had once vowed never to do.

You stand at a crossroads, Annatje Hoppe. There is no going back. And if you stand still, you will die.

She *had* felt dead then, at her very lowest, in those first weeks after she had arrived in New York.

A woman who has lost everything, as you have, has two choices. She can work to dismantle the system that stole her life, or she can try to fit herself again within the confines of that system, knowing full well that its mechanics—its injustice— might snatch it all away from her once more.

Anna had chosen to try again. To make herself fit. The Widow had accepted that. She had used her formidable resources to create a new identity, a new life for Anna. She had hired tutors, the discreet sort, to smooth out her English and teach her manners and singing and dancing and needlework, but she had insisted on other lessons too.

Anna knew that the desperate act of violence she had committed at Harenwyck had been a singular event, not part of her nature. The Widow had believed otherwise.

I must teach you to fire a pistol and kill neatly with a blade, because I do not know how to teach someone like you to accept injustice lying down.

The Widow had taught her more than that. She had taught her how to improvise weapons from whatever was closest to hand, how to pick a man's pocket, how to ride a horse bareback, and how to kill, if absolutely necessary, with her bare hands. But there was no certainty—even with the best technique—and there would be no protection in any of it up against a determined mob.

Which meant that Anna could no longer put off thinking about the manner of the Widow's death. The Widow's man of business, Mr. Sims, had appeared one day on Anna's doorstep with the deed to a house on Pearl Street that Anna did not want, and news she welcomed even less. The Widow would not be coming back. Ever. There were no details, just that one stark fact.

Anna had tried to refuse this unwanted inheritance, but the deed was already in her name. Mr. Sims declined to act as her agent in the matter and sell the wretched place, and there was no one else Anna could trust with that damnable, damning piece of property with the body in the basement. When fire had broken out during the American retreat, she had prayed that the house would burn, but fate had not obliged her. Fate never did.

The only thing that Anna could be certain of was that the Widow had died violently and ended in an unmarked grave. It was a grim prospect, and one she had to confront herself, since she now walked the same path, but at least she found that end preferable to the alternatives: dying in jail or at the end of the state's noose.

Forward.

Anna descended the back stairs to the kitchen. She had not expected anyone to be up, but Mrs. Buys was sitting next to the hearth and she still had one small fire lit, but not for cooking. It was meant to warm the crate sitting on the hearth tiles.

"I brought the plate down to wash," said Anna.

"No need, miss. My girls will take care of it in the morning. And we'll find you some more clothes. There are some nice enough things at the store in the castle. Not as fine as the gown you arrived in, may it rest in peace, but good enough until the patroon can get you new things up from New York. Now, come have a look at these little ones."

Anna approached the hearth. The crate was swathed in soft wool blankets. Inside lay a very large striped gray cat wearing a put-upon expression and nursing three kittens. A fourth slept sprawled atop her: Scrappy.

Gerrit had promised to go back for her mother and he had. No wonder he had looked tired. Anna could only imagine how difficult it must have been to find the cat and her brood in the woods. "Scrappy seems to have lost her taste for milk," observed Anna.

"Because *someone* spoiled her with fish and turkey, which are definitely not on the cat menu in my kitchen. Hopefully she will develop a taste for mouse," said Mrs. Buys. "We could use a good mouser about the place. We haven't had any cats at the house for years. The old patroon—God weigh his heart—hated them. There's something else for you on the table."

Anna brought her candle to the trestle. There, wrapped in another blanket, were her atlas and her book of engravings. There was also a very large box of capers on the table and a significant wedge of Parmesan cheese. With a surprising flush of pleasure, she recalled Gerrit's description of how his band divided up their plunder into gifts for their families and sweethearts.

"Would you like me to put these away, Mrs. Buys?" *Before the patroon sees them and knows you let his brother in.*

"There isn't any point, I'm afraid. The patroon is bound to notice the cat. Master Gerrit wants the girls to have two of the kittens. The two little black ones. Twins for twins, he said. His brother will scowl, but he'll give in."

"This feud between them," said Anna, "it's about more than the estate, isn't it?"

Mrs. Buys looked up. She had changed out of the bed jacket and petticoats she cooked in and was wearing a remodeled banyan. Another castoff from one of the ladies of the house, Anna guessed, just like the gown Mrs. Buys had lent her. "You're a sharp one, aren't you?" she said, but there was no disapproval in it.

She got up and bustled to the great *kas* opposite the hearth, where the better things were kept. "I won't have the maids gossiping about the family, but you're no maid."

The older woman opened the paneled doors and brought a china pot down from a high shelf. It too was a castoff from the house, chipped at the spout but too fine, with its painted flowers and gilded handle, to throw away. Anna realized she was being admitted to a very select society—those Mrs. Buys thought were good enough for the Van Haren hand-me-downs.

"Grietje and Jannetje are good girls. You'll have seen that for yourself. But they were young when their mother died, and there have been no real ladies in the house since to set an example for them."

"They are kind to each other," said Anna honestly, "and for that I suspect we have your example to thank, Mrs. Buys."

The housekeeper smiled, setting two mismatched but lovely Batavia tea dishes down on the table. "We've done our best, the maids and I, but we can't spend all day with them, and I am afraid that they do run a bit wild."

"I was told the patroon had a younger sister. Does she not take an interest in the twins?"

"Elizabeth. You'll have seen her portrait in the hall. Mistress Elizabeth ran away years ago. Truth to tell, it was all the old patroon's fault. He had *plans* for her, you see. Wanted her to marry a man twice her age, a burgher from Albany with money and a seat in the legislature."

Mrs. Buys clipped a generous lump of sugar off the cone for their tea. "Old Lord Cornelis and his crony had some scheme about anchoring floating mills at the Narrows and setting up as agent for every manor in the valley."

"I take it she did not agree to the marriage."

"No." Mrs. Buys sighed. "And the patroon was never a kindly man when thwarted. He beat her and she ran away, taking her maid with her. The patroon put it about that she eloped to New York, but I worked in the kitchen then, and I can tell you that pretty as she was, she had no suitors, not even secret ones. Servants know such things. Andries searched for her for months, but if he found her, we never knew it, and he didn't tell his father.

"Master Gerrit was in Leiden at school. When he came home the patroon tried his scheme again. He couldn't wed Gerrit to the burgher, of course, but he could marry him to the burgher's daughter. That poor girl was bought and sold like a sack of meal."

"Did she not *want* to marry Gerrit?" It seemed inconceivable to Anna.

"No. Sophia wasn't suited to Master Gerrit at all. She was quiet, shy, and did not enjoy his flights of fancy. She preferred Andries, it was plain to us all, and the feeling was mutual. But the old patroon wanted her money and her father's mills attached to Harenwyck, so it was the heir or no one for her. As if she had a say."

Mrs. Buys looked down into her teacup a moment. "Sophia would have done better to stand up for herself and run off like Elizabeth, I suppose, but she was a timid, biddable creature, and she did what her parents ordered. The only thing she took pleasure in was embroidery, but you won't find her work here. Gerrit never loved her, miss, but his brother did, and Andries couldn't bear to disturb anything of hers after she died. It's all back at the old house, rotting."

"I think I may have seen some of Sophia's embroidery at the old house last night. It was very fine," Anna lied.

"Was it? I've never had much use for anything beyond a darning stitch myself, but I suppose you are the expert. She certainly spent enough hours at it."

Anna was not surprised. She'd plowed her own unhappiness into similar pursuits those first few months after the Widow had found her, and had known her girls to focus deeply on such painstaking crafts when they were miserable over something.

"Do you think Mr. Van Haren would object to the twins making use of Sophia's old things?"

"I'm not sure. Better to ask first. The patroon doesn't like people in the old house. He's had offers to rent it, but he doesn't want tenants there."

And he made midnight—no, well *past* midnight— trips there alone. There was something—or someone— at the old manor that Andries Van Haren wanted kept secret, and that meant that, ghost or no ghost, Anna was definitely going back.

Twelve

Anna had no opportunity to return to the old manor the next day. Or the day after that. Andries Van Haren came home late that night in a foul mood that was not improved the next morning when he discovered the cat.

"I presume my brother brought the beast," said the patroon, in English, towering over everyone in the kitchen and peering into the crate with a jaundiced eye. "More of his peculiar largesse."

The maids and kitchen boys had scattered like so many marbles the moment he strode in. Anna stood her ground beside the box. "The young misses have already named them," she said, hoping to deflect a little of the patroon's ire from Mrs. Buys.

"I suppose that settles it, then." He did not sound happy about it. "Miss Winters, a moment of your time."

It was a command, not a request.

Anna followed him out the back door of the house where there was a pillared porch fully as grand as the one gracing the façade. It was her first opportunity to see much of the new manor, and what she saw was impressive. There was a garden here, laid out in the English style, a cultivated wilderness with grassy slopes stretching to a grove of trees. In the distance, hazy through the morning mist, stood a garden folly: a two-story teahouse built of red sandstone. The entire effect was such a contrast to the old manor—which had been thoroughly Dutch and practically medieval—that she could almost forget she was at Harenwyck.

"Mr. Ten Broeck tells me that you hold some very advanced ideas about female education," he said as they stepped onto the path that led to the folly.

"I'm not certain that my ideas are advanced as much as certain other people's are somewhat backward."

He laughed. That surprised her. It was not a smug or haughty sound. It caused her to turn and look at him. He was imposingly tall and erect, but there was a looseness to his posture, a relaxed grace that she had not observed before. Something like that of his father's in the hall portrait. This was in fact the most free and easy she had seen Andries.

This made her smile. He smiled back, and that surprised her even more. She had never seen any of the Van Harens—except Gerrit—smile. She suddenly evolved the conceit that the farther Andries Van Haren got from the manor, from the trappings of his patroonship, the less power the role exerted over him.

"Let us agree to call your ideas sensible, then."

"That will suit me fine," said Anna, "though I caution you as a single man to refrain from calling women sensible. Most do not find it flattering."

"But you are not most women, are you?"

In too many ways. "In the sense that I have no husband and no family of my own, I am not most women."

"That was not exactly what I meant."

"But they go hand in hand. When you are forced from the path most others take, you are unlikely to arrive at the same destination." This rang as true to her false tale of disappointed love and spinsterhood as it did her real history.

"And do you believe that we as a people—Americans, I mean—have been forced from the path? That, following now a separate course, we have a natural right to sever our ties with England?"

It was an overtly political question, and a refreshing novelty. Parents never asked her about her politics, because they presumed that as a woman she did not have any views of her own. Or at least, none worth airing. They might as well ask a kettle or a fish or a toddling child. But she was not here to talk about her views. She was here to discover the patroon's—and bend them to her will as the Widow might have done.

"Does it matter what my political views are, Mr. Van Haren? I teach singing and sewing. Neither subject provides much scope for political philosophy of any stripe."

"It is not your teaching that concerns me. Let us be frank with each other. We both know you are more than you would seem, that you are in contact with our mutual friends in Congress."

She had warned Gerrit that his brother was not stupid. She ought to have taken her own advice more to heart. "I have no friends in Congress," she said truthfully.

"But you know people who do," countered the patroon smoothly. "If you are here for more than the money they have offered you, Miss Winters, if you favor independence, if you truly wish to see America throw off Britain's shackles, then I would ask you not to include last night's encounter with my brother in your next letter to whomever pays you. This business with Gerrit is a family matter and will shortly be resolved, but outsiders might not see it that way."

Outsiders would likely question the firmness of the patroon's hold over Harenwyck. "The only one paying me to be here is *you*." It was the truth.

"But you will not deny that we have mutual friends."

"I would not call them friends. I won't deny that I was encouraged to accept Mr. Ten Broeck's offer, but my reasons for doing so are my own."

They had reached the end of the studiously unstudied path and come to the steps of the teahouse. The petite folly was a single room wide and deep, two stories tall, and decidedly Dutch in style, with a tip-tilted gambrel roof that gave it an antique air. Indeed, it might almost have been a monument to the old, abandoned manor.

The patroon held the door for her. The interior was cool and dark.

"I fear," Andries said, opening the shutters and revealing a paneled room painted butter yellow and furnished with cushioned window seats and a table and chairs, "that we have gotten off to a poor start, you and I. That is my fault. I owe you an apology for my behavior when I found you at the old manor. I was brusque. In my defense I shall say only that I do not often come upon damsels in distress wandering the woods at night."

He leaned against the window that looked out on the falling terrace. It was the sort of embellished wilderness the English so loved. Green grass rolling away in a cascade of gentle swells, pierced by natural-seeming staircases cut into the hillside.

"There are those who would say that a man's behavior in such circumstances—especially when they are *not* usual for him—is the measure by which his character should be judged."

"And what might those same people say when the man being fitted, liked a milliner's mannequin, for his 'character' has just been robbed by his own brother?"

"I expect they would say that Esau was unworthy of his inheritance—but the elder brother's sins do not absolve the younger's. As I recall, Jacob schemed and lied in order to steal Esau's birthright."

"Because he knew he could put the patrimony to better use. What, exactly, do you think my brother is going to do with my box of gold?"

Nothing. "I'm sure I don't know."

"He will give it away. *Foei!* He likes to play Robin Hood on the Hudson. No doubt it makes him feel better, temporarily, for abandoning his responsibilities, for running away to join the army and leaving his wife, his children, and the estate for others to worry about."

Anna did not like the idea of Gerrit as a man who would shirk his duties to wife and daughters. The estate was another matter entirely. "There are those who would not see Harenwyck as a responsibility to be manfully shouldered, but as an injustice to be set aright. The Wappinger and the Stockbridge Indians, for example. They still press claims to own much of your land, do they not? And then there are the squatters from Massachusetts. You had to drive them out with force last time, but they have a point: you have more land than tenants. That seems a grave injustice to a man who has no land at all.

"And there are those who would argue that the tenants—those who have cleared and planted the valley and built the barns and houses—now own the land they've worked by natural right. That it was a wilderness when their ancestors came here, and that they should no longer labor under a yoke their neighbors in other colonies do not bear simply because your great-great-grandfather paid their passages across the Atlantic."

It was a bold speech, she knew that, but under the circumstances, Anna saw no point in censoring herself. He knew why she was there, and he knew she was no ordinary schoolteacher. He might be a Rebel, but she was a leveler's daughter.

Andries cocked his head. "Is that a night with my brother and his followers talking, or is that the position of our friends in Congress?"

"It is my personal observation regarding this place, and the Hudson domains in general. Nowhere else in the colonies do so few men own so much land, or is so much wealth concentrated in the hands of such a tiny number of families. Your brother envisions a more free and equal valley." So had her father, of course, and he was dead.

"Yes, under my brother the tenants would find themselves more free to starve. His largesse with my gold makes him popular with the farmers, who think he is just returning their money to them from the greedy clutches of the landlord. It is always the same. Today they will spend his gold, and tomorrow they will have nothing to show for it."

"Certainly they will not have a great estate, like this one," she said.

"They do not live in my house, no, but its construction employed hundreds of tenants after the harvest was in, and for far more than the service days required of them. It lined their pockets in the winters when there was no other work to be had. And barely a tenth of the manor's profits end up in my coffers."

"Then where does the rest go?"

"Back into Harenwyck. Do you have much experience with farming, Miss Winters?"

More than you. "No." She had sown corn and harvested it, threshed wheat and milked cows and churned butter and carded flax until every muscle in her body ached. And, as often as not, she had still gone hungry to bed.

"It is a cash-poor business. My tenants pay me their rent largely in kind: in butter and eggs and flax. As part of their lease agreement, they must sell me their crops for whatever value I deem fair. In practice, if I do not offer them a price they like, they sell their corn under the table elsewhere."

"But you can take them to court if they do that. Or threaten to."

"Certainly that was my father's approach, but it is not mine. The manors do not have to be serfdoms. Once, they held out the promise of a new life. A man who could not afford to buy land could lease it and prosper here."

If he was willing to tie himself, his children, and his children's children to that land. *Perhaps.*

"Forgive me," she said, "but the farms on the road did not look so very prosperous to me." Burned out and boarded up. Lives shattered, as hers had been.

"You see the crux of the problem. To be cash poor during peace is an inconvenience. To be cash poor during war is disaster. Without money, I cannot expand my militia. I cannot buy the men that I *do* have sufficient powder and shot. I cannot fulfill the duties of the patroon and defend the families under my protection or their property from the Skinners and Cowboys, or from our neighbors in Massachusetts who are inclined to take by force what they have been unable to secure by law."

"Your situation probably suits General Clinton very nicely," said Anna. "He turns a blind eye while his 'foragers' ravage your farms, then demands your loyalty in exchange for his protection."

"He is playing with fire," said the patroon. "Neither Clinton nor the Americans truly understand the manors. Both sides want Harenwyck, in particular, because they both need control of the narrows at Harenhoeck. That means being able to march troops through the estate, transport material over land to keep the river secure. Neither of them will be able to do that if the tenants are in full revolt."

"Like they were in 'sixty-five," she said, "when there was no war."

"Again you are remarkably well-informed, Miss Winters."

Andries had been standing in the window this whole time, the farthest point possible from the door and from Anna. She had a suspicion about his behavior, and she set out to test it. Anna walked the perimeter of the room, closing the distance between them. "The trouble in the valley, then, was no secret," she said. And of course she had lived it.

The patroon moved in time with her—like opposing figures in a clockwork—to maintain the distance between them. "The *trouble* in the valley, then," he said, stepping to the next window, "was my late father. He thought that the patroonship existed at his will and pleasure, *to serve him*, but really, it is the other way around. The patroonships were granted to encourage settlement, to build a Dutch colony. Most of them failed early on because their proprietors failed to see that the essential element is not the land, it is the tenantry. My father's greatest mistake was believing that the patroon's job is to manage an estate."

"Isn't it?" She moved once more, and he did likewise, keeping the table, the chairs, and the floorcloth between them. She suppressed a sudden urge to vault over the furniture, upset his careful calculations of distance and reserve, and shatter his cold composure.

"No. A patroon's occupation is to manage *people*. It is leadership. The first patroon led five hundred souls across the Atlantic and into a new world and new lives. I want to do the same for the two thousand tenants we have now. But I cannot do it without money. Without hard coin, I cannot pay the tenants for the improvement projects I've in mind. Projects that could put cash into their pockets today and buy them richer futures tomorrow. Better, faster roads to get their goods to market. A ferry that will take them not just across the river, but all the way to New York and back. They make do with a part-time midwife and a 'wisewoman' in the woods, but they should have a doctor, paid for from rent the same way that the reverend is, and a school, funded likewise, for their children."

Anna had thought she had seen and heard too much in her young life to be shocked by anything, but the idea of a school on the manor for *tenant* children beggared the imagination. She could not help but wonder what her life would have been like if such a thing had been possible when *she* was a child. Cornelis Van Haren would never have countenanced it, of course. Would never even have considered it.

"And when those children decide they do not want to be farmers? Or they save enough money to buy their own land? What will you do then?" she asked.

"They can sell their leases to newcomers, or back to me."

"Or buy their land outright?"

"That would be neither to their benefit nor to the

estate's. There are advantages to size, Smith's 'economies of scale.' The estate must remain intact—they can buy land elsewhere, if they *must*."

He paused a moment, surveying the prospect from the window almost wistfully. "It is a peculiarly American mania, this thirst to own land. Most men would be better off as renters. Do you have any idea how many smallholdings fail every year? How deeply most farmers are in debt? The rent system transfers all the risk from the farmer to the landlord, to the patroon. A man can own nothing, not even a change of clothes, and if he signs a lease here, he can be sowing a field tomorrow. A smallholder is at the mercy of the market. If he reaches New York and discovers there is a glut of flax, he must take whatever price is being offered. He can go bankrupt overnight. An estate the size of Harenwyck, though, *sets* the price in the market."

"But with the risk comes a disproportionately greater share of the rewards," said Anna. "You take a tithe of their crop when they sell it to you, as a fee for bringing it to market. You take a tithe of their wheat and their corn when they bring it to your mill, for the service of grinding it, and they are not permitted to take it elsewhere. You charge twice or more what every necessity of life costs in New York, and you mandate that they must buy every necessity of life from you."

"But, Miss Winters, I *bought* the grindstone, and I *pay* the miller. I *pay* to transport all those necessities from New York, and the roads are dangerous, as you have seen firsthand. Yes, there is profit, as well as risk and responsibility, in my vocation, in leading people. How can it be otherwise?"

He paused again, seemed to suppress a sigh. "I shall not ask you to lie to your friends in Congress, Miss Winters. I ask only that you delay a few days in reporting the events of your arrival here."

She had not decided what she would communicate to Kate Grey, so she changed the subject.

"I am given to understand that you import things from New York besides necessities," she said. "Such as company." It was an entirely unsuitable subject for a gentlewoman to discuss with her employer, but they had been speaking as equals thus far, and if she was going to sleep under his roof she felt the matter should be raised. Still, she had not realized quite how much the idea annoyed her until now, and she did not like the feeling. Did not like *caring*.

"And which of your sources told you that?"

"Your brother leapt to a rather unflattering conclusion about the nature of my engagement at Harenwyck. He implied that you often bring prostitutes to the manor."

"Discretion has never been one of Gerrit's gifts," said the patroon flatly.

"So you don't deny it."

"Why should I? I am not married, Miss Winters. I betray no one by paying for companionship."

"You are the patroon. One might think it would be unnecessary for you to pay for such a thing."

"You mean because there is no shortage of women who would like to be the next lady of Harenwyck? The sort of woman desirous of marrying a patroon does not tend to be particularly interested in the man behind the title. Or were you instead suggesting that I exercise *droit du seigneur* upon the pretty maids who work at the manor house? That was indeed my late father's habit, but it is not mine. It may seem to you eccentric in a patroon, but I prefer my partners willing. The idea of cornering poor Tryntje while she busies herself making up the beds does not appeal at all. My father liked to pretend that the maids appreciated his attentions, that it was all a little game they played, to their mutual enjoyment. But he knew well enough their smiles were feigned, just as they knew that if they refused him, their positions in the household would be forfeit, and their families might even be evicted. The choice between submitting to your employer's advances and starving is no choice at all."

She knew that he spoke the truth about Cornelis Van Haren. She had been warned as young as twelve years old to stay away from the manor house and never to be alone with the old patroon. The tenants had all known what he was like. She had not considered that his family might know as well—nor how they would feel about it if they did. Andries Van Haren's empathy for the women in his employ seemed at odds with the aloofness he had displayed toward her, the careful distance he was keeping between them even now.

"The women you procure from New York," she said, "may have passing little choice as well. Few select that life when there is any other alternative. And some are forced into it with threats and violence."

"Believe it or not, Miss Winters, I do not have Mr.

Ten Broeck out scouring the Holy Ground for my night's entertainment. The ladies who visit Harenwyck are very well established in their profession, and are very well paid for their 'trouble.'"

"Now, perhaps," said Anna. "But the leap—or fall—from daughter or wife to prostitute is seldom a graceful one, and the landing is never soft. Some probably started out just like the maids your father cornered. Is there really such a great difference, Mr. Van Haren, in being the first or the hundredth man in line?"

"I suppose," said the patroon, with surprising candor, "the difference to me is that I did not push them when they fell. They may have few choices, but unlike the maids they *can* refuse me without fear of retribution. It is an honest bargain: my money for their . . . time . . . and no one is hurt, or deceived. That is more than I can say for my brother's style. He used to seduce our tenants' prettier daughters with scraps from the patroon's table."

She felt all the color drain from her face.

"You've no need to fear further encounters with my brother here," Andries said, misunderstanding her distress entirely. "I have set a strong guard. He won't get near the house again. The militia, under strength as it is, can at least protect the grounds and buildings. Indeed, if you were an ordinary servant, I would say that you have nothing to fear at all here at Harenwyck. I do not molest my staff and have never taken liberties with any of my dependents here on the estate. But then you are *not* an ordinary servant, are you?"

He took a step toward her, the first all day, and her mouth went dry. She had been so blind. Now she

understood their dance, his careful distance, his impersonal touch last night. This was not detachment, not
revulsion, it was *appetite* under tight rein, and just now,
kept barely in check.

"I try to be a good man, or at least a better one than
my father," said Andries Van Haren, who was not cold at
all. "But I am no saint, Miss Winters. And I doubt you
are one either. I cannot help but ask myself how much the
Rebels are paying you, and just how far they—and you—
are willing to go to secure Harenwyck."

He took another step forward. Her heart pounded in
her chest. Fear or desire, she could not have said. It struck
her all at once like a thunderclap, an awakening as unwelcome as it was startling. Seeing Gerrit last night had loosed
something in her, something pent up tight inside. For
nearly a decade she had hidden in the feminine world of
the school, a secular cloister where passion was something
that happened to other people. Now she was alone with a
man who, it seemed clear, fought daily to master his.

He closed the distance between them and caged her in
the window embrasure with his well-made body. "I wonder," he said, brushing her cheek with the pad of his thumb,
"whether I'm meant to seduce you, or you're meant to
reform me. Shall we find out?"

He bent to kiss her.

The Widow would have tilted her head back and
tasted his mouth and conquered by yielding, or seeming
to yield. She would have effortlessly transmuted this man's
desire for her into the outcome *she* desired. She would

have delivered Harenwyck to the Rebels the same way that she had delivered Trenton to Washington.

Here was more than carnal temptation. Here was the power to shape events, to alter nations, to topple kings. Anna had never doubted that the Widow had been motivated by a deeply held set of beliefs, but she had always wondered what moved men like André to play such dangerous games.

Here at last was the answer: *power*. It was a heady feeling, difficult to distinguish from—perhaps not unmixed with—arousal.

Anna sidestepped the patroon and edged toward the door. "I have lessons to organize, Mr. Van Haren."

He didn't move a muscle, but his eyes swept her from head to toe and it was all she could do not to shrink under his scrutiny. Finally he said quietly, "Have Mr. Ten Broeck send to New York for what you need. And don't let Hubble and Bubble lead you into too much mischief."

Now she did curtsy. Or at least she picked up her skirts and inclined her head just the slightest bit, because that abbreviated gesture helped put their interaction firmly back in the realm of the formal. It allowed her to glide from the room the way she taught her girls to and make a graceful exit.

As soon as she was outside, she lifted her skirts again and ran, whether from the patroon or the shade of Angela Ferrers she could not have said.

Thirteen

Anna bypassed the meandering garden path and crossed directly over the lawn back to the house, hitching Mrs. Buys' petticoats up so that she did not ruin the hems. By the time she had returned, Grietje and Jannetje were nowhere to be found, so Anna went to her room and began her list for Mr. Ten Broeck.

It was not short. She had literally nothing but the clothes on her back. She needed petticoats, chemises, jackets, gowns, stockings, and presentable shoes. Gerrit had returned her books but not her paints or charcoals—or her embroidery thread, which had presumably met a bad end on the carriage floor. The linen canvas for the twins' projects could come from Harenwyck—there would doubtless be some in the store at the castle—but the embroidery thread, the fine silk and wool in rich colors, would have to come from New York, and it would be several days at the very least before it arrived. Stitchery would have to wait. Likewise painting.

Drawing might hold more promise if the store had any paper. She hoped that it did. If she could persuade Mrs. Buys to lend them a pot she could show the twins how to make their own charcoal.

Anna went in search of Mr. Ten Broeck. When she had been a girl the estate manager had administered the patroonship from an office in the old castle. She stopped by the kitchens to ask Mrs. Buys the way, even though she had her bearings now and had traveled it many times, lest she appear to know more about Harenwyck than she ought. Anna did not think Gerrit would have vouchsafed her real identity to the housekeeper, but the woman was clearly observant. If Anna was not careful, Mrs. Buys would realize that she was no stranger to the manor.

She found the cook in the kitchen supervising two maids cutting and cleaning their way through six bushels of pumpkins. The baskets were stacked on the floor, filled with their bright orange bounty, a still life waiting for the artist's brush. Or hers, if she could find some paint.

Mrs. Buys gave Anna excellent detailed directions—and a shopping list of her own.

"Coffee, if they have any, which I fear they won't. Sugar, whatever the price. Even if Mr. Ten Broeck refuses and tells you that the tenants will riot if he runs out. New York, we hear, is short on fresh meat and butter and eggs. But here in the valley, we are all out of everything else. No tea, no chocolate, no coffee, no sugar.

Precious little salt. And that, in a few months, will mean no hams."

Anna assured Mrs. Buys that she would not come back empty-handed and took the mill path to the castle. The fort, or *kasteel*, as people called it, was as old as Harenwyck and looked even older. Like the Halve Maen it had been built from local stone. It dated from the early years of settlement, when the patroon did not live on the manor at all, but in a grand house in New York, and only visited Harenwyck from time to time to surprise his overseer and audit the account books.

The walls were three feet thick with nothing but slender arrow slits to pierce the gloom of the first two stories. The windows on the upper two floors, where the estate manager had his office and the store was housed, had been added later. Anna remembered how dark and cool it had been inside on summer days, a relief from the sticky heat of the fields and forest.

As *castles* went, though, it had always been a disappointment to her, especially after reading *The Castle of Otranto*. Harenwyck's stone fort had always been too prosaic to be romantic—although as Mrs. Buys told it, the late patroon's schemes to aggrandize his legacy sounded just as dark and destructive as Manfred's.

Anna found Mr. Ten Broeck in a storeroom counting his diminishing supply of sugar with the assistance of a slender young black man who was almost certainly a slave. The sight took her aback and disappointed her. She *liked* Mr. Ten Broeck, but her mother had been raised a Quaker and abhorred slavery. Her father had refused to defend tenants who owned slaves. In New York Anna did her best to follow her parents' example. She did not do business with tradesmen who owned human chattel, but there was no avoiding the scourge of slavery. She could not refuse students from slaveholding families, or she would end up with no students at all.

"I am sorry to interrupt." She handed over Mrs. Buys' list and her own.

Mr. Ten Broeck looked tired and his smile did not reach his eyes, but he dismissed his slave and took Anna's lists and read down them, nodding and murmuring, "Yes. We have that. Hmm. *No.* Yes. Possibly."

At last he looked up, removed his spectacles, and said, "Come, come," and led Anna up to the store.

In spite of Mrs. Buys' gloomy predictions, and in light of the Cowboys and Skinners wreaking havoc on the farms along the borders, she had not fully expected *this*. The main room of the shop was dangerously depleted of stock, nearly empty in fact. Where there should have been stacks of rakes, hoes, blades, pots, pans, and iron spiders, there were instead a few dusty pieces of equipment in odd sizes. The ones seldom used or needed. At this time of year sacking should have been stacked to the ceiling and bales of cord should have crowded the windows, but there was almost nothing for the patroon or his tenants to pack and tie their crops with. And empty shelves led to riots.

"Ours was not the first vehicle that the patroon's brother and his men waylaid," said Mr. Ten Broeck with a candor born of necessity. There was no hiding the extent of the problem. It was not just farm implements and equipment that were in short supply, it was the everyday luxuries of which the Dutch were so fond: the spices they baked with; the coffee they brewed, sweet and hot; the chocolate they drank in the morning.

Without further comment, Ten Broeck left her with a large, matronly woman who had charge of the store, returning to his office and work.

There was paper at least, which was a great relief. She could take the girls into the woods to hunt for wild vines to make charcoal. There was also stiff paperboard she could use to make stencils for theorem drawing on days when the weather was too poor to venture out.

The stockings available in the store were coarse wool, and Anna would have preferred none at all over the scratchy hose, but the woman who kept the store held up a finger to signal *one moment* and disappeared into a smaller room beyond. When she returned she had a box of fine silk stockings with clocking.

"If we leave them out they get snagged," she said in pleasantly accented English, unrolling the delicate silk carefully. "Farming hands aren't soft hands," she explained. "Mostly they're bought for weddings."

Anna knew, but she couldn't say that. Her parents, like most tenants, had each owned one good set of clothing. Her mother wore the same gown in which she had been married to church on Sundays. She always took it off as soon as they got home and folded it carefully in the locked chest where all their best things were kept. It had looked almost as fresh fifteen years on—when she ran off with her tin peddler—as it had the day she wedded Bram Hoppe.

Her father's suit had not been quite as well preserved. He had long since stopped going to church on Sundays, because he saw the reverend as little more than a mouthpiece of the patroon, but he had worn his wedding suit to meetings with the Wappinger and the Stockbridge Indians when they issued their own leases to Harenwyck land, as they steadfastly claimed they had a legal right to do since the Dutch had never paid them for it. And Bram wore it every time he stood up before the patroon on the minor charges the *schouts* harassed him with: most often public drunkenness or creating a disturbance. He wore it when he assembled the tenants to talk sedition, and he had worn it on the night the bailiffs arrested him one final time. He had worn it too in jail, and he had died in it.

It seemed that nowhere at Harenwyck could Anna escape the past. The store held other memories as well. As a child she had often accompanied her mother shopping for staples. There was never any money for luxuries like the bright silk ribbons that hung from spools on the wall or the good cloth shoes imported from London that the prosperous tenants sometimes bought. And they would never have been able to afford the ready-made silk petticoats in delicate shades of pink, lilac, and green that Anna selected today, or these gaily colored caraco jackets from Amsterdam in cotton sateen. Anna chose two and picked out several changes of lacing ribbons to match. She also picked out five chemises so she could have a fresh one every day without imposing too greatly on the laundress. And she selected a soft pair of cotton jumps to wear instead of her stays when she took the girls out looking for vines in the woods.

She justified the purchases to herself because even if she wrote to Mrs. Peterson today, her own clothes would not arrive for at least a week.

It was not the first time, of course, that she had been forced to acquire an entirely new wardrobe. She had arrived in New York after her desperate flight from Harenwyck with only the clothes on her back. For a week until the Widow arrived she had worn those same clothes, and they had practically been rags by the time Angela Ferrers came to her rescue.

The Widow had outfitted Anna for her new life with clothes suitable for a fashionable young spinster. They had been far more elegant than anything she had ever owned and the choosing of them had been an education in itself. Anna had never worn silk, had never owned a set of stays fitted just for her, had not known how to tell good cut from bad. She had always worn her mother's hand-me-downs and that Quaker lady had not seen the point in altering garments to fit. The Widow had not just taught her how clothes ought to lie on her body, but she had explained why some things flattered more than others, tutored her in how to choose color, pattern, and shape to enhance her best features and disguise or minimize any flaws. It was a set of skills she taught her own students, and because of it they were widely agreed to be the best turned out young women in New York.

Anna employed all her hard-learned acumen at the castle store to assemble a wardrobe that would both suffice and flatter until her own things arrived. She only wished that there were leather shoes available for walking about outside the manor house. She had destroyed her own on her flight from the farm, and the delicate silk ones on offer would be ruined in a single rainstorm. But when she asked the storekeeper for a pair she was advised to get *klompen* at the cider pressing.

"There's an old man who makes them. He sets up near the bonfire, and he'll carve them to fit your feet in a quarter of an hour. Better than leather shoes in the rain and muck."

Anna had sworn she would never wear *klompen* again, but she knew from experience that the woman was right. She'd envied the farmwives she had seen walking on her way to the castle—they'd looked far more comfortable in their clogs than she had felt in her worn-out shoes.

On her way out Anna stopped by Ten Broeck's office to thank him for the clothes and paper and collect Mrs. Buys' sugar and coffee. "How soon do you think we can expect a box of paints and embroidery floss from New York?" she asked. "I doubt the Skinners or Cowboys have much use for such."

Mr. Ten Broeck did not answer at once. "The roads," he said finally, "are very poor just at present."

"They were fine just a few days ago, and it has not rained."

Ten Broeck sighed. "I must think twice now about enrolling my daughters in your school if you will train them up to be so sharp. The patroon does not want it known widely, Miss Winters, but his brother has effectively cut us off from easy communication with New York. We do not have the men needed to protect the house and the tenants *and* mount a full escort for a courier. Two days ago the patroon sent his chariot to the city, and it was waylaid just beyond the borders of Harenwyck. The driver returned on foot yesterday morning. That afternoon, the patroon dispatched two riders, but they were turned back well before they even reached the old gate."

Anna had planned to write a masked letter to Mrs. Peterson for Kate Grey and send it on with the rest of the Harenwyck post. The code mask had been among the stencils she had lost with her baggage, but she knew its shape and dimensions by heart and could draw and cut a new one anytime—as could anyone who had been in regular contact with the Widow. Now, though, if she wanted to send her intelligence on to Angela's successor, she would have to find another way.

Use your instincts. That was what Kate Grey had said. Anna's instincts told her that the Widow had spent a great deal of time at Harenwyck during the last revolt. She would have had other contacts besides Anna's father. Anna must find them.

"What will the patroon do?" Anna asked.

"He will call upon his allies for aid."

Mr. Ten Broeck very purposely did not say which allies. He must accept the help of whichever side answers his call.

That would have been the Widow's appraisal of the situation. It was Anna's as well. The problem was that Anna was supposed to be acting for Kate Grey and the Americans. She was supposed to be serving as their eyes and ears, and if possible, their agent to convince Andries Van Haren to side decisively with the Rebels. She ought to relate everything she knew about Gerrit: the size of the force at his disposal, the location of his encampment, the nature of his feud with his brother. She ought, especially, to tell them about Gerrit's meeting with André and the overtures that dangerous gentleman had made on behalf of the British.

But to do so would be to betray Gerrit, whose aims were, in many ways, her own. Even if his methods were criminal and, depending one's point of view, treasonous. Nothing was as simple as she had hoped it might be on the road from New York.

"It would help tremendously," said Mr. Ten Broeck, as if glimpsing her thoughts in a dark glass, "if you could recall anything at all the patroon's brother or his men might have said as to the whereabouts of their camp. It would be best if the patroon could bring his brother to heel without recourse to outside aid—better for everyone on the estate. Once invited in, armies are damnably difficult guests to show the door."

She was supposed to be on the patroon's side—so long as Andries sided with the Americans. Kate Grey had strongly implied that independence would transform the manors and destroy the tenant system. Andries Van Haren had a bold vision to transform the estate in a different way, but Anna did not believe that he would give up power any more readily than his father had. He would not, as he admitted, sell land to his tenants. He would never dissolve the manor.

Gerrit would. The Americans ought to be backing him, but Anna was not naive. She knew that it was unlikely that those in charge truly cared about the estate, or the tenants. They wanted Harenhoeck and, with it, a stranglehold on the Narrows, and they would back whichever brother could deliver that strategic location to them.

"I am sorry, Mr. Ten Broeck, but they did not speak freely in front of me. Certainly not in English."

"Even names would help. We need to know more of Gerrit's associates. We can apply pressure through their families. The patroon has the power to evict tenants who disrupt the peace. Even if no one gives up Gerrit's location, a few *examples* . . . could help quiet the estate."

Examples. Naked force backed by the force of law. And it would all start again. The riots, the arrests, the deaths. For a moment she was back in that cottage, with the pistol in her hand and Vim Dijkstra's fingers curled cruelly around her hair. Her breakfast threatened to rise. With an act of will, she quashed the memory and said, "I am sorry"—when she was not sorry at all—"but these Dutch names all sound alike to me."

Anna took the long way back to the manor this time, through the forest path that no one now bothered to keep clear. It was hard going with her packages, but she did not care, because she desperately needed to be alone.

I cannot help but ask myself how much the Rebels are paying you, and just how far they—and you—are willing to go to secure Harenwyck. But that, Andries, was the wrong question to ask.

Anna had not come to Harenwyck for Kate Grey or

the Continentals or Congress. Kate Grey had threatened her with the bailiffs, but Anna too was one of the Widow's acolytes. She had disappeared once. She could do so again, transform herself into someone else—like Barbara Fenton—even slip across the sea and beyond the reach of the law.

A woman who has lost everything, as you have, has two choices. She can work to dismantle the system that stole her life, or she can try to fit herself again within the confines of that system, knowing full well that its mechanics—its injustice— might snatch it all away from her once more.

Anna had chosen to try again. The Widow had agreed to help her, hiring Latin tutors, arranging music lessons, finding a dancing master. But she had also insisted on training Anna in the art of espionage—and killing neatly with whatever weapon might be close to hand.

Schoolteachers, Anna had insisted, are not required to be crack shots or skilled lockpicks. Quite the contrary.

You will make a good schoolmistress, said the Widow, *because you are a quick study and have already learned to play roles as necessary to survive. But it is not a role you can play forever. Not so long as Harenwyck endures. What you did there was not a mistake or an isolated event. It is who you are: a woman who will not accept injustice.*

Anna had denied it at the time. She had wanted to put Harenwyck and the killing of Vim Dijkstra in her past, but she was coming to understand that what she had done would always be with her—and that the Widow might have been right about her after all.

Fourteen

After her trip to the castle, the next week flew by faster than any Anna could recall since childhood. She took the girls to the riverbank and searched for wild grapevines. She was shocked to learn that they had never foraged before. Spending an afternoon gathering blackberries had been one of the delights of Anna's childhood, before all the trouble started, and it was one of the things she missed most now that she lived in the city.

It took them a little while to find grapes, and along the way Anna taught Grietje and Jannetje how to tell the wild concords apart from their poisonous look-alike, the moonseed: a vine that appeared almost identical to the untrained eye. The main differences were the tendrils—moonseed vines did not have them—and the seeds themselves. Grapes had many, their poisonous imposter only one.

Anna was surprised to find moonseed vines that showed

obvious signs of cutting. No one foraging in the valley would make the mistake of thinking they were grapes. Someone had been harvesting them for other purposes, and Anna knew enough about the plant's uses to guess who and what for. The seeds could be made into a powerful purgative. On the estate, only Mevrouw Zabriskie was a skilled enough herbalist to dabble in such dangerous cures.

The twins collected a basket of vines and a basket of grapes. Anna hoped that the fruit would go some ways in compensating Mrs. Buys for the use of a pot and one of her fires to make the charcoal. The musky wild grapes made excellent jelly, and their frosty skins told Anna that they were near their peak for the season.

The irony of a finishing school teacher instructing the patroon's nieces in woodcraft and charcoal making was not lost on Anna. She was surprised, though, by how much she enjoyed these practical lessons. It harkened back to her own childhood, to the period before the riots, when her parents had been happy and she had been too.

Anna took the girls on rambles across the estate to teach them basic drawing skills. She believed the method superior to copying from plates, but it had always proved impractical in the bustle of New York. At Harenwyck they sketched pumpkins on the vine, fields and houses, ducks in the river. Anna showed Jannetje and Grietje all the little tricks for transferring what the eye saw to the page with as much faith as possible.

And she made them do something their grandfather, the old patroon, never did with anyone, ever: ask permission. When they sat down to sketch a particularly well-sited tenant cottage on a hill, Anna made Grietje and Jannetje knock on the batten door and ask the *mevrouw* of the house for her consent. The young farmwife was amused by the girls and brought them buttered slices of bread in the afternoon while they worked. When they were done, Jannetje descended the hill and presented the woman with her drawing.

When she came back up she said to Anna, "The *mevrouw* said she did not have any other pictures in her house." Jannetje furrowed her brow and then added, "But we have so many at the manor."

"Yes, you do," said Anna. Jannetje had glimpsed the gulf her father had seen the day Gerrit and Anna met. Anna wondered if Jannetje and Grietje would be able to see the injustice of it as sharply as Gerrit had. He had been raised as the heir, almost entirely insulated by the armor of privilege. Girls were different. They were not raised to rule. They were raised to be biddable and sweet like Gerrit's poor unloved wife. And if they rebelled they ended up like Gerrit and Andries' sister, Elizabeth, driven from her home, never to be seen again.

Anna had seen it happen to girls she had taught. Not many of them, fortunately. Families that thought female education—at least the sort Anna offered—worth paying for were more often than not reasonably enlightened. Most of her girls made good marriages to good men. Anna liked to think this was because she taught them to be astute judges of character. But there were always the girls whose parents had plans for them, who saw education for their daughters in the same light that they saw gowns for dances—as a necessary expense, or a necessary evil, to package their daughters as more appealing goods for the marriage market.

Grietje and Jannetje might lack polish, but Anna couldn't help but think that in some ways they had gotten lucky at Harenwyck. Mrs. Buys' occasional supervision and Andries' benign neglect had allowed them freedom to grow into distinct personalities. She doubted either would accept the first man she was presented with, no matter what the patroon dictated.

Unfortunately, by the end of the week no packages had yet arrived from New York, and Anna was feeling the distinct need to vary her curriculum. She had no opportunity to press the patroon to send another messenger to New York. She saw hardly anything of Andries that week, and when he did appear he was always dressed for riding and wearing the dust of the road.

"Out chasing his brother," sighed Mrs. Buys. "And much good it will do him."

When he was at home the patroon kept his distance from Anna and she did not know if that should make her worried or relieved.

The day of the cider pressing arrived. The excitement on the estate was palpable. Anna felt it too—a pleasurable anticipation that surprised and delighted her. She had not realized how much she had missed the rhythms of rural life, the rituals that celebrated the harvest and the turning of the seasons. The festivities would be held, as they had been for as long as anyone at Harenwyck could remember, that evening, in and around a great barn and outbuildings about a mile away from the new manor. Near the old church and burying ground she knew so well from her childhood.

It had always been a great occasion among the tenants, but Anna had not expected the patroon to mark it, or the girls to even be aware of it. When she had been a child, Cornelis Van Haren had appeared briefly for the very first turn of the stile, watching impassively as three strong men put the great stone wheels into motion. He had not brought his family, and he had not stayed for the dancing and drinking that followed. Anna had, even when she was too young to take part.

Gerrit had only come after Anna told him about it. She had been amazed that he had not known of it, the highlight of her year, as dear and special as Christmas. It was the finest spectacle the valley had to offer: hundreds of girls twirling in their best petticoats, musicians playing, everyone wearing their best shoes if they had them, or their finest clogs if they did not. The old patroon had only come to see that the work began on schedule, to watch proprietarily as the cloudy cider ran down the spout and into the barrels—not for the company or the food or the drink that all seemed so festive and rich to Anna.

She could remember watching him accept a doughnut hot from the pot, wrapped in the finest napkin Mrs. Ackerman owned. Old Cornelis hadn't even tried to look pleased with it. Anna had already eaten her *olykoeck*, and wished she could have another, but that was beyond her wildest dreams of avarice. The patroon had discarded his

untasted on the trail back to the house, tossing the doughnut and the napkin into the field like trash.

Later she had spied the fine linen gleaming in the
moonlight. She had wanted to pick it up off the path and
take it home and wash it, but her mother had scolded her.
They were not *that* poor. Anna's mother had jealously
guarded the subtle distinctions in wealth and status between tenants, right up until the day she left. But Anna
sensed early on that such distinctions meant nothing to
people like Cornelis Van Haren: the old patroon had
made it quite clear that the entire harvest festival was a
peasant affair.

So Anna was shocked when Andries Van Haren shed
his riding clothes for a suit of forest green velvet that set
off his pale blue eyes and golden blond hair, and called
Anna and the twins from their history lesson to get ready
for the festival. "I presume you will allow me to escort
you," said Andries Van Haren, offering her his arm.

"I did not realize that the family attended," said
Anna lamely. She'd planned on slipping out of the house
to meet Gerrit at the festival after the girls were in bed
and the servants had all left to don their best things, but
she could hardly refuse the patroon's invitation—at least
not without prompting unwanted questions.

"My father did not appreciate the charm of country
airs or *olykoecken* leavened with cider, but then he did not
have the sweetest disposition himself. Particularly in his
later years. My sister-in-law, Sophia, always wanted to go,
but she was too terrified of the old patroon to disobey
him. That is why I've taken Grietje and Jannetje each

year since he died, so that they might enjoy what their mother could not. She would have liked that. And I think it is safe to say that they are now *olykoecken* connoisseurs."

"The ones with bits of apple are the best. I can eat six," said Grietje proudly, her sharp ears catching the only part of the conversation that truly interested her, "without getting sick."

"Our father can eat a dozen," said Jannetje pointedly, daring the patroon to contradict her.

"He can," admitted the patroon. "That is one arena in which I refuse to compete with my brother."

There would be no sneaking anywhere, so she might as well enjoy her new clothes. Anna wore one of her Dutch chintz jackets laced with a green ribbon on top of a pink silk petticoat and felt very smart in it. The outfit would have looked rustic in New York, but it suited a country event like a cider pressing and made her feel . . . young.

She had not felt young—not really—since leaving Harenwyck. Andries Van Haren, she realized, was not the only one who carried outsized responsibility on his shoulders. She had been responsible for herself, alone in the world by eighteen, and soon thereafter responsible for a business and the welfare of a dozen or more young women.

Not tonight, though. Tonight she could be Annatje again in her heart, as she might have been if fate had not intervened. As she might have been if her father had lived. And tonight she could sample the adult pleasures she had been too young for then. She could drink strong beer with rum and maple syrup and kick up her skirts in one of the country dances that did not require couples.

It was madness, but she felt a surge of elation as she stepped out into the night air. The manor house was all but dark, the servants already departed for the festival. The patroon offered Anna his free arm. In the other he carried a crook and a lantern to light their way. Anna could smell wood smoke in the air and as they drew nearer to the old barn, she drank in the distilled scent of autumn: the sugary aroma of decayed leaves, the fruity musk of the apples waiting to be crushed on the great stone, the warm spices frying in the *olykoecken* pot.

Grietje and Jannetje ran ahead down the path leaving Anna alone with the patroon, and in closer proximity to him than she had been since that day in the teahouse. She was glad for the light. It was a dark night and the path was uneven and she did not want to lean too heavily on Andries Van Haren's strong arm. It was impossible to be unaware of his physical presence. The lantern gilded his shining hair, which was tied back with a dark green velvet ribbon to match his suit. His height, his sharp cheek-bones, and his blue eyes all conspired to make him appear a sending from faerie land, Oberon come to trick Titania.

Or to beguile Anna. She could not deny that she was drawn to him. It was more than his physical beauty that called to her. He was as passionate a reformer as his brother, and he was setting an example for Grietje and Jannetje that she approved, teaching them by word and deed that the tenants were people too. Where he had learned this, she did not know, but she was coming to understand that he was no longer the distant, aloof boy she remembered. And in the teahouse he had proved that he was not cold. Quite the contrary.

"Do you always attend the cider pressing, Mr. Van Haren?" She could not remember seeing him there as a child, though they must have been quite close in age.

"I have only begun to attend recently, with my nieces," he said. "As a boy I longed to come after my brother told me what it was like, but my father always discouraged the family from attending. I'm ashamed to admit that I was no more eager to risk his displeasure in that respect than Sophia."

"And is it everything you had hoped?"

"Everything and more. You will laugh when I tell you that I was twenty-five before I tasted my first cider *olykoeck*, and I am determined to make up for lost time. I hope you will not find the proceedings too bucolic."

"I am certain I won't. I'm fond of country dances. But I have to admit that your patronage of the festival surprises me. Even in New York the Hudson patroons are said to abide in feudal splendor, decidedly *apart* from the rustic pursuits of their tenants."

He turned to look at her and she was struck by the intensity of his gaze. "I mean to change that," he said. "The festival represents the very best of what the estate could be, what it should be: a community with common goals. Tonight at least, every soul on the patroonship should work and celebrate together."

Down the path and through intervening foliage, Anna

made out the first tantalizing glimpses of the kindling bonfire, casting light and shadows against the great barn in which the pressing would occur, and across myriad tiny human figures as though conspiring with the patroon to make his point. *Still . . .*

"Every soul?" she could not stop herself from asking. "Does that include Mr. Ten Broeck's slave, and others like him? In New York they are forbidden from gathering."

"New York fears another fire ever since the Negro Plot in 'forty-one. And, frankly, the city is right to be afraid. If anything, the lot of the blacks has deteriorated in the last thirty years. If I were a slave in New York, I would want to burn it too. Slavery is a sin no good Christian should countenance. And even if a man is not a Christian, he ought to find it an affront to human dignity. I will not allow any of my current tenants to buy new slaves, or new tenants to bring slaves with them into their leasehold. If they do so, they are evicted."

He had surprised her again. She had been ready to lecture him, but he had just voiced most of her arguments. "And the ones who already own slaves, like Mr. Ten Broeck?"

"My father hired Mr. Ten Broeck. It was perhaps the best thing he ever did for Harenwyck. Theunis is the finest manager we have ever had. I cannot accomplish what I want for the estate without him, but neither can I force him to free his slave."

"And what of the slaves belonging to the estate? I thought, like most patroons, you owned at least a dozen to work in the castle and man the mill and the ferry."

"My father's will manumitted all of his slaves."

She did not believe it. "That does not sound much like the late patroon, based on what I have heard of him." Old Cornelis would never have freed his slaves. Not in a thousand years.

"Sometimes people can surprise you, Miss Winters," said the current patroon.

He was certainly surprising her. "I was given to understand that your father's will went missing, and you were forced to rely upon the testimony of its witnesses to uphold your claim to Harenwyck in court."

"That was indeed the case."

He said it with a finality that did not invite further questions, and Anna suspected that was with good reason. Old Cornelis' last wishes—naming Andries as heir, liberating the estate's slaves—appeared to be entirely too close to his younger son's desires. Too close, perhaps, to credit. Convenient, then, that a will which seemed *unlikely* to memorialize them had gone missing. It seemed almost certain to her that Andries had bought the "witnesses" and their testimony with Harenwyck money. For enough gold or preferential treatment on the estate a man might swear to anything.

A man might be willing to see another man's brother disinherited.

And yet Andries had not done it *entirely* for personal gain. Harenwyck had owned at least a dozen slaves when Anna was girl. The number could have been twice as many by the time of the old patroon's death. The slaves had always done the hardest work: clearing land, turning the millstone when the river was slow, maintaining the roads. Andries may have lied under oath, but he had accomplished at least one just purpose. One that reduced his own inheritance through the loss of valuable human property.

"To answer your question honestly," the patroon said, breaking in on her thoughts, "you will not see any slaves here tonight. The tenants who hold slaves do not bring them to the festival, because they do not see them—or wish to see them—as *people*. It makes it easier, I suppose, to justify keeping one's fellow man in bondage. If my brother were to gain control of Harenwyck, Miss Winters, he would sell the land to the tenants. One in nine or ten of them owns slaves now. When they are freeholders, the patroon will have no say over what they do. I'd expect the number of slave owners, and of slaves, to increase, wouldn't you?"

Anna had seen the power of the patroon used to oppress. She had not considered it could be used to reform, to liberate.

The bonfire was already a roaring blaze by the time they arrived. Near at hand, a pot for *olykoecken* was bubbling, and Grietje and Jannetje made a beeline for the sugary confections. Not unexpectedly, the woman hooking doughnuts out of the pot with an iron crook was not Mrs. Ackerman, who had been seventy if she had been a day when Anna was a child. That good *mevrouw* had been replaced by a younger woman, one with a pair of helpers.

The two children sprinkling sugar over the doughnuts and rolling them in paper were about the same age as Grietje and Jannetje. They wore cheerful matching kerchiefs and aprons that were powdered with sugar. Anna was pleased to see the twins ask politely if they could take a turn at the job.

The *mevrouw* at the pot cast a worried look at the patroon. She did not want to put a foot wrong, to displease him. Old Cornelis would probably have had her whipped if she'd allowed his children to labor like peasants.

"So long as you work more than you eat," said the patroon, "I do not think there could be any objection." Grietje and Jannetje jumped up and down with excitement and set to learning their tasks. They sugared a doughnut for Anna, and then one for their uncle, who stood there and coughed theatrically until they sugared a second for him.

As they stood eating their doughnuts Anna saw a familiar figure separate herself from the crowd. It was difficult to miss Mevrouw Zabriskie in her brightly colored mismatched silks. She was selling posies of dried flowers, and when she came close Anna could detect the scents of lavender and jasmine even over the sweet perfume of the *olykoecken*.

The patroon bought three posies, one each for Anna and the girls. Mevrouw Zabriskie selected a bright purple one for Anna and pressed it into her hand. She took the opportunity to turn Anna's palm over and made a show of great interest in what she thought to see there.

"Where is your husband, *joung frau*?" asked Mevrouw Zabriskie.

"I don't have one," said Anna, tugging her hand back gently.

Mevrouw Zabriskie's grip tightened, and she tracked a tickling finger over Anna's palm. "But you have changed your name. I can see it here, in your broken life line. The end of one woman, the beginning of another."

Anna snatched her hand away rather too quickly. The posy dropped in the mud. "I am sorry," said Anna, "but you are quite mistaken. I have never been married."

Mevrouw Zabriskie looked into her eyes as though seeing her for the first time, and nodded. "As you say, *joung frau*."

But Anna knew that the cunning woman didn't believe her. Mevrouw Zabriskie clucked and bent to pick up Anna's dropped posy, her pale blond braids touching the ground. She pocketed the dusty bouquet thoughtfully and handed Anna instead a fresh posy from her bag.

Anna took it and smiled for Andries' benefit, but she did not like the way the old woman had scrutinized that dropped bouquet. She had looked as though she was putting it away for later, and Anna found the thought unsettling.

She put the cunning woman from her mind and followed the patroon on his circuit of the entertainment. Part of her wished she had been able to come here on her own as she had planned, anonymously, to hover on the edges of the crowd and relive privately her memories of this place, but it was impossible to be invisible at the side of Andries Van Haren. It was unfortunate that she could not refuse his invitation without inviting unwanted questions, arousing dangerous suspicions. If Gerrit was right and Jan had heard him call her Annatje, if Jan was plotting with his relatives, if they wanted a look at her, this girl who might be Annatje Hoppe, they would be able to look their fill tonight, and there was nothing she could do about it without attracting unwanted attention to herself. The patroon was squiring her around like she was a lady, and his sweetheart.

She suspected that the irony would be lost on the Dijkstras. Vim had not been an imaginative man, even in his cruelty. His clan's bullying had always been the opportunistic sort, licensed, even encouraged by the old patroon. His son was another matter. Anna was glad to see that men did not make way for Andries, obediently or sullenly, like they had his father, or for that matter, like the dragoons had for Banastre Tarleton at the Halve Maen.

The patroon led her into the barn—hulking and ancient—where the great press was ready to begin turning. There was a horse standing by to do the work later when the men became tired, Anna was glad to see, but it was not hitched to the gate yet. She remembered that it was something of an honor to start the press, reserved for the strongest or the most respected, or sometimes just the handsomest, men on the estate. For many years her father had been all three.

She felt memory threaten to overwhelm her, and she turned away from the sight of the press to watch Andries pop the last of his *olykoecken* into his mouth and wipe his lips on his sleeve. He crumpled the oily paper into his pocket and shrugged off his velvet coat.

"Would you mind holding this?" he asked. He pressed

the silk-lined velvet, still warm from his body, into her hands, and rolled up his shirtsleeves.

"You are going to take a turn at the press?" It was a tenant tradition—a *peasant* tradition—and it was unheard of, as far as she knew, for a patroon to take part.

He smiled warmly now. "Give me a lever and a place to stand, Miss Winters, and I will move the earth."

There were two burly men already waiting at the stile, one running to fat with the massy forearms and jolly red face of a blacksmith, and the other a muscular young man built along more classical lines. They made way for the patroon, but not like underlings. They slapped his back and offered him joking encouragement in Dutch. She noted how Andries called the older man by name—"Oosthuizen"—and he in turn addressed the patroon simply as "Mr. Van Haren."

It was then Anna knew Andries wasn't just going to join these other men in this traditional rite. He was going to *start* the press himself.

He was an exceedingly well-shaped man, but considerably lighter of build than either of the two tenants who had apparently been chosen for the honor, and he was going to have to get the great stone, weighing nearly three-quarters of a ton, moving.

She did not want him to fail.

She ought to find the twins. She ought to talk to them of Archimedes and simple machines and the workings of force, and balance and friction, but her heart was in her throat for the patroon of Harenwyck.

Her father would be turning in his grave.

Andries Van Haren stepped up to the stile and placed his palms on the wood, smooth with age, where her father's hands had once rested. A cheer went up, and the patroon laughed, and she felt as she had when Miss Demarest had taken her to the horse races. Anna had placed no bets that day, but Miss Demarest had. Somehow Anna had found herself caught up in the tension of the race, standing on tiptoe, craning her neck to see the course.

The patroon pushed. The stile did not budge. He pushed again. Nothing. He took a step toward the end of the stile to reposition himself, and Anna should have been explaining the law of the lever, the equation that translated force, distance, and fulcrum into work, but instead she was focused entirely on the man applying it.

Andries pushed. The wood creaked, rocked, and then began to move.

Andries Van Haren threw himself into that backbreaking labor. Through the fine lawn of his shirt she could see his muscles ripple. Through the silk of his stockings she watched his calves flex. The stone turned. A cloud of fruity mist exploded into the air and another, louder cheer went up. The two tenants who had been standing by now took their posts at the stile, and together the three men pushed until momentum lent them a welcome fourth hand.

The musicians struck up, fiddles and flutes soaring with Anna's spirits, and the dancing began in earnest. She watched as Andries and the other men circuited the great stone and the perfume of apples intensified. The fresh cider would be thick and cloudy, cool and refreshing. She could remember her father giving her a taste from his brimming glass when she was a girl. But most of it would go into barrels and ferment and come out in the first weeks of winter dry, clear, and crisp.

Anna's eyes returned to Andries at the stile. She knew on some level that his presence here was a calculated gesture. Indeed, she wondered whether more of this was orchestrated than met the eye. The two men he had joined at the press seemed happy and prosperous—favored tenants? Paid militiamen? But theater or not, the patroon's participation was effective. There was nothing he could do about the shortages at the store or the ravages of the Skinners and Cowboys, but symbolically he could say: *I am here; I am one of you; we are all in this together.* He was as canny a political mover, as skilled a showman as her father had been—and perhaps just as sincere.

But it was not enough, because he would never give them the one thing they truly wanted: land of their own. They had rioted for just the promise of it in '65, staked their lives on slips of paper written by an Indian sachem, and on the rhetoric of Bram Hoppe.

Most of the tenants might *like* this patroon, but the people of Boston had liked the King too. That did not mean they wanted to be ruled by him. Anna could see the eddies in the crowd, the ripples where men were passing beakers of fortified beer—and messages. These were the types of gatherings that men like her father had always used to recruit like-minded followers. In the dark corners of the barn men clustered and talked in low tones. Anna could guess what—or who—they were discussing. Gerrit would be here somewhere tonight, in this throng of thousands, trying to find his two hundred men.

And he would end up just like her father if she did not do something about it.

A cheer went up as the patroon relinquished his place at the stile to another man. There was a mug of beer waiting for Andries, dark and foaming. He drank it off and received the congratulations and back claps of his tenants, who seemed genuinely pleased to have him there. But even as they praised him and offered him doughnuts and skewers of meat, and a swig of something stronger from a jug—his eyes were searching the crowd.

They settled on Anna.

He set his empty tankard on a bench and threaded his way through the crowd to her. She held out his jacket. He slipped into the silk-lined garment and took her by the hands. "Let's dance."

He pulled her into the whirl. She knew how it was done, of course. The Widow had found discreet tutors to teach her all of the things that Anna Winters was supposed to know, including how to dance. She had practiced carriage and rhythm, the steps of formal and country dances, how to follow, and how—if needed—to lead while *appearing* to follow. And of course Anna employed an exceedingly good dancing master at her school, one who often prevailed upon her to join in during classes to make up the numbers.

She had danced with men before, but it had been nothing like this. She had never been so aware of the warmth of the hands that grasped hers or the pressure of a palm at the small of her back as he led her down, down, down the line and around to the end once more. Her heart beat in time with the music and her feet felt light as air even as they met the packed ground over and over, and she did not want it to end.

This was what dancing was for.

It struck her all at once that she had been living vicariously, observing life secondhand, ever since the night she fled Harenwyck. She liked teaching; she took pride in the academy and enjoyed the company of Mrs. Peterson and Miss Demarest, but she had hidden behind the school like a shield. Spinster teachers did not flirt or gossip or dance. Not like this. So many mornings she had stood outside the parlor door listening to the girls breathily recounting their adventures from the night before: the public dances, the private kisses, the letters and love tokens exchanged.

She had consoled herself that theirs were the pleasures of youth, that it was natural that girls should live so vibrantly at sixteen, seventeen, eighteen, and fitting that she should live so quietly, passions subdued and suppressed, at thirty-two.

It did not feel fitting now. Age, it came to her in a flash, was not the difference between Anna and her students. The difference was desire. For too long Anna had been afraid to want anything. Something had changed when she had entered the gates of Harenwyck. Something long dormant had woken in her. She would not lie to herself and pretend that it was only her reunion with

Gerrit. Or that Andries Van Haren's thinly veiled desire did not move her. It did. More than she cared to admit.

The dance ended and the musicians broke to drink their beer and eat their *olykoecken*, and the patroon led Anna out of the barn into the cool night air.

Her hand rested on the velvet sleeve of his jacket. She could feel the warmth of him and inhale the sandalwood scent of his skin. In the light of the bonfire she could see that his eyes were ablaze with the same excitement she felt. He led her past the fire, past the tables where the tenants were eating, drinking, and singing, and into the enclosure where the herbs were grown for the house. It was fenced on all four sides, and there was a trellised arbor at one end with a seat where the maids picked and spun wool on hot days. Andries brushed the bench clean and drew her down to it.

"There is nothing like dancing to stimulate the appetite," he said. His eyes were in shadow, but she could feel the intensity of his gaze like the warmth of a fire. His hands came to rest on her shoulders, traveled up her neck, framed her face, and tilted her head back like a chalice. His mouth covered hers with practiced—and all too effective— artistry. Warm and wet. Gentle and teasing. Heady and rich.

This was nothing like her childhood explorations with Gerrit, clumsy, thrilling, sweet. This was seduction, the skillful application of hands and lips and tongue—and when he lifted her suddenly to straddle him, of adult passions, honestly acknowledged. He ached where she ached, at least bodily, and he knew how to soothe them both. He gathered great handfuls of her skirts.

"I can't," she said. She wanted to, of course, because he knew exactly how to touch her.

"Shush. Let me do this for you. I expect nothing in return."

His hands were beneath her petticoats, drifting up her thighs. She arrested them through the layers of silk. "No."

"With my mouth, then. You'll like that," he promised.

"Oh God." She was certain she would. His nimble fingers had found the thatch of curls between her thighs. It was so tempting to allow this clever, beautiful man to minister to her body, but her soul belonged to his brother, and always would.

"I am sorry," she said, "but I cannot do this."

His knuckles brushed her slickness and she shivered with the pleasure of it. "But you want to," he said. "I can feel it."

There was a fierceness in his voice that was more than lust. She looked into his eyes and her heart broke for him. He was the patroon of Harenwyck, lord of two hundred thousand acres, but he was just like her. He had not wanted anything—not in the ways that mattered—for a very long time, and then it had been a woman forbidden to him by the laws of God and man.

"The girls—" she began, but he forestalled her.

"Are safe with Mrs. Buys. She will take them for the night. If you will not let me make love to you amidst rose petals and mint, we could go back to the house. Alone. The servants will not return until morning."

He had tried to strike a casual tone, as though the answer did not matter greatly to him—as though it would be the same if they stayed another hour and danced and ate *olykoecken* and he took another turn at the stile—but she caught the hopeful tension in his voice that told her it meant more to him than that.

If she had not met Gerrit again on the road to Harenwyck, she would have gone with him. Certainly the Widow would have. Probably Angela Ferrers would have maneuvered him into bed sooner.

I wonder whether I'm meant to seduce you, or you're meant to reform me. Anna did not know what Kate Grey had intended when she compelled her to Harenwyck. Perhaps Kate Grey had not known herself. What Anna knew was that she *liked* Andries, even if she did not wholly embrace his vision for the estate. She liked him enough that she could not bring herself to play the Widow's games. And she did not want to hurt him, this man who had everything and nothing at the same time.

She pushed his hands away, and he made no effort to stop her as she slid from his lap and smoothed her petticoats. "I think I will stay a little while longer, Mr. Van Haren," she said, "and have a pair of *klompen* made. They will make a wonderful souvenir of my adventures in the highlands when I return to New York."

He did nothing to hide his disappointment but bore it manfully and well, and that made her like him even more. He stood up and bowed to her—the patroon of Harenwyck bowing to Bram Hoppe's daughter—and said, "I'll take my leave, then, and have a bath and a glass of brandy in peace for once."

Then he kissed her hand, and she knew that she

would have gone with him, elated from the dance, were she still not in love, after all this time, with his brother.

She watched Andries Van Haren go, threading his way carefully through the crowd with a word for each man he knew. Nothing could set him further apart from his father than what she had just witnessed, nor convince her more that his feud with Gerrit was not entirely about the estate. Neither Van Haren wanted to hold the patroonship in the tyrannical grip that old Cornelis had exercised.

Both brothers wanted reform—and they were both willing to hold the lives of Harenwyck's tenants hostage to gain possession of the whole estate. A fractured patroonship was of no use to the British, or to Kate Grey and the Rebels. Andries was right in some ways. Harenwyck did not need a Robin Hood, but better schools and better roads would not change the injustice on which the estate had been founded. Between them, Gerrit and Andries were going to tear the patroonship apart and lay waste to countless lives in the process.

Only compromise could avert that outcome, because a peaceful division of the land could render the estate far less appetizing to the armies hungrily circling it. The Americans and British each wanted a strong ally, beholden to them, at Harenwyck, authorizing and supporting a military garrison at Harenhoeck. If Gerrit and Andries were to reconcile, were to strike a bargain, *neither* would welcome soldiers onto the estate, and forcing the issue by arms—whether Rebel or government—would not only threaten unrest, but risk the enmity of all the patroons in the valley.

Only Anna was in a position to broker such a bargain. To put the independence of two thousand families ahead of that of a nation—and herself. Because if she brought Andries and Gerrit together to divide the estate, Kate Grey and the Rebels would expose her, and the law would take its course.

To have any chance of success, she must discover proof of her growing suspicions about Sophia Van Haren. If such proof existed—and, knowing young women like Gerrit's late wife from her years of teaching, Anna was almost certain it did—it would be at the old manor house. Mrs. Buys, all unawares, had given Anna a clue. She ought to go there now, while everyone was at the cider pressing, but she did not relish exploring that mournful house with its table of *doed koecks* in the dark. And the dancing *had* given her an appetite, the sort she had thought she would never have again after New York, but she did not hunger for Andries Van Haren. It was his brother she wanted, and always would.

It was easy to find the *klompen* maker. He had set himself up in front of the old brick shed opposite the meat roasters. Anna remembered him from her childhood. He had been old then, and he did not seem very much older now in his blue apron with his long-fingered hands. He sat upon a rough-hewn stool beside his workbench with his feet upon a chopping block, finishing the decoration on a pair of infant's clogs. There was a tub of soaked wood beside him, chunks of maple, birch and ash too short to make good lumber and heaped almost as tall as Anna.

Beneath the bench was a row of finished *klompen* lined up in pairs from largest to smallest.

"Vil je een par klompen, mevrouw?"

She had to bite her tongue to keep herself from responding in the same language. For a moment she felt the presence of her father behind her, urging her forward. He'd brought her to the *klompen* maker for a new pair of shoes every fall and insisted they be painted, even though she would outgrow them in a year.

"I'd like a pair of clogs, please," she said, shaking off the memory and pointing to the smaller pairs at the carpenter's feet.

He shook his head and switched to English. "Those will not fit you."

Anna was fairly certain she could fit into one of the finished sets, but if the *klompen* maker was willing to cut a pair just for her, there was nothing she would rather do than watch. His skills had fascinated her as a child, and she could remember looking on for more than an hour as he shaped the wood like butter, pair after pair.

He chose a block of maple first and contemplated it, turning it this way and that. Then he shook his head and set it aside. He selected a piece of ash next, but this was not to his liking either. The pile was completely rearranged by the time he found the block he was looking for, a pale slab of soaked birch, and set it deliberately on the packed earth in front of him. "There." He pointed to the block. "Stand, please."

Anna took her shoes off and stood upon the block

while the *klompen* maker traced her feet with a pencil. "Sit," he ordered, pointing to the stool he had just vacated.

She sat. He placed her block upon the stump and chopped. His ax moved up and down like a kitchen knife and within minutes he had shaped the block into the rough form of two clogs.

He moved to the bench and took up his drawknife, the handle worn and smooth, the long blade sharp as a razor. In his hands the wood seemed soft as fruit. He peeled each *klomp* like an apple, pale curls of birch falling softly to the ground like dogwood blossoms, until he had two pointed toes and two neat heels. His spoon drill scooped out the insides as fast as one of Mrs. Buys' pumpkins, and in less time than it took Anna to eat her second *olykoeck* he presented her with two shoes, the tops decorated with carved lappets and buckles.

She stepped into the *klompen* and wondered how something newly made could feel so familiar. The insoles were pale and pristine now but gradually they would darken with the print of her heels and toes and become indistinguishable from the last pair her father had bought her. "Thank you," she said. Mr. Ten Broeck had given her a purse for expenses. She fished in it for a coin, but the *klompen* maker shook his head.

"I will not take money from Bram Hoppe's daughter."

For a second she was gripped by fear, but there was no one nearby to hear, and in the quiet the enormity of it hit her. There were still people here who had loved her father.

"I remember you," she said.

The *klompen* maker smiled. "Then that is payment enough. You'll find him in the usual place." He did not have to say who *he* was. And she knew their usual place.

The church had been one of the first structures built at Harenwyck. It was almost as old as the stone arch, but not nearly so old as the blockhouse. The walls were local fieldstone, the windows were picked out in white paint, the shingle roof sloped down and tilted up in a shape as familiar as the back of Anna's hand.

Gerrit was leaning against the stone wall at the back, looking up at the stars, when she came around the corner, and it was difficult to believe that after visiting this place in her dreams for so many years she was finally back. His coffee hair was tied loosely at the nape of his neck, and the tail snaked over his shoulder in a lazy wave. He wore a suit of soft homespun linen the color of molasses. With his hat pulled down he would have been able to pass unseen among the crowd at the cider pressing.

"Did you enjoy *dancing* with my brother?" Apparently he *had* been there.

"Yes," she said honestly. "I have never danced like that, with a real partner. Only dancing masters and students."

"The irony is that I *never* wanted to be patroon—until I saw you dancing with Andries tonight, the tenants bowing and curtsying to you, and all I could think was: that should be me, with you on my arm. And then when I saw him lead you to the arbor, I thought, one well-aimed shot and I will be patroon. He has no heir but me."

"That would have been a far safer path than turning

outlaw and robbing coaches, but you did not take it, because he is your brother, and while he might be wrong about a good many things, he is not a bad man."

"Andries *is* better suited to be patroon of Harenwyck than I am. The issue is that there shouldn't be a patroon at all."

"I take it you were recruiting," she said, crossing the churchyard in her sturdy new *klompen*. "How many men agreed to join you?"

"Sixty."

"That is not enough. John André wants two hundred," said Anna. "And every time you beat the drum at an event like this you run the risk that some coward will betray you to your brother for a purse of gold." There had been spies and informers at the Halve Maen the night her father was taken. And she was not the only one at the cider pressing with eyes and ears.

"I will not have to beat the drum again. Once word gets out of what I offer, I will have my two hundred men. More probably."

Fear threaded through her. "Gerrit, please don't tell me you are offering them Wappinger leases."

"No. Not new landlords with newer, fairer leases," he said. "Your father tried that. You were right. He was blind in some ways. No court will ever find in favor of Indian land claims, because the precedent could unravel the fabric of a whole nation. Whose farm was not once the domain of one tribe or another? But my claim jeopardizes no one's wealth but my brother's. I am the patroon of Harenwyck, Annatje. Andries has stolen the estate from me with lies and bribed witnesses. The Rebel courts accepted his calumnies because it suited them to do so, because it would suit them to control Harenwyck through him. But the outcome, in a *British* court, is bound to be in my favor. If I win British sponsorship, I can offer those who join me something far more than fair leases. As the real patroon of Harenwyck, I am free to dispose of my land exactly as I wish. Sell it, or give it away."

"You will pay them in freeholds," she said. It was brilliant. It was her father's legacy come to life. It was a dream she had shared with hundreds, indeed with thousands up and down the Hudson. And it was going to get Gerrit killed.

He pushed himself away from the wall and prowled toward her, his coattails brushing the headstones, and it was as though time had collapsed. She was seventeen again, and he was everything she wanted. "Annatje, I did not come here to talk about freeholds."

She moved at the same time. He met her among the graves, and she came into his arms as though years had not passed between this meeting and their last.

His body was warm, a sharp contrast to the night air, and his mouth tasted like fresh apples, and she did not think she could ever drink in enough of this new Gerrit, familiar and changed. A body she knew and had loved and had wanted to know better. She had desired him so very much—with a hunger that kept her up at night when they were young—but always he had stopped just short of that ultimate joining with her. They melted into each other now, hip to hip, thigh to thigh, as they used to do, and just like then—just like *always*—he broke away and stepped back.

"I like your new shoes," he said, running his hands over her face like he still could not believe she was real. "I liked your old ones too. They were sunny yellow. I did not believe that you were dead when I came home from Leiden, but they showed me your clogs and told me . . . they told me that you had drowned yourself in the river."

"That was the Widow's idea."

"It was a good one. *Annatje, Annatje,*" he said her name over and over like he was conjuring her. "Tell me what happened after I left."

She remembered all the things he liked. She kissed his neck softly, and heard his sharp intake of breath. She had always known how to bring him close, so close to losing control. She nipped his ear, and he groaned. Her fingers slid down his hard chest to the top of his breeches, and his hands met hers there and stopped them.

"Annatje, you must tell me what happened, how you escaped and came to be here, or else I will think I am making love to a ghost."

She could feel the tension in every muscle of his body. He was trembling with it. He wanted her as badly as she wanted him, as badly as they had wanted each other when they were seventeen. If she seduced him now, overcame his reservations, he would receive her story differently.

Lovemaking is a tool. And a tool can be a weapon. The Widow would have advised her to draw Gerrit Van Haren's warm, strong body down into the grass between the graves. Afterward she could tell him about the things she had done. The bond formed between them, the tenderness of two vulnerable bodies meeting flesh to flesh, would elicit his sympathy, trigger his natural protectiveness.

She would not manipulate him like that.

And silence was not an option. He was following too closely in Bram Hoppe's footsteps, and he needed to know precisely where they led.

Fifteen

Harenwyck, 1765

There was going to be rough music that night. Annatje's father called it an expression of the will of the people. Her mother would have called it mob justice. But then Mehitable Wing had run off with a Huguenot tin peddler from New Paltz, and there was no one to gainsay Bram Hoppe now.

Annatje was happy that she was gone. Her mother had always been whipsawed between the Quaker rigidness of her upbringing and the radical ideals of her husband, whose leveler philosophy took the seductive revelations of George Fox to their natural conclusions. Annatje's mother said she had been following her inner light when she married the "unconvinced" Bram Hoppe, but the Society of Friends had not seen it that way. They had promptly cast her out.

That spurning had left its mark upon Annatje's mother. Mehitable had been raised in a sect of nonconformists whose bulwark against the outside world had been their profound sense of community. She felt its lack like a missing tooth, and she was forever tonguing and prodding it. She clung to her Quaker love of simplicity, and Bram Hoppe's dazzling oratory, the way men flocked to hear him, was anything but plain.

Annatje wished her mother had left *a year ago*, rather than six months, and never found out about her meetings with Gerrit. It was no comfort to Annatje that her mother had beaten her for her imagined sin of fornication and then become a fornicator herself. Gerrit was still gone, and Annatje was left with no one but her father. They had always been close, she and her father, but in the wake of Gerrit's departure for Holland, and her mother's shameful flight, Annatje's love turned into fierce devotion.

She took up the housework abandoned by Mehitable, and the hopeless household accounts. Not that they were difficult to balance. Everything the Hoppes earned when they sold their crop to the patroon, less his tithe for grinding their corn at the mill and his percent for taking it to market, was spent. Between food and fuel and seed, all of which, according to the terms of their lease, must be bought from Cornelis Van Haren, and the rent they paid him, there was never anything left to save toward improvements, let alone land of their own.

The system was designed to keep them tied to their leasehold forever, cogs in the patroon's wealth machine, and Annatje had never felt its injustice more keenly than the Sunday morning when Gerrit had failed to appear in church. Afterward she overheard the patroon informing the minister that he had sent "the boy" to Leiden for university, and he would not be back for years.

There was an ocean between them, one whose breadth she had traced with her finger in the pages of the atlas. The same ocean Henry Hudson had crossed in the *Halve Maen*. But Gerrit would see the world she had only experienced on paper, and she was bound to Harenwyck by the terms of a lease signed by Willem Hoppe, her great-great-great-grandfather, a long-dead Dutchman who had crossed that same ocean.

Unless her father prevailed.

The Widow visited twice after Annatje's mother left. She came on her own the first time and drank whiskey, neat, with Bram. She was dressed like a good Dutch *mevrouw* in clogs and a broad-brimmed hat and a threadbare apron, and Annatje could not have told her from the farmwife next door tending her cabbages. Except that Annatje could sometimes feel the Widow's sharp eyes on her as she moved about the kitchen. Something about that gaze—about the quality of her attention—reminded Annatje of the falcon Gerrit had shown her last winter, or more familiarly, of a cat sizing up its prey.

When her father got up to go outside the Widow said, "You do not have a country accent, I notice."

She had lost it speaking to Gerrit, but she could hardly say that. "My father is very well-spoken," she said.

"But not well tutored. Not in the accents of Amsterdam, anyway. He sounds like what he is. An intelligent, self-educated Dutch farmer, born and bred here in the valley. *You* sound like something else."

"I'm just Annatje," she said.

"More than that, I think. You know how to keep your counsel. I could make use of you, *just Annatje*, if you were willing to leave Harenwyck."

"I can't leave. My father needs me." There was no one else. And, of course, Gerrit would be coming back.

"At the moment, yes," said the Widow, "but it is impossible to say what the future holds. If you change your mind, you will be able to find me, or someone who can reach me, at my house in New York. It's on Pearl Street. Green clapboard, white door. You will always find it open to you."

The Widow said nothing of their exchange when Bram Hoppe returned.

The next time Angela Ferrers came she brought a lawyer with her. Mr. Lindsey was young, ambitious, and eager to make a name for himself in New York politics. He had studied law at King's College and argued a recent case—successfully—against the Crown. The Widow did not return herself after that, but the lawyer became a regular guest in their home, working late into the night with Bram Hoppe and leaving in the wee hours of the morning with a case of documents under his arm.

Annatje's mother had never liked it when Bram gathered a "committee" of tenants and led them on a "visit." His mob would call on neighbors who refused to stand firm against the patroon on the price of corn, or worse, new tenants who dared to take up leases after old, progress-minded ones had been evicted. Bram Hoppe would call the coward out of his house—or drag him, if need be—and the assembly would try him for his crimes. They were always found guilty, of course, and the committee would haul the miscreant out to a tree and fix a rope around his neck to symbolize their verdict. Sometimes they even hanged him a little. Just until he thought it might be real. Then they would drop the man to the ground and let him run a gauntlet of his outraged neighbors homeward.

Mehitable judged that to be violence—though Bram maintained that it was largely the shamming of violence—and she refused to attend, but she used to go and listen to him talk at the Halve Maen. Now Annatje took her place.

That night her father sat in the center of a circle of pulled-up chairs, his friend from when he had campaigned in the last war against the French, Sachem Daniel Ninham, at his side. They talked about the "dignity of man" and "natural rights," about land stolen and honest men: Wappinger men—of Sachem Daniel's tribe—who farmed and had families just like they did, and had been swindled.

As *they* were being swindled.

It was also a kind of music, this talking. Not rough, but smooth: her father in his beautiful tenor, and the sachem in his bass tones.

They talked, and they wrote out leases. Every farmer who stepped forward and recognized the legitimacy of the sachem's claim to the land that made up Harenwyck received a hundred-year lease for the grand total of one dollar. Angela Ferrers' lawyer was there to witness the documents, and he was going to stand up in court for the sachem and Annatje's father and argue that the patroon had no right to his land. When all the leases were signed they would make a list of those tenants who had not accepted them, and then the rough music would begin in earnest.

Everyone at the gathering could see that Mr. Lindsey was no country lawyer. He wore silk stockings and silver buckles on his shoes and spoke the good Dutch that Gerrit had tried to teach Annatje. He was going to be heard in the court at Albany, and he could not be ignored because he was not an ignorant tenant. He was the son of a prominent New York merchant with friends in high places. The Hudson patroons had always been able to get their way in the New York courts because they not only had money and power, but acted in concert and toward interests that did not conflict with those of other powerful men. It was an easy thing to deny justice to a poor tenant farmer, a much trickier matter to cross the son of one of New York's most influential families.

That was why the *schouts* came the next night, tall, strapping Vim Dijkstra and a dozen well-armed bailiffs, because the patroon knew he must not let these men bring him to court. Not in a case that would attract public scrutiny, that could not be dealt with quietly, out of the sight of the English government in New York. The *schouts* broke down the doors to the Halve Maen, which were closed for a private meeting: just Annatje's father, the lawyer, the sachem, three of their most trusted allies among the tenants, and Annatje.

They dragged Bram Hoppe in his best suit of clothes out of the taproom. Annatje chased after them but the *schouts* were deaf to her cries. They took the lawyer too, when he demanded to see their warrants. For that, they gut punched him, in plain sight of onlookers, on the threshold of the Halve Maen. He doubled over wheezing and then they dragged him—unprotesting now—down the stairs, and flung him into the mud that pooled there.

They shackled Bram Hoppe in the same irons that the castle sold for use with slaves, and chained him to the bed of a cart. The vehicle had last held chickens. Annatje could smell the pungent odor of their droppings.

It was done with such speed and violence that the cart was already being struck up by the time the Halve Maen's landlord and his family heard the disturbance and emerged from the kitchens. They stood at the top of the stairs, under the sign painted with Henry Hudson's *vlieboot*, screaming in outrage. Annatje was only a few steps ahead of them. She half ran, half fell down the stairs to reach her father.

"Get word to the Widow," he said, his shackled hands clutching hers. The cart began to move. "Tell her everything that has happened."

"How?" Annatje was running at the back of the cart to stay with him. All she knew about the Widow was that she had a house on Pearl Street in New York.

"Remember what I bought for her," he said, remaining obscure in case the bailiffs overheard. "Go home, Annatje. You're a clever girl. You'll figure it out."

"I don't understand," she pleaded, feeling salty tears start in her eyes.

But that was all they had time for. The cart picked up speed and broke their connection. Annatje pounded after it, but could not run fast enough. The cart dwindled into the night taking her father away with it.

It was the last she ever saw of him.

She walked back to the Halve Maen in a daze.

The sachem was waiting there for her, resignation in his dark eyes. "They will not release him," he said with the fatalism of a man who knew something of English courts and English law.

"Why do you say that?"

"Because they did not fear the lawyer."

"My father has a friend in New York. She will help. I must go home and figure out how to reach her."

"Has your mother come back?" asked the sachem.

Mehitable wasn't coming back. Bram had put it about that she was visiting her family in Pennsylvania, but Annatje did not think anyone believed it. Perhaps Daniel Ninham only thought it right to ask.

"No."

"Then you cannot stay at Harenwyck, Annatje. Not alone. Come home with me to Stockbridge. We have a lawyer there who may be able to help."

"We already have a lawyer," said Annatje. And he had silver buckles on his shoes. But Mr. Lindsey was no longer lying in the mud. In fact, he was nowhere to be seen at all.

Mr. Ninham shook his head. "They will arrest him too if he challenges them. That is what the English do when they become too frightened to respect their own laws. Too frightened of what their own law might require."

"My father told me to go home." It was printed in her memory like the plates from one of Gerrit's books. Get word to the Widow. Go home. Remember what he bought for her. *Figure it out.*

She went home. It had rained the night before and the mud sucked at her *klompen*. The sachem followed her all the way there, shook his head at the sad little brick cottage with the fragile batten door and poor old shutters, bolt and latches long since broken. But there had been no point in repairing them, or getting a proper lock for the door, because there had never been anything inside worth stealing.

Daniel Ninham made up the fire and went to the shed for a hammer and nails and found lumber somewhere in the kitchen garden. Annatje watched him nail the shutters closed and reset the flimsy bolt on the door. He did these things with the familiarity of a man who knew her house well, because he had been there many times, and she had the terrible presentiment that he believed this would be his last visit.

"You should come with me, Annatje. There is nothing for you here."

"My father said to go home."

"Men are not always wise in a crisis."

"You don't think he will be back, do you?" she asked, the words catching in her throat.

"I think I would want my daughter to leave and save herself. I think my friend would want me to save his daughter in spite of her stubbornness. I think that if you stay here, I will lose you both."

If she cried, if she showed him how frightened she was, he would make her go. She knew that. So she fought back the lump rising in her throat and said, "I'll be fine, Mr. Ninham. And I promise you that I will get my father back."

The sachem sighed. "You take too much after your father. I only hope, for your sake, that you take a little after your mother, and that you'll have the sense to run before it's too late."

He did not try to make her go. He found her father's pistol in the chest at the foot of the bed, carefully filled it with his own powder and shot, and placed it on the kitchen table. She was grateful for that. Gerrit was gone. Her mother had abandoned her. Her father had been taken from her. She had to get him back. She had to get word to the Widow.

The riots began the following afternoon. Annatje did not learn this until later. All day she searched the house for some clue as to how she was supposed to contact the Widow. There were precious few cupboards. They had never been wealthy enough to own a *kas*. But there were shelves surrounding the open hearth, and she searched these for a scrap of paper or notebook or token of some kind. Annatje emptied the salt box and unwrapped the sugar cone. She turned the mattresses over, picked open the stitching, and emptied the straw filling onto the floor and found nothing. She checked every loose brick in the walls and turned her arms black with soot exploring the jambless chimney.

With Gerrit she had always felt so clever. She did not feel so clever now, standing in the wreckage of the home she had kept so faithfully for the past six months, with her father gone and no idea how to do as he had asked.

It had taken her the morning to dismantle the cottage. She had taken everything in the house apart in a panicked frenzy. It took her the whole afternoon to put it back together, and her sleepless night began to tell on her long before she was done. She felt as though she were floating, every movement dreamlike and slow. She wished she *were* dreaming, that she could lay her head down on her pillow and wake up to find her father home.

Evening fell and she had only the shelves left to restore to order. She had moved their contents to the table to examine every box, every bottle, every paper package. Now she was putting everything back in place. The sugar, the sugar tongs, the box of tallow-dipped rushes, the chipped earthenware plates, the Widow's bottle of whiskey.

It came to her in a flash of insight. Her father had bought the backwoods whiskey for Angela Ferrers because he knew she liked it. There was only one place on the patroonship to get home-brewed whiskey, only one place that the Widow could have acquired a taste for the local mash and distillation: from Mevrouw Zabriskie, who brewed gin and other ardent spirits at her cottage in the woods.

Annatje needed to write her letter and deliver it now. Her father had already spent one night and one day in jail. Without money or friends he might be held in the sort of conditions that would eventually make a trial unnecessary. And now she could not find the paper or remember where she had put it after her wild search of the house. She found the ink, homemade stuff that streaked and ran, but it would have to do. The paper turned out to be on the shelves. She wrote as quickly as she could, then folded and tied the letter closed with string. They had no wax candles, only rush lights.

She put on her cloak and her *klompen* and took up the pistol that the sachem had loaded for her, because nothing must stop her from delivering the letter tucked flat inside her stays. She was ready to go, on the brink of departure, when she heard the horses approach.

It was Vim Dijkstra and another *schout*, one of those who had taken her father. Annatje watched them through the cracks in the shutters as they dismounted and approached the door. Dijkstra rapped sharply on the warped boards and shouted, "Annatjc Hoppe! Come out!" A big, hectoring voice for a big, bullying man.

She froze, afraid to move a muscle lest they hear her. She willed them to go away.

"Go check the barn." Dijkstra's voice. He was circling the cottage, searching for some sign of occupancy. Annatje could hear him pass by each window through the weathered shutters. She heard his heavy boots crunch into the pebbles outside the door, and then it burst open without warning beneath the impact of his shoulder. The sorry old repaired bolt snapped off and clattered to the ground, and Vim Dijkstra filled the doorway.

There was hardly any light in the cottage, but the moon outlined his tall, heavy silhouette. "Come out!" he barked again.

Annatje did not move. "You cannot arrest me. I've done nothing," she said.

"You're not arrested. You are evicted. But if you don't come now, then I *will* arrest you."

"Come where?"

"The patroon has ordered me to load you on the ferry. We don't want to see you again on Harenwyck. Now, you can ride with me, girl, or I can drag you behind my horse the whole way."

"No, thank you. I can find my own way off the estate." And she could not leave until she had delivered her letter into the hands of the Widow's contact. Her father was relying on her. She was all he had. He was all *she* had.

"*No, thank you,*" he mocked, flutingly. "Always putting on airs, thinking you're better than the other tenants just because the patroon's boy diddles you silly behind the church."

He reached for her, and Annatje dodged and tried to get around him to the door. His big fist shot out, connecting with her stomach with terrible force. Pain exploded inside her. All the air rushed out of her lungs. She crumpled to the floor, unable to scream, unable even to breathe.

"Looks like you need taking down a peg or two," sighed Vim Dijkstra, "just like your bastard father." He kicked her, and she curled into a ball, and he kicked her again.

"The patroon said it would be a fine thing all around if his boy Gerrit didn't have your pretty face to moon over when he comes home."

Dijkstra plucked a dull knife off the rack on the wall. "Thing is, he might run off in search of it, knowing that one. So, as I see it, I wouldn't really be doing my job if I let you leave here with *both* those pretty gray eyes."

She could still barely breathe. Her father's pistol, loaded and primed, remained tucked inside her jacket. Vim Dijkstra crouched beside her. The knife rose in the moonlight. He tangled a fist in her hair, wrenched her face violently to one side, and touched the cold nicked blade to her scalp.

She clutched the pistol in her numb hands and aimed, as best she could, dead center at the shadow looming over her . . . and fired.

The report was loud in her ears, but muffled by Dijkstra's bulk. His body jerked grotesquely, then collapsed atop her, and she struggled to get out from under it. Wet warmth slicked her hands. Blood. The gory hole in his back told her plainly that he was dead. The shout from the barn told her plainly that she must go, and go now.

She had killed a man.

She bolted out the door.

A dark shape on the path was hurtling toward her. She darted around the corner of the house and ran for the road. A few seconds later she heard Dijkstra's companion shouting, "*Moord!*" Murder.

From the road she heard other riders approaching. Their shouts soon joined his like the homing cries of birds, and a dozen mounted men converged on the house.

Annatje fled into the forest. She could not deliver her father's message to the Widow's associate now. The house and the *schouts* were between her, and her objective, and the only direction she could run . . . was away.

There was just one option now. She must reach the Widow herself at her house on Pearl Street in New York.

Numb, cold, all sounds distant and muffled to her ears, Annatje stumbled through the forest all night, her second without sleep. She could not manage a third. At dawn she collapsed in the shadow of a stone wall that marked the edge of some forgotten leasehold. When she woke it was nearly evening again—she had slept away the whole day— and a woman was standing over her. The *mevrouw* wore a red kerchief on her head and a flour sack apron, and she said, "The *schouts* are out searching for you."

She was the wife of one of the rioters. Her husband had been taken too. She told Annatje what had happened during the day and the night that she had been frantically searching her cottage for some link to the Widow.

Word had spread of Bram Hoppe's arrest and there had been a full-scale uprising. A thousand tenants, men and women, had marched on the patroon's house and demanded his release. It had not been like the peaceful delegation her father had led, and Annatje had marched with, the previous year. This had been an angry mob— some armed, some bearing torches—and they had threatened to burn the patroon out.

The *schouts* proved more organized, and ruthless, than the leaderless tenants. The patroon's men had dispersed the mob, driven them back into the woods or to their homes; and now the army was on the estate, rounding up the rioters and evicting people from their leaseholds. The *mevrouw* in the red kerchief gave her a loaf of bread and a purse full of pennies.

"The *schouts* will not wait for the law. They mean to hang you for killing Vim Dijkstra, and you can be sure they have the patroon's blessing to do it. Keep off the roads, girl. Go across the country. Travel only at night. And run as far and as fast as you can."

Annatje did. She walked for days. South and farther south, stopping to wash and drink from little brooks and streams because they would be looking for her near the river. She navigated by the stars Gerrit had taught her, and when the bread ran out she ate wild grapes because she must save her coins for the ferry.

There would be soldiers at the landing. She knew that. And they might be on the lookout for a fugitive Dutch girl. She had left home wearing two petticoats. She untied the worn one on top and climbed the wall of an orchard in the dead of night to gather a bushel of dropped apples. When she paid her fare and boarded the ferry, she wore a smile she did not feel and carried a sack over her shoulder, and so became a farm girl intent on selling fruit for some extra coin in the city.

When she knocked upon the Widow's door on Pearl Street, she had not eaten anything *but* fruit in three days. The woman who answered was not the Widow, but she was about the same age as that lady, something indeterminate between thirty and forty. She was tall and rail thin, with bony hands.

She did not want to let Annatje in.

"The Widow," Annatje began, using the only name she was sure her father's ally answered to, "said that her door would always be open to me. I must get her a message. Urgently."

"She has not been here for two years," said the woman, in an incongruously small, high-pitched voice. "I have no idea when she will be back again. Maybe never." She said this last with a tight smile that made it plain she resented the anxiety and uncertainty of keeping house for a woman who did not regularly reside there.

"But you *can* get her a message," insisted Annatje.

"I can, but there's no telling how long it will be before she replies—if she wishes, or is able, to reply at all."

"I'll wait." And she stepped across the threshold of the open door.

The woman's name was Mrs. Duvel, and she grudgingly served Annatje a meal of stale bread that was clearly meant for crumbs. When Annatje expressed a desire to sleep she led her up a back staircase to a third-floor chamber with nothing but a straw pallet on the floor. Annatje knew it was a slight, but she did not care. She had not slept indoors for a week, perhaps more. She no longer knew what day she had left Harenwyck.

When Annatje stepped past Mrs. Duvel into the pool of light from the landing window the housekeeper stopped her. She gripped her chin with a gnarled hand and turned her face this way and that, examining it like a cracked egg.

"Not this room after all, I think," she said, turning around and beckoning Annatje to follow her back down the stairs.

The first room had been at the front of the house, on the third floor, facing the street, with all the attendant dirt and noise that entailed. This new room was on the second floor, at the back and much quieter. It held a hired man's bed and the ghost of some musky perfume. There was no other furniture in the room.

Annatje did not know why Mrs. Duvel changed her mind, and she did not much care. She wanted to crawl into the bed in her travel-worn clothes and sleep for days, but Mrs. Duvel insisted she bathe and change. She brought her water and a chemise and stood by while Annatje washed the dirt of the road from her skin and hair. Then Mrs. Duvel took away her dirty clothes and battered clogs to clean them.

Annatje slept. She woke several times that afternoon, despite her exhaustion, shaken from sleep by the clap of the front door slamming closed or the crack of the back door swinging shut. They were distinctive sounds, and they marked the housekeeper's comings and goings. Annatje wondered if she bothered to close doors more softly when her employer, the Widow, was in residence.

It was evening before she woke fully. Mrs. Duvel had not returned with her clothes. The air in the room had grown stale. Annatje attempted to open one of the windows, but they were all stuck. She tried the door and found it locked.

It might be a sensible precaution for a woman who lived alone and found herself saddled with an unwanted visitor— if that visitor had been a man or a physically imposing woman, but Annatje was neither. Dread crept upon her in stages. The Widow had told her to come here, but that had been months ago, and according to Mrs. Duvel, Angela Ferrers had not been here for two years.

It was morning by the time a key turned in the lock, and Mrs. Duvel appeared. She had a man with her. He was dressed something like Mr. Lindsey, the lawyer, in a suit of finely woven wool: not the kind you loomed at home but the sort you bought at the castle, dyed a deep dark blue. The buckles on his shoes were pinchbeck, and he wore fine silk stockings and a gold ring. His hair was the color of old straw and tucked up under a wig that even Annatje recognized as very old-fashioned and out-of-date.

He looked Annatje up and down the way the estate manager looked at cattle. He pursed his lips and announced, "A guinea. No more, though," and Mrs. Duvel asked him to wait in the hall. She closed the door behind her and spoke in her high-pitched voice.

"My employer does not even pay me enough to keep up this house and manage all of her affairs here, let alone to feed an extra mouth."

Annatje stood up. "I did not mean to impose," she said stiffly. "If you will give me my clothing back, I shall leave."

"And go *where*? You are the Dutch girl the bailiffs from the valley are searching for, aren't you?"

Annatje said nothing and Mrs. Duvel smiled her thin-lipped smile. "You owe me for your meal and the shift, girl, for the use of this room, and for my silence."

"The Widow will pay you anything I owe."

"*The Widow* isn't coming back. Most likely she is dead. You can continue to take advantage of my kindness and do as I say by way of recompense, or I will fetch the law and let them know that there is a murderess sheltering under my roof."

Mrs. Duvel left. The man in the old-fashioned wig entered once more.

She lay in the sagging bed on the stale linen and stared up at the ceiling while a stranger handled her the way she had handled sheep when they needed shearing: as a dumb beast. With Gerrit her body had been warmth and light, a source of astonishing joy. With the straw-haired man she was cold. She was meat. There was the dry cold of his fingers pinching her nipples and the wet cold of him striving between her legs, sharp at first and painful and then just a coarse, sandpapery sawing at her soul, to the grating sound of the bed ropes creaking.

Her body was not her own in that room. That is how she thought of it, how she had to think of it, when she could think of it at all. She had sold her body in exchange for some stale bread and a shift and the fragile hope that Mrs. Duvel would not call the bailiffs down on her for another day. That by staying alive, by *enduring*, the time would come—the Widow might return or some other chance might arise—when she might save her father.

On the days when Mrs. Duvel could not find a customer,

she did not feed Annatje or bring her water. Annatje had thought it would get easier, but each man was worse than the last: more humiliating, more dehumanizing.

After a week, Annatje decided that she would prefer to take her chance with the *schouts*, find some other way to contact the Widow—if she was still alive—and rescue her father. But she discovered that the windows were not just stuck, they were nailed shut, and Mrs. Duvel kept the door locked. When Annatje declared that she would not service another man and bade her call for the bailiffs if she must, the housekeeper simply locked the door and left Annatje alone, with no food or water, for three days.

On the fourth day the Widow returned.

Annatje heard the front door open below and close with a soft swish quite uncharacteristic of Mrs. Duvel's loud comings and goings. She pressed her ear to the floorboards. There was fast movement below, Mrs. Duvel rushing up from the kitchen to meet some visitor, and then voices: the Widow, measured, neutral, inquisitive. Mrs. Duvel: high, fast, nervously self-justifying.

Annatje listened as feet climbed the stair. Soft steps in light shoes. She had experienced the world outside her room almost entirely through sound for the past week, learning to judge who approached her by the weight of their tread on the stairs, sometimes by the sound of their breath in the hall.

The key turned in the lock. Annatje jumped up from her listening place on the floor. The Widow entered, though for a moment Annatje did not recognize her. She was not the Dutch *mevrouw* of the cabbage fields that

Annatje had known at Harenwyck. This was an English beauty in Spitalfields silk with fly fringe robings. Her hair was powdered to match the oyster hue of her gown, and she wore a citrine on a ribbon around her neck that was big enough to choke a pigeon. The pale glittering effect of the ensemble lit the shabby room and made her look an angel.

When she saw Annatje, barefoot in her dirty shift with her unwashed hair, her handsome face became very cold for a moment, then the expression was gone, replaced by a polite mask. Annatje wished she had the trick of that. She feared everything she had lived in the past two weeks was writ plain on her face, including the naked desire, swiftly checked, to throw herself into this woman's immaculate arms and sob.

"I am sorry I could not come sooner," said the Widow. "Word of your father's circumstances reached me when I was no little distance away, and it took me longer than I would have liked to reach Harenwyck. By that time your father was already in Albany, and so I was obligated to travel there before I could come here."

She closed the door, softly, behind her. "I am glad you found me, Annatje, but before all else, I must know *exactly* what has been taking place in this house during my absence."

Annatje did not have the vocabulary to describe everything that had happened, but the Widow supplied the words where hers were lacking, and allowed certain silences to speak for themselves.

"Wait here for a space," said the Widow. "The door

will not be locked, but I think you might prefer to remain inside the room until I return."

The Widow swept out of the chamber in a cloud of silk and gardenias. She left the door slightly ajar, and it took all of Annatje's will not to bolt from the hated room, down the stairs, and out into the street.

Instead, she listened to the Widow make her way to the parlor below and ring the bell, and then to Mrs. Duvel's heels snapping upon the floor. The Widow's voice this time was clipped. From the rising and falling of her tone, it was apparent that she asked three questions. Annatje could not make them out. Mrs. Duvel's replies were equally indistinct, but heightened in pitch and intensity—until her words were quite suddenly cut short by the almost musical sound of something breaking, a teacup or some other delicate, resonant object, followed by the soft thump of a heavier object against carpet.

Then there was silence.

Annatje backed away from the door and sat upon the unmade bed. She tried to shut out the sounds that followed and their import. If Angela Ferrers was an angel, today she was the kind with a fiery sword.

The Widow returned a quarter of an hour later and bade Annatje follow her into a room that, though only across the hall, felt as though it belonged to a different house. Painted roses papered the walls. Striped carpets lined the floors. The carved bed was covered in dimity drapes, and there were softly gathered shades filtering the light through the windows.

"There are clothes in the cupboards," said the Widow.

"There is water in the basin. You will find soap and tooth powder and most necessities in the drawers. Everything should be serviceable, if suffering from a lack of proper housekeeping. When you feel refreshed, please join me downstairs."

Annatje washed and dressed. The soap was scented with gardenias, the Widow's signature, and Annatje guessed this room was hers. The clothes in the cupboards ranged from Quaker simplicity to damask ostentation. Annatje chose a gown that wrapped around the body and closed with a tie because its shape did not demand stays and her ribs were still bruised from Vim Dijkstra's "lesson."

When she looked at her face in the glass it appeared unmarked—yet completely changed. Hunger had stripped the youthful fat from her cheeks and sharpened her chin. A week on the road had bleached her hair from mouse brown to honey gold. And her eyes would never be the same. They *knew*.

She looked, in fact, a different woman.

She descended the stairs to find the Widow in the back parlor, an elegant room Annatje had only glimpsed on her way in. She was boiling water in a copper kettle over the fire. Everything, including the kettle, appeared very fine but blurred by a layer of grease and dust. The only dust-free surface in the room was the mantel. There was a gilded set of four porcelain vases sitting atop it, rearranged to disguise the fact that a fifth had very recently gone missing. Nothing could hide the ring left behind by the absent vessel. The paint around it had changed color in the sun.

"Where is Mrs. Duvel?" asked Annatje.

"Mrs. Duvel is no longer in my employ," said Angela Ferrers, lifting the brass kettle off its hob.

"I did not hear her go out." The sounds of the doors were distinctive. She knew them well. Mrs. Duvel had not left the house.

"And you will not see her again," said the Widow.

She had thought she had crossed a threshold in the room above, entered the adult world irrevocably, but that had been merely an alteration to the body—a violation, yes, but ultimately, as meaningless as cutting her hair or clipping her fingernails. She had *killed* a man at Harenwyck, but that had been self-defense.

This was something different.

"Mrs. Duvel failed me," said the Widow. "She should have sent word to me immediately when you arrived, but she kept your presence here secret, for her own purposes, her own gain. I cannot forgive that, even if I blame myself. I placed trust in her because she proved, on several occasions, to have few qualms and strong nerves. But her judgment in this matter was sorely lacking."

"If Mrs. Duvel did not send word, how did you know that I was here?" asked Annatje.

"I didn't. I received news of your father's arrest from a friend at Harenwyck."

Annatje guessed who that friend might be, but she said nothing.

"It was only once I reached the estate that I learned what happened with the *schout*. Do you know, the patroon had his whole militia out hunting you, and the army too?

I had not thought it likely that you would evade them and survive the journey, but I hoped that you might, so I came here."

The Widow lifted the copper kettle off the fire and poured water into a dish of yellow flowers and black kernels. Anna recognized the contents: tansy and moonseed. Mevrouw Zabriskie brewed something like it for the maids at the manor. It didn't always work, and the effects weren't pleasant, but it had been more than one girl's salvation.

"Is that really necessary?" asked Annatje.

"The choice is entirely yours," said the Widow. "And it is not without risks, but the risks of childbirth are greater. Only you can decide how to weigh the odds that you have fallen pregnant this past week against the unpleasantness contained in that cup."

"My luck has not been very good of late," said Annatje, and she drank the sour brew down in one go.

"You are a very resourceful young woman, Annatje." The Widow spooned ordinary black tea now, rich and soothing, into a pot. "You have the intelligence and will to become anything you want. You have survived ordeals that would break most others. Now the question before us is what you would like to do next."

"I want to help my father."

The Widow paused with the teapot in her hand. "Ah. Forgive me, but I thought you knew. That Mrs. Duvel might have . . . Annatje, your father is dead."

It couldn't be. Only two weeks had passed. It could not be more. "But there has been no time for a trial."

"There was no trial. They say Bram Hoppe died in jail. He may have died on the very night of his arrest—in any case, I rather doubt he actually reached the jail alive. The patroon could not risk it. They had already buried him by the time I reached Albany. The official cause was a fever, and they tried to keep it quiet as long as possible—to avoid sparking further riots—but they could not keep his death secret for long."

Annatje wanted to deny the facts being placed before her, or, failing that, press for details, ask a hundred questions, but she was unable to speak.

"I am sorry, Annatje. I underestimated Cornelis Van Haren. He has put down the rioters with such brutality, so many arrests and beatings, that Harenwyck and the other manors are unlikely to rise again in this generation. Not unless another Bram Hoppe emerges to lead them, and I do not think we will see your father's like again soon. I may not be here when the opportunity next arises to finish his work, his revolution, but *you* could be."

"No," said Annatje flatly. Her father was gone. She would never see Gerrit again. There was nothing for her any longer in the place she'd called home. Nothing but memories. "I am done with the manors. Done with Harenwyck. And I want no part in your intrigues."

"Very well." The Widow did not try to change her mind. "I will do everything in my power to help you build a new life, whether that means clinging to the familiar, or striking out in a new direction. First, though, we must make sure that no one goes looking for Annatje." She nodded toward a neatly folded pile of clothing sitting on a chair against the wall. Her clogs rested atop it. The ones her father had bought for her just that year. They were as fine as the ones made for weddings, had been much admired at the last cider pressing, their tops carved with snowflakes and stars, their heels adorned with her initials: *AH*. Annatje Hoppe.

"Harenwyck," continued the Widow, "is extraordinary in some ways, but quite ordinary in others. Almost all rural communities have a place that becomes a focal point for despair. Where the failing farmer goes to fling himself from a great height, or the girl with a swollen belly and no husband goes to drown herself and her babe. Where a runaway Dutch girl—father in jail and *schouts* on her trail—might go to end her misery."

"I would never do such a thing. *Dum spiro spero.*" Gerrit had taught her that. It was Latin. She had always wanted to learn more. "While I breathe, I hope."

The Widow smiled, pleased. "*You* would not, but many—a great many—would. The patroonships are more prone to tragedies, large and small, than most communities, Annatje. And so, I think, there must be such a place at Harenwyck."

There was. "The Narrows," said Annatje. It was where Maarten, her father's oldest friend, had drowned himself two years ago. After two disastrous harvests, and enough genuine and trumped-up charges—public drunkenness and disorderly conduct—that eviction must have appeared imminent.

"Harenhoeck," said the Widow. "Very well. Annatje Hoppe will die at Harenhoeck. Her clogs will be found on the rocks. The *schouts* will stop looking for her, and everyone will forget the little Dutch girl who was wanted for murder."

They were the last tangible reminder she had of her father, but they were just things.

"I do not think I can ever forget," said Annatje. She was not speaking of Vim Dijkstra. She felt no remorse for his death, only a cold kind of horror. And she was not thinking of the men upstairs, though she wanted to leave that house and never set foot in it again. She was thinking of her father, and her last glimpse of him, and his plea to her.

"Never forget," said the Widow. "But never look back. The only way from here is forward. There are Dutch communities in the Jerseys where you might feel at home, pleasant towns with good freeholds. With a few small alterations to your appearance and some well-placed introductions, we could find you a husband."

"No."

"Not all men are like the ones who frequented this house," said Angela Ferrers.

"I know." Some were like Gerrit. Or perhaps only Gerrit was like Gerrit. Her memories of their breathless explorations in the barn had survived miraculously untouched, separate and apart from the sordid things she had experienced upstairs. She would cherish those memories. "But I have no desire to farm again, or keep house. I like books. And learning things. Maps. And art. Latin," she added impulsively.

The Widow considered. "You could teach girls. You

would also need to learn the feminine accomplishments, which sadly do not include Latin and geography, but fancy needlework and painting flowers on velvet are easy enough subjects to master if you put your mind to it. And as long as you offer tuition in these areas, there will be scope for you to teach other, more enriching subjects as well."

The Widow put her considerable resources to work building Annatje a new identity and a new life. She hired tutors to eradicate her Dutch accent and perfect her English, to teach her French, Latin, even a little Greek. There were dancing, drawing, and painting masters, the sort who usually taught the mistresses and bastards of wealthy men and so understood the value of discretion.

There was one woman who was not a tutor, but a genuine member of the class Annatje was learning to ape, who came to teach her needlework. She brought a roll of canvases with her, some finished, some barely started, all of them the sort of large landscape compositions meant to grace a fireplace mantel. Her family name was never spoken, but Hannah appeared to be a genuine friend of the Widow, and they all took tea together after lessons, Annatje, the Widow, and this lady. It was Annatje's first real experience of the easy feminine companionship she later found at the school, and it was a balm to her soul.

There were other lessons, in subjects that would never be learned or taught in any finishing school, and Annatje had studied them gladly as well, because she was determined to follow the Widow in one respect at least: she would never be anyone's victim again.

At the end of six months' time, the silkwork picture that would ensure her success as a finishing school teacher was complete.

"And so Annatje became Anna," she finished. "I taught privately for three years and then opened the academy. The sampler hangs above the fireplace where I teach my girls needlework. The Widow gave me money to buy the house, but I paid it back soon enough. I had no intention of ever returning to Harenwyck until the Widow's successor turned up at my door."

Anna had never told anyone all of it. Not even Angela Ferrers. Not like that. To the Widow she had related a series of events, as though they had happened to someone else. Emotion, she had soon learned, carried no weight with that formidable woman.

That did not make it weightless. Quite the contrary. And she had borne that burden with her for so many years—an indissoluble mix of outrage, shame, and grief—that she had forgotten what it was like to be free of secrets. Now, no matter what Gerrit thought, even if he turned from her in disgust, the burden was lifted. The only person whose reaction really mattered to her knew all.

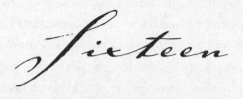

Sixteen

Gerrit had known she was remarkable from the first time he saw her, clomping across the lawn in her yellow clogs. Her sharp gray eyes had taken in everything around her and had helped to open his own.

They were fixed on him now, and he realized that she was waiting for him to say something. Almost any words he could think of would sound like consolation, or worse, absolution, and she did not need that from him. He wanted to tell her that she was the most remarkable woman he had ever met—because she was—but that would sound patronizing. And he wanted her to know how damned grateful he was to her for surviving—so they could be to-gether now—but that sounded selfish.

Finally he said, "This is the point where Barbara Fenton's Dutchman should have set his chin and sworn vengeance against all her enemies. But you've already taken care of Vim Dijkstra, and my father found his own way to dusty death. Your Widow made a neater job of Mrs. Duvel than I likely would have. Have you no enemies left?"

She looked him in the eye and said, "John André."

He opened his mouth to make some retort, but her expression told him that she was serious. "Annatje—"

"He was responsible for the Widow's murder. I would not be alive if not for her. But I do not ask that you kill him—I do not even want that on either of our hands. I ask only that you walk away from him."

"That is the one thing I cannot do."

"You can't trust him, Gerrit. Not when the stakes are your very life."

"I don't need to trust him, but I do need his six hundred men. Annatje, ask me for something else. Anything else."

"I want you safe, Gerrit. I have lost everyone who was dear to me to this place. I will not let Harenwyck destroy you too."

He believed her. "I have it the wrong way around, don't I? It isn't you who needs saving from villains— excepting my brother—it's me. You've already faced all your demons and lived to tell the tale."

"Not all of them."

She took a step closer. Her clogs gave her petite frame a few extra inches of height, but she still had to stand on tiptoe to press her lips to his. They were warm and soft. He set his hands lightly on her shoulders, exquisitely aware, after all she had told him, of how she might feel about men who took instead of offered, of all the ways he could do this wrong.

"Annatje, has there been no one else, in all this time?"

"No one." Her hands slid up his chest. Her every touch set him on fire, but it must be her touches that led them. He understood that. "Unless you count your brother kissing me just now in the arbor."

"I must rethink killing him," said Gerrit. "Have I any other rivals?"

She laughed. It was a musical sound. He had not heard it since the last time they had stood in this place. "The Widow tried. Oh, how she tried. She told me it was like falling off a horse, and that I must get back up or I would never be able to ride." A giggle escaped her soft lips. "She was a subtle woman, but I could always spot the paramours she sent my way from a mile off. I did not want any of them. I felt nothing in that way, until I came back here. Do you understand?"

She took a step closer and fitted her body to his, hip to hip, thigh to thigh. He did understand. He had not been celibate since their parting, but physical desire had come uncoupled from tenderness, from love, until now. He took her hands in his, kissed them, and tugged her down the grassy slope to the hidden grove where the oldest tombs lay.

The tombs were built from the same red sandstone as the gates of Harenwyck, and Anna knew that here she would cross another threshold. The men and women lying quiet beneath this earth had passed from life to death, but Anna would pass from death to life here and be reborn.

She remembered the broad sepulchre on which they used to lie. It was as wide as a bed, its inscription long since worn away by the rain. Only the supple carving along the edge remained. The moonlight made the peeling layers of sandstone look stitched together, like sheets of scuffed red leather.

Anna hitched herself on top of the stone and tugged Gerrit close. He kissed her on the mouth, along the edge of her jaw, in the hollow of her neck. She expected him to slide onto the stone beside her, to tangle limbs with limbs as they used to do, but he surprised her by dropping to his knees and folding back her skirts.

She knew what he proposed to do, and was unsurprised to find she liked the idea very much. "They must be teaching far more than Calvinism at Leiden these days," she said.

"They have a telescope there for one thing, but I am hopeful that I can make you see stars without it."

He was right. He kissed his way up her thigh, and when he put his mouth on her it was with delicate skill. More than that: He knew, from intimate acquaintance, no matter that it was years ago, exactly how to read her. He knew how her muscles twitched, how her belly quivered, how her breath hitched when she was climbing, when she was close. He knew how to draw out her pleasure, and the low rumbling in the back of his throat indicated that what he was doing pleased him almost as much as it did her.

The crisis left her dizzy but excited, reaching for him

with eager hands. When he climbed up on the stone beside her, he too was trembling, but he let her guide him onto his back and moaned when she freed him from his breeches and straddled him. They moved together like that, slickness against hardness, until they found where they fit, until they could strive together for what they both sought.

Afterward they lay tangled there, heartbeats slowing, bodies cooling, and he said, "If we were married, we could do this every night. Perhaps in a bed. Possibly that would be softer."

"Are you asking me to marry you?"

"Yes. Unless it is against your leveler principles. In which case I'm asking you to live in sin with me. Both options include a bed."

It was not against her leveler principles. It was the daydream, secret and forbidden, she had never shared with anyone: to marry Gerrit Van Haren, the boy who had brought her cookies and maps and books and kissed her beneath the stars. It had been impossible then. She'd understood that even before her mother had beaten her for her foolishness. It was just as impossible now, for entirely different but equally compelling reasons. For a few seconds, though, while his words still lingered in the air, she could stand in the space between the question and the answer and imagine a future with this man who was friend, confidant, and lover.

The words stuck in her throat. She forced them out. "I'm sorry, Gerrit, but the answer to both questions is no."

He was in no position to marry anyone, and neither was she. The nephew of the man she had killed was skulking somewhere about the estate, perhaps preparing to expose her. There was also the matter of the crafty Rebel spy mistress who had blackmailed her into coming to Harenwyck in the first place, and could set the bailiffs on her at any time.

But those were not the grounds on which she was refusing him. She was refusing him because it was the only leverage she had to make him see reason. "You won't live long enough to marry me," she said, "if you go on distributing freeholds to the tenants. Your father got away with murder because that sort of murder was in every landlord's interests. They will *crush* you, Gerrit, as they crushed my father."

He rolled off the stone and began buttoning his breeches. "Surely, after everything you have suffered, you must see that so much power, over the lives of so many, should not rest in the hands of one man."

She helped him tuck in his shirt before sliding off the stone and straightening her petticoats. "Your brother is not the old patroon." She had been convinced that her story could persuade him.

"No. Andries is not like my father. Andries is not even a truly bad man. It is the order of things, the *system*, that is wrong, and I mean to destroy it, Annatje. To finish the work your father started before mine had him murdered."

She took his hand and began leading him back up the hill to the church. "Like Gaius Gracchus finished his brother Tiberius' work? If you do that, your story will end the same way. Gerrit, let your brother have Harenwyck. Let him give it to the Americans. Let *them* break up the estates. Do that and there is nothing—nothing at all—to stop us leaving here together."

"The Americans have put a Virginia planter—a slaveholder and landlord of vast acreage—in command of their army. They will never break up the manors, Annatje. The men in Congress are not levelers like your father. They want different men in power, but they do not want to change how that power is concentrated. If the patroonships are to be dissolved, someone other than Washington and Congress will have to do it."

They reached the top of the rise where the smaller graves stood in the shadow of the church. "You may be right, but why, Gerrit, must that someone be you?"

"For years I thought that I could never be free of Harenwyck, that it would cast its shadow over my life so long as the tenant system kept so many farmers yoked to its plow. I could never see past that, though, past the moment when the estate was divided into freeholds and sold. I could not picture myself living in that absurd mansion, or anywhere else for that matter, and trying to raise Grietje and Jannetje on my own. But I can now, because of you."

"Gerrit, I am a murderess. If I do not deliver Harenwyck to the Rebels, that fact is bound to come out, and it will taint every young woman who has passed through my school. You cannot possibly want me educating, let alone raising your daughters now. *I* am the ghost of Barbara Fenton, haunting Harenwyck in my tattered finery."

"You are not Barbara Fenton. She killed in cold blood, out of revenge. You killed in self-defense. A brute of a man who beat you, then threatened you with a naked blade. It is not at all the same thing. And you did not choose what happened to you in that house."

"I could have—I should have—fought and run screaming out the door."

"And died in jail just like your father, as you almost certainly would have. *If* you even escaped Dijkstra and that house at all."

He took her hands in his. "Annatje, it would not matter to me if you had sold yourself on the street for a scrap of bread. You did what you had to do to survive, and I am glad of it, because we can finally be together. I want us to make the kind of life we talked and dreamed of when we were young, to plot it with books and maps and charts of the stars. But I cannot wake up next to you, Annatje, knowing that Harenwyck abides. Not when my father had yours butchered to preserve it."

"You see? I *told* you she was going to meet him."

The small piping voice came from the other side of the churchyard, and it belonged to Gerrit's younger daughter. Her eyebrows were roof high in smug satisfaction, while Jannetje pouted beside her, arms crossed over her chest in vexation, or disappointment.

"You were right," said Jannetje. She stamped forward and looked up at her father, her little chin raised pugnaciously. "Why haven't you come to see *us*?"

For a moment Gerrit looked stricken. Then he said, "I have not come to visit you because I did not want you to have to lie to your uncle about it, but I am very glad to see you now." He dropped to his knees and opened his arms, and both girls flew into his embrace without hesitation.

They were a study in contrasts, Gerrit and his daughters, golden-haired and fair where he was dark. He hugged them tight, and Anna could see how much it cost him to let them go at last, knowing he could not keep them with him.

"Grietje, Jannetje, you must not tell Uncle Andries that you saw me, or that Miss Winters was here with me. Do you understand?"

"Uncle Andries says you are trying to destroy Harenwyck," said Jannetje.

"He is right. I mean to divide up the estate, and sell the tenants their land, so the men and women who do all the work can keep the fruits of their labor. The way it is now isn't fair. Soon you will be old enough to see that when you visit the castle and the farms."

"Uncle Andries says you think it's wrong for people to be rich," said Grietje.

"It isn't wrong to be rich, if you come by your wealth honestly, through hard work, but the leases at Harenwyck are designed to make us rich by keeping hardworking men poor. And that *is* wrong."

"But I don't want to leave our house," said Grietje.

"We don't have to sell the manor house. Or the farms that are part of the Van Haren manor proper. But two hundred thousand acres is too much land for any man to claim and control. Such avarice has been the downfall of empires before."

"Like Rome?" asked Jannetje.

"Just like Rome," agreed Gerrit.

"We have been reading Mr. Gibbon's *Decline and Fall*," explained Anna.

"It is not as boring as it sounds," said Jannetje. "But it is not as good as pirates."

"Reverend Blauvelt would tell you that Gibbon was worse than pirates," said Gerrit, instantly elevating the *Decline* to the twins' new favorite book in the library. "He lays the blame for the fall of the empire squarely on Christianity, though I think he would acknowledge that the *latifundia*, the Roman patroonships, played a strong supporting role."

Anna suspected that Gerrit was right about the reverend. She had sat through only one of his sermons, and found him to be even more of a stick than the divine who had presided over the church in her childhood.

Gerrit made the girls promise to say nothing of their meeting to Mrs. Buys and return to the housekeeper before they were missed. "It would be unfair to ask her to lie for you," admonished Gerrit. And the patroon would have only so much patience with her loyalty to his renegade brother.

When they were gone, he turned to Anna and said, "You are very good for them."

"And you love them," said Anna, "even though they aren't yours."

His face told her that it was still a raw wound. "Did someone tell you?"

"No. I guessed." Her voice dropped to a soft sympathetic tone. "Gerrit, they do not look like you."

"They look like all the Van Harens *except* me," said Gerrit. "My father, who never had much use for any of his own children, Elizabeth, Andries, and myself included, adored them. He took such delight in the girls, in fact, was always so smug about them, that I think he knew Andries had cuckolded me. It was like a private joke to him. He never much cared for me, and my happiness meant less than nothing to him. It was Harenwyck he loved. Sophia, bringing her father's floating mills, was meant to ensure that Harenwyck's wealth and influence continued to grow. He didn't care a fig if the girls were mine or my brother's. All he really wanted was to be certain that heirs of his blood would inherit the estate."

Anna suspected that old Cornelis had been even more conniving than Gerrit realized, but she had no proof. She wasn't sure she wanted any.

"Why did you marry her, Gerrit?"

"Because you were dead, or so I believed. And she hung on my every word, and I thought she liked me, came to think she loved me. She didn't. Not really. She was already a fixture at Harenwyck by the time I came home from Leiden. Her father and mine had by then come to some kind of bargain. One that was more to old Cornelis' benefit than anyone else's, if the sourness of Sophia's father was anything to go by. He did not seem exactly pleased with the situation, but he was committed to the match. I asked Sophia once why she did it—why she let me, made me, believe she loved me—and she said that she didn't have any choice."

"Many women don't," said Anna.

"Should it matter whether Grietje and Jannete are my daughters or my nieces? They were the only good thing to come out of my marriage, and they are not to blame for the sins and weaknesses of their parents."

"It *shouldn't* matter," said Anna. "They are good girls. A pleasure to teach. I shared our old atlas with them."

"Is it still there?" he asked, brightening. "Up in that mean little cabinet of books that passes for a library?"

"A little older," she said, "but still there. Like the *klompen* maker."

"Salomon Beck marched on the manor with your father. He can be trusted. The Dijkstras, unfortunately, cannot. Jan has not returned to the blockhouse. It is possible that he has left because he sees me as a traitor and has no desire to fight for the British."

"But you do not think that is why he has left."

"No. He hasn't been seen about the manor for days. I do not know what he is plotting, but it is nothing good. We have moved our camp, in case he is planning to betray us, but there is nothing I can do to protect you if you remain at the manor house."

"Are you suggesting I play Maid Marian with you in the woods?"

"Not in the woods with me, no. My father was never able to make his scheme for floating mills at the Narrows work, but he built three of them, anchored off Harenhoeck. We are camped in one of them now. It is habitable, but that's not where I'd like to see you either."

"Where, then?"

"Annatje, my brother likes you. That much is obvious. Convince him to let you take the girls to New York. At least until I can deal with Jan and the Dijkstras."

"I can't leave. Not yet. Not until I have persuaded your brother to give Harenhoeck and the Narrows to the Americans, or they will expose me as Annatje Hoppe, murderess. And if you go on robbing his coaches you will push Andries right into the arms of the British."

"And you into his?"

He was not being playful now. She could see how deep the hurt went, how betrayed he still felt by his brother.

"I am not Sophia, Gerrit. I have always wished we had been reckless together in the barn that year, that *you* had been my first, and not some stranger."

"Our *firsts* don't matter," said Gerrit taking her into his arms. "It is our lasts I care about, Annatje, and as soon as I have Harenwyck in my possession, I swear that we will be each other's."

The great manor house was dark and quiet when Anna returned. Only a single lantern burned beside the kitchen door. She let herself in with the key Mrs. Buys had given her and felt her way through the dark up the stairs to the main hall. In the wan starlight that filtered through the windows, painted patroons stared down at her in judgment.

Good and bad, the lords of Harenwyck were all immortalized here, but nowhere on the estate was even the crudest memorial that her father had ever lived.

There was light coming from the parlor door at the foot of the stairs, and Anna was surprised to find Andries, still in his velvet suit, sitting in a chair before a fire that was almost burned out. The patroon looked up when Anna appeared on the threshold, and his pale blue eyes searched hers as though seeing her for the first time.

"Apparently Barbara Fenton is not the only ghost haunting Harenwyck," he said.

She did not follow his meaning. She stepped inside the room, but he remained seated. If she had not come to know him this last week, she would have taken it for more of his hauteur, but she recognized it now for what it was: admission into a familial sort of intimacy he shared with only a select few.

"I received unexpected visitors tonight. Rie Dijkstra and her extended clan."

The room was still warm from the dying coals, but suddenly Anna felt very cold. "Who are they?" she asked blandly.

He ignored her question.

"They came to me with an extraordinary offer. Rie's nephew Jan is part of my brother's band of outlaws. But you know that already. What you don't know is that young Jan is willing to deliver me Gerrit in exchange for the murderer who killed his uncle. In exchange for you, *Annatje*."

Seventeen

Anna took another step into the room. *Forward.* "What did you say to her?"

Andries Van Haren looked up. "Nothing, at first. The idea sounded so outlandish, but of course, it explained everything: how you knew Harenwyck well enough to escape from my brother and find the manor in the middle of the night; why the Americans sent you. They needed someone who could understand this place. And I had never really met you when we were children. Elizabeth and I didn't pay any attention to the tenants. Our father's dutiful children, in this at least. We simply weren't raised to see you as people. Gerrit did, though, and our father hated that. Old Cornelis was already difficult enough—no, impossible—to please."

He sounded distant, caught fast in the grip of the

past, but it was the present that Annatje feared. "So what did you tell Rie Dijkstra?"

The patroon smiled wryly. "I relied upon my upbringing. My father's example proves useful on occasion. I told her that I ought to have her whipped for her insolence, that she had forgotten her place, that she had no business slandering her betters. I told her that Miss Winters of Miss Winters' Academy was a well-known lady in New York, a genteel Englishwoman with unassailable credentials and a verifiable family pedigree."

Anna realized that she had been holding her breath. Relief flooded her. Evidently Andries had given a performance worthy of the old patroon—for her.

"Was she convinced?"

"No. She saw you at the cider pressing tonight and said she would swear in a court of law that you are Annatje Hoppe. I threatened to revoke her pension if she dared commit such an offense against a member of my household."

"But obviously you know that she is right. I *am* Annatje Hoppe. Why are you protecting me?"

"Do you have to ask?"

He wanted her. She knew that. But he was not using her predicament just as leverage to bed her. And he was too focused, to driven, too intent on Harenwyck's future to jeopardize it.

"Flattering," she said, "but not the whole truth. I think the time for lies is past, don't you?"

He turned from her to look into the fire, and she realized the patroon of Harenwyck, this proud, haughty man, could not meet her eyes. "For the same reason," he said, staring into the flames, "that I am trying to keep the estate out of Gerrit's hands and hold the manor together. To make amends for the sins of my father. I was there that night, the night your father died."

The world turned upside down. Anna felt for the chair opposite Andries to steady her. "How? *Why?*"

The patroon poked at the blaze and stared into it as though the fireback were a window to the past. "Gerrit was always a disappointment to our father. Old Cornelis thought that his heir was weak. A dreamer. Unsuited and unfit to be patroon. No son of his, he used to say. You can imagine how much our mother appreciated that.

"My father was determined to make sure that I didn't turn out soft like his firstborn. The night Bram Hoppe was arrested he roused me out of bed. He had one of the *schouts* with him. They made me get dressed and saddle my horse and then follow the *schout* into the woods. He took me to the clearing beyond the old sandpit. The bailiffs had a man there, and I thought from afar that he was standing on his tiptoes, and that everyone was playing some kind of madcap game.

"I had never set eyes on this man before. When I got up close I saw that he had a noose around his neck, and my father's men were taking turns raising and lowering him from a tree. Every time they let him down they set upon him, beat him again. His face was so battered. So misshapen from the punishment that to this day I do not know what he looked like. Not really."

The room spun around her. She could not tell which

way was up. Strong arms caught and lifted her and the spinning became far, far worse as she was carried across the room to something smooth and soft. The sofa. It had to be the sofa, but she could not see it because her vision would not answer. When at last the room stopped swimming she was looking up into the concerned face of Andries Van Haren.

"I am sorry," he said, kneeling beside the sofa. "That was thoughtless of me. I have never told anyone about that night before, not even Sophia. I was so ashamed. Ashamed that I stood there and did nothing, that I just watched a man die."

"How old were you?" asked Annatje.

"Fourteen."

"There was nothing you could have done." But Annatje thought about all the things she could have—should have—done if she'd been the woman then that the Widow made her afterward. *Forward*.

"It was not just that night," said Andries. "Not something I could put behind me and forget. There were more than a dozen men in that glade with me. I never saw Bram Hoppe's face, but the faces of his killers were printed on my memory. For nearly a decade, while my father was still alive, I saw them on the estate, at the castle buying seed, working on the new house, attending church, carrying their children on their shoulders as though they were blameless men. Murderers, all of them, hiding behind the authority of a murderous patroon. Every time I encountered one of them, it reminded me of my own cowardice. When my father died I evicted all of them, on one pretext or another, with the help of Mr. Ten Broeck. I did not move against the Dijkstras because Vim was already dead, at your hands, and I did not think that his relict and family should have to pay for his sins. A mistake," he said rising, "soon to be corrected."

"If you evict them now they will take it as proof that I really am Annatje Hoppe." She shivered, whether from the thought of the mob or the chill of the far side of the room she could not say.

"They are already convinced it is you," said the patroon, rising and crossing to the fire. "And I don't believe they are much interested in proof, apart from the facile kind that will raise and move a mob. I cannot afford that now, not with the manor cut off from New York by my brother, Gerrit. There will be no rough music. Rie and Ida Dijkstra will be taken to the ferry first thing in the morning and banished from Harenwyck."

Anna watched him kneel beside the hearth and methodically begin to layer wood atop the dying coals. He was saving her life, at no small cost to his ambition. "You will lose your best chance to catch your brother and put an end to his rebellion," said Anna. Every step she took, it seemed, dragged her further away from her goals of delivering Harenwyck to the Rebels and extricating Gerrit from danger.

"If I cannot deal with my brother without the connivance of a clan of bloody-minded extortionists like the Dijkstras, then I do not deserve to be patroon."

"What about Gerrit? Are you going to warn him that there is a traitor in his midst?"

Andries Van Haren paused in his labor and became perfectly still. The room became pin-drop silent. "Is he your lover?" asked Andries.

He was protecting her at great cost to himself. He deserved the truth. The Widow would have accounted her a fool. "Yes. I love Gerrit." She found an unexpected joy and wonder in speaking the words, breaking a silence she had kept for more than a decade.

"I suppose he thinks that is poetic justice, then, because he believes that I cuckolded him."

"Did you?"

"No. Never. Not even after Gerrit left Sophia here alone and miserable, married to a man who did not want her. For the past eleven years my brother has steadfastly believed me to be guilty of a sin I did not commit. That is between us. But he is jeopardizing *everything* I am trying to accomplish at Harenwyck. I may not be the profligate sinner he paints me as, but neither, as I told you, am I a plaster saint. He has surrounded himself with a band of opportunistic ruffians for the dubious purpose of wresting the estate away from me. Brother Gerrit can watch his own back."

The girls slept late the next morning. Anna did not sleep at all. She spent the night lying in her great carved bed and staring up at the canopy. She must write to Kate Grey. She had to say something of Gerrit and the situation on the estate. *The patroon's brother has formed an alliance with the British. If he raises two hundred men Tarleton will invade the estate with six hundred and the narrows at Harenhoeck will be lost to you.*

But the patroon's brother was the man she had loved since girlhood, and delivering such a missive was as good as aiming a pistol at his heart. And time was running out. News of the freeholds Gerrit was offering would spread like wildfire. Very soon, Gerrit would likely have his men and the British would invade Harenwyck—unless she could somehow convince him to reconcile with his brother, Andries. The key to that, she suspected, lay at the old manor.

The silence of the house became oppressive as the morning stretched without the bustle of cooks and house-maids. Everyone was sleeping off a night of indulgence—except Anna. The whole plantation was likely to be in the same state of torpor, which meant that Anna could return to the Van Harens' old manor unseen.

It didn't take her long to reach the abandoned house, and she did not meet a soul on the road or along the path. Only here and there did a chimney smoke, tentative puffs that spoke of fires too long banked being brought to life.

It was the deep porches that made the house look so forbidding, Anna decided. When she had been a girl the manor had been a site of ceaseless activity. The slaves in the kitchens had come and gone from the great double doors below the porch, and the air had always been perfumed with cook fires. Anna remembered the flowers in pots that used to line the stairs, the fruit drying in the sun.

All that was gone now, and only a pile of broken

crockery remained heaped against one wall as a reminder of the life that had once bloomed there. Anna climbed the stairs. They creaked, but the sound was not as loud as it had seemed by night, drowned by the music of crickets and birdsong.

Inside, the sad dining room was just as she had last seen it, mouse-eaten chairs askew and a thick blanket of dust covering the ugly table. The parlor opposite was prettier than she had realized, with the delicate green paneling glowing softly in the morning sun.

The *doed koecks* were gone. The table had been dusted. The wax from that lone candle had been removed. The item she had come for was still there, though. Sophia Van Haren had been an unhappy bride, but before she became the lady of Harenwyck, she had been a schoolgirl like Mary Phillips and Becky Putnam and all the others Anna had taught. And because the natural inclinations of the human heart were so often at odds with what was expected of genteel young women, they all had secrets, things they knew they must not share with the world. Desires, undertakings, deeds that were of the greatest moment to them. Girls like Becky Putnam kept love letters—unless they were lucky enough to have teachers like Anna who insisted they be burned—like a miser his gold, because tangible things such as ink and paper were sometimes the only refuge for, and reflection of, their true selves.

If Anna was right about Sophia Van Haren, she would not have gone to her grave without memorializing the truth that had defined her adult life: the name of the man who had fathered her daughters.

The clumsily embroidered fire screen was covered in a thick layer of dust. Anna lifted the framed embroidery off its pole and laid it on the game table. The canvas should have slipped out the top of the frame easily—had it been professionally mounted—but the fabric had never been stretched tight and humidity had caused it to bunch and become stuck in the frame. Anna used the knife she had brought to pry the mitered corners of the frame apart and release the silkwork picture.

She peeled the picture from the card to which it had been glued, and found what she was looking for behind the canvas. The document was written in a girlish hand, the sort of round, looping script that Anna taught her own charges. It was signed in the same hand, by Gerrit's late wife, Sophia; and witnessed by Gerrit's missing sister, Elizabeth Van Haren, long after that lady had supposedly fled Harenwyck. There was another name as well, one that was unfamiliar to Anna: Lettitje Bronck. Her halting, cramped signature suggested she had little education and was unused to writing.

Anna folded the mildewed document and tucked it safely in her pocket. She knew where she must go now, but she needed to make a thorough investigation of the rest of the house first.

There were three empty chambers at the back of the ground floor that had once been bedrooms—the two grander having once boasted tester beds, by the marks on the bare floors—but nothing of their furnishings remained. Another parlor behind the dining room had also been efficiently stripped.

Anna lit a taper she had brought with her to descend to the kitchens, and when she opened the shutters, she could see that the thrifty servants had left nothing useful behind. At least not on the shelves. But there was a cord of seasoned wood stacked next to the hearth and a pile of ashes inside the yawning bake oven. The bricks, as she had suspected, were still warm.

Someone was using the bake oven here; someone who did not much fear the patroon's displeasure. Few tenant cottages had bake ovens, it was true, but few tenants would be bold enough to trespass in the patroon's house for the pleasure of a hot, crusty loaf. Even fewer would dare use the front door when they came to borrow the oven, but the double doors from the kitchen to the yard were barred from the inside with balks of timber.

Anna knew the path through the woods, but she had never taken it. Her mother had forbidden her to consult Mevrouw Zabriskie. Mehitable had called the Pole a witch and worse. Anna knew that other girls on the estate used her cure for cramps, and she'd had it once herself: a musty-smelling tea brewed from lady's mantle, lovage, and valerian. It had tasted foul, but it had worked in less than an hour.

There were other reasons to visit Mevrouw Zabriskie. She told fortunes and served as a midwife, and sometimes she could help if you *didn't* want to have a baby. Anna suspected that the old patroon had tolerated her presence on the estate for that very reason. The new patroon, Anna had decided, had his own reasons.

Mevrouw Zabriskie's hut looked the part of a witch's

cottage. It was one of the only structures at Harenwyck not built of stone or brick. The steep thatched roof gave it an antique air, and the drying racks outside—heavy with bundles of herbs and other things Anna did not care to examine too closely—added to the clearing's eldritch aura. And drying in trays on the ground were the moonseed berries she had taught Grietje and Jannetje to tell apart from wild grapes. In the right dose, it could have medicinal properties. In the wrong dose, it killed.

The ill-fitting batten door to the cottage stood open. It took a moment for Anna's eyes to adjust to the dark interior, but once they had she saw that apart from the building material and more cramped dimensions, it was much like that of any other cottage on the manor: a single room with a jambless hearth and a sleeping loft above. The walls, however, were lined with bottles of dried herbs and chicken feet, tiny bones and nameless powders, and there was a crude stone mortar and pestle on the table. Only the cheerful chintz curtain hanging from the chimney rather undermined the unsavory aspect of the room.

Anna almost laughed—until she spied the posy she had dropped last night, suspended from the chimney by red string. The end was charred, as though someone had crisped it on a salamander.

"Come to have your fortune read, have you?"

Anna turned in the doorway to find Mevrouw Zabriskie behind her. She was dressed, as always, in mismatched finery: a bright yellow silk jacket over an orange striped petticoat—with a brace of hare hanging from a thick leather belt at her waist. Something about these limp, scrawny, glassy-eyed creatures made Anna's stomach turn and heart sink.

"No," said Anna. "I wish to talk to the witch of the woods."

"You've found her, then."

"I meant the other. The patroon's sister, Elizabeth Van Haren. It was her I saw on the path near the patroon's house last week, wasn't it? If she's living in these woods, then you know where."

Mevrouw Zabriskie looked her up and down. "If you want my help, you must let me read you first."

"Very well," said Anna. It was all superstition and nonsense, but she knew country people, because she had been one, and it was never wise to spurn their ways. She followed Mevrouw Zabriskie inside.

"Cup of tea?" asked the *mevrouw*.

"What kind?" asked Anna, suspiciously, recalling the moonseed drying outside.

"Black. Bohea," replied Mevrouw Zabriskie.

She pulled a very Dutch tin canister painted with bright flowers off the chimney ledge and opened it for Anna to sniff. It was the freshest, richest tea Anna had smelled since the war started. Maybe she *was* a witch.

The old woman put two teacups and saucers down on the table. They matched the chipped pot in Mrs. Buys kitchen *kas*. When the tea had been poured, Anna placed her hand palm up on the table.

Mevrouw Zabriskie shook her head. "You grip your secrets too tightly, young miss, for me to read your palm." She produced a battered deck of cards from her pocket and spread it on the table. The backs were painted dead black, nicked and chipped. *Tarot.*

Anna noticed now that the cunning woman wore rings on every finger, all of them mourning jewels or *memento mori*: a macabre garden of skeletons, snakes, and twisted hair. She gathered the old cards into a stack and cut the deck, then turned over an utterly prosaic suit card: the two of wands. Anna let out a breath that she did not know she had been holding.

"Two of wands. I have read you before."

Anna felt a shiver travel down her spine. Mevrouw Zabriskie *had* read her fortune as a girl, at the Halve Maen, while her father plotted insurrection. But of course that was not what she meant. "Yes. At the cider pressing," said Anna. "Last night. You read my palm."

Mevrouw Zabriskie shook her head. "Not last night. Not your palm. These cards, they know you. They know your past." She peeled a card off the top of the deck and laid it on the table. "Know your present." Another card, this one closer to Anna. "And your future." A final card, inches away from her heart, which was beating fast even though she didn't believe in such things. She had lost her faith—in almost everything—the day she learned of her father's death.

The cunning woman flipped the first card over. "*Justice.* But upside down it means *in*justice."

"What spinster does not think she has been ill done by?" asked Anna. She knew how fortune-telling worked. The Widow had shown her, because it was a useful tool with those who did, or wanted to, believe. Tarot was a form of theater, part illusion, part suggestion, part appeal to emotion, a sleight of hand abetted by a little knowledge of the subject and a fine-tuned understanding of human nature. Mevrouw Zabriskie would know that Anna was a teacher, unmarried, and unlikely to be happy about it.

"There are seventy-eight cards in this deck," said Mevrouw Zabriskie. "Fifty-six of those are suits. Twenty-two are trumps. The trumps do not show themselves for trivial disappointments."

She flipped the next card over. "And you, it seems, have not been so very disappointed recently, yes?" said Mevrouw Zabriskie. *The Lovers* were naked and very carnally entwined. She and Gerrit had made love with their clothes on, with perhaps less serpentine contortions than the coupling depicted on the card, but it had been no less carnal for all that.

Mevrouw Zabriskie looked up at her through thick blond lashes. "Finish your tea."

Anna wanted to refuse, but she wanted to see Elizabeth Van Haren more, so she drank off the last of her tea. Mevrouw Zabriskie beckoned with one beringed hand, and Anna passed her cup across the table. The cunning woman placed the saucer over the cup and flipped both upside down.

All Anna saw was a brown mess of unfurled leaves, but Mevrouw Zabriskie, of course, would pretend to see more. No doubt a tall, handsome man with piercing eyes. That would cover most of the population of the valley—seen through the eyes of love, anyway.

The cunning woman curled her lips into a pleased smile and cackled. "Your lover is the patroon."

Mevrouw Zabriskie was a charlatan, just as Anna had thought. "You are saying that because you saw me with him last night, talking and dancing. It is an excellent guess, but it is also wrong."

"I did not mean Andries Van Haren."

That gave Anna pause, because she believed Gerrit *was* the rightful patroon. Anna did not credit second-hand recollections of a conveniently missing will, and she doubted anyone else really did either. Perhaps there was something in the tarot. Or perhaps Mevrouw Zabriskie heard everything that happened on Harenwyck because she delivered its babies and washed its dead.

The old woman flipped over the last card, the one closest to Anna.

"*The Hanged Man*. It seems there is a noose in your future."

That was not her future. It was her father's past. *He had a noose around his neck, and my father's men were taking turns raising and lowering him from a tree.* "The cards are allegories," said Anna. "They're not meant to be taken literally. They are only paper," she added to reassure herself.

"Just like a treaty, or a deed, or a will. Or the testament folded in your pocket. *Only paper.*" Mevrouw Zabriskie pinched another card off the top of the deck. "*The Tower.* A house made uninhabitable by death."

Anna saw the house on Pearl Street flash before her eyes. She plucked the card out of Mevrouw Zabriskie's fingers and threw it on the fire. The terrified figures falling from the tower on the card's face seemed to move and writhe before the fire consumed them.

Mevrouw Zabriskie set the deck down. The reading was over. Anna knew it was only the passage of clouds, but she had the sense that the cottage grew brighter when the old woman relinquished the deck.

She said nothing of the loss of her precious card. "If you want to take tea with me again, you know where to find me."

"And what about whiskey?" asked Anna. There was no place else on the patroonship where the Widow could have developed a taste for the stuff, where her father could have bought that dark glass bottle.

"You're one of hers, then," said Mevrouw Zabriskie. "I should have guessed. She didn't believe in the cards either, but they *knew her*. They can tell you where to find her body."

Not even Mr. Sims, the Widow's man of business, had known that. All she needed now was what the *mevrouw* had agreed to provide: where to find Elizabeth Van Haren.

"No, thank you," said Anna, her throat dry despite the tea. "I am on the trail of different ghosts today."

The cunning woman gave her directions leading deep into the forest. The path was little more than an Indian trail. "Look for the hatchet marks," Mevrouw Zabriskie said.

Anna walked for an hour. The cottage, when she found it, was ancient, its timber bones as old as the estate itself. An abandoned leasehold, no doubt, one of those early farms that failed, where the tenants had succumbed to disease or starvation or Indian attacks, or simply run away in search of better prospects. It might easily have belonged to Barbara Fenton and her Dutchman, if they had ever existed, but it belonged to the patroon's sister now, and the girl with whom she had run away.

They were sitting on a table outside the cottage shelling beans when Anna approached. Elizabeth Van Haren was marked by her gilded hair, visible beneath a farmwife's kerchief. Her companion had a darker complexion and thick hair, black as a raven's wing. They both wore homespun, and if Anna had come across them without foreknowledge she would have assumed them to be peasants.

They exchanged looks with each other when they heard her approach, but they did not rise to greet her. Elizabeth Van Haren went on shelling beans and said, "Are you lost, Mevrouw?"

"My name is Anna Winters. The patroon hired me to tutor Grietje and Jannetje. I am also a friend of Gerrit's, and I am here to talk with you about his late wife."

"And what would I know about such things?"

"Everything, I should think." Anna unfolded the testament in her pocket and spread it on the table beside the pea pods.

Elizabeth's hands stilled. "Where did you find that?"

"Hidden in the embroidered screen."

The patroon's sister sighed. "We searched for it after she died, but we could never find it."

"That is because your father never sent you to be

educated at a finishing school. Young women become very clever at hiding things from their teachers," said Anna.

"We tried to convince her not to do it, that the truth would only hurt the twins in the end, but Sophia hated living like that, with everyone thinking she had betrayed Gerrit so lightly. She held out hope that she might be vindicated some day, once the old man was dead. She knew he would never let the real story be known while he lived. She was terrified of him, and with very good reason."

Elizabeth Van Haren paused to point to Anna and mime drinking. Her companion nodded and smiled, and disappeared into the cottage.

"Lettitje Bronck, I take it? She is not your servant, nor just your friend. I teach girls, Elizabeth, and there is no shame in honest words or honest passions."

Elizabeth's pale eyes widened slightly in surprise, but she did not flush or spout reflexive denials. She simply nodded.

"Lettitje is deaf," explained the patroon's sister. "My father's doing. He found us *together*, and he beat her for it. I feared for her life. He raised his hand to me only when I said I wouldn't marry his odious miller. There was nothing for us at Harenwyck. So we ran away. Only we weren't very good at it. We didn't bring food or money or clothing. We just fled into the night. And of course no one from the estate would help us, for fear of my father."

"No one except your brother," said Anna.

"No one except Andries," agreed his sister. "Gerrit was away at school. Mevrouw Zabriskie took us in, but we knew she could not keep us. The patroon had his *schouts* out scouring the countryside for us. Andries found the cottage, and fixed the roof and the doors, and he kept our secret. He brought us food, until we were able to begin producing our own. We thought we had thwarted the old man, and were going to live happily ever after, but then my father brought Sophia to the estate."

"For Gerrit to marry," supplied Anna.

"No. *For himself.* He wanted the mills. And he wanted her. It was only when she fell pregnant that he got the idea of marrying her to Gerrit. You see, he never believed that Gerrit was his son. Without reason, so far as I know, although I'm sure my father gave our mother cause enough. But my father was convinced his wife had cuckolded him. It galled him that his heir was a bastard. He couldn't prove it, but he devised a plan to put things 'right.' If he could marry Sophia, pregnant with his own child, to Gerrit, then his blood heir would be sure to inherit Harenwyck in time. And he'd revenge himself on the wife he thought betrayed him by cuckolding her bastard son."

The calculating greed and cruelty of it turned Anna's stomach. "Why did you let him do it? Why did Andries? Why didn't you warn Gerrit?"

Elizabeth looked down at her hands, and her voice was wistful but resigned. "Because Gerrit would never have married her if we had. And my father and Sophia's made it plain they would turn her out on the street if she did not persuade Gerrit to fall in love with her. Can you imagine it? It would have destroyed her. A frail girl like that, pregnant and penniless? She wouldn't have survived a day. Andries begged our father to let him marry her—he was so in love with her, poor boy—but our father wasn't having that. His line, his petty 'revenge,' was all that mattered. And Andries couldn't run away with her, because of *us*."

Lettitje came back with a tray and three wooden beakers of small beer. Anna noticed how Elizabeth's face brightened again when she reappeared. It was not so very uncommon to encounter such relationships when you taught young girls and moved in a world of spinster ladies.

"Gerrit will want to know you are alive and well. Your father is dead—why must you live out here, like this? In seclusion?"

Elizabeth looked back at her, again with a trace of surprise. "Andries is not my father," she said firmly. "You wrong him greatly if you think he would not have me come back home—that he has not asked us more than once. To live in the manor, with Lettitje as my lady's maid. But I *love* my brother, and he loves Harenwyck. The times could not be worse for such a thing, such a kindness. One whiff of scandal, of *decadence*, in the hall could destroy all that he's trying to build, damage him and the legitimacy of the patroonship itself in the eyes of the pious and discontent. Who would respect, who would serve, such a man, with *such* a sister?"

The bitterness that colored Elizabeth's voice for a moment disappeared as she took Lettitje's hand in hers and held it tight. "Besides," she said, "we've grown accustomed to the quiet, and to appreciate the freedom of living together—not as lady and maid, but *honestly*."

For a long moment, Anna looked at the two women with newfound respect, and content that they'd found, at least, a measure of happiness in spite of everything. Then she returned to the matter at hand.

"Gerrit *needs* to know about Sophia, about your father," she said. "He is raising a militia to march on Harenwyck, and he is doing it by offering the tenants freeholds. He and Andries both want to reform Harenwyck, but they will never come to terms with this open wound between them."

"I do not think an ordinary schoolteacher would care so much about her place of employment, or her employers," said Elizabeth Van Haren astutely. "Which one of them are you in love with? Andries or Gerrit?"

"Gerrit," said Anna, without hesitation. "And if he goes on like this, he is going to get himself killed."

"You have my permission to tell him," said Gerrit's sister, "but I would advise you against it. Andries didn't cuckold him, but he made a cuckold of him by letting the marriage proceed. To believe that your brother has lain with your wife out of lust and jealousy is one thing. To discover that your father has out of malice and spite is quite another. It is possible that you will be able to bring my brothers together—and it is equally likely that this news will only serve to drive them further apart."

Eighteen

Anna left the cottage with Sophia's testament tucked inside her stays. She had thought she would discover a truth there that would defuse the conflict brewing between Gerrit and Andries, but now she wasn't quite so certain. Andries had kept the truth from his brother for the same reason that he refused to sell land to his tenants: he thought he knew best. He simply believed that he knew what was best for others better than they did themselves. He did not see, or in some cases care, that he was robbing them of their right to determine their own destiny.

It was impossible for Anna to deny that he had done some good. His sister and her lover were living a safe if secluded life. But Anna was not as certain as Elizabeth that she and Lettitje could not have survived, even thrived, on their own *beyond* the borders of Harenwyck. They were content with their isolation now, but had they gone to New York and set up housekeeping as spinster sisters, say, they might have enjoyed a wider society than secret visits from Elizabeth's brother and Mevrouw Zabriskie could provide.

And their seclusion had its own perils. Anna doubted she had been the only one to see "Barbara Fenton" in the woods at night. Country people were not as a rule tolerant. If they discovered the two women living there in the woods, they might punish them with rough music. Annatje had seen the *mevrouwen* of Harenwyck drag a man accused of adultery naked through the estate and nearly drown him in a well. Andries had protected his sister and Lettitje from the old patroon, but she doubted he could protect them from his tenants if they had a mind to do them violence.

It was late afternoon and the sun was low on the horizon when she climbed the granite stairs of the manor porch. They sparkled in the waning light. She was surprised when no servants appeared to greet her or pull wide the grain-painted doors. She had remembered lazy mornings after the cider pressings, certainly, but not lazy *afternoons*.

Inside she could tell immediately that something was amiss. The great house was cold and dark. Normally the maids went from room to room making up the fires and banking them when the family moved to another part of the house, but no warmth emanated from the parlors or the grand dining room. The sconces in the entrance hall had burned down the night before and not been replaced.

Anna found Jannetje and Grietje in the library, poring

over Gibbon in the last light of the day. Gerrit might have stolen or destroyed the majority of her school equipment, but his tantalizing characterization of *The Decline and Fall*—*worse than pirates*—had made Gibbon good for a fair few more lessons. She lit a lamp for the girls and went to find the patroon.

The door to the small office he kept behind his bedroom was ajar and light spilled out. Anna could hear voices speaking in Dutch.

"I do not like it, sir," said Mr. Ten Broeck.

"The tenants always start work late the day after the cider pressing," said the patroon dismissively.

Not this late, thought Anna. *Never this late.*

"The grooms have not come to work at all. I had to saddle my own horse to tour the estate. Only the home farms show any signs of activity, the ones within a short ride of the manor, the holdings of your *schouts* and militia and favored tenants. The ones who are indebted to you for their prosperity. Go farther than a mile or two from the house, and there is no one stirring."

"You are reading too much into a night of overindulgence," said the patroon. "I am not prepared to believe that it is the End of Days just because my tenants have taken the morning off."

"This is your brother's doing," said Ten Broeck. "One of the footmen said he was at the cider pressing last night. He was promising the tenants freeholds."

"And how many of them," said the patroon reasonably, "can afford to buy their land? Precious few."

"He is not *selling* them," said Ten Broeck. "He is giving them away in exchange for service in his so-called militia. If they march on the house, we may not have the men to repulse them. If they march on the house and come with wives and children in tow, armed with scythes and pitchforks, the men we *do* have will not fire into such a crowd."

The patroon said nothing at first. Then, his voice flat: "What are you suggesting I do, Ten Broeck?"

"You have already tried the Americans. Their promises are empty. They do not have the men or the powder to spare us. Declare for the British. Take their oath. There is a British warship anchored near the Narrows. Send word to it. Act now, before it is too late to preserve the patroonship."

"How is it that you know about this British warship, Ten Broeck, while I do not?"

"You have been unreceptive to British overtures, Mr. Van Haren, so I stopped putting them before you. But I have kept the channels of communication open in your name, in case it came to this. There is a certain Major André. He is said to be thick with General Clinton, his deputy adjutant general, and acts with his authority. His offers of aid are generous. Six hundred men to fight your brother, if you but take the oath."

It was the same offer John André had made to Gerrit at the Halve Maen, and Anna had no doubt that the British agent would treat equally—fair or foul—anyone who secured him control of Harenhoeck and the Narrows.

"Mr. Ten Broeck," began the patroon, but just then Anna heard feet upon the stairs behind her. Someone was coming. She smoothed her skirts and knocked upon the half-open door.

"Come," said the patroon.

Anna entered. The patroon smiled when he saw her and rose. Ten Broeck popped up guiltily as well.

"Where is everyone?" she asked, in English.

"The servants get a late start the day after the cider pressing," said the patroon, forestalling Ten Broeck from pressing his arguments. "A local tradition. I am sorry if you've been inconvenienced. Mrs. Buys is short staffed. I told my nieces to make up their own fires."

"They are too engrossed in Gibbon to be bothered by the chill," said Anna.

"Are they?" asked the patroon. "Perhaps the End Times *have* come."

"Not quite, but it will seem so when we have run through all the books in that library. And I can well see to my own fire."

"No need, Miss Winters," said the patroon. "I will do it for you. I wanted a word anyway, about your supplies from New York."

Mr. Ten Broeck did not look pleased when the patroon abandoned him to lead Anna down the hall. He made up the fire in her room and then drew her away from the door to speak in low tones.

"I do not want to alarm you unnecessarily, but it would be best if you kept the girls inside for the rest of the day. I dispatched *schouts* to evict Rie and Ida Dijkstra this morning, but they have not yet returned from the ferry. It is most likely just a product of the general lassitude. If the ferry master was not yet up they might have had to wait, and depending on the delay, they may elect to remain at the landing until morning. In any case, until they report back, I'd prefer that you and the girls stay close to the house."

"I understand," she said. But she promised nothing, because she knew she would not be able to honor such an undertaking if Andries sent for André and Tarleton. She would need to warn Gerrit. And she would be obligated to alert the Americans.

In the morning Anna woke to find her room cold, and no tea waiting for her. She dressed and went downstairs to find Mrs. Buys alone in the kitchen, cutting up a chicken.

"Mr. Ten Broeck says this is Gerrit's doing, but I do not credit it," said Mrs. Buys. "He wants the patroonship, right enough, but he's no plotter, and he would not risk the dear girls' safety with a riot."

Mrs. Buys hacked a wing off the chicken and sent a morsel of raw meat flying onto the floor. A black ball of fur streaked from the hearth to catch it. Scrappy. It was a small comfort to Anna to find *someone* unmoved by the present tensions, but her attempt to scratch the kitten behind one ear was met by a tiny, proprietorial growl.

"Everyone wants something to have and to hold," said Anna, sparing a last look at Scrappy and her prize. "But I don't believe Gerrit would do anything to put the girls in jeopardy." Not intentionally, anyway. But he might make the mistake the British and the Americans were making. He might think the estate—or the mob—could be controlled by one man.

Anna helped Mrs. Buys for an hour. She took her tea in the kitchen and kept the girls inside. She had the stiff board and the paper she had bought at the castle store, and she showed the girls how to cut stencils for theorem paintings: the cheerful sort with fruit and flowers, and the doleful kind for memorial pictures, the gravestones and urns and anchors.

"But won't they all look the same if you're just making your picture up out of stencils?" asked Grietje.

"No," said Anna. "The stencils are only outlines. No one can tell you how to combine them, where to put the apple and where to place the pear, how to color or shade them, whether the fruit is soft and ripe or hard and green. That's why no two ever look alike."

The girls became engrossed in their projects and Anna cut a stencil just for herself, one to mask her long-deferred letter to Kate Grey, when she knew what she must write in it.

After the midday meal Mr. Ten Broeck arrived with his family in a cart piled high with furnishings, clothes, dishes, silver, a very excited dog, and what appeared to be every small thing of value from his home. His slave had driven them.

"We saw lights in the field last night," explained Ten Broeck. "It is starting."

Andries came home from his morning tour of the manor with a dozen men carrying muskets and rifles. He positioned them around the house. Ten Broeck's girls huddled together nervously. Their mother retired to a bedchamber and would not come out. Jannetje and Grietje ran from window to window arguing strategy with one another and badgering Anna to teach them Latin so they could read Caesar and tender their uncle some useful defensive advice.

The patroon retired to his study. Anna found him there cleaning a pistol.

"You think Mr. Ten Broeck is correct, don't you?"

"Don't you?" he asked. His manner was controlled, but taut with suppressed anger, as though he saw himself beset and betrayed by those who should most welcome his leadership and reforms.

"I'm not certain. A riot does not seem to me Gerrit's style. What do you plan to do?"

"Ten Broeck wants me to take the British oath."

"And will you?" She did not want him to.

"What choice have I? I cannot get a message to the Americans. My brother has seen to that."

"Perhaps you can't," she said. "But I can."

"How?"

"I have a contact on the estate." Mevrouw Zabriskie had been in the Widow's confidence. She would have a reliable means of sending messages. But that was not Anna's secret to share.

"Even if you could get word to the Americans," said the patroon, "and they had the men to help us, they could never get here in time."

Anna had known this was coming. She braced herself inwardly.

"Then tell your brother the truth. About Grietje and Jannetje. With some understanding, some hope of forgiveness, you and he could find a compromise."

Andries' lips tightened into a thin line, and his complexion seemed suddenly ashen, but his gaze was level. He saw that she *knew*, Anna realized, if not how, and declined, for the moment, to pursue the whys and wherefores.

"Gerrit will never listen to any offer that comes from me," said the patroon. "And why should he? I didn't cuckold him, but I deceived him for eleven years."

Anna suspected Andries had in mind the "burned" will and his insistence that Harenwyck was his rightful patrimony as much as things relating to Sophia and her children, so she pressed on, trying to point up rifts that could yet be bridged.

"To protect someone you cared for, those who could not protect themselves," she said. "Sophia, the girls . . . even the tenants. In that way, you and your brother are very much alike, Andries. What you did was wrong, but you and Gerrit were young when you made many of those decisions, and your reasons are the kind he would understand."

After a space, when the patroon said nothing, she continued.

"If you speak to him, *explain*, you could offer him a compromise. Sell freeholds to the tenants who have enough money to buy the land they are leasing. Build your school and hire your doctor and make your improvements for those who don't. Or split the estate between you so each of you can order things in the way you see fit."

Andries seemed surprised at this last suggestion, but something in his blue eyes suggested he saw in it a possible way clear. But when he spoke, his voice was low, resigned. "You may be right, but this is pure fantasy. There is little time, and I do not even know how to find my brother at the moment. Or why, come to that, he'd believe anything I might say about Sophia and our father after all these years."

"I do," said Anna. "I can take an offer from you to work out your differences, or, failing that, to divide the estate, to him, along with *this*." She unfolded Sophia's testament and placed it on the table.

The patroon read it, fingertips smoothing the paper out. Then he placed his palms flat on top of the document as though he could absorb some trace of the woman he had loved through her written words.

"How did you come by this?"

"It was hidden in the pole screen Sophia embroidered." Off Andries' astonished look she added, "It is a common schoolgirl hiding place. I have been to see your sister—it was her you were going to meet that night at the old manor, wasn't it?"

"If you have been to see my sister then you know why she insists upon discretion."

"Her secrets harm no one. They are safe with me. Sophia's testament is another matter. Your sister gave me her permission to share this with Gerrit. I would like yours."

He folded the paper carefully. "Sophia wanted to tell Gerrit. So many times, she wanted to tell him. We convinced her not to. We were wrong. I know that now. She died with this on her conscience. That was my doing."

"Because you thought you knew what was best for

her and Grietje and Jannetje." As he thought he knew what was best for the tenants on the estate.

He closed his eyes and took a deep breath. "Take one of the *schouts* with you. And give this"—he handed her back Sophia's testimony—"to my brother."

Anna tucked the document inside her stays. "I won't take the *schouts* with me." If Gerrit refused, she would *not* betray his hideout to the patroon. If Gerrit refused, Andries would turn to the British, and Anna would have to go to Mevrouw Zabriskie and send word to Kate Grey. "But I *will* take that pistol."

On the road, mounted on the pony that the patroon had saddled for her, Anna could see why Ten Broeck was so worried. No one was in the fields. There were no women in their gardens. No children walked the path to the castle with baskets of eggs or produce to trade for spices or salt or nails.

Anna had seen the estate like this before, during the turbulent year of her father's revolt. There were two thousand leaseholders at Harenwyck. Barely a fraction of them would take up arms. Most of the tenants would bar their doors and windows and hope the violence passed them by, that their neighbors would not seize the opportunity to avenge some past slight, real or imagined, under the cloak of a riot.

Even the castle was shuttered, no doubt on Mr. Ten Broeck's orders. The Widow would have called this a mistake. Anna did as well. Shuttering the store said that normal life had been suspended, that order had given way to chaos and misrule. Andries Van Haren's goodwill and good works should have gone a long way to keeping the estate quiescent, but that depended on keeping up an appearance of control.

Anna made good time on the main roads, but as soon as she turned off on the track leading to the Narrows she was forced to slow her mount to a walk. Harenhoeck was a lonely spot, the land too rocky and steep to farm, and the path was seldom used. No doubt the old patroon would have improved it if his scheme for the mills had come to fruition, but it hadn't, and whole stretches of the rutted track remained barely passable.

The way climbed steeply through thick forest and then descended as a rocky path that led to a long dock. Anna did not recall the dock from her childhood. She saw no signs of a camp, but the path here had been cleared recently, the brush freshly cut back. The sun was already beginning to set, burnishing the tops of the trees orange. An owl that was not an owl hooted somewhere above. Gerrit, obviously, had set a lookout, so she was unsurprised when the ruffian named Pieter appeared at the water's edge to meet her, his thatch of white blond hair catching the last of the fading light.

He eyed her warily. "You're not going to start a stampede again, are you, *mevrouwtje?*" he asked in Dutch.

"I don't know. Do you have enough sheep on hand?"

Pieter sighed. "I suppose if any woman is a match for him, it's you."

He helped her dismount, beckoned her onto the dock.

Anna had only been on a boat twice in her life, the ferry to and from Manhattan. Those crossings had been relatively smooth. The dock pitched and heaved underfoot, responsive to rough waters of the Hudson at this narrowing. She felt like it was going to throw her off. There was no railing: just a long row of rotting planks, barely six feet wide, resting on pontoons stretching out into the churning water.

The planking led to a chain of three low structures: floating wooden millhouses, anchored all in a row. The first was cavernous and dank. The sluices were closed but Anna could feel the river rushing past beneath her feet. The giant wheel, locked in place, loomed over them in the darkness.

The second house was heaped with boxes, the spoils of Gerrit's banditry, and contained no wheel. Perhaps it had in fact always been intended more as a warehouse, or perhaps it had never been completed.

The third millhouse was warm and dry, heated with stoves and lit with good beeswax candles—stolen, no doubt—and filled with a small band of men playing cards and cooking skewers of meat and making music on country instruments, a fiddle and a lute.

The music stopped abruptly when she entered, and the card players looked up, Gerrit among them. He smiled when he saw her, and despite everything—all the danger and uncertainties ahead—she felt a quick smile touch her lips in return, simply to see his face again and find him alive and well.

"So you have come to play Maid Marian with me at last?" he asked in Dutch.

Something was amiss. She knew how riots began, what plotting looked like, and it did not look like this. "Gerrit," she said. "I've come because your brother, Andries, thinks you're about to march on the house, but you're not, are you?"

"No," he said, rising to take her hands in his and draw her to him. "No, I'm not. I barely have a hundred men enlisted yet. And they're not interested in attacking the manor on their own. They'll rise if and when the British arrive, but they're not going to antagonize the patroon without a fair certainty that they will win. It was ever thus on the manor," he said wryly, "as I'm sure your father knew."

"I don't understand. No one is in the fields. There are no servants at the manor. Something is happening."

Gerrit's concern was plain. "When did this start?"

"Yesterday morning, after the cider pressing."

"Whatever it is, Annatje, it is not me."

She felt a prickle of unease run down her spine. "Then why is there a British warship in the river carrying your John André?"

"We were supposed to rendezvous Saturday. By then I had hoped to have my two hundred men so André would give me Tarleton's six hundred."

"Major André has made the same offer to your brother, although Andries need only take the oath in exchange for British troops and protection."

She stopped the question forming on his lips with a lifted hand. "Gerrit, there is something I need to show you," she said.

He must have read the look on her face because he lifted a lantern off one of the hooks on the wall and led her wordlessly around the great wheel to the other side of the millhouse, where a folding desk and a campaign bed had been set up and a stretched canvas afforded them some privacy.

"Your wife wrote this," said Anna, "because she hoped that someday you might know the truth about her. About why she acted as she did."

Anna unfolded the paper and laid it on the desk. She did not want to hover over him while he read it, so she crossed to the camp bed and sat beneath the looped-back worsted draperies. They smelled musty from the damp, but the mattress itself was dry. She watched as Gerrit read the letter, then read it again.

"It is signed by my sister, Elizabeth," he said, puzzled. "*After* she fled Harenwyck."

"Andries found her after she ran away. She has been living on the estate with her maid." Anna was not sure how much to tell him about his sister, how much he might have known or guessed.

"*Why?* Why did they never tell me that it was my father? Sophia, Andries, Elizabeth? None of them."

"Because they knew—feared—you wouldn't marry Sophia, and Cornelis promised to destroy her life," she answered, "like he destroyed so many others. They should have told you, let you decide for yourself whether to marry

Sophia or confront your father. But consider this—Andries was willing to make his own sacrifice: to let you think him an adulterer to protect the woman he loved, and he has kept that secret to protect her daughters. For good or ill, everything he has done since you returned has been an effort to undo some of the harm your father wrought. Your brother's way may not be the right way, but you both want what is best for Harenwyck and the people who live there, and that is not the chaos of a riot."

Gerrit looked up at her, nodded. He was shaken, but with all he'd just learned, she felt a little proud to sense understanding wrestling with the anger and the hurt. "You are right, of course," he said, after a moment, "but I am not the one stirring unrest."

"But you *were*, two nights ago, at the cider pressing. You were giving out freeholds, Gerrit, in exchange for insurrection. You have sparked something. Now someone else must be fanning the flames. Your brother has only a dozen men. Scarcely enough to protect the house and your family."

"I don't even have that many myself, Annatje, not at hand. I can hardly call up the men to whom I promised freeholds in the cause of defending my brother."

Gerrit opened the lantern and consigned Sophia's testament to the flame.

"What are you doing?"

"Sophia was lucky to have Andries. She was not like you, Annatje. Not strong, not resourceful or self-reliant. She would not have survived my father's wrath, let alone thrived and built a new life from the ashes, as you have.

And so we—we would not have Jannetje or Grietje at all. Andries was right to keep Sophia's secret from the world, if not from me."

"When he thought you were the one orchestrating the unrest, he was willing to offer you half the estate to quell it."

"Generous of him," Gerrit said drily. "But that may be moot as I am not the one behind it. And I've no idea who is."

"Whoever it is will gather their mob at the Halve Maen," said Anna. They always had. It was far easier to convince men to march in the cold, to face the *schouts* and court the patroon's wrath, when well fortified with beer and rum.

"You're most likely right. But there's no guarantee such men would be swayed by my pleas to stand down and disperse."

"No, but they might be swayed by those of Bram Hoppe's daughter."

Nineteen

Gerrit knew what she was thinking, and he did not like it. Not at all.

"No, Annatje. *I* am going to row myself out to the British warship downriver, where I shall promise my first-born to John André in exchange for however many men he can give me, or even just a brace of cabin boys and a cook with a gamy leg and a marlinspike. *You* are going back to the manor with Pieter and Edwaert and the rest of the men, where you will stay inside and not be called upon to demonstrate your mastery of that pistol you have tucked into your skirts."

"We have no choice about treating with Major André," agreed Anna. "Your brother wanted to keep the British out of Harenwyck, but not at the expense of so many lives and livelihoods. And you should indeed send your band to the manor house. Andries' men are stretched thin there. But I must go to the Halve Maen."

She was right. He knew she was right. But he had just found her again after so many years that he did not want to let her go, not on a night so like the one that had stolen her from him in the first place.

"If you must go, then some of my men go with you."

"Grietje and Jannetje are at Harenwyck. When I left there, Andries' *schouts* were away, and his militia cannot be relied upon. They are tenants as well, and have to live with their neighbors. The girls have only your brother and Mr. Ten Broeck to rely upon, and you remember how well Ten Broeck acquitted himself in my defense when you stopped our carriage. All the men must go to Harenwyck. I can take care of myself."

"I know you can," he conceded. "But, Annatje, I have only just found you again. To be reunited, against all odds and reason . . . I *will not* lose you a second time."

She stood up, and he realized it was the first time he had ever seen her in the proximity of a bed. He did not want it to be the last. He wanted to buy a very large tester, hang it with the darkest, stuffiest curtains he could find, and shut out the world, close them alone within. Only then they could not look up at the stars. Perhaps he could paint stars on the canopy.

Anna stood up on tiptoe—she was back to wearing her boring shoes and he missed her clomping *klompen*— and kissed him on the mouth.

"You are the boy who taught me to read a map," she said, "now become a man. Mine. You are my compass and my North Star, and I swear to you, Gerrit Van Haren, I will always find my way back to you."

She had already done as much once, he must allow, so he was in no position to dispute it, but that did not mean he had to like it.

For once he was glad that his "merry men" were first and foremost opportunists. They did not require a great deal of convincing. The manor house had to be protected because Andries had capitulated, and Gerrit was going to get half of the manor. There would be land—ample land—for everyone. They would probably have defended George Washington's chamber pot or General Clinton's jakes from a column of Gibbon's Huns for similar stakes. In the end, it made no great difference to them.

Gerrit insisted Pieter at least accompany Anna to the Halve Maen, because he was his oldest friend and could be relied upon.

"If there is the least sign of trouble, take her straight to the manor."

"What if she doesn't want to go?" asked Pieter, eyeing the pistol at her waist.

"She is unlikely to shoot you, Pieter."

"I suppose I shall be safe enough," Pieter said with a martyr's sigh. "So long as there aren't any sheep."

Gerrit gave her a leg up onto her pony. "We don't have to stay at Harenwyck," he said, "when this is over." He wanted to talk about the future because that made it real. It conjured a tomorrow, *tomorrows*, when he was desperately afraid he would never see her again. "We can go to New York. Back to your school, if you like."

"I'm not sure that would work," said Anna. "A conspicuous lover would ruin my spinster's reputation."

She was joking, but she was also right. "Then we'll have to get married."

"Is that another proposal?"

"Yes. Hear me out this time. We can go to New York. Or we can find a little house somewhere, one of those rambling old Puritan manses with steep gables and tiny rooms like I imagined Miss Winters had been raised in. We can make it that house—paint it yellow and put dentils on it and fill it with books. Harenwyck has made enough people miserable. Too many. I thought that in order to escape its shadow, I needed to destroy it utterly, but that has only served to place me on the same road as my father, destroying everything in my path to possess more land than any man should control—no matter that my intent was to sell it all in the end. If Andries will divide the estate with me, I can make one thousand tenants free men tomorrow, and go down in history as the only man who has wooed a bride with the great estate that he will *not* bestow upon her."

Her eyes were shining now. A trick of the light, or unshed tears. He hoped the latter.

"I have no desire to be lady of Harenwyck," she said. "Nor would I ever ask you to give up your ideals. All I require is that you not be quite so reckless with your own life in pursuit of them."

"Does that mean your answer is yes?"

"Yes."

He watched her ride off into the night beside Pieter

with a feeling of sudden elation. She was going to be his wife. He was going to have a real wife. A partner, a help-meet, someone who would inspire him to be his best self. He was going to reconcile with his brother. He was going to break up his half of Harenwyck. His daughters—and they would always be that to him—would have more than a teacher. They would have a mother and friend. All he had to do was strike a bargain with the dangerous gentleman aboard the man-of-war in the river.

He rowed himself out to the frigate anchored below the Narrows. It had never occurred to him that André might not be there, not be immediately accessible. He was treated with courtesy and led to a cabin that smelled like hemp and tar, and in which he could stretch his arms and touch both walls with his fingertips at the same time.

Apart from jail, it was perhaps the worst place Gerrit had ever been, and he'd only spent two nights in the lockup, whereas sailors spent months and sometimes years at sea, a good portion of it in these or worse conditions. His voyage across the Atlantic to Leiden had been cramped, but the British navy appeared to make both an art and a science of discomfort. He would never understand the appeal of it all.

A midshipman offered him rum, which he refused, and ale, which he accepted because he was thirsty. An hour passed before John André appeared. This time he was dressed in scarlet regimentals with epaulets that confirmed his rank as major.

"I was not expecting you so soon, my lord," said André, in Dutch, on entering the tiny cabin. His hair was wet, Gerrit noted, as though he had toweled off and dressed hastily after a swim in the river. Perhaps he had.

"And you were hoping perhaps that my brother might come instead," answered Gerrit, in English, remembering what Annatje had told him about the British overtures that Mr. Ten Broeck had been entertaining. This man was not his friend, no matter how candid and friendly he appeared.

Major André pulled up a chair and poured himself a beaker of ale. "I wasn't, actually. I have never met your brother and have nothing that I know of in common with him, whereas you and I share similar educations and experiences. But my occupation allows very little scope for sentiment. My first priority has always been to secure the Hudson for the government's interests. If your brother had been willing to take the oath, then, understand, I would have been obligated to strike a bargain with him instead of you. Since he did not prove willing, it was in British interests to strike a bargain with you, against him. That doing so dovetailed with my own personal preferences was nothing but a happy accident. Of course, matters have changed somewhat since you and I last spoke."

"How so?" asked Gerrit. He did not really care, he discovered, if this glittering officer threw the support of the British behind Andries. He did not care so very much if he got all or half, or none, of Harenwyck. What he wanted was to guarantee the safety of the estate and the people who lived on it tonight. His daughters, his friends, even his brother, and Annatje. Always Annatje. She *could* take care of herself, but he wanted to make it so that she never had to again.

"The Americans have fortified a point downriver that neatly trumps control of Harenhoeck. It is there that I must now turn my attention. Colonel Tarleton and I no longer have six hundred men to offer you, Mr. Van Haren, even if you were able to raise two hundred tenants by Saturday."

"I do not need six hundred men on Saturday," said Gerrit. "I need sixty, *tonight*, to put down an uprising."

"Even if I could secure you sixty men, I wouldn't do so," said André, drinking deep from his beaker of ale. "An insurrection against your brother is only to your benefit. If the tenants riot and march on the manor house tonight, you will be patroon tomorrow. It is an economical and elegant solution to your problem, and one, in point of fact, I have gone to no small trouble to arrange."

It took a moment for his meaning to penetrate. Gerrit set down his beer. "What have you done?"

"It became obvious to me as soon as I reconnoitered the fortifications that the Americans are building at West Point that the position is superior in all ways to Harenhoeck. My superior, General Sir Henry Clinton, ordered me to abandon negotiations with you, and ensure we remained on good terms with the patroon for Harenwyck's continued provision of butter and beef. But I had made representations to you, and I am—whenever I can be—a man of my word. So I sought another way to put the patroonship into your hands, without disobeying my superiors or committing British forces."

"So you engineered an uprising." His stomach turned over at the thought. Bram Hoppe had raised the tenants to fight injustice, to redistribute power in the valley. Major André had done it to effectuate a mere regime change, to again concentrate power in a single man: himself. "Who are the ringleaders?"

"A disgruntled tenant family called 'Dijkstra' with a grudge against the woman your brother is keeping at the manor. The very one you waylaid on the way to Harenwyck, as a matter of fact. At the heart, there are two very fierce Dijkstra matriarchs and one bloodthirsty young man. All my hard work nearly unraveled yesterday morning when your brother Andries tried to evict them, but even that, in the end, worked to our advantage, once I dealt with their escort at the ferry. The thwarted eviction was a helpful example of the patroon's injustice, and also that his power was not absolute: rallying cries for the Dijkstra women to recruit followers. A multitude of followers. Tensions, as you know, have been running very high."

"Call it off," said Gerrit, his words hoarse in his own ears.

André's surprise seemed genuine. "Call it off? Don't you want to be patroon, Mr. Van Haren? *Gerrit?* This is your opportunity to dismantle the estate. Or keep it if you like. With such an inheritance, a man could do anything. Anything at all. If you had been born with less, mayhap you would not be so quick to cast such fortune aside."

"You have no notion of what you have done."

"I have delivered you Harenwyck."

And put Annatje in the gravest danger. "I must go," said Gerrit.

"You would be far better off to stay out of it until the insurrection runs its course," advised André, but Gerrit was already on his way out of the cabin, toward the gangplank.

André did not attempt to stop him, but trailed along behind, not disliking his role, it appeared, as the unheard voice of reason. "Return to Harenwyck in the morning, Gerrit. Or better, late afternoon. As lord of the manor. Put things right . . . as *you* see fit." The major lingered for a time at the rail, with an air of puzzlement or mild reproof, watching Gerrit begin to row himself back to the dock.

As he bent to the oars, back warming to the effort and lungs drinking deep of the night air, Gerrit hoped against hope that Annatje and Pieter had been delayed, or returned there for some reason. He needed to see her, to lay eyes on her, to know that she was all right. If she wasn't still in the mill, she was riding straight into the hands of her persecutors.

Though he made good time, it seemed an age before he arrived back at the dock. He ran through all three cavernous structures calling her name, but there was no answer; there was no one there at all.

Cursing the time wasted, he saddled his horse and rode hard for the Halve Maen. Each minute on the trails and road seemed an hour, an eternity. And when he arrived he found all in darkness, the doors barred and windows shuttered. Gerrit hammered on them until he roused the Duyser family, but the tavern keeper insisted he had closed at midday. He knew about Rie and Ida and Jan and the trouble they were raising, of course, but had wanted no part of it, not for him or his. It was too wild, too risky.

Neither Mynheer Duyser nor any of his family had seen Pieter or Annatje. There was only one other place to look for her: at the manor.

At first Anna thought that the lights were the windows of the Halve Maen, but as they grew closer she realized that there were far too many of them and they were too low to the ground.

"I don't like the looks of that, *baas*," said Pieter, reining up and scanning the way before them. He had been calling her that since they left the mill. "Nor the sound of it, neither."

They were on a flat stretch of road bordered by cornfields, the stalks cut to stubble in the recent harvest. A great mass of men and women seemed to coalesce out of the darkness less than a hundred paces away, moving noisily, inexorably toward them. There was nowhere to hide.

"No more do I," admitted Anna.

Moments later, they were close enough that Anna could distinguish the faces of the tenants at the front of the column. There was a tall, gaunt woman leading them. Her eyes fixed on Anna in recognition.

"Annatje Hoppe!" she cried out, voice wild as a crow's

caw. The lanky woman had a mane of red hair turning ash gray and a scythe in her hands. And Anna had no doubts—none at all—as to who she must be. The rioters were being led by Rie Dijkstra. The sister of the *schout* she had killed.

"Ride!" Anna shouted to Pieter.

She did not wait to see if he followed her instructions. The mob was not after him. She turned her horse and urged it to speed. She knew better than to look back. That was one of the things the Widow had taught her. *When someone is chasing you, never turn around. Those are seconds you will never get back, and if your adversary is quick enough, they will be your last.*

Her adversaries were not quick, but they were well armed. Anna heard a dozen or so shots ring out, felt something whistle past her cheek and—more poignantly—a bullet graze her calf.

Only to strike deep in her mount. The pony screamed and stumbled. Anna squeezed her legs tight around the saddle and clung to the beast's mane, hoping she would not be thrown, but the force of the pony's convulsions was too great, and she pitched forward bodily onto the packed earth.

Her shoulder smacked the road, and something in it popped. Her cheek smashed into the ground and was cut by rough stones. The impact knocked all the air from her lungs, and she could not draw breath to stand, but she knew she *had* to move.

They were on her before she could recover her breath. Cruel fingers dug into her scalp, just as Vim Dijkstra's had done all those years ago, and dragged her head up. Rie Dijkstra spat in her face, but still Anna could not will her lungs and body to answer.

Then air came back in a painful rush. And with the pain, like the first breath of a second birth, came a flash of hope. Someone grabbed her jaw, swung her face around into the light of a lantern; a fist came out of the darkness to connect with her chin.

Hope died aborning, and Anna knew no more.

Twenty

Gerrit reached the manor to find his men in place beside the militia. Edwaert came to take his horse.

"Have Annatje and Pieter returned?"

"No, *baas*." Panic seized him. If she was not at the mill and she was not at the Halve Maen and she was not at the house, then it was not an uprising at all. The Dijkstras' *only* goal was Annatje. André thought he had been using Rie and Ida, but they had been using him.

"Gerrit!" His brother's voice called to him from that absurd porch. Gerrit saw his daughters peering out from behind Andries, and Mrs. Buys looking worried beside them.

Gerrit took the stairs two at a time. "It is not an uprising," he said to his brother. "It is not about the manor. It is about Annatje. You sent Rie and Ida Dijkstra to the ferry, but the British killed the *schouts*. Now Rie and Ida have come back and I fear they have taken Annatje. She was on her way to the Halve Maen with Pieter, but she never arrived. You have to send the militia out to search for her."

"And leave the manor defenseless?" Mr. Ten Broeck shouldered his way past the girls and Mrs. Buys.

"I will stake my life on it," said Gerrit. "They are not coming here. If I knew where they were taking her, I could use my own men, but the estate is too large to find her with just a dozen searchers."

"Rie came to me two nights ago," said Andries. "She had recognized Annatje. She wanted to make a trade. She offered me you, in exchange for Anna." Gerrit had not known that part. Annatje had not told him. "Rie wanted to try Anna, the way Bram Hoppe used to try tenants, and then hang her, but she did not intend it to be a sham execution. They will take her to the place Bram Hoppe used to play his rough music. That is where Vim Dijkstra killed him."

"How do you know that?"

"I was there. Father made me watch."

There were so many things he had not known, but now was not the time for them. If they got Annatje back he would reconcile fully with his brother. "Where?"

"The clearing near the old sandpit. I'll come with you. We can take the militia, but we must leave a guard on the house."

Gerrit agreed. The sandpit was two miles, if they cut across the fields. There were not enough horses for the militia, but Gerrit's men had mounts. He prayed they would be fast enough.

. . .

Annatje tasted blood. The blow that had knocked her unconscious must have been only seconds before, but already the world had shifted. She was looking up at the stars. And her arms hurt. That was because her captors were dragging her. They had left the road and were crunching through the forest over pine needles. Her muscles tensed automatically, but she forced herself to go slack because it was to her advantage that they think her dazed.

Count them. She knew that was what she must do—what the Widow would have done first—but her head swam as she tried to tally the moving bodies. She had an impression of thick farmers' calves and heavy homespun petticoats. More petticoats than stockings. She should not have been surprised. Her father had made rough music because it was the only justice available to the powerless and dispossessed, and women were so often that.

She tried to get her bearings. She knew she had to take her first chance to escape, and that if she was fleeing from a large number of attackers while concussed—which she very likely was—the direction she ran in would be more important to her survival than any other factor. She must run *toward* help, not away from it.

But the swishing of petticoats was distracting, and the velvet one kept changing places, moving around. *Velvet.* That meant something. She could not remember what. Anna tried to follow the shimmering petticoat, but it kept disappearing, until she looked straight up and found herself staring into the eyes of Barbara Fenton.

It was a hallucination, Anna was sure of it, but a vivid one, because the beauty put a finger to her ruby lips, as though she were playing hide-and-seek with King Charles in the palace, and signaled for silence. Her baroque ringlets hung from her high, clear brow and brushed Anna's face, and she mouthed *This way* and pointed into the woods.

It was a hallucination, but it was all Anna had to go on right now, and if she was going to die, she was going to die fighting. With a burst of energy, she wrenched her arms free from her captors and broke into a run.

Or a semblance of one. She stumbled but her fingers were so numb that she could not feel the pine needles of the forest floor, and she picked herself up and kept going. She did not look back. The girl in the velvet gown was in front of her and she knew that if she followed her she would find her Dutchman.

Like a pack of dogs her captors gave chase, shouting. But there was more shouting now from ahead of her, and someone was calling her name. "Annatje!"

The witch in the velvet gown disappeared, and Anna burst into a clearing filled with light and noise. Her knees gave out and she fell to the ground, and it felt like the beach beneath her, all sand but warm and dry, and there were strong arms folding around her and she was resting her head against a familiar shoulder and she was home.

"Gerrit," she said.

He spoke her name over and over like a litany and rocked her and held her close.

"How did she know which way to run?" That was

Andries. He was standing over her, and she was too tired to look up, but she answered him:

"It was the witch in the velvet dress," she said. "Barbara Fenton showed me."

"She is delirious," said Gerrit. "Annatje, can you ride?"

"No." The idea made her feel ill.

He carried her back to the manor. The girls were very excited to see her and ran to the library in search of a medical treatise to tend her cuts and bruises. When they returned with a book on animal husbandry Mrs. Buys banished them and helped Anna to wash and put on a fresh chemise and climb into bed. There were probably a great many things that had to be done, but she did not care, just then, about any of them.

Except for Pieter. She asked Mrs. Buys what had become of him. "The militia found him on the road."

"Alive?"

"Alive enough to eat two chickens and a pie I was saving to serve tonight."

Sometime later the door opened and Gerrit climbed into the bed beside her. She reached for him.

"You're not well enough," he said.

But she was.

She had never woken up beside anyone before. It was a wonder to stretch her arms and touch the warm, bare flesh of the best friend she had ever had, who was also now her lover.

"What will you do about the estate?" she asked.

He gave a loud, unconvincing snore.

She kicked him.

"I was asleep," he lied.

"You cannot sleep all day, and the problem will not solve itself."

He pulled her into his arms. "I spoke with Andries last night. We agreed to divide the estate. He will keep the farms that prefer to remain leaseholds. That is the majority of the land. But he will agree to sell to any tenant who can afford to buy. The manor is his, along with the adjacent farms, but the old house is to be a school for the tenants. Or whatever you would like to make of it."

"And the Dijkstras?" she asked.

"Evicted for good this time, along with their supporters. They ought to pay a greater price for what they did last night, but a trial would dredge up too much of the past. Their influence on the estate is finished. They will not be back. And you and I, my *klompen* girl, have to get married."

Gerrit spent the day closeted with his brother and three lawyers drawing up an agreement to divide the estate. Mr. Ten Broeck was notable by his absence. "Andries could not forgive him for treating with the British in secret," Gerrit explained, when he visited the kitchen to see his daughters and purloin a plate of *koekjes*. Anna had decided that the girls' lessons must continue. Shortly, there would be enough upheaval in their lives. For now she wanted them to enjoy the security of the familiar. "He has been given a week to remove himself and his family from the estate."

In the afternoon, while the girls sketched, Anna wrote a masked letter to Kate Grey. She related a rough outline of the events that had occurred at Harenwyck, with certain facts and names omitted, that the patroon had elected to provide the Rebels full access to Harenhoeck, and concluded by stating that she hoped and assumed her obligations had been discharged.

At dinner Anna announced her intention to retrieve Sophia's embroidery, the chair and table, fire screen and loom, from the old house. "They should not be left to rot." And Andries must not spend his evenings, after she and Gerrit left for New York, sitting in that dusty, decaying house with his dead lover's things.

"Take Pieter with you," said Gerrit. He looked like he expected her to protest. She didn't. Nor did she relate the tale of Barbara Fenton. She had decided that the apparition had been the product of her own mind, conjured by need and desperation. Anna had grown up at Harenwyck. As a girl she had known those woods well enough to find her way home in the dark. The ghost could only have been memory given form and put in the service of survival. Even so, she would always be grateful to the shade of Barbara Fenton, real or imagined. That did not mean that she had any wish to meet it again.

At the end of the week she received a missive from an unexpected quarter. Mr. Sims had been the Widow's man of business. It was he who had conveyed to her the deed to the house on Pearl Street, the one where Anna had spent those wretched first days in New York kept prisoner by Mrs. Duvel—and where the Widow had buried her venal

DONNA THORLAND

servant's body in the basement. Mr. Sims wrote to tell her that the house had burned down.

Anna checked the date of the fire against her memory and discovered that it had occurred on the same day she had consigned Mevrouw Zabriskie's eerie tarot card to the flames. *The Tower. A house made uninhabitable by death.* She did not mourn its demise in the slightest. And she gladly accepted Mr. Sims' generous offer to handle the sale of the property for her. He had not been willing to do so a year ago, and in his change of heart Anna detected the hand—and blessing—of Kate Grey. She could return to Manhattan and the school without fear, of blackmail or exposure. Her old sins, such as they were, were truly buried and burned.

Anna and Gerrit were married in the old church at Harenwyck. She was too excited to eat breakfast before the ceremony, and when her stomach rumbled during the exchange of vows loudly enough to interrupt the reverend's droning Dutch service, Gerrit broke into laughter and kissed his bride, and told the scandalized divine to get on with it. Pieter stood—shifting his feet in his pinched dress shoes but beaming like a disreputable, thatch-haired angel at his old *baas* and his beloved—as Gerrit's best man.

The following week Anna and Gerrit traveled to New York and took up residence as man and wife at the school. They brought Scrappy with them, predictably much put-upon by the move. Pieter followed a week later, claiming he was done with farming and ready to give city life a try.

Anna resumed teaching, and a month after that Andries brought the girls to Manhattan to enroll at the academy.

That spring the Rebels confiscated Harenwyck, despite the patroon's steadfast support of their cause. Mr. Ten Broeck's correspondence with the British surfaced at an inopportune moment, when Congress was in need of money, and they ordered the seizure and sale of all that remained of the estate. Much of it was bought by other patroons. Among them, Andries' new father-in-law, an upriver landowner with a hundred thousand acres of his own.

Gerrit wished his brother joy with his new bride, but the day after the lavish nuptials, he entered upon a new career in politics and, to no one's great surprise, became a tireless campaigner for land reform. It was a crusade for which the time had finally come, and for which he had his wife's full and committed support.

The school prospered in the wake of the war, buoyed by a vogue for female education and republican virtues. Anna added Dutch to the curriculum, even though there was little call for it. And once a year, Gerrit Van Haren, who might have been patroon of Harenwyck and lord of two hundred thousand acres, made a journey on foot to the valley where he had been born and returned with a gift for his cherished wife, made by hands that had shaken her father's: a pair of clogs for his *klompen* girl.

AUTHOR'S NOTE

The pervasive foundation myth of early America is the elementary school version of the first Thanksgiving: Pilgrims, Puritans, and the Mayflower; pass the turkey, please. If we trouble to think of the native peoples who were here before the English, we count ourselves enlightened, and pass the pumpkin pie. It's a comforting, comfortable fable, but seven years before Mary Chilton touched Plymouth Rock—if she ever did—the Dutch were already established on Manhattan Island. They brought with them from the Netherlands perhaps the most open, tolerant society Europe had ever seen, and prefigured the melting-pot character of the New York we know today. New Amsterdam was annexed by the English Crown in 1664, but the Dutch didn't go anywhere. Their culture and language persisted, in places, into the twentieth century, and their radical political ideas helped shape debate during the American fight for independence—and beyond.

But Dutch settlement was also steeped in mercantilism. Paradoxically, the manorial system they established on the Hudson River to encourage colonization introduced a feudalism to the New World that had long since died out in Western Europe. The Dutch West India Company doled out vast tracts of land up and down the river and its tributaries to a handful of "patroons," whose holdings, rights, and privileges survived the transition to English rule surprisingly intact. And the system proved astonishingly persistent. Though the patroonships were riven by tenant uprisings during the Stamp Act crisis and in the midst of the Revolution, it would not be until the 1850s that the last of the great manors was dissolved.

RECOMMENDED READING

Alexander, Kimberly S. "Myra Montgomery's World: Haverhill, Boston, and Beyond." *Historical New Hampshire* 67, nos. 1 and 2 (Fall/Winter 2013).

Blackburn, Roderic H., and Nancy A. Kelley. *New World Dutch Studies: Dutch Arts and Culture in Colonial America, 1609–1776: Proceedings of the Symposium*. Albany, NY: Institute, 1987.

Countryman, Edward. *A People in Revolution: The American Revolution and Political Society in New York, 1760–1790*. Baltimore: Johns Hopkins University Press, 1981.

Edmonds, Mary Jaene. *Samplers & Samplermakers: An American Schoolgirl Art, 1700–1850*. New York: Rizzoli, 1991.

Fabend, Firth Haring. *A Dutch Family in the Middle Colonies, 1660–1800*. New Brunswick: Rutgers University Press, 1991.

Fingerhut, Eugene R., and Joseph S. Tiedemann. *The Other New York: The American Revolution beyond New York City, 1763–1787*. Albany: State University of New York Press, 2005.

Goodfriend, Joyce D. *Before the Melting Pot: Society and Culture in Colonial New York City, 1664–1730*. Princeton, NJ: Princeton University Press, 1992.

Goodfriend, Joyce D., Benjamin Schmidt, and Annette Stott. *Going Dutch: The Dutch Presence in America, 1609–2009*. Leiden: Brill, 2008.

Humphrey, Thomas J. *Land and Liberty: Hudson Valley Riots in the Age of Revolution*. DeKalb: Northern Illinois University Press, 2004.

Johnson, James M., Christopher Pryslopski, and Andrew Villani. *Key to the Northern Country: The Hudson River Valley in the American Revolution*. Albany: State Universty of New York Press, 2013.

Nash, Gary B. *The Unknown American Revolution: The Unruly Birth of Democracy and the Struggle to Create America*. New York: Viking, 2005.

Panetta, Roger G. *Dutch New York: The Roots of Hudson Valley Culture*. Yonkers: Hudson River Museum/Fordham University Press, 2009.

Postma, Johannes Menne. *The Dutch in the Atlantic Slave Trade*. Cambridge: Cambridge University Press, 1990.

Rink, Oliver A. *Holland on the Hudson: An Economic and Social History of Dutch New York*. Ithaca, NY: Cornell University Press, 1986.

Rose, Peter G. *Food, Drink and Celebrations of the Hudson Valley Dutch*. Charleston, SC: History, 2009.

Shattuck, Martha Dickinson. *Explorers, Fortunes & Love Letters: A Window on New Netherland*. Albany, NY: New Netherland Institute, 2009.

Shorto, Russell. *The Island at the Center of the World: The Epic Story of Dutch Manhattan and the Forgotten Colony That Shaped America*. New York: Doubleday, 2004.

Tuchman, Barbara W. *The First Salute*. New York: Ballantine, 1988.

Schulte Nordholt, J. W. *The Dutch Republic and American Independence*. Chapel Hill: University of North Carolina Press, 1982.

Walters, Kimberly, *A Book of Cookery by a Lady*. Woodbridge: Kimberly Walters, 2014.

The Dutch Girl

RENEGADES OF THE AMERICAN REVOLUTION

DONNA THORLAND

A CONVERSATION
WITH DONNA THORLAND

Q. I had no idea that feudal estates like the patroonships ever existed in America. How did these come into being?

A. The Dutch West India Company wanted more than trading posts in America, but colonization was an expensive business. To encourage settlement without incurring expense, they came up with the patroon system. Starting in 1629 the company began granting the title of patroon to invested members who met certain conditions. Patroons were required to build a manor house and recruit and transport settlers to the New World. In exchange they received land grants with extraordinary rights and privileges, including the ability to create and administer civil and criminal courts and appoint local officials. For every fifty settlers over the age of fifteen that a patroon brought to New Netherland, he received a grant of land sixteen miles along one side of the Hudson or eight miles along both sides "and so far into the country as the situation of the occupiers will permit."

Q. Why did farmers choose to live within the patroonships? Why didn't they buy their own land?

A. Farmers took up leaseholds because they had no other choice. Most of the land in the Hudson River Valley was owned by the patroons. Scarcity drove up prices so that what little land was available was too expensive for small-holders to buy. Lease terms often seemed attractive at first, especially to new arrivals in America. In the middle of the eighteenth century a man might rent roughly two hundred unimproved acres from a patroon for about three pounds a year. He'd receive a discount for the first few years while he was clearing the land and building a house and barns. After that, though, he would pay his full rent and discover that conditions on the estate made it difficult to get ahead. He was obligated to use the patroon's mills for his lumber and his grain, and he had few choices but to purchase his seed, equipment, and most finished goods from the patroon's stores. Many leases ran for three life terms, meaning that his son and grandson were bound to the land by the same terms.

Unrest, given the spirit of the age, was almost inevitable, and Annatje's father is loosely based on the revolutionary William Prendergast, who was jailed for leading revolts against the Hudson Valley landlords in 1765 and 1766. Riots followed his arrest. He was sentenced by the patroon-dominated New York courts to be hanged, drawn and quartered, beheaded, and burned. Several attempts were made to break him out of jail. Prendergast was so popular that no willing executioner could be found. He was pardoned by King George III, most likely a move to defuse tension in the valley. Ten years later, during the

Revolution, the British would encourage tenants to revolt against landlords who chose the Rebel side.

Q. Highwaymen are fixtures of swashbuckling adventure fiction, but the novel suggests that real highwaymen were active in the Hudson River Valley during the Revolution. Can you describe the conditions in the region during this period?

A. By the end of 1776, Washington had been forced to evacuate New York and the British were firmly in control of Manhattan. That left Westchester County with the British Army camped on its doorstep. The political sympathies of the population were mixed, and no strong local Rebel government emerged in the area, leaving the country south of Dobbs Ferry prey to ceaseless raiding, mostly by irregular loyalist units, often referred to as Cowboys. Interestingly a mythology grew up in the nineteenth century, largely created by James Fenimore Cooper for his Revolutionary War novels, that the Cowboys were opposed by a similarly ruthless Rebel band called the Skinners—but the term appears in only one diary entry for the entire duration of the war. The Skinners make terrific drama but suspect history. If they existed, they were most likely another loyalist band similar to the Cowboys. What is certain, though, is that lawlessness prevailed in what became known as the Neutral Ground. When John André was captured with the plans for West Point stuffed in his boot, it was casual bandits with only a loose affiliation to the Continental Army who waylaid him.

Q. The silkwork picture that hangs in Anna's academy sounds remarkable. Did schoolgirls really create art like this?

A. Yes. Anna's silkwork landscape is modeled on a picture embroidered by Hannah Otis (1732–1801) called *View of Boston Common*. It's an extraordinarily accomplished work, made around 1750 out of wool, silk, metallic threads, and beads on a linen ground. Hannah's older sister Mercy served as the inspiration for my previous book *Mistress Firebrand*. You can view the picture at the Boston Museum of Fine Arts Web site. English and American schoolgirls, in addition to academic subjects, learned both practical and decorative skills—polite accomplishments—such as dancing, singing, playing the harpsichord, painting, needlework, and drawing.

QUESTIONS
FOR DISCUSSION

1. The novel has many elements that place it in the Gothic tradition: a remote house; a powerful, landed aristocrat; a heroine separated from her home and family. How does it conform to and defy the conventions established by books like *Jane Eyre* and *Rebecca*?

2. What do Anna's *klompen* symbolize to Gerrit? Do they mean something different to Anna herself? What do they mean to you?

3. How did you feel about the choices Annatje made to survive after she left Harenwyck?

4. Kate Grey blackmails Anna into traveling to Harenwyck, but Anna acknowledges, if only to herself, a debt owed to the Widow. Do you think Anna made the journey to save herself from exposure as an imposter, or for more complicated reasons?

5. The Widow told Anna that she would make a good teacher, but that it was not a role she could play forever, because of her strong sense of social justice. Was the Widow right?

6. Andries Van Haren has a vision for reforming the patroonship that will provide his tenants with schools, doctors, better roads, and more favorable markets for their goods. Would you choose the security of tenancy under a regime like Andries', or the independence—and uncertainties—of life as a freeholder?

7. Gerrit resorts to highway robbery to destabilize his brother's regime. Is he more or less justified than the partisan bandits terrorizing the Hudson River Valley on behalf of the British and Rebel armies?

8. Did Anna really see the ghost of Barbara Fenton in the woods, or was it a hallucination?

9. Barbara Fenton's tragic romance with her Dutchman serves as a counterpoint to Anna's happy union with Gerrit. Anna and Gerrit both find meaning in the story. What is it that Anna learns from Barbara's tale? What is Gerrit's lesson?

Photo by Peter Podgursky

After graduating from Yale with a degree in classics and art history, **Donna Thorland** managed architecture and interpretation at the Peabody Essex Museum in Salem for several years. She then earned an MFA in film production from the University of Southern California School of Cinematic Arts. She has been a Disney/ABC Television Writing Fellow and a WGA Writer Access Project Honoree, and has written for the TV shows *Cupid* and *Tron: Uprising*. Currently a writer on the WGN drama *Salem*, Donna is married, has two cats, and splits her time between Los Angeles and Salem, Massachusetts.